HOPING
for
HOPE

HOPING
for
HOPE

Lucy Clare

DUTTON

DUTTON
Published by the Penguin Group
Penguin Putnam Inc., 375 Hudson Street, New York, New York 10014, U.S.A.
Penguin Books Ltd, 80 Strand, London WC2R 0RL, England
Penguin Books Australia Ltd, Ringwood, Victoria, Australia
Penguin Books Canada Ltd, 10 Alcorn Avenue, Toronto, Ontario, Canada M4V 3B2
Penguin Books (N.Z.) Ltd, 182–190 Wairau Road, Auckland 10, New Zealand

Penguin Books Ltd, Registered Offices: Harmondsworth, Middlesex, England

Published by Dutton, a member of Penguin Putnam Inc. Originally published in Great Britain in 2001 by Warner Books, a Division of Little, Brown and Company

First American Printing, March 2002
10 9 8 7 6 5 4 3 2 1

 REGISTERED TRADEMARK—MARCA REGISTRADA

LIBRARY OF CONGRESS CATALOGING-IN-PUBLICATION DATA

Clare, Lucy.
    Hoping for hope / Lucy Clare
        p. cm.
    ISBN 0-525-94637-3
    1. Middle aged women—Fiction. 2. Pregnant women—Fiction 3. Married women—Fiction. I. Title.
    PR6103.L37 H66 2002
823'.92—dc21   2001037117

Printed in the United States of America
Set in New Baskerville
Designed by Eve L. Kirch

PUBLISHER'S NOTE
This is a work of fiction. Names, characters, places, and incidents are either the products of the author's imagination or are used fictitiously, and any resemblance to actual persons, living or dead, business establishments, events, or locales is entirely coincidental.

This book is printed on acid-free paper.

This is for James, Phoebe, Henry, Thomasina,
Agnes and, of course, for Veronica—with my love

Acknowledgments

Helenka Fuglewicz for her support, her enormous energy and her sense of humor. Julia Forrest for her early editing and valuable encouragement. Dr. Victoria Hartnell for answering all the medical questions. Ursula Mackenzie for her enthusiasm and her faith in me. Viv Redman for so cleverly and so patiently sorting out the final manuscript. Kate Vaughan for endlessly discussing my ideas. Lizzie Frizzell and Katherine Fox for reading the early drafts. And James, so positive, so kind to me and so good at making tea. Thank you.

HOPING

for

HOPE

Chapter

ONE

It was, by anyone's standards, a watershed of a week. Or, more accurately, a week of watersheds. It had started quite promisingly with the purchase of a much sought-after pair of bright red Doc Martens, but it had deteriorated alarmingly after that. Liddy Claver would not forget this particular week—ever.

"Council cutbacks, I'm afraid," Rosa, the head of the Adult Education Institute, said with a sigh. "No more evening classes in anything that is not going to further this country's industry—and jewelry making is not a prime target for resources." She pronounced it *re*-sources, which at that particular moment annoyed Liddy rather more than the implications of her redundancy.

"I'm sorry, Liddy," Rosa went on, wearily dragging her beige cardigan round her chest as though for protection. "Adult education is being moved to another site and there is no accommodation for your classes. Computers yes, car maintenance yes, one upholstery class for the bored middle classes yes, but jewelry making no. I am so sorry." She shrugged helplessly.

Liddy, in a mirror image, shrugged back.

"Oh, well, I shall just have to find some other way of earning my living," she said with a faint but brave smile. "At least I'll have more time to make my own stuff, I suppose."

"Thank you for all your work. Your classes have been very popular," Rosa said formally.

Well, not that popular obviously, Liddy thought as she clattered down the stone stairs of the primary school, or I would have been moved to the new site along with car maintenance.

"I thought perhaps I should consider HRT," she said to the doctor. "I'm sure I'm menopausal because I haven't had a period for months." She paused, remembering how her eldest daughter had recently castigated her for calling it "the curse."

"You really should stop calling it the curse, Mum, it's like talking about O levels."

"I get terrible backaches, I'm moody and I've put on a bit of weight," Liddy went on now.

The doctor raised a delicate eyebrow.

"You've always had a little trouble with your weight, though, haven't you?" she said in a slightly accusatory tone, "and certainly there is often a thickening at this time of life. You are how old?"

"Forty-nine. Fifty the day after tomorrow."

"And do you know when your mother started her menopause?"

Liddy shook her head.

"No, she died when I was much younger, when I still believed myself invincible. I was never going to be menopausal, of course, so I wouldn't have thought of asking her about it." Liddy made a face to convey self-deprecation. "Anyway," she added, "it wasn't the sort of conversation my mother and I ever had."

The doctor gave a wintry smile. She had been Liddy's doctor for over seven years, but Liddy still found her disconcertingly uncozy and uncommunicative. Liddy was depressed that this was the woman with whom she had to discuss the possibility of going on HRT.

"I'm not really very happy about the idea," she said. "It seems such a big step. I hate the idea of mucking about with my hormones. And bleeding every month—and even growing hair, someone told me."

"How much do you know about the drug?" the doctor asked severely. "Have you read up about it?"

"No, but my friends and I seem to have stopped discussing education and parking problems and now discuss HRT and osteoporosis."

The doctor took a leaflet out of her drawer and handed it to Liddy.

"Well, you'd better read this and come back when you've decided."

"What do *you* think?" Liddy asked, desperately looking for professional guidance.

"It has to be your decision and you do need to have all the facts to make it."

Liddy wanted to ask the doctor whether *she* was taking HRT; she wanted to ask all the silly little questions that were so important. Will I get fat? Will I really look younger? Will I want sex all the time? Will I bleed a lot? Will I get hairy nostrils?

"It's all in there," the doctor said almost irritably, gesturing to the leaflet Liddy was turning around nervously in her hands. "Anyway, I'll take a look at you while you're here. Weigh you, take your blood pressure. Do you check your breasts regularly?"

Liddy winced as she stood on the scales. Why do you always weigh more on doctors' scales than on your own?

The doctor listened to her heart and chest, took her blood pressure and then deftly spread her hands over Liddy's breasts.

"I know. Even *they*'ve put on weight," Liddy said with a guilty smile.

"Slip your shirt up and lie down, would you? I'll just take a look."

Liddy lay back. The doctor palpated her stomach and Liddy thought she saw a thoughtful frown cross her face. Liddy felt the palms of her hands become sweaty and her heart start beating quickly.

My God, Liddy thought in a white panic, she's found a lump and it's cancer. She's found an enormous tumor. It's in my stomach, which is why I've got fatter and why I feel tired all the time and it will be inoperable and I'm going to die . . . and I haven't even made a will.

"Could you be pregnant?"

Such a simple question, easily answered almost without thought.

"Me? No, absolutely not."

The doctor reached out for a blue box and unraveled a long probe. She covered Liddy's stomach in cold jelly and held the probe on to her white flesh. The sound of slurpy swirling filled the room and Liddy became aware of a regular beat coming through the gurgles. The doctor looked at her questioningly. "Can you hear that?"

Liddy nodded. "Sounds like my heart."

My God, she thought wildly, tumors don't have heartbeats. So it's my heart. I've got something wrong with my heart. I shall have to have a bypass or a transplant and I shall never be able to go upstairs again.

The doctor spoke in a deadpan voice. "That's a fetal heartbeat, Liddy. You are pregnant."

She looked at Liddy as if to gauge her reaction, but at that moment Liddy reacted not at all. She just stared back at the woman.

Still supine, Liddy looked up and watched the doctor's arm as she leaned over her and picked up a tape measure from the shelf above. The doctor's short sleeves moved and, from her submissive position, Liddy could see her white bra underneath and she felt as though she were prying into the doctor's private places. The doctor measured her from the top of her uterus to her pubic bone. This was suddenly so familiar.

"About thirty weeks, I would say, but the scan will confirm your dates. It *is* unusual to conceive at your age," the doctor went on in her clear, clinical voice, "but your blood pressure is more or less normal and you seem perfectly well. The worry is the baby having had no prenatal care. You must have a detailed scan immediately and see the consultant obstetrician. We need to know how the baby is."

Liddy sat up. "But I can't be. I've had all my babies. I'm a grandmother. I'm much too old now."

"Well, you're not, obviously. It doesn't often happen, but it is quite possible, as you have proved."

"But I can have an abortion, can't I?" Liddy felt as though she had stepped outside her body and was watching a pregnant someone else asking these questions.

The doctor shook her head. "I'm afraid not; it's definitely too late. You wouldn't find anyone prepared to terminate at this late stage."

Liddy sat as in spasm, her brain refusing to function as she watched the doctor make a telephone call to the consultant obstetrician.

"She should be seen as soon as possible," Liddy heard the doctor say from somewhere distant outside her head. She watched her fill out a form, write a letter and put the papers into an envelope.

"They'll see you at the clinic ten o'clock tomorrow. They're expecting you. Give them this"—she handed Liddy the letter—"and make an appointment with me next week."

The doctor opened the office door for her and for a brief, soft moment reached out to Liddy in sympathy. It was almost as if she didn't know how to begin acknowledging the magnitude of what her patient had just found out.

"It's a shock for you, I know. But you're healthy and I hope, I'm *sure* we'll find the baby is, too. Your previous pregnancies were all quite straightforward, weren't they?"

But those pregnancies were in another lifetime, Liddy thought as she stumbled out of the room. She had this strange feeling that the pale green walls of the doctor's office had completely filled her head—she could see only pale green, hear pale green, feel pale green.

Liddy sat in her car in the parking lot and her brain slowly cranked into life. She thought in short, sharp sentences.

So I haven't got cancer or heart disease. That's good. I am pregnant. No, that's not good. My husband and I have not had sex for five years.

Mary poured Liddy a glass of wine. "If you've been drinking your way through six months of pregnancy, one more bottle isn't going to harm it. It'll help with the shock," she said firmly.

Liddy had fled straight from the doctor's office to Mary's house. Mary—her very dearest friend with whom she shared everything. She had been painting in her studio when Liddy had rushed in, blurting out her news in blind terror.

"And Martin will know it's not his," were Mary's first, succinct words as she turned to put her brushes into a jam jar of turps, then gently led Liddy into the kitchen.

"How could this happen to me?" Liddy shook her head.

Now that she had told, it suddenly became real and permanent—the fuzzy pale-green dream in which she had been enveloped since being in the office had broken up and Liddy thought she had never felt such panic and distress. The worst thing was the realization that no one, not even Mary, could make it better for her.

Mary spoke slowly and thoughtfully in her gentle voice. "I

suppose there is always the possibility you may not be so far gone as the doctor thinks."

"She seemed pretty certain."

"Well, you are going to have to think this through, Liddy, before you have the scan—you should know what you're going to do, because I think sometimes it's easier to make plans while there is still a possibility that you might not have to use them."

"Why was I so stupid?" Liddy whimpered. "Why didn't I *think?*"

Because Liddy had never thought to think. She had been too transported by the brief, glorious affair with pretty Barney—the same age as her son—who had found her sexy, desirable and seemingly irresistible. And who had made her laugh with his mad energy and bad jokes.

He had arrived in her jewelry class last September—wandered in, tall and slouching, in a scruffy tartan jacket, his thick straw hair beaded with autumn rain and his stubbly face creased in a wide smile. The five young mothers and two young girls in the class had all looked up at him with interest. Only Geoffrey, the elderly man who was trying to make a silver-wedding present for his wife, remained head down over his work at the bench.

"Jewelry?" Barney had asked briefly.

Liddy had nodded and they had smiled together, both recognizing something in the other.

He was a cobbler by trade, making clogs, boots and leather bags, selling them at markets and music festivals. He wanted, it seemed, to increase his repertoire and learn the basics of jewelry making. With the arrogance of youth, he had arbitrarily decided that he could easily learn all that was necessary to make jewelry, so he had paid for only one term.

By the middle of the first term, Barney had signed on for

the rest of the year and he and Liddy had had their first fuck, up against a wall in the classroom after everyone had gone home. They had only just not been caught by the caretaker rattling his keys.

For Liddy, whose sexual urges had apparently lain dormant for five years, it was a most exhilarating experience. She still often replayed the memory of the immediate sexual frisson between them, and remembered the electric moment when the flirting became something more; when she realized that her life had been ambushed and that an affair with Barney was not only possible but also inevitable.

Her greatest surprise was that in the end it was no surprise. It was as though she knew the moment she saw Barney what would happen between them.

"Why?" she had asked after the first time. "I'm fat and forty-nine."

"You're not fat, you're just big. And I knew you the minute I walked in here. Just like you knew me," Barney had mumbled into her neck. "I've never met a woman like you before. You're generous and you're sensuous. You know what to do with your body—and with mine."

She felt silky and beautiful once again: her skin glowed, her hair shone—she cared what she looked like and she liked how she looked. Her heart jumped and her hands shook when she caught sight of him. Awake, she thought about sex with him, and in her sleep he insinuated himself into all her dreams. And every day for three months she smiled plump, contented smiles into her mirror.

Barney, he told her, lived with his girlfriend and also with a lodger who seemed to spend all his time in front of afternoon television learning how to make chocolate cakes and restore old cupboards. It was because of the sedentary nature of the lodger that Barney and Liddy spent the next few months having furtive sex in the car, the municipal park, the attic of a building site and in a garage.

It was such good sex, too—once Liddy had realized that Barney, a child of the curiously repressed nineties, could be released from such a conventional attitude to the physical act of lovemaking. As her confidence grew, she began to redis-cover her long-abandoned hippie philosophy. Barney's youth and strength seemed to liberate her free spirit and, from out-side her head, she could see herself behaving like an irresponsible young woman. But inside, his obvious admira-tion for her became a heady drug that she simply could not resist.

And it wasn't just sex. The more they talked, the more Liddy felt released to be what she considered her real self. No longer limited to being a wife, a mother and a grandmother, she became someone else: someone young, thoughtless and care-free—her own creation. It was like being on a roller coaster that was going faster and faster. The ride stopped only when it became clear that Barney was convinced he was in love with her and was quite prepared to ditch his girlfriend. Liddy was scared then. His declaration of love made her realize that she, too, was in danger of becoming seriously attached. Suddenly their relationship was becoming frighteningly real, no longer a game. Sanity replaced the brief madness that had captured her, and Liddy, with much sadness and needing a great deal of strength, put a stop to their relationship. Feeling as though she were returning a wonderful Christmas present, she tried to unravel the affair without diminishing the relationship that Barney thought they had. It was one of the most difficult things Liddy had ever had to do and also served to remind her never to repeat the experience. It was, in the end, an acrimonious parting, one that Barney, unable to accept that she was not prepared even to think about leaving her husband for him, failed to achieve cleanly and, for a while, he hung around

Liddy's classes being alternately aggressive and pleading. Then one day, he didn't turn up; he just disappeared and Liddy, whose head and heart, for those few months, had been completely hijacked by Barney, felt empty and dull again.

That had been over five months ago.

"How *could* I have not known that I was pregnant?" Liddy asked Mary. "I feel like a bloody stupid teenager."

"Didn't you feel sick at all? Have you not felt it move?"

Liddy shrugged. "I don't think so. I don't remember. Any twinge or anything, I just put down to my age. I've had heartburn occasionally, but I thought that was just wind and I've often had that. I have put on a bit of weight, I suppose, but you know me, always getting fatter and then dieting. Done it all my life. But I should at least have wondered. Being pregnant just never occurred to me." She buried her hands in her head and the tears fell through her fingers. "Oh, God, what am I going to do, Mary? I've blown everything. I thought I'd got away with it. I knew I didn't deserve to, but I thought I had and that Martin would never know about Barney. Oh, God, God, *God*. I can't tell him about it."

She was aware of Mary getting up from her chair and heard her open a cupboard. Her movements slow and deliberate, Mary opened a bag of chips, shook them into a blue pottery bowl and placed them by Liddy's elbow. She touched Liddy's arm lightly in an uncharacteristically tactile gesture.

"You will have to tell him," she said. "There is nothing else you can do."

"But it's not fair; he'll be devastated. We haven't had sex for years."

"Liddy, it takes two *not* to have sex just as it takes two to have sex," Mary said severely.

"But it *is* my fault," Liddy wailed. "I did go off sex for a while and Martin agreed to back off and not having sex became a habit with us. It was Barney who made me want it again, but somehow afterwards I never tried with Martin and now it's too late, I've hurt him too much. I'm so scared of what he'll say."

Mary stood up, towering over Liddy and demanding her attention.

"Liddy, you've got to listen to me. I've something to tell you and it's really important."

Liddy lifted her head and looked at Mary who spoke in a low matter-of-fact voice.

"I found out something yesterday and I was going to talk to you about it this evening. I don't know how you'll react to this, but apparently Martin is having an affair."

The shock she felt, Liddy realized, was at the lack of shock with which she received the news. Had she recently written that storyline in her head to make herself feel better about Barney or had she already thought? Guessed? Known?

"Who?" was all she asked.

"Fay Jackson. Lizzie Wilson saw them together at the Black Swan and, being Lizzie, asked a friend of Fay's outright. The friend didn't know who it was, but she knew that Fay has been having an affair with a married man."

Fay Jackson. A family friend. Their children had been at the same school. She owned the dress shop next to Martin's bookshop and, for God's sake, she was the same age as herself. Liddy was surprised at that and shaken, too. She realized that if the idea had been at the back of her mind that Martin had someone else, then that someone else was young—someone for lust, not for life.

Mary broke the silence. "So now how do you feel?" she asked in a measured voice.

"Are *you* surprised?"

"I don't know. It's interesting, though, isn't it? This is another element to your situation that you've got to think about." Mary always had a way of sounding curious but dispassionate, of opening up intricate lines of thought that could possibly lead through to a conclusion and a solution. Mary the thinker. Liddy had relied on Mary's trains of thought for years. Just as Mary had always valued Liddy's natural spontaneity.

They had been solid friends since they met the day their eldest children started nursery school. They recognized the bond between them as they watched each other for the first time in the playground. They were two sides of the sixties fashion revolution: Mary with her straight angular-cut hair and somber geometric clothes, Liddy with long tumbling hair and messy rag-bag skirts. Two women, both creative, spending long philosophical hours discussing life, listening to each other, dissecting and sorting out their lives together. It had been Liddy who comforted Mary when her husband was killed in a climbing accident and it had been Mary who had supported Liddy through her stormy relationship with her troublesome second daughter. They knew each other very well.

"I probably imagined," Liddy began slowly, "somewhere at the back of my mind, that he did have someone. I know he always enjoyed sex and he's obviously not been getting that from me. So, if I pictured her at all, she would have been young, blond and fluffy. The awful thing is, I was probably assuming that I could get us back together again when I bothered to put my mind to it. How arrogant is that? But my redundancy has been looming for some time and I suppose I was concentrating on that. But Fay, now I know it's Fay—she could be *me*."

"A bit more of a sophisticated you," Mary said with a smile.

Liddy poured herself another glass of wine.

"This is so peculiar. I don't really know how to feel about it all."

"You could start by telling him about the baby, particularly knowing that he hasn't been honest with you either."

Liddy was surprised to find that with Mary's disclosure she had momentarily put her pregnancy to the back of her mind.

"One doesn't cancel out the other, though, does it?"

"How would Martin feel about bringing up someone else's baby?"

"At our age? I should think he'd be horrified." Liddy was remembering a conversation she and Martin had had many years ago. "Actually, I know he wouldn't even contemplate it. We had a conversation once about adopting a baby and he said then he could never have someone else's child. His parents adopted his brother, you know, and he turned out to be very disturbed—virtually destroyed the family."

Mary hated not knowing the end of things.

"What happened to him?"

"He died just before we got married."

"But this is half your baby. It's not all stranger. Now, Lid, I'm only playing devil's advocate here, but suppose, just suppose," Mary said slowly and thoughtfully, "Martin used your pregnancy as a reason for leaving you? You've got to think that possibility out, too."

"So he could go and live with Fay, you mean?" Liddy felt a lurch of panic. How had she let her and Martin slip away so? "I don't want that." Her voice trembled uncontrollably. "I love him. I can't lose him, not now, after all these years. We've always been together, we've brought up three children, we're *friends*, but"—she stopped and made a face—"maybe, I suppose if I'm being honest, we haven't been particularly friendly lately. We seem to live together more like housemates than lifemates. Sort of two self-contained and silent islands. Now it appears he's found someone else to talk to. God, it would be all right if he was screwing a not very bright young girl, but Fay, now he could live with her." Liddy felt like a rabbit caught in the headlights of an oncoming car.

"I can't bring up a baby by myself, Mary, I just can't. I'm too old and I'm too tired—I'll be seventy when it's twenty. I can't face it Mary, I can't . . ."

"Mrs. Byford? This is Marjorie Turner. We've just moved into Malting Cottage and I'm told you're organizing the village fête."

Laura drew out her fête file from the shelf under the telephone.

"Yes, that's right," she said briskly, a pen already in her hand.

"I can make a tray of fairy cakes and half a dozen loaves of bread for the cake stall, if that would be helpful."

Laura watched her husband walk across the yard and registered to herself that she must take his Barbour into Frenton to have the zip mended.

"Oh, that would be marvelous, thank you so much," she gushed. "Now will you deliver or shall I collect?"

Marjorie Turner wanted to talk and she began to offer fruit cakes, Victoria sponges and help with the children's face-painting. Laura was torn between hanging on to the telephone as Marjorie kept upping her offers of help, and curtailing the call so that she could move on to her next task of the day.

"Well, that is so kind of you. If you could bring all the baking round here early on the morning of the fête, it will give my team time to price it up. Thank you *so* much."

She put the phone down, finished writing the list of promised cakes and help and slammed the file shut with a sigh of pleasure. It was going to be a good fête. Now she had to move along; she had a list as long as her arm—all to be done before she met the school bus.

Laura allowed herself a minute to enjoy the smell of roses and beeswax polish in the hall. She had once read a literary description of a shiny copper vase full of plump garden roses on a polished hall table and the image had always stayed with her. She wanted that image to be hers and now it was reality and she never failed to feel a kick of pleasure when she stood here, in the flagstoned hall of the Queen Anne farmhouse that had been in Fergus's family since Domesday. She could hear Connie vacuuming the children's bedrooms upstairs, the chickens chucking outside the window and she could smell the casserole in the Aga. This was her world—almost everything she had ever wanted.

Laura gave a sigh of satisfaction and consulted her list. She had to deliver an ice cream order to the vicarage, pick up the meat from the village butcher and finish the new curtains for the spare room. But first she must ring Miranda about the surprise party.

The kitchen door crashed shut and Laura heard Fergus plod across the kitchen into the farm office.

"Laura," he roared.

"Coming." She hurried into the office and found Fergus hurling bits of paper around in his customary manner.

"I can't find the Mallets' invoice. Bloody fools have sent the wrong feed order."

"Calm down, darling, I'll find it for you—there you are: filed under *M* for Mallets." She handed it to him triumphantly.

His face creased into a charming grin.

"You're a star," he said, bending down and kissing the tip of her little nose. "What would I do without you?"

"Go bankrupt, probably," Laura said prosaically. She smiled up at him, but Fergus had already gone.

She refiled the scattered papers—creating order where there was disorder, her favorite occupation—and went back to the hall to ring Miranda, party file in hand.

"Miranda, it's me, Laura. Is this a good time?"

On the other end of the phone, Miranda sounded distracted.

"If it's quick."

Laura never expected a salutation from her somewhat spiky younger sister. She had always felt lumpen and ordinary next to fragile, willowy Miranda, who was so beautiful, yet so highly strung and sometimes so acerbic in her manner. From earliest memory, Laura had been slightly in awe of Miranda and, now as then, she took refuge in being the eldest child, looking after her brother and her sister, her family. Laura felt comfortable taking charge—organizing, delegating, helping and bringing the strands together. It was what she was good at.

"It's about the party," she said now. "You've spoken to Dad, have you? He's got it organized, has he? He's got to keep Mum out of the way for the whole day."

"It's all arranged. They're going shopping in the morning to buy her a dress and then have a late lunch at Craneton Lock." Miranda sounded bored. "Mum's friend Judy is doing the catering and she says they'll be there by midday."

"I really think we could have managed the food between us," Laura grumbled.

"Well, I don't," Miranda said crisply. "I've got better things to do with my life than stuff little bits of phyllo pastry with pesto."

"Well, I'm bringing ice cream, of course."

"Of course," Miranda breathed.

"I've arranged for the drink to arrive at four, plus glasses and ice." Laura looked down at her sheaves of paper. "But I think we should all be at home by eleven."

Laura, the one sibling with a real family home of her own, was the only one who still called their natal house "home." "We'll need to move furniture and make the place look presentable. Would you tell Alex? Today—and for Heaven's sake, make sure he's concentrating."

Miranda sighed heavily over the phone. "Laura, can't you? I'm really quite busy at the moment. And Richard and I are going out tonight."

Laura bit back a curt remark along the lines of Miranda didn't know what busy was: she should try running three children, one of whom had Down's syndrome; a farm; a homemade ice cream business and numerous village commitments.

"Oh, all right," she said irritably. "I'll ring him. I just hope I don't get Mungo, he's so . . . so camp."

Alex, the youngest in the family, had been Laura's baby. A round and ridiculously pretty little boy, he had good-humoredly allowed his sister to lug him about like a real live doll. She was devoted to him.

But Alex had had to grow up and, somewhere so deep inside her that she could never voice it, Laura felt confused and saddened by his homosexuality.

"Mungo is hardly as camp as our brother," Miranda said affectionately. She had no difficulties with their younger brother's sexual proclivities. Now she gave in gracefully to her sister's demands. "It's OK, Laura, I'll ring him. And stop worrying—it'll be a great party and Mum doesn't suspect a thing. Must go, the other phone's ringing. See you on Saturday."

Laura sighed slightly as she put down the telephone and tripped off to the dairy to pick up the ice cream order.

There was only one phone in Miranda's office, but Laura didn't know that.

Laura is so *family* minded. It's so important to her, Miranda thought grumpily, as she leafed through the pile of paper on her desk, counting the editorial pages that had just come up from the magazine's design department.

She picked up the phone and dialed Alex's mobile number. "Alex, it's Miranda."

"Mirry, sweetheart, bless, I was just thinking about you yesterday."

"Constructively, I hope."

"Oh, very. I was looking at a new mag that's just out—high-powered working woman's stuff. You should be writing it. You must send them your CV immed*iatement.*"

Miranda sighed.

"Alex, sort your own career out, not mine. Anyway, why aren't you at work?"

"How do you know I'm not?"

"You sound at home."

Alex squealed with laughter.

"You're quite right. We are at home. Mungo has a very important audition this afternoon and I've thrown a sickie so that I can stay with him and keep his mind off it."

"I don't want to know," Miranda said firmly. "I'm just ringing you on Laura's orders. She's gone into overdrive about this bloody party. She wants us all on parade by eleven in the morning, and that includes you and Mungo."

"Oh, good for Laura," Alex said warmly. His voice turned a little wistful. "But I do wish she would *try* and bond with Mungo a little bit. Last time we were all together it was a bit embarrassing, I thought."

"I suppose we're right to believe that Mum wants a surprise fiftieth birthday party," Miranda said quickly, refusing to get into the minefield of Laura's attitude to Alex's boyfriend.

"Ooh, yes, of course she does. Who wouldn't? Everyone loves parties. I want a bonanza of one when *I'm* fifty, God forbid."

Miranda heard the shudder in Alex's voice.

"Please don't be late, Alex, and for goodness' sake try not to bait Laura this weekend. No limp wrists and screeching. You only do it to annoy, you know you do."

"I'll be good, promise," Alex assured her solemnly.

Miranda smiled as she rang off. She was very fond of her baby brother, quite fond of Laura, too, really nowadays. But it hadn't always been like that. Miranda, only eighteen months younger than her sister, had strived through her childhood to be like Laura, lovable, friendly and homely. She had desperately wanted to be ordinary-looking, to have thick blond hair and a healthy, rosy, round face with a dusting of freckles. She had wanted to be able to do the right things with dolls and Wendy houses, to bake tidy jam tarts, to play snap without getting cross, and she had wanted to be small and compact like Laura, too. But she had grown tall and thin with dead straight, noncolor brown hair and her face was pointy and pale. She was so different from the other two, her mother would joke that she was a foundling. "My beautiful doorstep child," she would say. A loving remark, Miranda knew that, but no one had realized how the feeling of being different had grown up with her. She had taken refuge in a bitter sense of humor, sharp remarks; in a solitary life, writing angry little stories for herself and in an eating disorder that left her thinner and pokier than ever. Miranda knew herself to be ugly, yet Richard, like so many others before him, never tired of telling her how beautiful she was.

She attempted to bring order to the paper in front of her and thought about the problem of Richard.

"So when are we going to do the deed?" he had asked, only last night as they cleared up the Indian takeaway they'd eaten late, when they had both got back from their offices. He had come up behind her and held her tightly in his arms. "I think two years is probably a long enough engagement, don't you? I'm a conventional man. I want you to be my wife."

"Why?" she had asked. "We're fine as we are, aren't we? We've got everything we need here." She looked round at their smart little flat. "Why get married?"

"Babies?" Richard had said hopefully with a smile in his voice and Miranda's heart had thudded. Her nemesis was hovering just around the corner—babies. The idea of an alien body inside hers, taking control of it, then the emergence of such a body through her own and the confusion it would bring into her world terrified her and made her feel physically sick every time she thought about it.

She managed to distract Richard from the subject for weeks at a time, but then, like last night, he would begin to talk earnestly about babies. He was over ten years older than she; he wanted to be a father while he was still young enough. Miranda simply wanted a career in writing—and Richard—with no added complications. She never ever wanted a baby, but she didn't dare tell Richard that.

She picked up the phone and dialed the number of the glossy magazine of which Richard was publisher. A magazine considerably more prestigious than the one for which she worked as a subeditor.

"Richard Butler, please. It's Miranda."

Alex clambered back into bed still giggling.

"The point of a mobile phone is that you don't have to move to answer it. *It*'s mobile, not you," Mungo said, turning over onto his back and holding out an arm for Alex to nestle in.

"I left it in the kitchen last night." Alex looked up into Mungo's face adoringly. "If you remember I had other things in my hand when we came in here." He leered suggestively.

"Who was it anyway?" Mungo asked, his big hands stroking Alex's blond head.

"It was Miranda about Mum's party on Saturday. You are coming, aren't you?"

"What, miss a chance to get on your elder sister's nerves? I don't think so."

"I've promised Mirry we'll play nicely."

"Then so we shall," murmured Mungo, his hand slipping down between Alex's legs.

Alex had met Mungo at a party full of screaming queens in

black leather and studded collars. Alex, new to this particularly
camp scene, had felt nervous among such gay strength and
camp aggression. Mungo, his large frame dressed simply in a
well-cut Hackett suit and a bottle of designer beer in his hand,
had stood out as a piece of comparative normality and Alex
had naturally gravitated to him. Afterwards, Alex was to think
that it had all seemed completely meant: Mungo was an actor,
Alex had always thought that he wanted to be one; Mungo was
big and dark, Alex small and blond; they shared a liking for
opera, Scrabble, *Coronation Street* and Marmite sandwiches.
Mungo seemed perfectly happy to listen to Alex burbling on
about his attempts to grow an oleander bush from a cutting
and Alex listened wide-eyed to Mungo's theater chat. They
passed the whole of the evening together and Alex, who had
spent the last six months celebrating his newfound promiscu-
ity with absolutely anyone who took his fancy, invited Mungo
back to his studio apartment.

Sex with Mungo came as a revelation to Alex. He found
that sex could really be lovemaking—gentle, intelligent and
selfless. He fell devotedly in love.

The next morning Mungo had spoken severely to Alex
about his morals and the company he was currently keeping.
He had suggested that he do something serious about training
to be an actor and they had then gone out to find a flat
together. Mungo had also bought two King Charles spaniels
with beautiful deep-brown seal's eyes, which Alex felt was the
greatest symbol of love and commitment. That had been over
a year ago and they were still blissful: the flat was full of dog
baskets, gay videos, Alex's potted plants and Mungo's gym
equipment. At twenty-nine, Mungo was four years older than
Alex and slowly and conscientiously building up his body and
his career as an actor. Alex had got himself a job in a ticket
agency and was working on audition speeches for drama
schools.

"Have we thought of a birthday present?" Mungo asked as he was getting dressed sometime later.

Alex, sated, lay back against the pillows.

"No, we haven't, actually. I'll mosey round Camden Lock while you're at your audition."

Mungo took some bills out of his wallet and put them on the bedside table.

"Well, here's my contribution. Get her something really nice. I like your mum."

The fiftieth birthday party that Laura, Miranda and Alex were organizing was to be yet another surprise for Liddy in a week already packed full of surprises.

Chapter

∽

T W O

There was no last-minute reprieve for Liddy. She had only a
hazy idea of the date of her last period, but she knew
exactly the three months during which she could have conceived. More scientifically, the scan showed the baby to be
approximately thirty-two weeks and with no obvious complications, although the consultant pointed out gently that it would
be pointless doing any of the conventional tests since it was too
late to terminate anyway. Liddy made it quite clear that she did
not want to know the sex.

"How could I have not known that I was pregnant all these
months?" she railed at length to the consultant, who appeared
inappropriately calm about the situation.

"It's not that common, Mrs. Claver, especially with someone who has been pregnant before, but it can happen,
particularly to the larger-built woman and particularly at
this time of life when you're really not expecting it. Now,
the important thing is to take care of you and the baby. I
want to see you every week. It's not easy carrying a baby at
your age."

"I seem to have managed it so far without much disruption," Liddy said grimly. The consultant didn't smile. She wondered if he ever did.

"On the evidence of the scan," he continued gravely, "the baby seems perfectly healthy and probably due around the middle of August, though I would say it is quite small for its dates."

Liddy's other babies had been quite small, for which she remembered always being very grateful when she heard about friends delivering monsters. She had known immediately that she was pregnant with Laura and had been irritated and impatient with the doctor for making her wait for two missed periods before confirming the pregnancy. She hadn't, it was true, looked pregnant till very late, which had disappointed her, longing as she was to have the experience of wearing smocks and showing off her newfound fecundity. The other pregnancies were the same, although with them she didn't really have time to think about it.

"I'm not surprised it's small," Liddy said bitterly. "It's hardly been nourished and cared for. It's lived on a diet of wine, cigarettes and Weight Watchers food."

The consultant frowned; then his face gave way and a small crease of a smile hovered around his mouth.

"Babies are tough little things. However, Mrs. Claver, I suggest you give up cigarettes and alcohol immediately and start eating sensibly. Time to diet afterwards."

Afterwards. *Afterwards* just didn't bear thinking about.

Liddy drove out of the hospital, through the little market town, past her own house and out toward the bridle path over the fields where she often walked. It was nearly the longest day and summer had eventually come to the Midlands; the rusty earthed fields which had lain bare during the winter were now squares of thick green interspersed with odd patches of yellow rape, glinting acidly in the sun. She walked slowly up the gentle hill toward the ironstone church at the top, suddenly and acutely aware of her baby inside her. It was a real, alive and, according to the scan, a whole little person and she absolutely didn't know how she felt about it. She instinctively wanted to protect and love it, but she didn't *want* it. And she didn't want the pain and hurt that it was going to bring to those around her whom she loved.

Rage at her own crass stupidity boiled over inside her. How could she have been so bloody unaware? Barney had been divine—just divine. Flattered by his youth and beautiful body, she had had a wonderful game. And it *was* a game, though she had only realized that just in time to stop it from slipping unobtrusively into something more serious. She had never had an affair before, never planned to, never been tempted, yet Barney had somehow pushed the right buttons and she had not regretted the affair or the end of it. She had been jaded and disillusioned. Fifty loomed, along with possible redundancy; she felt that her jewelry designs mirrored her life and had become colorless and unremarkable. And she and Martin had drifted apart, either through idleness or boredom, she didn't know which, but she had intended to find out and make it better—she really had. But now. Now this. It was unfair, so utterly unfair. She wanted to scream her anger up at the sky. Why? Why? Why did this have to happen to her?

Liddy sat on a bench in the quiet graveyard—"the grave garden," Miranda used to call it when she was little—and wondered if she might wake up in a minute to find that none of this had happened. She held her hands over her stomach, which she could see now truly was a lump. She wondered if she really could feel the baby kicking or whether it was her imagination working because she knew there was a living thing inside her.

She looked across the valley below her: a tractor ground up and down a field and a few cars streaked along the ribbon of curly gray lane.

She tried to think in straight lines as Mary would. The baby was—there was nothing she could do about it. It just was. But Martin, Martin *and* Fay—that made her stomach lurch and her heart turn over. While she had stopped bothering about Martin, someone else had started. From where she was now, Liddy could look back on Barney as a brief aberration, but Fay was, possibly, quite a different thing. Barney wasn't Fay, he was a roll in the hay. Liddy shook her head as if to get the ridiculous rhyme out of her head.

An unreasonable anger against Martin rose up in her—how could he? With Fay? Not when he loved Liddy. They'd always loved each other, hadn't they? Could she confront him and use his disloyalty to mitigate her own? Could it really be that Martin was looking for a way out and the baby would be it? Did he perhaps not love her anymore, after all?

Liddy stood up and began to walk back down the hill. She was terribly scared—scared that she would lose Martin and alienate her children, scared that she would end up all on her own with a fatherless baby that she was too tired and too old to look after. She was scared that something would be wrong with this uncared-for baby and that it would be her fault. Her punishment. She was also, she realized, scared of physically giving birth: the pain, the danger to the baby and herself—and all this fear and panic she was feeling had been brought about by her own utter stupidity.

Liddy had only one other good friend close enough to tell about the pregnancy and her husband's affair. Judy had known about Barney and, during the liaison, had taken vicarious pleasure in a woman of a similar age having an affair with someone young enough to be her son.

"It's what should be prescribed for every menopausal woman," she would sigh enviously. "I wish I could find one."

But "*Sh-it*" was what Judy said when Liddy told her about her pregnancy. And then, "I'll buy you lunch after the hospital."

Liddy was grateful for any excuse not to go home—somehow not being at home gave her a brief feeling of being someone else, someone not involved in this drama.

Judy was already at the wine bar. She watched Liddy make her way to the table.

"Do you know," she said cheerily, "almost overnight, you've started looking pregnant. You're even beginning to waddle."

Liddy had noticed that as well.

"I'm going to be fifty tomorrow," she said. "People don't get pregnant at my age. I should have lost all my estrogen or whatever it is women need to have babies."

"True, but he had young, virile sperm, didn't he? Your fading estrogen probably didn't stand a chance against that," Judy said.

"Well, I wish he'd kept his thrusting virile sperm to himself, or in his girlfriend." Liddy snorted and then gave a faint smile at her own lack of reason.

"You didn't at the time, if I may say so." Judy looked at the menu. "God, this is crap. I should be running a restaurant really, not a lousy catering company. Come on, Lid, choose something healthy; we'd better feed the little thing."

"Don't give it an identity, please, Judy. I can't handle that at the moment."

"You know, you could have it adopted. Childless couples are crying out for babies." Judy liked rapid solutions.

"Oh, no, I couldn't go through with that," Liddy said with conviction. "I mean, what would it be like to abandon a baby? I couldn't. I know I would think about it every day, being brought up by someone else. I just couldn't bear it."

Judy frowned and Liddy remembered, too late, how Judy's sister had put her baby up for adoption many years ago when she was a teenager.

Judy's pained expression shocked Liddy into recognizing how much a personal crisis makes for self-obsession. But she still couldn't stop herself going on. It was as though if she kept talking, she could drive out the panic.

"What will it be like going through the whole thing over again? I never was a very good parent, you know, not when they were growing up," she admitted honestly. "Martin was a much better one. He looked after them while I concentrated on my jewelry business." She made a face and said ruefully, "Of course, that failed in the end, too. I shall be so old, I *am* too old for God's sake. I'm a grandmother. That's what I should be. Giving the babies back to the parents when I'm fed up playing granny."

Judy visibly shuddered. "No sleep, never going out, baby buggies, croup—asthma, actually; they all have asthma nowadays because of the pollution. Then, of course, it's teenagers, drugs, AIDS, taxi service in the middle of the night, loud music—"

"Yes, thanks, Jude, shut up now."

"Look." Judy leaned forward, speaking seriously. "I'm really surprised about Martin and Fay. I mean, they are both *so* not the sort of people to have an affair. I think it's nothing, a moment in time, like yours was. I honestly don't believe that Martin will let you do this on your own, whatever the circumstances. He is such a kind, generous man and he adores children, and I know he loves you. You two have just always been together." Judy stopped for a moment and added with a sigh, "Heavens, you're the envy of all your friends; you share too much, you and Martin. I really believe that."

And Judy made Liddy believe it, too. She surprised herself by stopping at the gates of the primary school on the way home and watching the mothers talking together in the playground as their children spilled out of the school in noisy heaps, flapping paintings and cardboard models around them.

She wondered what it would be like to be one of them again.

* * *

Mary, however, was not quite as confident as Judy.

With a desperate urge to avoid Martin until her thoughts had begun to reassemble themselves into some logical form, Liddy spent the evening with Mary. She wondered if it was in her imagination that Martin seemed relieved that she would be out.

Now that she had been to the hospital, she knew there was no escape. There were no more *whys*, no more *if onlys*.

Their discussion turned solely to Martin.

"Don't assume anything, Liddy," Mary urged. "As well as you might think you know someone, you simply can't always tell how they will react. Martin may be having an affair and it may be something that just happened and not a major affair, but you don't know and you won't until you start talking."

"But I know Martin. He's so . . . . so"—Liddy searched for the right word—"*loyal.*"

Mary grimaced. "I don't know and nor do you until you ask him. But you've got to think. Your affair may be over now, but you're actually confronting him with something much bigger. It's going to be a lot for him to take on board."

Yesterday afternoon Liddy's world seemed to have stopped spinning and since then she had created at least three different conversations with Martin, all with different outcomes. Somewhere in her zigzag lines of thought had crept in the possibility of the baby not surviving. Then she had considered her own children and hated herself for almost wishing a new life dead. Her *own* children, she had called them. Wasn't this baby her own as well?

She felt as though her head were full of spaghetti.

"I don't want to tell him. I don't know how to," Liddy moaned.

Mary was silent for a moment. "You have to, Liddy. Abortion is not an option now. You can't pretend the baby is not there."

"I could run away," Liddy said half seriously.

Mary looked at her with a raised eyebrow. "Oh, yes. Where to?"

Just for a moment, Liddy saw a way out.

"I could go and stay with Amanda in France," she said defiantly. "You've met Amanda. We went to school together."

"You wouldn't want to have a baby abroad, Liddy, be reasonable. Anyway," she added with a smile, "born in France, wouldn't it be liable for National Service? What about family?"

"I've only got the lesbian great-aunts in Cornwall."

"Do the lesbian great-aunts like babies?" Mary inquired tentatively.

"No, I shouldn't think so; they like cats—but my great-aunt Cleo is my only living relation."

"The other one isn't, though. How would she feel about it?"

Liddy thought about Cynthia—Cyn; not a real aunt, but Cleo's partner who had been with her for so long she had become an honorary great-aunt.

Cleo was in her early nineties, Cyn was six years younger, and these redoubtable women lived in a large house in Cornwall with sixteen cats and various itinerant seagulls. But until fifteen years ago they had lived in an elegant doll-size mews flat in Kensington, stuffed full of beautiful furniture and scruffy stray cats. Throughout her childhood Liddy had loved to visit: in her young eyes they were a glamorous couple, so different from her plain, rotund mother. Cleo, tall and elegant in beautifully cut expensive suits and dresses; Cyn, short and squat, so masculine in tailored trousers and a white shirt buttoned to the neck with a large cameo brooch. Both with hair that seemed sculpted to their head in stiff, geometric waves and sometimes with a blue rinse, sometimes a ginger one, depending on the season. To a child like Liddy, their thick eyeshadow and red lipstick, applied regularly wherever they went, were symbols of the highest sophistication. She had always wanted a powder puff like Cleo's, soft, long-haired and attached to a silk handkerchief—she could still smell the sweet scent that surrounded the ritual of Cleo powdering her nose. Soon after Liddy's mother died and much to all their friends' mystification, Cleo and Cyn had moved down with the cats to a small seaside village where they were viewed with amazement and suspicion by the villagers. Cleo, it transpired, had longed for a country garden all her life, but Cyn made no pretense of being anything other than a Londoner under sufferance in the country.

"Ghastly place, the country. So parochial. So bloody twee," she would grumble. "Can't think what Cleo sees in the place."

Liddy's lips twitched now as she contemplated Cyn's reaction.

"Cyn would probably tell me to 'bugger orf.' They'd take me in if I was having a clutch of kittens, of course." Liddy shook her head suddenly as if to stop her mind riding the fantasy.

"I need time to think," she said piteously.

"You don't have time, Liddy," Mary said crisply. "Talk tonight."

But Martin was in bed asleep when Liddy crept home.

And the next day was her fiftieth birthday.

Because Sunday, it appeared, was the only day all their children could come up for a birthday lunch, Martin and Liddy had agreed that they would celebrate her actual birthday quietly at home, just going out to dinner in the evening. It made it worse that today would have to be the day to talk.

Liddy only managed sleep as the early morning light seeped in round the curtains. Martin woke her up with a cup of tea, a large bunch of flowers and a package.

"Happy birthday, darling." He leant over and kissed the top of her head as she struggled out of heavy sleep and tried to marshal her thoughts. He sat beside her while she opened her present—a beautiful gold Longines watch. Liddy was touched—such a perfect present, something she had always wanted, but was it, she now wondered, guilt gold? It felt so strange.

They opened her birthday cards together, laughing at the silly ones and crowing at the largesse of Aunt Cleo's check. Liddy was bewildered at how they could both be so normal, each with their own apocalyptic secret squirrelled away inside. It was as though they were automatically falling into a loving behavior pattern that was historical and embedded naturally deep in them both.

"We could go to the Caribbean for weeks, courtesy of Aunt Cleo," Martin said, looking at the check.

"But you'd hate that."

"I probably would," he said cheerfully. "Perhaps we could go to the west coast of Ireland instead."

"Martin, you hate to leave Market Ketton for more than a day."

"I do," he admitted. "However, I'm being very brave for your birthday. I'm leaving Hannah in the shop and taking you to Leicester to buy a new dress, then lunch at Craneton Lock."

"A new dress—what do I want a new dress for?"

"Every woman wants a new dress, don't they? Anyway Laura told me I was to buy you one for your birthday. And you know we always do what she tells us."

"But you've given me the most beautiful watch." She must stop this birthday, find or make the space in which to start talking, but Martin seemed determined to be in charge of the day; he was moving too fast, almost hassling her, and she couldn't find a way in to stem his flow.

"And so now you're going to get a beautiful dress, too," he said firmly.

If I can find one to fit, Liddy thought gloomily.

"Martin, let's just stay here," she pleaded.

"Absolutely not. This is your half-century and we're going to celebrate." He hustled her upstairs to get dressed. "Come on, hurry up," and he disappeared into the garden.

Cleo rang up.

"Happy birthday, darling," she said in her rich throaty voice, always such a big voice from such a wispy, finely shaped person. "Have you a lovely day planned?"

"We're going shopping, would you believe, then out to lunch. The children are all coming up tomorrow."

"Oh, darling, that's lovely. Cyn sends her love, of course."

Liddy could hear Cyn muttering in the background.

"I don't know why everyone makes such a fuss of birthdays. Bloody ridiculous nonsense."

"You heard that, I expect." Cleo laughed down the phone. "Anyway, darling, I shall be thinking of you all day. Have such fun."

Fun was probably not high on the agenda today, Liddy thought as she got dressed. She put on her red Doc Martens and tried to recapture a little of the peace of mind she had had on Wednesday when she bought them. The day before everything changed. She chose a large glass brooch, one of her own designs, to secure a long scarf that she wound around her shoulders and let flow down the front of her dress. Now that she knew, her pregnancy suddenly seemed blindingly obvious.

"Hurry up, Liddy," Martin called from downstairs, jangling the car keys in his hand. "We've got to go."

"For goodness' sake, Martin, we've got all day," she grumbled as she reached the top of the stairs.

"Have you got your makeup?" he asked suddenly.

Baffled, Liddy looked at him.

"What a bizarre question. Have you ever known me to be without it?"

Martin looked up at her with an expression of such affection and tenderness on his face that her heart nearly broke into little pieces—there and then—all over the hall, the large hall that was stuffed full of the familiar bits of furniture and junk that had been collected during thirty years of family life.

"No, I suppose not," he said with a grin. "You're right. Now, come on, let's go."

The extraordinary thing was that Martin genuinely seemed to be enjoying himself as they battled round Leicester town center. It was almost like old times: they made the same comments on the people they passed, laughed at the same little jokes, looked into shop windows and longed for the same things. Martin bought an expensive modern laundry basket for their bathroom. Was this the action of a man who wanted to set up home with someone else? Liddy had to keep reminding herself that it couldn't be real. She wanted to get the whole thing over with; she was acutely conscious that she had gone up one dress size at least and that everything she tried on made her look like a bag of washing. By midmorning she was tempted to blow the whole thing and suggest that they bought a dress at Mothercare.

They found something eventually: a large floating dress from Monsoon that cost a fortune.

"I think that's definitely a frock, not a dress. Do you remember your mother always called them frocks? Such a funny word, *frock*," Martin said.

"Oh, no, it's a dress; don't you remember? She thought a frock must have smocking," Liddy said definitely and looking at Martin, she caught him grinning at her.

"I think you look beautiful in it, whatever it's called." And just for that moment, she believed him.

"You need some shoes to go with it," Martin said as they left the shop.

She only realized afterwards, of course, how desperate Martin was to spin out the day.

Laura was on a roll. She had harried Fergus and the children out of the house so early that morning that they had had to sit in the car for nearly an hour, parked round the corner from the house, waiting for her parents' car to sweep out of the drive. Fergus had slept solidly beside her in the passenger seat throughout the journey.

Everything was going according to plan: Judy had arrived with two young girls and was busy in the kitchen; Alex had arrived with armfuls of flowers and was dexterously arranging them in flamboyant arrangements; and Mungo and Fergus had been set to arranging garden furniture.

Laura was vacuuming the stairs when Miranda and Richard arrived.

"Miranda and friend reporting for duty." Richard tapped her on the shoulder and dropped a kiss on the top of her head.

"Bless you." Laura looked up in grateful affection. She was fond of Richard, admired his strength in dealing with Miranda. "The children are icing the cake in the kitchen. They are probably driving Judy mad. Would you two go and make peace?"

"Delighted to. Come on, Miranda, child duty."

Miranda only barely concealed a shudder.

"I must go to the loo first," and she escaped upstairs. Miranda and Richard both knew that she would not be joining him in the kitchen.

Mungo arrived in the drawing room looking for another job as Alex placed the last vase of flowers on the chiffonier.

"God, I'm talented," he said, stepping back to admire his work, his feet in first position, ballet-style, to annoy Laura who had bustled in pulling the vacuum cleaner behind her.

"Alex, you two can move the sofa and armchairs out of here

and put them in the study." Laura always seemed to avoid using Mungo's name—as if by the omission, she could pretend he was not part of Alex.

"I think she'd resent anyone who took you away from her, whatever sex they were," Mungo had once remarked phlegmatically.

"Couldn't we do something a little less butch, Laura darling?" Alex purposefully simpered in a high voice. "They look dreadfully heavy to me."

Mungo kicked him.

"Lay off your sister, you little beast. This is happy families time," he murmured out of the corner of his mouth. Alex blew him a kiss before picking up a large armchair with consummate ease.

Laura looked down at her list and shouted from the French windows, "Fergus, Fergus, I told you—the bench goes under the tree."

"Uncle Richard, Uncle Richard," clamored Tamsin and Rebecca, as Richard walked into the kitchen. Jake, Tamsin's twin and a more serious ten-year-old than his sister, was less ebullient; he merely looked up from the large bowl he was stirring and grinned at his uncle. Richard hugged the two little girls and then did a high five with Jake.

"Hello, kids—I've come to help with Granny's cake. It's looking good."

"Jake won't let me have a go." Tamsin, so like her mother, was outraged.

"You make the letters all wobbly," Jake said, squeezing the icing bag with vigor and concentrating on writing, his tongue hanging out.

Rebecca, aged seven, enthusiastically waved a spoon thick with multicolored icing sugar, her typically flat round face alight with pleasure and shining with sugar crumbs.

"Taste Uncle Richard 'slicious." Since attending a mainstream school three days a week, her speech had improved enormously in the last year, but Richard had to listen hard as she gabbled animatedly at him, and her movements were uncoordinated, powerful and wild.

Richard took the spoon from her and gave it a tentative lick.

"Ummm, delicious."

"Granny doesn't know it's her party," Tamsin said. "I've made her a pincushion, for pins."

"A calendar bag," Rebecca said indistinctly.

"She means she's made a lavender bag," Tamsin said, naturally translating for her sister.

Richard helped them finish the cake, expertly including all three children and preempting any arguments. He was washing Rebecca at the sink, having to use all his strength as she fought against the operation, when he noticed Judy watching him.

"You're obviously born to fatherhood, Richard," she said admiringly.

"I'm looking forward to the experience," he said with a smile and ushered the children out of the kitchen.

Fergus was hovering in the hall.

"Come and see Granny's cake, Daddy." Tamsin pulled at her father.

"I think we might show Daddy a little later when they've finished in the kitchen," Richard suggested tactfully. "Let's go and play in the Rough, shall we?"

"Yeah." The suggestion was greeted with loud approval. "And, Daddy, you come, too."

Fergus looked round guiltily and then turned to Richard. "Good idea. Let's keep out of the way for a bit."

"It'll be useful to keep the children busy." Richard helped out Fergus.

"Absolutely." Fergus smiled with relief.

"I'm going to find Uncle Alex." Jake peeled off as the small party made its way across the garden.

The Rough was a large area of long grass at the far end of the garden with rusting swings and a climbing frame. Surrounded by twisted fruit trees and with a rotting summerhouse, it was secluded and private, an age-old family place for hiding away.

At the sound of Laura in the distance shouting at Alex, Fergus raised his eyebrows at Richard. "Laura is in her element with this party," he said affectionately. "She loves family get-togethers. Thank God for Miranda insisting on caterers, though. Laura was horrified, of course."

Richard smiled and helped Rebecca unravel herself from the bars of the climbing frame. "Well done, Becs, that was very high up."

"I suppose you and Miranda will be having some of these little nightmares soon," Fergus said to him, nodding at the children.

"Mmm, I hope so," Richard said noncommittally.

"You want to get on with it. Get the worst bit over and done with."

Rebecca rushed at her father, grabbing his hand and gibbering excitedly at him.

"Babies improve with age, I find." He bent over Rebecca, trying to understand what it was she wanted him to do.

"She wants you to climb up with her, Daddy," Tamsin said in a superior voice from the top bars.

Fergus grinned ashamedly at Richard. "I'm not always very good at understanding what she wants, I'm afraid. Laura and the children, of course, are wonderful with her."

"Fer*gus*." Laura's voice sounded alarmingly nearby.

Fergus grimaced and then, as if afraid that Richard might think him disloyal, he grinned. "She calls, I go." He disappeared through the trees.

Moments later, there was a rustling in the bushes and Alex and Jake arrived, laughing, beside Richard.

"Uncle Richard." Jake, carrying a bat and ball, tugged at his elbow. "Will you bowl at me?" He smiled affectionately up at Alex. "Uncle Alex is really *rubbish* at cricket."

Miranda and Mungo were sitting at the garden table when Richard and Alex returned to the lawn with the children. The sunshine was weak and watery through a haze of cloud, but the air was still and warm. The fruits of everyone's labors were evident by the tables and chairs set out on the large terrace outside the drawing-room French windows.

"Is this anarchy, then?" Richard inquired as he sat down.

"Not at all," Miranda said crisply. "We're just waiting for our next orders." She looked up at the sky. "I hope Laura's right to put tables out here, I thought the forecast said rain."

"Not till much later. People are coming at six. It'll still be OK by then, I should think," Richard said. "We need them for the overspill."

"I've probably done my back in moving all those heavy sofas," Alex grumbled good-naturedly. "I must visit Mum's greenhouse if there's time this afternoon. I want to take some cuttings and her hibiscus needs repotting." He smiled winsomely at Mungo. "You can join me in the potting shed if you like," he offered.

"God knows, we'll all have plenty of time to spare this afternoon," Miranda said. "There's nothing else left to do: everything's been done. The drink and glasses are being delivered earlier than planned. I've just rung the wine place. Something about the champagne being cold enough." She made a jokey face. "Command from head office, of course."

Fergus came across the lawn with a large cool box, followed by Laura with two baskets and a rug.

"Lunch," Fergus said, plonking the box onto the table.

"I knew we wouldn't be able to use the kitchen," Laura said, "so I packed us a picnic. I thought we all deserved a decent lunch. Open the wine, Fergus. Let's all have a drink."

Everyone looked at Laura with admiration and gentle forgiveness for the morning's orders.

"Oh, good call, Laura darling," Alex said with affection. "You are brilliant!"

Miranda agreed with a smile. "Yes, well done, Laura."

Alex raised his glass to her. "You're impossibly bossy; you have always been that—but nothing in this family would get done properly without you. How much we do love you."

Laura blushed and smiled for a moment at her baby brother, then shook herself. "Don't be silly," she said gruffly, and began to hand lunch to the children sitting on the rug beside the table.

"How's Mum going to get her party dress on then?" Alex asked, piling salami and cheese onto his plate. "She's got to look her best, if she's going to make an entrance."

"It's all organized," Laura said.

"Natch," Alex mumbled, his mouth full.

"Dad is taking her to have tea with her friend Eileen first." Laura ignored her brother. "They should have bought a dress this morning, that was the plan, but we have a plan B." She preempted Alex by holding up her hand and smiling at him. "Don't you dare say it, Alex. Eileen whipped Mum's blue dress from her wardrobe last week, so if they haven't bought anything she can wear that."

"And won't Liddy wonder why she's got to get dressed at Eileen's?" Mungo asked.

"She'll be told Dad's taking her out to a smart dinner—it'll work. Even if it doesn't, I know she'll be thrilled."

Miranda made a face. "I'd hate a surprise party."

"I went to a surprise party once," Fergus said, "and the girl was told she was going out to supper. When she arrived and we all jumped out from behind the furniture, she was horrified. All she kept saying was, "I haven't eaten yet. I want to go out to supper." I've always been a bit wary of surprise parties ever since. You never know how the person is going to feel."

"Are you all right, Mirry? You look tired," Mungo said as he and Miranda carried the picnic stuff back to Laura's car.

"I'm fine," Miranda said. "I'm just not good at family *things,* if you know what I mean."

Alex watched the two of them walking across the lawn.

"God, I love that man," he said.

"I'm glad for you, Alex," Laura said stiffly. She gave him a little smile as he looked at her sideways. "No, I really am, honestly. I suppose I just don't understand it, that's all." She got up from the table. "Now I must go and see how Judy is getting on."

Alex stood up and put his arm round Laura and kissed her cheek.

"You know, Laura, you're what Aunt Cleo would call 'full of *cope.*'"

"Sometimes I wish I wasn't, though," Laura said with a deep sigh and went off to the kitchen.

Left alone round the table, Richard and Fergus finished their drinks. Fergus lit his pipe, sat back in his chair and looked at Richard. "Nice family, don't you think?" he said contentedly. "So normal and uncomplicated."

Richard raised an eyebrow and stared silently out across the garden.

Martin and Liddy chose to eat outside on a table overlooking the lock. Martin ordered champagne and Liddy looked hopelessly at the full bottle and wondered how she was going to avoid drinking it.

Sod it, she thought. I drank through all my other pregnancies, so what the hell, and accepted the full glass gratefully.

"I'm driving, so I'll only have a couple of glasses," Martin said, "just to toast you on your birthday." He raised his glass. "Happy birthday, darling. I don't want *anything* to spoil your day." He sounded really quite fierce and looked at her so meaningfully that Liddy began to believe that he knew she knew about Fay and he was commanding her not to destroy this day that he had so carefully planned.

"I'll always love you," he went on, "and our three lovely children."

To Liddy, his words seemed suddenly like a termination, a farewell.

She wanted to scream at him, I'm sure you're lying to me because it's my birthday. Isn't it really Fay you love now?

"And," he went on, "I'm serious about us going away. I've been thinking about it for some time. We haven't had a proper holiday for years, not just us."

Martin talked—all day he had talked—almost as though he was determined not to leave a silent void for Liddy to jump into. Liddy was confused by Martin's declaration of love for her, for the plans he was making for them both; she even wondered whether, perhaps, it was all wrong and there was no Fay after all. Or was he playing some elaborate game with her? That was not Martin's way—games playing had never been his suit. But if he did love her as much as he appeared to, was it enough to accept what she surely must tell him today?

Martin went on talking and somehow the meal passed and she could never quite start saying out loud what she wanted to say.

"Come on. Let's go for a walk," Martin said when he had paid the bill.

"Can't we just go home," protested Liddy desperately. "I really need to sit down and talk to you properly. *Please*, Martin." She was begging now.

"Not now, Liddy." Martin spoke roughly. He forced a smile which became more genuine as he spoke. "It's your birthday and it's a beautiful afternoon. Come on."

Martin's heart was as heavy as his feet as he plodded down the towpath. Today was proving to be the strain that he had hoped desperately it would not be. It was so ironic that it was today of all days that Liddy wanted to talk. For months he had waited and hoped for her attention, her interest and her love. He had so much about which to talk and now it was the wrong time, the wrong occasion, and he could have wept with frustration.

They walked along the dark oily canal, the air heavy with summer smells. Ducks scuttered out of the reeds and, as they passed the triple lock a richly painted barge waited to go through. Liddy looked down, through the narrow windows, and wanted to be safely cocooned in the tiny cabin.

"Listen to the birds," Martin said, slipping his arm through Liddy's. "Do you know, I don't think I've heard a cuckoo at all this year. 'In June they change their tune,' he quoted. "But I've never known what they change their tune into."

Liddy plodded beside him, letting him ramble on, hating every moment that passed full of her silence, yet quite unable to speak.

"Now then. *Are* you having a good day?" Martin snuggled his arm farther into hers and looked earnestly into her face.

"Oh, yes, it's lovely here," she said hopelessly.

It wasn't until they had left Eileen and were driving back to Market Ketton that something in Liddy finally snapped.

Eileen had opened a bottle of champagne and she and Martin had been most insistent that Liddy change into her new dress for dinner. Liddy had submitted wearily and just longed to go home, get into bed and leave this muddled day behind her.

"Oh, shit," Martin said, turning off the dual carriageway. "We'll have to go back to the house. I've left something there."

The way he said it made Liddy's heart sink.

Oh, God, not another present, she thought.

"Look, I'm really tired, Martin," she said. "Let's go out to dinner another evening. Honestly, I've had a lovely day, but I'd be happy just to have a boiled egg in front of the television, really I would."

"Don't be silly, darling. I want to take you out to a really special meal. I've booked the table. We're going to the Peacock. We spent a night there, years ago, do you remember? Your mother looked after the girls and I think it was then we conceived Alex, didn't we?"

"Stop the car, Martin," Liddy interrupted loudly.

He turned to look at her, puzzled.

"Go on. Stop here, just here."

Martin swerved the car into a parking place on the hill just above their house and Liddy got out and leaned against the hood. Looking down, she could just see the bottom of their garden.

Martin came and put his arm round her.

"What's the matter, darling, are you all right?"

The words that first came out of Liddy's mouth were the wrong ones but she couldn't stop them coming.

"Fay Jackson is the matter."

Martin caught his breath and his arm slipped from her shoulders. He stood quite still, staring down at his hands, his knuckles whitening as he clenched them together.

"You have been having an affair with Fay, Martin—I know you have."

Martin felt the blood pound in his ears. Not now, he wanted to yell out. This cannot happen *now*. It just can't.

"Yes," Martin said eventually in a monotone. "I have. Oh, God, Liddy—," he started. Liddy spoke over him.

"So what was today's charade about, then?"

Martin turned to look at her, his eyes large and wild in his stricken face.

"But it wasn't a charade." He sounded desperate. "I wanted us to have a happy day like we used to. I love you, Liddy. I always will."

"So why Fay, then?"

"Oh, Jesus, I don't know." Martin rubbed his eyes. "You and I seem to have stopped being friends in the past couple of years. We are so apart, leading different lives. We just seem to be separate people nowadays. We've even got out of the habit of kissing and once that happens . . ." He shrugged hopelessly.

Liddy was surprised at the anger that suddenly seemed to be pouring out of her, completely out of control.

"So you decided to take up with Fay—to replace me."

"I was so lonely," he said piteously. "You didn't seem interested in me anymore and she just happened to be there." It was, Liddy thought, an age-old cry, ever wailed between once-loving couples. "She was there when I felt that it was raining all around me," he went on. "It was as though my head was covered with heavy gray blankets that I couldn't get through."

"But she's my age," Liddy said bitterly,

"When it started, I wanted *you* back, don't you see? I've been feeling that things are changing in my life. I wanted to talk to you about it, but I couldn't get to you. You don't seem to be interested in me anymore. We seem so very far away from each other."

Liddy looked at Martin as he spoke so softly and so sadly. He looked heartbreakingly old and heavy; her anger subsided into a powerful desire to get everything said, to get everything into the open and to start the fight for what they had lost. Unexpectedly, a picture of the new laundry basket he had bought came into her head and she clutched at it as a ridiculous symbol of hope. They did love each other. They would get through this. It would be all right after all.

"Martin," she began in a low voice, looking down at her hands as she threaded her fingers together, "it's all right. It's not just you. I've done the same. It was a very short affair—just a silly fling with one of my students, long over now, but I believe that happened for the same reasons. It often happens to couples of our age. We've been married so long, we start to take each other for granted and that's when we begin to hurt each other—"

Martin made to interrupt her.

"Liddy—," he said hopelessly.

The champagne swilling inside her bolstered Liddy's determination to be heard and she cut across him.

"Look, please, we can't do this here. Let's forget about dinner and just go home and talk through everything properly. Come *on*," she said abruptly, striding round to the driver's seat and starting the engine.

"Liddy—" Martin was saying something as he went round the car to the passenger seat. Liddy, with no thought of the Breathalyzer, put her foot on the accelerator and skidded across the road into the opposite curb.

"Liddy, watch it!" Martin shouted and leaned across to grab the steering wheel.

Liddy batted off his hand and drove the short way into their drive, pieces of gravel flying up around the car wheels as she shuddered to a halt.

"Liddy, listen to me," Martin said urgently. "It's your surprise birthday party. There are masses of people in there. Everyone's in the house."

But Liddy was past hearing anything. She flung herself out of the car and almost ran toward the front door. Martin's words hit her only as she opened the door and went into the large hall. She was momentarily aware of a hushed silence, as though someone was holding their breath—suddenly she could feel people.

"Happy birthday, Liddy," came a roar, as a crowd of familiar faces emerged from behind furniture and doors.

Tears of frustration rolled down Liddy's cheeks.

Chapter

THREE

"Granny, Granny, it's a s'prise, it's a s'prise. You didn't know, did you? Did you?" Liddy's grandchildren clutched at her waist.

"Happy birthday, Mum." Laura's shiny round face loomed up beside Liddy as seventy people sang "Happy Birthday" to her. "You didn't guess, did you?" she asked anxiously.

"Absolutely not, darling, it's . . . just wonderful."

Liddy never knew how she managed to get through the nightmare that was her surprise birthday party. Afterwards, she was to hold in her mind the image of Martin, pale, hunched and tense, smiling and laughing nervously as he wandered through the groups of happy affectionate faces. And also a very clear picture of Martin and Fay together. From the doorway of the dining room, she had watched Martin speaking earnestly to her as he ushered her out of the front door soon after they had arrived. As Fay stepped over the doorstep, Liddy saw Martin stroke her hand, and then his fingers close tightly and briefly around it. Like a photograph—a freeze frame—the two of them looking at each other was printed on the back of her mind, while her face set itself in a silly smile as

her friends and family came up in a seemingly endless stream
of kisses.

"Did you really not know?"

"Hasn't your family done well?"

"Wonderful food. . . ."

"We nearly gave the game away last weekend, didn't you
notice?"

"Look at your pile of presents. . . ."

"Doesn't your grandson look just like Martin?"

"What a wonderful surprise this must be for you . . ."

"Lovely to see so many old faces . . ."

"Great party, and you really didn't know anything about it?"

Liddy wondered when her head would fall off with all the
nodding and smiling that she was doing.

"Are you OK?" Eileen came up and whispered to her. "You
looked so terribly unhappy when you left after tea."

Liddy looked into her friend's anxious face.

"Yes, yes, I'm fine; just shocked, you know. It's all such a
wonderful surprise," she said. She had now repeated the sentence so often, she hoped that it had become convincing.

When the initial babble around her had died down, Liddy
sought out Mary in the garden.

"You're meant to be my friend," she muttered through
clenched teeth. "Why the hell didn't you or Judy tell me?"

"How could we? Your family have been planning this for
ages. Would you have told me?"

"I need to talk to you and Judy—*please.*"

"Mum, you're wanted in the drawing room." Miranda interrupted them. "Now," she said impatiently.

"You've got a cake, Granny, and we iced it," Tamsin said,
leading her to the table in the center of the room.

"So I did, did, did, did . . . ," clamored Rebecca.

"Ladies and gentlemen," Alex tapped his glass with a fork

and spoke in a mock-pompous voice, "it has fallen upon me to propose a toast to my favorite mother in the world." He looked at his mother lovingly and said in his normal voice, "I just want to say, Mum, that everyone is here because they love you, and want you to have a happy birthday, but no one loves you as much as Dad, Miranda, Laura and I do. Thank you for every-thing you've done for us in all these years. Here's to the next fifty. Everyone—I give you Liddy and a happy birthday."

Liddy could feel the tears in her eyes as the room resounded with the toast picked up by the guests. She looked across at Martin, who raised his glass silently to her, a faint, nervous smile crossing his sad face.

"Speech, speech," was the inevitable call from somewhere on the floor. Liddy moved forward as though she were being propelled on remote control like one of Jake's electronic cars.

"Just thank you. I had no idea about this party and I had no idea I had so many good friends. And such a big thank-you to these three." She stretched out her arm toward her children, standing together around her and then, tentatively, toward her husband. "And to Martin, of course. I drink a toast to you all."

She took a drink and Rebecca dancing around her nearly knocked it out of her hand.

"Candles, candles."

"There are fifty, Granny. We counted," Tamsin said.

Martin looked at his family gathered around the cake and felt apart from them all. He listened to Alex's little speech and heard the lazy warmth in his voice, he saw Miranda standing stern and awkward beside her brother—there but somehow almost not there—the light falling across her fine face. He watched Laura, looking slightly tired and strained, he thought, glancing around the room, constantly troubled that everything was as it should be. His eyes fell upon Liddy, standing between them; the low evening sun sparkled the bright colors of the scarf that she had tied round her thick curly hair. He heard her heavy bracelets clack together as she lifted her glass and the sleeves of her new dress fell back to reveal a suntanned forearm. Everything about her was so familiar and Martin found that the saddest thing of all.

This had had to happen sometime. But not today. Liddy had always been going to know about Fay in the end. He was going to tell her. *Wasn't he?* The revelation that Liddy had had an affair came as little surprise to him, now that he thought about it, and he felt a curious kind of safety in the knowledge that they had both been unfaithful. But something was changing in his life: he was fifty-five, their children were settled and didn't need him anymore; the lease on his shop was up for renewal and he wanted something different—he didn't know what it was exactly but he was absolutely sure he didn't want his life rumbling on unchanged until he died. He wanted to think that Fay was a symptom rather than a cause, but he couldn't be sure of that. He had wanted to think aloud, to make decisions about the future, but Liddy had seemed so far away from him. Fay, though, was always there and now the time had come to explain to Liddy about her. The weight of what he wanted to say was pressing down on his chest so that he felt he could hardly breathe.

When the cake had been borne away to the kitchen, Martin drew Liddy away from a group of people.

"Come into the garden with me," he said in a low voice. "We really need to talk."

Liddy looked at him with blank eyes. "Liddy." He shook her arm. "Please."

She looked at him bleakly.

"How can we?" She gestured toward the room of party guests. "We've got so much to talk about. We can't. Not now. When they've all gone."

"But the family are staying the weekend," Martin said desperately.

A guest came up to Liddy, and Martin saw the momentary desolation in her face mirror his own, as she turned to greet the guest with a forced smile.

And he hated himself for needing to go upstairs and ring Fay.

"It was lovely food, you are kind," Liddy said later to Judy.

Judy made a face. "You didn't really need this now, though, did you? I think you've done terribly well. No one would know what you're really feeling—or Martin. He's doing all right as well."

"He doesn't know," Liddy said in a small voice. "I haven't told him yet . . . not everything."

"Oh, *Liddy!*"

Liddy felt her legs were about to collapse under her.

"He was being so loving," Liddy said. "I don't understand it."

She and Mary were in Liddy's bedroom. The party was still in full swing, but Liddy had ceased to be the center of attention, so she and Mary had slipped upstairs. Mary was sitting on the lavatory as a reason for them being there. They talked quietly, aware of Laura, farther down the landing, putting her now fractious children to bed.

"Liddy, you don't stop loving someone just like that."

"He looks so sad, though."

"About the baby, sad?"

"I didn't get that far."

"Oh, *Liddy!*" Like Judy. Mary frowned at her.

"We had just started talking and I was driving home to come back here when we got hijacked by this party. He told me he had only begun with Fay because we had grown apart and he was lonely and I said I knew how he felt because that was why there was Barney."

Mary looked at her sideways. "Was it?"

52

Liddy shrugged. "I'm sure it was, subconsciously. Our marriage had become sick, but I know Martin and I love each other. So together we *can* sort this out. We just need to sit down and talk quietly and sanely about it. I know it won't be easy. It'll be horrible and I'm dreading it, but I want to do it now and get it over with. It's the waiting that is stressing me out. But apparently the children are staying for the rest of the weekend—" Liddy's voice rose slightly and her shoulders began to shake. "—so we won't have any proper time to ourselves till tomorrow evening. I can't wait that long. I'm so tired, Mary, I am *so* tired."

Mary got up and sat on the bed beside Liddy.

"Come on." She gave Liddy's arm a shake. "Of course you're tired. You're about to have a baby, apart from anything else. Give yourself a break, but you must hold it together till everyone's gone tomorrow. Come on, Lid," she urged. "You've done brilliantly so far and you sound confident that it is going to be all right with Martin, so I'm sure it will be."

Liddy, in her distress, failed to hear the small note of doubt in Mary's voice.

"Mum," Laura knocked perfunctorily on the bedroom door and tripped in, "I need another blanket and the children are waiting for you to say good night to them."

Liddy felt a wave of anger at her family hemming her in, demanding from her when all she wanted was to curl up and sleep and leave someone grown-up to take charge and sort all this out for her. The baby inside her was like a time bomb, making her feel claustrophobic and panicky.

"There's a spare blanket in the linen closet," she said, wearily getting to her feet. "I'll come and give the children a kiss now."

"What a happy weekend," Laura said on Sunday afternoon, as she settled more comfortably into the passenger seat of the car. "I really think Mum enjoyed the party, don't you?"

"I think she did," Fergus said fondly and reached out and

patted her knee. "You did a really good job organizing everything so smoothly."

Laura acknowledged the praise with a small smile.

She glanced to the backseat at the three children, all of
them deeply asleep—little thin necks bent over, barely supporting heavy heads; sticky, grubby hands clenched; the late-
afternoon sun flickering over them in rolling shadows as the
car bowled along the tree-lined country lanes. Her eyes lin-
gered over Jake and she resisted the temptation to lean over
and stroke his smooth slightly flushed cheek.

"Fergus." She lowered her voice. "Jake is very unhappy
about going back to school tomorrow. He told Alex again this
morning that he really hated it."

Ever since Friday, when Jake and Tamsin had come home
from their boarding schools for the weekend, Laura had been
waiting for an opportunity to open this particular conversation. It had to come while Fergus was away from the farm in
order to get his full concentration and he enjoyed driving on
long journeys; he and Laura always had their most productive
conversations in the car.

But now she saw his jaw clench slightly as he spoke.

"Nonsense. This is his third term—the best: summer, swimming, cricket." Fergus's heartiness made Laura wince.

"He's never liked it. All his friends live near us. He really
does want to stay at home and go to a local school," she persevered.

"What, and miss out on the experience of boarding school?
The schools round us can't provide the opportunities that
Brampton does. He's very lucky to be there, and he will realize
that," he added more gently, "he really will. And we're bloody
lucky Ma pays for him—and for Tamsin. She loves Elmfield,
you know she does. She never stops talking about it."

"But Jake is different," Laura argued. "He genuinely doesn't
enjoy boarding, not like Tamsin does."

"He's just taking longer than Tamsin to settle in, that's all. You wait, he'll be longing to go back in September, I promise you."

This had become a well-worn argument and one that always left Laura feeling as though she and Fergus were speaking two different languages. The fact that none of her family was ever sent away to school gave her a distinct disadvantage in the argument. This was the first time in their marriage that the disparity of their backgrounds was so evident.

"Please listen to me," she pleaded. "I'm right. I know I'm right. He's genuinely not happy. He's changed since he's been away."

Fergus briefly touched her knee again.

"Laura, love, of course he's changed. He's gone away to school. He's beginning to grow up. That is healthy and how it should be. I know we've always agreed that the children are your department," Fergus went on, and Laura wondered exactly when that agreement had been made and whether she had been present at the time, "but believe me, you do make the best friends when you're away at school—it welds you together like nothing else. You'll see, it's the very best of experience that we can offer the twins."

"Except *we*'re not offering it," Laura said resentfully. "Your mother is and it seems to have been her decision all along."

"I don't want thanks, darling." Vivien had grandly waved away Laura's attempt to speak. "All Byford boys go to Brampton. In fact, Fergus's great-great-uncle was a schoolmaster there. And of course I shall do the same for Tamsin," she said graciously. "I've heard Elmfield is very well thought of for girls."

"They're twins. They should be at school together." Initially Laura had been firm and confident that the decision would be hers and Fergus's.

She and her mother-in-law had a conventionally sticky relationship. Vivien, while making clear the social gulf between the Claver family and the Byfords, had recognized in Laura a perfect replacement for herself in the care and management of her beloved eldest son. For his part, Fergus, conditioned as he was to being dominant on the farm and having his personal life ordered by a woman, had merely transferred himself seamlessly from his mother's administration to that of Laura's. "We usually . . . we've always . . ." were constant remarks from Vivien at the beginning and Laura battled to retain her own identity—to do things her own way and not just to inherit Vivien's mantle. She believed that she had been successful in achieving the right balance between Byford family tradition and bringing her own customs and beliefs to the family: she wanted her children to have the same loving, free and open childhood as her own—a perfect childhood. In the early days Fergus had supported her and she had reveled in his quiet undemanding kindness. Now the twins' education had proved to be an unexpected battle and Fergus had stopped listening to her. She felt that they were drifting apart and she was weary of the fight and feeling increasingly isolated.

Vivien's forcefulness and unquestioning commitment to boarding school, her son's obsession that Rebecca should never hold back his eldest children and the twins' own initial enthusiasm for the idea had left Laura with no allies in this issue. She was taken up with Rebecca's care and somehow the battle had slipped away from her. It baffled Laura that Fergus and Vivien seemed to think it was perfectly all right for small children to spend two-thirds of the year in an unnaturally formed community, cared for by adults with no familial ties. She simply could not make Fergus understand how alien it seemed to her and how much it broke her heart to see them both go away. She was the only one who knew that Jake was sick every time he had to go back to school.

"It might be good for Rebecca, too, to have Jake at home." Laura now dangerously persisted on another tack.

Fergus frowned at her before looking at the road again.

"You can't hold back the others just for Rebecca. That wouldn't be fair," he said stiffly.

Laura watched her husband retreat into himself—just as he always did when the subject of Rebecca came up. Laura, from the moment she began to recover from the difficult birth, had gradually come to realize that there might be something wrong with their third child. When the tests had confirmed Rebecca's Down's syndrome, she had wanted and expected that she and Fergus would grieve together, supporting and giving strength to each other. But, after the interview with the specialist, Fergus had disappeared out of the hospital and when he returned some hours later, Laura had seen the shutters already closed down over his eyes. So she went through her time of shock, of disbelief, of anger, of guilt and of weeping all alone—and she was on her own again in the hard task of trying to heal her family's hurt and supporting them in the acceptance of this new person who would need so much. She knew their life would never be the same again. Laura's own family had embraced Rebecca with positive, loving energy that had gone a long way to getting her through those early months. She had not realized that Fergus would forever see Rebecca as a reminder of what he perceived as their failure. The Byfords had always produced whole, perfect children—he had let down his family, and most particularly, Vivien, his mother. Laura knew that Fergus, in his own way, had grown to love his youngest daughter but he was not always comfortable with her. He preferred to ignore Rebecca's special needs where he could and it had always been Laura, on her own, who, in the early years, had traipsed round doctors and therapists with her. Somehow, Fergus could never find the time to leave the farm. It seemed to Laura that it was always she alone who struggled to keep the family whole and happy and this lack of support was beginning to make her increasingly resentful.

Jake and Tamsin going off to boarding school had underlined Rebecca's constant dependence on them and Fergus seemed fearful of that dependence.

"Listen to me, *please*, Fergus," she wanted to cry out yet again.

Quick to curtail this particular conversation, Fergus leaned over and squeezed her knee.

"Don't worry, Laura. They'll both be home again for the holidays before you know it."

"Just like visitors," Laura said between clenched teeth. Every time they came home she could feel the twins becoming more distant: they were now part of a world of which she knew nothing and it seemed to take them longer each time to slip back into her world.

"Not like visitors." Fergus shook his head. "Like family, a perfectly normal family. You'll see, Jake will be longing to go back by the end of the summer holidays, I promise you. You'll wonder what all the fuss was about. And," he added soberly, "obviously we'll always have Rebecca at home. You have much more time to cope with her now the others are away, and think of all the work you do for the village. They couldn't survive without you, you know that. You never stop."

But she wanted to stop. She wanted to spend quiet, gentle time with Fergus, just for themselves. She wanted them to have an open, giving, intimate marriage like her parents had. She could find the time to stop and work on their relationship—the trouble was, Fergus couldn't. He was always too busy on the farm.

So Laura expanded her work to fit the time that might otherwise be spent in self-pity.

Fergus had come to the end of this conversation. He saw Laura sit back in her seat and tried not to see the bleak expression on her face. To clear his head, he executed an ambitious overtaking of a lorry on a roundabout. He loved Laura: she was everything he wanted in a wife and a friend and he believed that she had taught him a lot. He envied her her upbringing; her arrival had brought a natural warmth and emotional honesty into his cold, upright family. He loved the way she *cared* so much for everyone; he loved her when she was serious, when she laughed; he loved her decisiveness and her certainty. Which was why he hated her being so upset over Jake. Laura's positive strength often left Fergus feeling sadly inadequate. She seemed to be wanting more from him than was in his power to give. He wanted always to walk beside her, but sometimes he felt he had to run to keep up with her and lately she was constantly just out of his reach. He took Laura's hand, which was clenched on her lap. He held on to it tightly.

"I love you," he said awkwardly.

"I like family parties, especially yours," Richard said as he maneuvered his sleek car into the fast lane of the motorway.

Miranda grunted noncommittally and looked out the window and, as usual, wondered at the utter monstrousness of the British motorway—its bleak ugliness, a container for tense, huddled humans contained, in their turn, in small metal boxes more lethal than a firearm. Always a nervous passenger, she held on to her seat belt as Richard pressed his foot on the accelerator.

"Laura is an amazing person, you know," he went on. "She's very efficient, but she's also kind and thoughtful. I get the impression she has a lot on her plate, and she was looking a bit strained. But I think their children are delightful. Do you know what Tamsin said this morning? . . ."

Miranda retreated deep into her head, trying not to hear Richard talking.

She leaned forward slightly and clasped her stomach: it felt full and distended and she hated it. She had been so careful this weekend to look as though she were eating as much as everyone else. Sometimes, she thought, just watching people eating and drinking made her feel pogged and fat. Miranda knew her parents watched her, even after all these years, and it annoyed her because she did eat normally nowadays—just not as much as everyone else. This weekend she hadn't been able to exercise properly and she felt stiff and sluggish.

She looked at her watch and interrupted Richard. "I might get to the gym tonight if the traffic's not too bad."

"Miranda, we've got to talk about the job *tonight*." Richard spoke seriously. "I thought you were seeing David tomorrow."

Miranda sighed. In the three days since she had been offered the editorship of a magazine outside London, the implications of her desperately wanting the job had hung over them both like a thick, black cloud.

This discussion was inevitable and if they had it now, she could probably get to the gym later.

"Look, it's not for very long." Miranda had been rehearsing this in her head. "A year, eighteen months, maybe, just enough to get it on my CV and to give me the experience."

"What, to come back and edit *Vogue*?" Richard asked caustically.

"No, I just need the experience. I need to move up a rung."

"Why don't you try for some other publication in London? Or this lot will offer you another rung up eventually: they're not going to dump you just because you refuse this job. They obviously think a lot of you. Why don't you wait for that?"

"Because I don't want to wait. I want to be an editor now and this is my chance," Miranda said stubbornly.

"Miranda, I thought you wanted to write. Do you know what a magazine editor's job is nowadays? It's administration, budgets, spreadsheets, staff interviews and appraisals. Trust me, you don't want to be an editor, my darling, you want to be a proper writer. And what about the short stories you've been working on? I thought they were going well. You won't have time for them as an editor, believe me."

"But if I took this job, I'd get a better paid and more inter-esting job when I get back to London."

"I'm sure you would, but you used to talk about being free-lance. What happened to that idea? We can easily manage financially, you know, and you can concentrate on the stuff that you really want to do."

"But that's the point, Richard. I really want to do this. I would be mad not to take it."

"Well, it has to be your decision," Richard said unhappily. "I suppose it's just that I'm feeling sad that you seem quite happy to go and live in Leeds while I live down here. I love you, I don't want you to go." Richard took her hand and stroked it.

"I don't know why you love me. I'm very difficult," Miranda said aggressively.

Richard chuckled. "Difficult? You're a high-maintenance hell, my sweet, but I think you're worth it which is why I don't want you to go away from me."

"But I'll be back most weekends. It's a monthly publication, not weekly."

"Oh, no, please. This is me you're talking to," Richard exploded suddenly and uncharacteristically. The car wobbled dangerously near the crash barrier. "I'm in the same business, remember. You and I both know perfectly well you won't either be able to, or want to come back very often, not once you're really involved, and, as a publisher myself, I would take a very dim view of an editor of my local magazine whose heart was really two hundred miles away in London. Or," Richard sounded menacing, "perhaps that's the point, is it? Your heart is not in London any longer. You *don't* want to be with me."

"Oh, Richard, of course I do," Miranda protested angrily. "You know I do, but you also know that this is about bloody babies and *me* having them and *me* staying at home to look after them."

"Yes." Miranda could hear the unhappiness in Richard's

weary voice. "Yes, you're right, it *is* also about 'bloody' babies."
He emphasized the word *bloody.* "I'm thirty-five years old,
Miranda. You know I want babies, and before I'm old enough
to be their grandfather. It's obviously not happening as soon as
we would have wished, but it would be well nigh impossible if
you're going to spend the best part of next year in Leeds."

It was always the same when Richard had been in the company of children.

They drove in silence. Richard put on a tape and Haydn
filled the car. He took some deep breaths and yet again silently
castigated himself for being too intense. It was, he felt sometimes, a treacherous path he trod with Miranda. She was like a
summer butterfly—catch her and she struggled, let her free
and she returned.

Richard's hand fumbled for hers.

"Christ, I'm sorry," he said forlornly. "I don't mean to hassle
you, darling. Forgive me? I must be more patient. I know it will
happen when the time is right."

But it won't, it won't, Miranda screamed inside herself,
because you have no idea what I've been doing for the past
eighteen months.

"I thought your mother looked rather tense," Mungo said as he
drove deftly through north London.

"She's put on a bit of weight," Alex said, "but she looked
fine to me."

Mungo glanced at Alex affectionately. "You wouldn't notice
if she grew another nose, you selfish little faggot."

"I would so," Alex said hotly. "I love my mother to distraction."

"That's what all the queens say." Mungo laughed.

Alex leaned against the car window and fell asleep in a
moment. Mungo looked across at him and smiled to himself. Alex was like a puppy: excitable, enthusiastic and

utterly dedicated to the gratification of his own physical needs. Mungo was surprised at quite how much he was beginning to love him. They had had, he considered, a nice weekend with Alex's family. Apart from anything else, he and Alex had been allocated the same bedroom, with no fuss or even comment. Not, in his experience, a common occurrence in most parental homes. He liked the Clavers, though it never ceased to amaze him how normal they all seemed as a family and how uptight they were individually. He supposed that was the same with most families—except, of course, his. He had severed all connection with his relations when he announced he was gay. He wondered if anyone else had noticed the tension between Liddy and Martin. Alex obviously hadn't, but he thought that both Miranda and Laura had seemed a bit on edge.

Funny things, families. Thank God he need never have one again.

Mungo found a parking place in a leafy Kensington road and reached over to stroke Alex's cheek. "Come on then, Pigeon, let's be reunited with our babies."

They rang on the bell of a small house completely submerged in heavy succulent wisteria and the two dogs leapt up and down at the men when the front door was opened.

"Hi, had a good time?" Karen made her way through the brown and white waggling bottoms of the dogs to give them a kiss. "Come in and have a cup of tea. This is Charlotte, known as Ship," she said casually, nodding toward a young girl standing by the fireplace, "as in a ship that passes in the night."

The girl grinned at Karen and playfully kicked out at her with a large biker boot. "I *don't* think so."

"This is Mungo, my husband, and Alex, his wife," Karen said as she went into the kitchen. She put her head round the door and winked at Ship. "And I'll leave you to work that one out."

Alex bent down and cuddled the dogs.

"Have you been a goodums for your Aunty Karen then, Kylie? And, Danni, are you a good boy, too?"

Karen made a sick noise from the kitchen, "Yuk, shut up, Alex. They've been perfectly happy, which is, I know, all you care about. I, on the other hand, seemed to have spent the weekend walking round Kensington Gardens collecting shit in plastic bags. I can't believe it all came from those two. I bet I was picking up other dogs' mess." She emerged from the kitchen with two mugs and handed them to Alex and Mungo. "I'm very good to you two. I spend all week in a vet's office looking after other people's manky animals and then I take your two smelly pooches for the weekend. You owe me a bottle of wine at the very least."

Alex produced a bottle of champagne from behind his back and waved it at Karen. "They don't smell and we've brought you this, you tetchy old dyke."

Karen received the bottle with a smile. "Thank you, and any time, you know that. So, tell. How was it? Was she surprised?"

"It went superbly," Mungo said, sitting down on the least uncomfortable piece of modern furniture that Karen owned. "Laura bossed, Miranda was edgy and Alex charmed everyone. How was your weekend?"

"Well, Ship was my weekend." Karen sat on the sofa and pulled the girl down beside her, "and very satisfactory it was, too. We went to Chris Tolmey's party and—oh, do you know?—Huey and Dave were there and they think they're pregnant."

"No." Alex leaned forward in excitement, nearly spilling his drink. "Who's the womb?"

"Louise Griffiths. She was so funny about it. They really did use a turkey baster. Huey and Dave sat in one room, Louise in the other and some friend of hers ran between the two."

"So who's the father?"

"That's the point. They mixed the sperm up so it could be either."

"Two fathers. That's going to look good on the birth certificate," Mungo said dryly.

"No, I think they've agreed Huey's going on that."

"That's brilliant," Alex said and turned to his partner with a grin. "Should we have a baby, Mungo? Would you do that for us, Karen?"

"No, I bloody wouldn't, no matter how much you offered me."

"How much is Louise getting?" Alex asked.

"None of them would say, but quite a substantial sum I would guess, wouldn't you?" Karen turned to involve Ship in the conversation.

Ship nodded. "Personally, I can't think of anything that I don't want more than having a baby." She grinned. "But then I teach in a boys' school and I have a very jaded view of children. Knowing what they do to each other just makes me wonder whether all hetero males shouldn't be neutered at birth."

"Actually, I think it would be great to have a baby." Alex looked thoughtfully at Mungo.

"Oh, yes, and who would look after it, please, who would finance it?" Mungo inquired.

"Well, I might be able to get some sort of work from home. I can earn and look after it."

"What happened to drama school, then?" Karen asked.

Alex made a rueful face. "Oh, I don't know. It was just an idea, but I think I would like Mungo and me to have a baby one day. We'd be a real family and we could get a house with a decent, proper garden."

Mungo took Alex's hand. "Or, alternatively, sweetie, you could get a life," he said kindly.

*   *   *

Liddy and Martin waved to the departing cars in the soft Sunday afternoon sunshine. She had a vision of them in a picture from a Janet and John reading book. *"Happy Mummy and Daddy wave good-bye to Laura, Miranda and Alex after a splendid weekend."*

Except they weren't and it hadn't been. She and Martin had kept the balls in the air by throwing themselves into playing happy families—autonomously. Not even in bed, after the party, had they been able to talk. All energy between them had been drained out by the long and grueling day, and the knowledge that they were surrounded by their family prevented them from embarking on the colossal issues they knew lay before them.

"Thank you for a lovely party," Liddy had said, hating her polite voice that came out without warning.

"I hope you enjoyed it," Martin had replied in a deadpan voice.

It was like a giant thunderstorm waiting to break, rumbling around in the distance.

Sunday had been taken up with the family; breakfast and lunch for eleven people had to be provided and Liddy went through the preparations on automatic pilot.

"So you really did enjoy it, didn't you, Mum?" Laura said anxiously, as they peeled potatoes together in the kitchen.

"Oh, darling, I did, so much," she lied. "It was such a nice idea and a special thank-you to you because I know you probably did most of the organizing."

Laura preened herself slightly.

"Well, everyone mucked in," she said modestly, "but it's easier for me. You know what they say, 'Always ask a busy person to do something.' My mother-in-law would say it's because I have short arms. She says"—Laura altered her voice into mock grand—"she only ever employs servants with short arms and legs, because she finds those sort tend to have more energy."

Liddy smiled with her daughter. "I don't know about short arms, but you've always had a lot of energy. Even as a little girl, you were always busy doing something, usually domestic. I couldn't count the amount of times you redecorated the doll's house!"

"I've always liked doing homely things, you know that," Laura protested.

"You should make some time for yourself."

"I'm sure I do," Laura said doubtfully, "although," she added in a wistful voice, "I don't really need it for myself. I'd like Fergus and me to be alone together more, but he's always so busy. He can't even get away for a family holiday this year. Anyway," she spoke briskly, "I look after my children, that's what I do with *my* time. I miss the twins dreadfully, but Becs takes up a lot of my energy. Did I tell you we've been offered respite care? I've refused, of course. I mean, I don't think it's really meant for people like us, do you?"

"It might be good for you and Fergus to have a bit of space without her occasionally," Liddy suggested. "Fergus can't work every hour of the day, surely?"

Laura made a dismissive gesture and gave a hollow laugh.

"Oh, he can. I do most of the paperwork, but he always seems to find things to do for the farm. But anyway, Fergus isn't a great "together" sort of person. And you know he's never been a great talker."

Liddy could hear suppressed irritation in her daughter's voice. Laura looked out of the kitchen window, watching her children playing on the lawn. "Do you think Jake is really all right, Mum?" she asked anxiously.

"Yes, darling, he seems fine. Look at him out there. He's having a wonderful time teasing his sisters. I know you hate the twins going away. I do sympathize. We never even thought about it. But Tamsin obviously loves it and Fergus is probably right, Jake will settle down soon. You've done so well and they are a lovely, happy family."

"Yes, but everything changes," Laura said gruffly and, still staring out of the window, added with a strained little laugh, "Gosh, do you remember I always said I was going to have seven children? That would take some doing now."

Liddy knew there was a hidden agenda in their brief conversation. She knew that her eldest daughter had never found it easy to admit to any vulnerability she might be feeling. Now Liddy sat at the kitchen table, miserably aware that she just could not summon up the energy to find out what was making Laura so strung out; she was failing to offer the support and comfort that her daughter was, in her diffident way, asking from her.

Later, sent out by Laura to sit in the garden with a drink, Liddy wandered down to the Rough and came across Miranda doing a workout. Sweaty, red-faced and completely absorbed, she was, Liddy thought, probably completely unaware of Rebecca and the next door neighbor's daughter, three-year-old Sadie, behind her, copying her movements.

As Liddy drew nearer, she could hear Rebecca thumping her feet into the ground, mumbling a jumble of numbers. Little Sadie beside her was in a world of her own. "Stretch arms, stretch legs." The little girl held out the edges of her skirt as if to curtsy. "Stretch skirt," she murmured.

Liddy laughed out loud and Miranda stopped, startled. The two girls stood still.

"What are you two doing here, Becs?" Miranda demanded, so fiercely the little girl blanched.

Liddy rescued her.

"Becs, darling, would you and Sadie like to go and help your mum with the beans? And Sadie can stay to lunch, if you'd like, but you must ask her mother," she called after the little girls who scampered away through the bushes.

"I think you scared poor little Rebecca a bit," Liddy said with a reproachful smile.

Miranda glowered.

"I just wanted a bit of privacy," she grumbled. "Those children get everywhere."

"Darling, they're only children and very nice ones, too. You wait till you have your own." Liddy was about to change the subject, but Miranda picked up her sweatshirt that was hanging over the climbing-frame bars.

"Oh, don't you start, too," she said crossly as she strode away across the grass.

Confused by her younger daughter's outburst, Liddy sat miserably on the bench outside the summer house, listening to the sound of Sunday: birds in the trees above her head, a distant lawn mower and the sound of chinking glasses and chatter from the terrace.

There was rustling from the overgrown bushes and Alex appeared with a drink, a bowl of chips and a broad smile.

"I knew I'd find you here. Well now, he*llo*." He sat beside her and linked his arm with hers. "Happy to have us all here?"

Liddy gave him a kiss.

"How are the auditions going?"

Alex made a face.

"Not the best. They're over till autumn now, anyway." He changed the subject quickly. "Can I take some of those extra sweet pea seedlings from the greenhouse? You're not going to use them, are you? I'm going to try them in a pot on the balcony."

"I should think so, but sweet peas are your father's domain, so ask him. They're his favorite flowers."

A troubled look came over Alex's face. "Good Heavens, don't tell me I've got something in common with Dad after all," he said in a glib, brittle voice. He got up and forced back his smile. "I'm going to open some more bottles. Are you coming?"

"In a minute." She gestured to her glass. "I'll just finish this."

"OK," Alex said cheerfully. He bent over and kissed her. "Love you lots."

Would you, if you knew? Liddy wondered.

Left alone, Liddy sat thinking about her three children. Each one had obliquely expressed some pain to her this morning and she had singularly failed to respond to any of them. She was so imprisoned in her own pain, she couldn't struggle out to listen to what they were saying—let alone to what they were not saying.

She walked toward the house down the shady overgrown path, stopping for a moment at the edge of the lawn to watch her family spread out before her.

Alex was standing by the French windows teaching Jake how to pop a champagne cork. Mungo, Fergus and Miranda sat in deckchairs with the Sunday papers and she could hear Laura and Richard talking in the kitchen to the accompaniment of clashing saucepans. Martin was laying the garden table, helped by the little girls. Liddy felt outside the magic circle. Guilt and remorse from a long way back welled up within her. She had always been an absent mother in a way; she had never had the patience like Martin to stop and sift, to listen, to give. It was a terrible admission that perhaps she hadn't always been a good mother—and now she was going to have to bring up another child and this time she might be doing it on her own. Her failures—in the past and those to come in the future—horrified and scared her.

Liddy's last thought that morning, as she moved forward to join her family, was an overpowering desire to seek solace with them and ask for their love and support. But she had, by her own actions, made this family too frighteningly vulnerable for that.

*   *   *

And now their children had all gone home, leaving a great cavernous hole just waiting to be filled.

"You must be exhausted," Martin said as they went back into the house. "Go and sit down and I'll make some tea."

Liddy lay on the sofa, her mind a complete blank; the mountain that lay before her seemed insurmountable. She wanted to lie down on the nice puffy sofa and be transported somewhere else—away from here, away from Martin and, most of all, away from her body and the secret inside it.

"You probably don't want to look at any more food this weekend"—Martin came in with a tray—"but I've brought some birthday cake in anyway."

He fussed around her, pulling a table up beside her, letting down a blind to stop the sun shining in her eyes. She struggled up to a sitting position in a surge of emotional energy.

"Martin, I have something to tell you—," she began.

She thought she saw panic flash through Martin's eyes as he interrupted her, speaking quickly.

"I knew, yesterday, before you said it, that you knew about Fay. I'm sorry you didn't hear it from me—you should have done, I've been wanting to tell you for some time and I was going to, but I couldn't spoil yesterday."

Something in his tone of voice led Liddy to believe that he was going to tell her that his affair with Fay was over, that the rediscovered honesty between him and Liddy would now make Fay redundant in his life.

Which made what Martin went on to say an even greater shock.

"It's very beguiling, you know," he spoke in a low voice, "suddenly finding someone who loves you so much at a time when you are feeling particularly unloved. We have become very close, Fay and I." Martin was turned away from her, staring out of the window, his shoulders hunched. "Liddy, I do love her. I'm sorry, I can't help it, she has become a very important part of my life."

"But *I* love you," Liddy burst out, almost unable to grasp what Martin was saying.

He turned round then and looked at her.

"I've loved you for over thirty years," he said sadly. "I still do. We have shared so much and that can never go away. The thing is, Liddy"—and his voice became strong and decisive—"I feel I've reached a crossroads in my life. I think it's been looming for a while, but when I got the letter about renewing the shop lease, it made me think. Do I really want to be here doing this for another twenty years? I don't think so. I'm fifty-five years old. I want to do something different. I want my time. Well, I hoped it would be *our* time, but you weren't here to discuss it with me—"

"I've not been away, Martin," Liddy interrupted. "I've always been here."

Martin looked at her almost as though she were a stranger.

"Liddy, you know what I mean. You've not been *here*." He tapped his head, "for us. And I missed you when I needed you. And the thing is, Fay *was* there."

A tear rolled out of each eye and ran silent and unchecked down his cheeks and Liddy, too stupefied to say anything, had time to wonder at the symmetry of them. She wanted to reach out and wipe them away—make it better, but it was as though her arm was pinned down; she just couldn't move it toward him—then the opportunity passed, she hadn't touched him and she knew that, in that moment, they had moved yet further apart.

He dashed his hand across his face and spoke resolutely in one breath, denying her an interruption.

"I need some space, I need to think, to work things out. Make decisions. I didn't expect or want this to happen, but I need time to get things straight in my head." He was telling her, not asking.

Everything had changed—suddenly. Martin appeared to be saying, brutally and emphatically, that he needed to decide between her and his mistress—that it would not be an easy decision. Liddy could feel reality slipping away from her—she was losing everything.

"Martin." Her heart was thumping. "Listen, you're not thinking straight. We grew apart for a bit, I know we did, but I love you. We can get it all back. I didn't plan to have an affair any more than you did. But it wasn't serious. He was just a kid and it's been all over for months."

Martin looked at her coldly then, as if contemptuous of her transient infidelity.

"But for me and Fay I think it *is* serious, Liddy. I'm sorry, it just is. You are both part of my life, but I know I can't have you both."

Shock had momentarily driven all thought of the secret that she held from Liddy's mind. She was going to lose Martin. She couldn't tell him about the baby just now; it would color his decision—delete all possibilities except one; it would be like handing Martin to Fay. There was blackness all around her. She mustn't lose Martin, he must want *her*.

She flung her pride down in front of him.

"I'd rather share you than lose you. I love you, Martin. I want us to be together. We can, can't we?"

He shook his head sorrowfully, but he spoke robustly and his words were explicit. "Liddy, I honestly don't know. I wish I knew what I wanted. I need some time to think things through, get everything—not just you and Fay—everything about my life and my future in perspective. I know I should have talked to you before, but—" he rubbed his head and his hair stuck up; he looked like he did in the mornings when he woke up in bed and Liddy loved him so much—"I just kept putting it off and the whole thing began to run away from me. Then there was your party and the children were determined to do it for you and I went along with it. I'm sorry this has happened, Liddy, I really am sorry and I know I'm probably being very selfish, but I'm going to go away and work out exactly what I do want."

The telephone rang then. It was Avril, who looked after Cleo and Cyn. She was ringing because Cleo had had a couple of dizzy spells over the weekend, but had refused to see the doctor. Avril was of the opinion that she might have had a small stroke and she thought that Liddy, as Cleo's only relation, should come down for a few days as soon as possible.

For both Martin and Liddy, the call came as a timely release. The tension, the secrets and the decisions could be put on hold for just a few more days.

Chapter

FOUR

T he chain ferry cranked its noisy way across the river like
some lumbering prehistoric monster. Liddy got out of her
car and looked at the small village of Portlisk spread vertically
up the hill. Cleo and Cyn's house was perched at the top,
standing out like a beacon, white and square; the garden slop-
ing right down onto the rooftops of the row of houses below it.

"Oh, darling," Cleo had said robustly when Liddy had rung
her, "it would be lovely to see you, it always is, but there is
really no *need* for you to come down. I'm perfectly all right. I
just had a couple of dizzy spells, that's all. Dear Avril is just
making a fuss and a bother."

But Liddy had insisted. She had this idea that if it was she
who went away and Martin who stayed at home, he might come
to realize how much he would be losing if he left her.

They had lain beside each other all night, silent and deep in
their own secrets. In the morning they had parted from each
other with mutual relief.

"I'll just stay a few nights, see that they're all right, and then
we'll . . . ," she petered out uncertainly.

Martin nodded.

"I'll be here when you get back. Take care."

"I love you," she had bleated at him through the car window and he had blown her a small, sad kiss.

She went to see Mary on her way out of town. "He loves her," she said resentfully. "He loves Fay. He says he loves us both. It was such a shock. I thought he loved *me*. I hate her. I feel as though I'm in competition with her."

"And the baby?"

Liddy's shoulders slumped. "How could I tell him? Mary, he's deciding whether to stay with me or go to Fay. I don't want him to be so angry that he leaves me without thinking about it properly or, for that matter, chooses to stay with me just out of pity or a sense of duty. He says he wants to do something different with his life and he wants time to sort out what. I want him to be with me, but if he knew that I was pregnant with another man's baby, he wouldn't even think of me. I would be sending him straight into Fay's arms."

"But he has to know eventually."

"Of course he does. I want him to know. But now we've got a couple of days apart for the emotional temperature to go down. He can have his space and we can both have some time to think calmly. I've got to be back later this week for the doctor and the hospital, anyway."

Liddy looked at Mary. "I love Martin so much. Why did I ever get involved with Barney? I must have been completely mad."

Mary's mouth set in a downward line and she shrugged. "It happens, Liddy. Not just to you. Everyone makes choices—bad ones and good ones. Occasionally the consequences turn a bad choice into a good one and sometimes it's the other way round. Barney was what you wanted at that time. He made you happy. But wrong time, wrong place sort of thing. It's human nature. You can't go back and make it right. You've got to concentrate on going *forward* and making it right."

Liddy drove away, hunched over the steering wheel, her knuckles white with pain.

"You've put on weight," Cyn said roughly, as she held her papery cheek out for a kiss. "And that is really a quite dreadful skirt, Lydia. You're much too old to dress as Gretel."

Liddy was not courageous enough to respond by telling Cyn that she had also grown more portly in the past few months. She was relieved to see that Cleo, although thinner than ever, seemed to show no signs of physical impairment. The two women were like leftovers from a different time. They never really seemed to change; just a few more lines on their faces, the thick powder stuck into slightly deeper troughs, their hair thinner, lipstick and eye shadow applied a little less accurately—but the same dear people: Cleo gentle and giving, Cyn pugnacious and demanding.

The familiar meaty smell of cat hit Liddy as she went into the White House. It was teatime and the sitting room was a mass of seething fur as all the cats converged around the tea tray. Afternoon tea was a time-honored ritual—created by Cleo—and every day, for aunts and cats, everything stopped for tea. There was, as usual, a wooden tray with curly brass handles and an embroidered traycloth on which sat a fine selection of Marmite, fish paste, cucumber and sardine sandwiches, cut into tiny triangles with their crusts removed, little squares of homemade gingerbread and slices of Battenburg cake. Tea was Earl Grey, poured from a silver teapot with a curly handle into the finest bone china and served with a sliver of lemon. It had always been the same—like a doll's tea party—for as long as Liddy could remember. As a child she would stand in their little Kensington galley kitchen and watch fascinated as Cleo made her Marmite sandwiches, mashing the butter and Marmite into a light-brown squish on a flowery saucer before putting it on the bread. Sitting, that afternoon, in their low, long sitting room, high above the glittering river busy with boats, the sun pouring in through the large picture windows, tea laid out before her, the cats purring around her feet, just for a moment Liddy felt transported back to the safety of her childhood.

But she was no longer a child. As Cleo poured the tea Liddy thought that her movements were slightly slower, more tremulous, and she reached out to help.

"Sit down, darling, I can manage," Cleo said quickly.

"I really don't know why you've decided to turn up," Cyn grumbled. "There's nothing wrong with Cleo. It's a lot of fuss about nothing. We can manage perfectly well without your interference."

Cleo frowned at Cyn and turned to Liddy.

"Was it a lovely party, darling? Tell us all about it," Cleo said eagerly when she had dispensed tea and plates. "Of course, Laura asked us, but you know how lazy we are and it is such a long journey."

"It was a lovely party and a complete surprise. I had absolutely no idea."

"I really don't understand why all you young people make such a fuss about birthdays," Cyn said, feeding a paste sandwich to a large tortoiseshell cat with no tail. "What's so special about being fifty?"

"Don't be so curmudgeonly, Cyn darling." Cleo reproved her with a loving smile. She turned to Liddy. "Now, darling, tell me how the family is—"

"Oh, God, must she?" Cyn groaned. "It'll be a litany of how wonderful her children are, how special the grandchildren." Cyn caressed a large cat on her lap, who was delicately drinking tea out of her teacup. "There's nothing so tedious as a proud mother."

"Actually, I'm pregnant," Liddy was surprised to hear herself say.

Cyn spluttered into her tea. "Oh, my God, how revolting."

Once she had started, Liddy told the aunts the whole sorry story. She had not intended to tell them and, even as she spoke, she was bemused that she was blurting it out so. Afterwards, she was to realize that this was yet another plea to another quarter for confirmation that her world would be righted. It came as something of a shock to her that she did not immediately receive this confirmation from the aunts.

Cyn was the first to break the silence when Liddy had stumbled to a halt. "Well, I must say, that wet husband of yours has gone up in my estimation a bit. A mistress. Didn't think he had it in him."

"Cyn. *Shhh*," Cleo said distractedly.

There was a silence, broken only by the distant sound of pounding metal against metal from the shipyard way below them. The thumps went through Liddy as, head down, looking at her hands in her lap, she waited for Cleo to speak. What had she expected? Not, she thought afterwards, quite the stricken look on Cleo's face, or the old and weary way her usually straight shoulders slumped into the sofa. Or the distinct feeling that she seemed almost physically to distance herself from her.

"Oh, Liddy darling," she murmured almost to herself, "what have you done?" She looked up. "What about this young boy, the father?"

"I shouldn't bother worrying about him," Cyn rumbled from her chair. "Better off without bloody fathers in my experience."

"He doesn't know. I haven't seen him since January. I don't even know if he still lives in Market Ketton. It only lasted a few months." Liddy wanted to justify herself to her great-aunt.

"Obviously quite long enough," Cyn said acidly. "Anyway, I thought you lot all had access to unlimited birth control?" Cyn's face wrinkled with distaste. "I can't stand pregnant women. They only ever talk about their bladders, and in my experience babies turn everyone around them into soppy, brain-dead individuals."

Liddy turned to Cleo, wanting her to respond, but her aunt's expression was blank; all vestige of shock had gone, leaving her face an empty canvas.

"Poor Martin, poor, poor you. I can't bear it for you both. The whole thing is quite dreadful." She seemed so devastated and so near to tears that Liddy found herself being terribly positive.

"I'm sure Martin and I will be able to get through this. We've been together so long, we have so much that ties us together."

"If Martin had any spirit at all, he'd leave you alone to sort out your own mess," Cyn said sourly.

"Cyn. That is a simply wretched thing to say. This is family." Cleo rose to her feet and began to clear the tea tray crossly.

"Happily not mine," Cyn said sulkily, picking up a magazine and ostentatiously holding it up in front of her face.

Liddy rose to her feet to help clear the tea.

Cleo held up her hand. "No, you sit here. I must go and feed the cats."

She left the room with a retinue of cats stalking behind, tails swishing. Liddy and Cyn sat in silence.

"Your mother was a selfish woman, too," Cyn suddenly said from behind her magazine. "Ghastly woman. Never had a thought for anyone other than herself. You're just like her."

Liddy chose to remain silent. Cyn put down the magazine and fumbled a cigarette into an ivory cigarette holder.

"She always regretted not being able to have a baby, you know. Of course, nowadays, it wouldn't have happened." Cyn looked at Liddy fiercely. "You don't know what I'm talking about, do you?"

Liddy shook her head and Cyn sighed. "Typical of your

family, chatter, chatter, chatter about the weather, and the color of Aunty Bedsocks's new bathroom—all the things that don't matter—and sweep the dark bits under the carpet. Cleo had a hysterectomy when she was a young woman."

"I never knew that," Liddy said.

"Why should you?" Cyn said crossly, and then added confusingly, "Your stupid parents weren't interested in anyone but themselves."

"Why?"

"Why what?"

"Why did she have to have a hysterectomy?"

"Oh God, I don't know," Cyn said dismissively, waving her arm and dropping ash down her front. "I can't stand all that medical stuff. Anyway, she had it all taken away and with it, the chance, as she saw it, to get married and have a baby."

Liddy digested this information, half listening to Cleo in the kitchen cooing at the cats as she fed them.

"I'm sorry. No one ever told me," she said apologetically.

"It's too late to be sorry now, Lydia. Don't waste your breath. You've upset Cleo. Your grandmother was her favorite sister and Cleo always thought of your mother as her daughter. She was very fond of her. Personally, I never understood why. I always found her an appallingly dreary woman. Anyway, Cleo always says she's very fond of you, proud of you, too. She will take this latest drama of yours very hard indeed." Cyn raised her penciled eyebrows heavenward and drawled, "So I'm extremely sorry that you didn't have the manners to keep the details of your sordid little life to yourself."

"Well, Miranda, have you had a chance to talk to Richard?" Miranda's boss, David, looked at her across the table, his elbows making dents in the thick white tablecloth. It was Monday lunchtime and the restaurant was half-empty—just a whispering couple in the corner and a four-man business lunch at the table by the window. Miranda fiddled with the packet of breadsticks and wished the heavy smell of Italian food didn't make her feel so sick. "I really need an answer by the end of the week," he pushed. "Miranda, I *need* someone strong in editorial up there. You've got a lot of potential, a good career ahead of you. I know you're doubtful about leaving London, but it's only a year's contract and Leeds is only a couple of hours away. You would have an experienced deputy who knows the area. It is an excellent opportunity that you would be foolish not to take up."

Miranda thought how much she wanted the job—and for so many reasons. Ever since the job was first brought up, she had been dreaming about turning a failing magazine round. She could do it: she had the ideas, she had the energy and it was a step up the ladder. The more she heard about the job and thought about it, the more she wanted it—and it would have the added advantage of deferring Richard's plans.

"Look, I can give you until Friday. We'll meet again then," David said, picking up the menu. "Decision day, OK? Now, let's order and get that out of the way and I'll tell you more about Leeds."

While David talked, Miranda picked at the smallest and simplest salad the restaurant had to offer and dreaded the thought of speaking to Richard.

It was worse than she imagined because Richard was already white with anger when she arrived home.

He was sitting at the kitchen table, head bowed and something clenched in his hand.

"Hi, darling." She flung her briefcase down on the kitchen table and leaned over to kiss the top of his head. He stood up and moved away from her, as though needing a large space between them. He threw a crumpled package onto the table.

"So?"

"So? What?" Miranda said bravely as her heart plummeted and her hands began to shake.

"Look at it." Richard's voice was so tight, it sounded as though the words were having difficulty coming out through his mouth. "As if you needed to," he added.

Miranda picked at the screwed-up cardboard. She didn't need to look at it. She knew perfectly well that it was the packaging for the morning-after pill that she had taken three days ago.

"How did you find it?"

Richard looked at her incredulously.

"That's what matters, is it? How did I find it? Not that I have and that I want to know what the hell you've been doing?"

Miranda sat down heavily.

"I'm sorry," she said inadequately.

"Oh right . . . right, you're *sorry*. Sorry you took these?" Richard swept the package on to the floor. "Or sorry that I've found out? That I happened to be looking for a Visa card slip in the dustbin outside and found this screwed up in the bottom of a Boots bag?"

"Sorry about it all," Miranda said truthfully, unable to focus on anything except the rotten twist of cardboard on the floor.

"Is this the first time, or are you in the habit of killing our embryos?" Richard got up and leaned against the sink, arms folded across his chest, his dark eyes glaring through her.

"Look, I probably wasn't pregnant. I just wanted to make sure."

"I believe that wasn't quite the question."

Could she tell him now? Could she tell him how in the last two years she had had two abortions, how she had had to go to two different private hospitals, and then to endless family-planning clinics across the other side of London to get a supply of morning-after pills?

"For someone who has never been on the pill in case it makes you fat," Richard said, "you are remarkably ignorant about this." He kicked at the box contemptuously. "This is the same drug—just a much higher dose."

"But I'm not ready, Richard. I can't have a baby now." Miranda's tears began to roll down her cheeks.

"You mean it might get in the way of your high-flying career?"

"No, it's nothing to do with that."

"Why, in the name of God, didn't you tell me you didn't want a baby? We could have discussed it. Why have you let me hope each fucking month?"

"We will have one, I promise, we will. Just not now." Miranda unconsciously clutched at her stomach and wanted to tell him how frightened and disgusted she was at the thought of her stomach growing with something inside her. She couldn't do it: she knew she could never lose control of her body; it would balloon up, stretch and become someone else's body, no longer hers to direct. How could she explain to Richard the panic she felt at the idea of carrying a baby; how it would make her dirty and spoilt?

"Don't leave me," she keened like a child left at the school gates.

Richard looked at her and the silence between them seemed dark and heavy.

"Miranda," he said in a calmer voice. "We have to sort this out." He rubbed his eyes wearily and turned round to open a bottle of whisky.

"Here," he said roughly, handing her a glass. "I suppose you *can* drink with your death pills. For such a neurotic little eater, you seem remarkably cavalier with the pills you throw down yourself," he added cruelly.

"You bastard. That was a bastard thing to say." Miranda began to shout.

Richard put up a hand. "Sorry," he said in a tired voice. "I'm sorry. That was a gratuitous remark."

But as Richard's anger subsided, Miranda welcomed her own surge of anger. It bubbled out of her at last, making her feel alive and dominant. She had always been able to deal with her anger; it was her security. While she was angry, she was safe, impregnable, no one could get to her.

"How could you say that to me, Richard? I can't help my food thing and I never said I wanted babies," she screamed at him. "It's my body. I can choose what I do with it."

She smashed the vase in the middle of the table with her arm and it crashed to the floor, the water flooding over the tiles and onto the package.

"And it's my sperm. I can choose what I do with that," Richard said coldly, moving his feet to avoid the water, "and believe me, I will."

"Are you saying you only live with me to have babies? What happened to two people loving each other and having a life together?"

"Well, what indeed? In my book, having a life together usually entails communication. You know, sharing hopes and fears, that sort of thing. I shared my hopes with you, but you apparently were unable to share your fears with me. That smacks to me of a vast lack of trust, wouldn't you think? I don't know how long this has been going on—" Miranda looked up to say something, but he stopped her. "And I *really* don't want to know. But for nearly two years, I have been thinking that we were trying for a baby. How do you think this makes me feel?" He rubbed his face again and picked up his bunch of keys. "I've got to get out, Miranda. I need to get my head round this and I can't do it here. I'm going for a walk."

Miranda got up.

"I'll come with you. We can talk."

Richard looked at her with distaste.

"Bit late for that, don't you think?"

"No, it's not." Miranda was in a panic now. "We can talk.

We'll go up to the heath." The next sentence came tripping out before she could stop it. "The exercise will do us both good."

Richard curled his lip at her. "Exercise? God, you really are a neurotic bitch, Miranda. Exercise is not exactly in the forefront of my mind at the moment and I want to be on my own."

He turned and slammed out of the flat and Miranda heard his feet thumping down the communal stairs of the house. The silence he left behind pressed in on her ears and Miranda hated herself with a passion.

"Who was that?" Fergus said sleepily from the depths of a deep sofa, as Laura came into the drawing room.

"Miranda."

"What did she want?"

What indeed? Laura wondered. Her sister usually only rang when she needed something. She had rung on the pretext of finding a cardigan that she had lost over the weekend, but Laura was unsure what exactly it was Miranda was asking of her. She never rang for a chat, yet this time, sounding more tense and nervy than usual, it seemed that she might be wanting one.

"Mum's gone to Cornwall to see the aunts. Dad can't find it at home," she whined. "I thought you might have picked it up."

"I haven't. I'm sorry."

A silence fell between them.

"Did you get back all right on Sunday?" Laura asked banally.

"Yes, of course." Another silence.

Laura took a deep breath, knowing that she was opening herself up to inevitable rejection.

"Are you OK?"

Miranda's voice immediately turned hard. "Of course I am. I'm just trying to locate this cardigan, that's all." There was a small pause then, casually, "Had a bit of a row with Richard last night—you know the sort of thing . . ."

Laura, sensing Miranda's sadness hidden behind the non-chalance, persisted with her sister, as she always did.

"Oh, Miranda, I am sorry. Do you want to talk about it?" Too late, Laura realized her mistake in sounding sympathetic.

"No, I don't. It's nothing." Miranda's voice became dismissive, warning Laura off prying.

Laura sighed. It was always the same with Miranda; she so often seemed to be crying out for something, yet any approach toward her sent her scuttling back behind a screen of remoteness, rudeness and, sometimes Laura felt, cold superiority. Retreating from the inevitable rejection if she dug any deeper, Laura chattered on about the party, the portable phone tucked under her ear as she whisked around the kitchen gathering together the ingredients for a loaf of bread.

"I really must go." Miranda's bored voice eventually interrupted her, midsentence, and, summarily dismissed, Laura had felt disadvantaged, as though it was she who had kept Miranda on the phone, thus preventing her from doing more important things.

Fergus, uninterested in the telephone call, settled back into sleep on the sofa and Laura went disconsolately back into the kitchen to finish the bread. She put on a CD of Brahms *Requiem* as she kneaded and thumped the bread dough crossly—her sister never failed to make her feel *wanting* in some way.

Even now that they were all adult, Laura felt responsible for her siblings. She had always known that she was not ravishing and interesting like Miranda, that she did not have Alex's easy charm with people and that she did not have an iota of her mother's artistic talent. Laura had always been a skillful needle-woman, and as a child spent hours making perfectly stitched dolls' clothes, but she was never artistic. She had loved to watch as Liddy, with swift, easy pencil lines, sketched a jewelry design on paper and then brought it to life with metal and stones. However much Liddy encouraged her and no matter how hard she persevered with her small square hands, she was always aware that the final result lacked the initial imagination to make it into anything other than a piece of almost technically perfect work.

No, her talent had always been looking after people: caring, organizing, protecting and making an easy path for others more charismatic than herself. It was a role she had come to enjoy, to feel proud of. Alex happily accepted her care and protection as his natural right, but Miranda was temperamental; she craved attention and then cruelly rejected it and the person giving it. Laura, never given to tempers herself, had always been scared of Miranda's tempestuous outbursts and over the years she had learned almost to abase herself in an attempt to avoid them. She put the kettle on and wished wistfully that Miranda was the kind of sister who would ask *her* how she was. Then she would have told Miranda how worried she was about Jake; how his brave little letter that morning had brought tears to her eyes and how Fergus had just said patiently, "I've told you before, Laura, he'll pull through. Everyone feels like that to begin with. He'll thank us for it. You wait till he gets into the rugger team next term."

"But it's nearly a year and he still isn't settled," Laura had snapped at him pointlessly. "We *must* discuss this, Fergus. We've got to help Jake. We must talk."

But Fergus had just said, as he pulled on his farm boots, "The best way we can help him is to encourage him to stick with it."

"Why should he stick with anything? He's only ten years old, for God's sake," she had yelled at his back view as he crossed the yard.

She could also have told Miranda that she had got her

period that morning and how much she wanted a fourth child; how each time she bled heavily, she wanted another baby a little bit more and this want was beginning to color her life. And she could never share her pain with Fergus because, more and more, even if he was here, he was, in some way, absent. After Rebecca was born, Laura had accepted having three children; then four years ago she had become pregnant accidentally and miscarried. It had devastated her.

"Try again," everyone had said—everyone, that is, except Fergus who refused to condone risking what he considered another failure.

"We don't need any more babies, Laura," he had said. "We had our pigeon pair and then you insisted on Rebecca. . . ." He had paused and the inference that Rebecca was their punishment for greediness hung solidly between them. "We would be stupid to risk another child like Rebecca," he had added and, no matter how often she brought up the subject and in how many different ways, whether gently, pleadingly or whether in sudden anger, had refused to discuss the subject ever since—that was the hurt that Laura always carried around with her. Never a particularly passionate man, Fergus had been reluctant to resume their lovemaking after her miscarriage, and even now it was more often Laura who made the initial moves between them. For the past few years Laura had collected her pills from the doctor and silently flushed them down the lavatory, disguising from Fergus and from everyone else her sadness when she bled each month and the terrible feeling of loss when, unbeknownst to anyone except the doctor, she had miscarried a few months ago. No one knew what she was doing, how lonely she was and how empty her womb felt.

She suddenly wanted her mother.

Hoping fervently that she would not get Aunt Cyn, who never failed to unnerve her, Laura telephoned Cornwall.

"I don't know what to do about Jake, Mum," she burst out.

"He's so unhappy at school and Fergus will not discuss it properly. What shall I do? I feel so helpless."

Liddy talked to her, suggested that she tried again and again with Fergus until he listened but, afterwards, Laura felt a hard ball of dissatisfaction and disappointment lodged inside her. She had the definite feeling that her mother had been slightly distrait throughout their conversation; that she had taken refuge in platitudes and had given Laura none of the sympathy she expected from Liddy.

Laura made the tea, walking briskly round the kitchen on the balls of her feet, making herself think about something more pleasant. Poor young Mrs. Fairley, for instance, who had no money to speak of and who was on her sixth child. She needed help with getting the two little ones into playgroup and Laura was at the moment negotiating with the playgroup leader to let them in on free places. She was confident that she would succeed and she thought she might make a collection of the children's old toys to take to the family. Not, though, the baby clothes that she had so lovingly stitched for her three babies; she wouldn't take them. They had been carefully washed, ironed and tissued, and were in a trunk up in the attic waiting for just one more tiny baby.

Alex had also received a letter from Jake. He gave it to Mungo to read.

"It sounds a bit stiff upper lippish, poor little bugger," Mungo said, as he handed the letter back to Alex.

"Buggeree is probably more like it," Alex said, screwing up his nose.

"Oh, get over the stereotype, sweetheart," Mungo said, shoving a heavy script into his briefcase. "Boarding schools are not like they used to be. I wish I'd gone to one." He gave a cursory glance over the kitchen. "I think I've got everything. I'm outta here. Wish me luck. I hate read-throughs. Half the cast know each other from way back and noisily trot down memory lane, while the other half stare at each other and pretend to do the crossword."

He dropped a kiss on Alex's forehead. "See you this evening. Don't know what time—we've only got a week's rehearsal for this."

Alex cleared up the breakfast things in a desultory fashion, piling up the china into an already full sink. His shift didn't start until two and he was depressed at the idea of spending the afternoon at the ticket agency alongside all the students in their gap year who talked, bright-eyed and enthusiastic, about their treks round the world. He didn't want to go trekking: no, he wanted to be going off to a read-through; he wanted to share in Mungo's working life; he wanted to be an actor. It was always bad when Mungo first got a job; all Alex's insecurities came rushing up to fill his head. Would there be an old boyfriend there? Or worse, would there be someone new with whom Mungo might fall in love? Bloody actors—they shared an exclusive, incestuous world that shut out lesser mortals. Alex wouldn't be allowed to meet any of the cast before the first night, so he couldn't check out any potentials until, one day, it might be too late.

Kylie and Danni snuffled around his feet as he sat on the sofa having a cigarette, gloomily contemplating his failure to get into drama school. He reached across, picked up the phone and dialed his best friend.

"Druse, it's me."

"Ah, hello me." Drusilla's sleepy voice struggled with forming the words.

"I've woken you up," Alex said, completely without contrition.

"Of course you have—you always do. Mungo's read-through, is it?"

"Oh, darling Druse, you know me so well. I just feel so *left out.*" Alex's voice ended on a plaintive whine. "Can we do lunch? Early. I've got to work at two."

There was a pause at the other end and Alex could hear the soft burr of murmuring voices. He wondered idly who was Drusilla's current lover.

"OK. That funny little Italian round the corner from your office at twelve. But I can't be long, really I can't, because I said I'd meet Polly at Harvey Nicks for a bit of retail therapy."

Alex knew she was lying. He found a porn movie in the stack of videos under the television and lay back on the cushions with a dog on each knee.

"So who is it?" he asked Drusilla when they met later.

"Who's what?"

"The person you were in bed with this morning and who you're going back to bed with this afternoon."

"Charlie. Married. Old enough to be my father. Very good in bed and very, very rich." Drusilla sighed with satisfaction. "He has a business lunch he couldn't get out of, but we've got a little time before he goes off to his dreary wife in Oxford. I absolutely adore him. Now, what about you?"

"I hate my job. I'm a failure and I don't want Mungo to be working."

"Oh, selfish boy."

"I know," Alex sighed. "Why am I so jealous?"

"Because you're bored and not interested in anything but him."

"We could have a baby."

"Could we?" Drusilla looked baffled.

"No, not you and me. Mungo and me."

"Darling. Now, how can I explain this to you?" Drusilla spoke slowly and clearly. "You and Mungo cannot have a baby. It is biologically impossible."

"Ditz," Alex said affectionately. "No. Rent a womb time." He looked at his friend.

Drusilla put up her hands. "Don't look at me. My womb is not for hire. I do sex, not babies, and you'd better believe it. Anyway, what do you want a baby for?"

"It would make us a proper family."

"Oh, I see. You can stay at home and be a mother," Drusilla drawled sarcastically, "and that will be sure to keep Mungo faithful, just like Charlie is and most every other man in the world. Get real, honeybun. Anyway, I thought you were planning to go to drama school."

"Well, I am, but so far I can't find a drama school that shares the same agenda."

"You can't have a baby just as an alternative plan," Drusilla persisted.

Alex had never been good at being told what to do. In a fit of contrariness, he pushed the idea forward.

"But I want a baby," he said stubbornly. "Why shouldn't I have one?"

"Primarily because you're shagging another man." Drusilla picked up the menu and then looked at him over the top.

"Now, let's eat." She twinkled at him. "I love you to pieces, Alex. You're my best, best friend, but you really can be a spoilt brat."

"I'm not so," Alex protested.

"Yes, you are, you dumb blond. You're too charming for your own good. This is all about you not being stretched, not having anything interesting to fill that pretty little head of yours. So you hate your job. Quite right, so you should, it's a crap job. If you can't be an actor, find something else, something that amuses you and that exercises that perfectly good brain of yours. Behave like Mungo's equal, not like a fawning puppy."

"You're a bully, Dru," Alex said affectionately. And, after lunch, went back to sell tickets for plays that he wanted to be in.

*　　*　　*

Liddy was upstairs in Cleo's bedroom on the telephone to Martin. Their conversation was disconcertingly businesslike.

"How is Cleo?" Martin sounded concerned.

"I *think* she's OK, really. But I can tell that Avril is worried."

Avril had looked after Cyn and Cleo ever since they had arrived in Portlisk and had, over the years, become friend and confidante to the two old ladies. In her mid-fifties, she was a small, compact woman, honest and straight-talking.

"Cleo trails around after Cyn all day. It's too much for her at her age," she had said on Tuesday morning when she came in to work. "She oughta get Doctor in. I'm telling you. I'm sure she's taken a small stroke. My mother was the same, a couple of dizzy spells, said she was fine, but I knew. There was something different, slower about her, if you know what I mean. It's a warning, you see. Doctor put Mum on to an aspirin a day and she lived for another three years," and Avril had stumped upstairs with breakfast trays.

"But I get the impression that Cleo and Cyn think I'm rather superfluous to requirements," Liddy now said to Martin.

"You must make sure they're really all right." Liddy felt Martin urging her not to hurry back. "Cleo should see her doctor as soon as possible, and Avril may have rung because she feels she needs more help."

"How are you?" Liddy asked tentatively, forcing herself not to ask the questions that she really wanted to ask.

"Fine, fine, I'm fine." Martin spoke unnaturally.

She wanted to ask him if he was missing her—like she always used to, before this ring of darkness had settled around them both—but she was too afraid of the answer.

"Well, I'll phone you tomorrow and let you know when I'll be back."

"Yes, do that." Martin's voice softened slightly. "Take care of yourself."

Replacing the receiver, Liddy tried not to read a sense of

finality into Martin's last words. She remained sitting on Cleo's bed, looking at the framed sepia photographs around the walls: fuzzy pictures of a calm woman dressed in white muslin, surrounded by little girls with long curly hair and sailor-suited boys with serious faces. Had this matriarch suffered with a similar heavy heart at some time in her life? Had she resolved her crises and had they become small and unimportant or even forgotten in the passage of time? Liddy fiddled idly with Cleo's old teddy bear, laid tenderly on top of the bedspread, as it must have been for so many years. A modern soft toy of E.T. sat beside it, looking strange and out of place in the room. Two cats spooned together at the end of the bed peered at her with arrogant green eyes. She stared out the window, thinking of Martin and watching Cleo floating round the garden in a large straw hat with a trug over her arm, snipping at roses, looking just like a photograph of Vita Sackville-West.

She attempted again to get Cleo to the doctor.

"Don't worry about me, darling," Cleo said firmly. "Avril is such a worrier. Anyway, I think poor old Cyn is hatching a nasty cold. I'm much more concerned about her." She looked at Liddy anxiously. "You must go home and sort out this wretched mess you've got yourself into."

"I don't know what else I can do," Liddy said to Avril. "She insists that she is perfectly fine and I can't force her to see the doctor. And I must be home by Friday, I really must," she added desperately.

Avril looked at her shrewdly. "Yeah, my lovely. I heard you were in the shit, you silly cow. You'd better hope it's stillborn," she added cheerily. "That's your best bet, I reckon."

As if reminding Liddy that she had, briefly, had the same thought, the baby batted around and Liddy found herself instinctively stroking her bump protectively, as though getting to know the small life that had grown inside her for so long without her knowing it.

*　　*　　*

Avril sent Liddy into the nearest town to buy cold medicaments for Cyn. Wandering past a maternity and baby shop, unfortunately called Happy Days, she noticed a plain black dress in the window, and on impulse she went into the shop and flicking through the rails of clothes found herself quite absorbed in the choice.

"I always buy maternity size, too," a large, elderly shop assistant confided in her. "I find the elasticated waistband so much more comfortable—much easier than dieting."

"Actually, I really am pregnant," Liddy said, and watched an expression of confusion, followed by awe, then excitement trip in quick succession across the assistant's face.

Her name was Joan, she told her, and she thought it really rather intriguing to be having a baby at fifty: they became quite friendly and conspiratorial and, carried away by the woman's enthusiasm and gaiety, Liddy collected a pile of things for the baby while they discussed their children and grandchildren.

"It's all so different from our day," Joan said, holding up an odd-shaped feeding cup. "Well, of course, I'm much older than you, but everything changes so quickly; all this sterilizing equipment and safety stuff and then there are gadgets to make food hot and others to make it cool." She rolled her eyes. "Honestly, these modern mothers don't know the half of it. They should have seen child-rearing in the fifties—they'd wonder how any baby survived."

Joan packed up the parcels in a pretty Moses basket that she persuaded Liddy to buy. "Go on," she said. "It's so pretty. Much nicer than those rucksacks youngsters carry their babies around in."

Afterwards, Liddy realized that Joan had been the first person to treat the imminent arrival of her baby with any degree of delight or even normality.

She also found a small craft shop down an unexpected alley-way and fossicking through sheets of silver, stones and beads, she suddenly had a desire to design a piece of jewelry in cele-bration of the baby—just as she had done with her other babies.

And tomorrow she would go home to face Martin.

Chapter

F I V E

But Liddy's departure from Cornwall was delayed. Cyn's cold turned heavy, and the next day she took to her bed.

"She only has herself to blame—all that smoking." An anxious Cleo was uncharacteristically cross with her partner.

Cyn was a demanding and imperious patient; she lay in her bed, surrounded by cats, wheezing and coughing and constantly ringing an annoying little bell. Liddy and Avril were concerned by the extra work imposed on Cleo; Cyn only wanted Cleo to look after her, and no matter how often Liddy and Avril offered both women vehemently refused offers of help.

"Cleo is the only one who knows what I like," Cyn croaked.

"I don't want her upset," Cleo said wearily.

Pressurized by Avril, Liddy could see no alternative but to postpone her hospital and doctor's appointments and stay on for a few more days to support Cleo, who was obviously relieved and grateful at her decision.

Cleo called the doctor and Cyn raged at Cleo and then at the doctor, calling him an incompetent man.

"It's debatable whether incompetence or man is the greater insult," the doctor said wryly.

Even at the height of her illness and unable to breathe easily, Cyn managed to demand and to complain with her customary fluency.

"I thought people were meant to be soft and sweet when they were ill," Liddy found herself saying with asperity when Cyn had reduced Cleo to tears over some argument about a meal she didn't like. "Didn't you ever read *What Katy Did?*"

Cyn, who always appreciated a fight-back, smiled at Liddy. "Frightful book," she shuddered. "I don't see why I should be grateful just because I feel as bad as buggery." Then she added gruffly, "It's probably a good thing you're here, after all. Cleo can't manage me and the cats on her own, not at her age."

In a last-minute bid to keep herself and her baby fit enough for the birth, Liddy walked up to the cliffs—slowly and panting heavily, she arrived at the top and sat on a bench with a brass plaque dedicated to Kathy and Alfred.

Idly contemplating Kathy and Alfred and trying to get her breath back, she watched a solitary male figure in a beaten-up jacket and matching cap walking toward her with an elderly cream-colored Labrador lumbering around at his heels.

Liddy looked across the sea; there seemed to be a yacht race around the headland and the boats, whipped up by a saucy wind, bounced and bobbed across the waves.

I think I'd have liked to have been a sailing sort of person, Liddy thought idly, watching the small figures on deck fling themselves around under the flapping sails.

She must have either spoken aloud, or her lips had moved because the man and the dog appeared in front of her.

"Sorry?"

She looked up at him blankly. The sun was so bright behind him, she had to make a visor with her hand.

"Oh, sorry," she said automatically. "Was I talking out loud? Sorry."

"My fault, I thought you said something to me."

He moved round so that she could look at him without being blinded by the sun. He was, she thought, probably about her age, a little older perhaps, with thick gray hair crunched down under his cap. In repose, his face was smooth, peaceful and ascetic. Liddy thought he looked rather like a remote Pre-Raphaelite Christ, but when his calm expression crunkled into a smile, the image was immediately broken and it became a friendly, approachable face.

"Shall we stop apologizing to each other. *Sorry* must be the most overused and often most insincere phrase in the English language." He held out his hand formally. "Robert Trevland. Are you on holiday?"

"Liddy Claver. I'm staying with my aunt, Cleo Nye."

"Ahh, and with the redoubtable Miss Trenton."

"Do you know them?"

Robert's dog emerged from a gorse bush and lolloped up to them. Robert pushed her away.

"Go on, Bonnie—find the rabbits." He gestured shyly that he might sit down beside her and Liddy moved up to make room. "Not really. They occasionally used to take part in village life when they first came here, but I'm afraid Miss Trenton probably found us all unbearably provincial. Miss Nye and I often have a chat when she comes down to the village, but Miss Trenton usually stays above like a snarling dragon protecting its princess. Her reputation goes before her. They're all terrified of her."

Liddy defended Cyn. "She's not so bad when you get to know her."

"Are you staying down here for long?"

"I came down because Cleo hasn't been well and now Cyn is enjoying a very bad cold. I'm hoping to go home in a few days. You live in the village, do you?"

"Yup. Have done for ten years. It's quiet and cold in the winter and the holidaymakers are hell in the summer, but it suits me." He noticed Liddy shift her body to accommodate the baby's movements. "You look uncomfortable. Do you want to potter a bit?"

"I don't walk very fast."

"No, I imagine you don't," he agreed. "When's it due?"

He asked so naturally and Liddy answered without thinking, "In about seven weeks." She paused for a moment, looking down at herself in her new black dress with surprise. "I suppose I do look pregnant now," she said almost to herself.

Robert glanced at her with amusement.

"Why? Are you trying to disguise it?"

"It's rather difficult . . ."

They walked slowly along the cliff toward the village, the wind blowing their hair across their faces and Liddy talked.

They reached a second bench and sat down and she finally crumbled to a halt.

"Sorry, you didn't need to know all that," she apologized, suddenly shy and awkward in front of a stranger. "I can't seem to keep it to myself. Every time I tell someone I think, or rather hope they're going to say it's not so terrible as it seems." She looked at him piteously. "Now I've just told a complete and utter stranger. I'm so sorry."

"Would you like a cup of tea?" Robert asked. "My cottage is just down there." He called the dog and held out a hand to pull Liddy up.

"If it would make you feel any better, I could tell you the story of my life—that's not particularly edifying either."

Robert was a cartoonist turned detective fiction writer.

"Cartoon work dried up when I came down here," he explained. "I was out of the mêlée and lost my touch. I started writing detective stories and they seemed to work." He was, he told her, a widower in his late fifties with two sons who lived abroad.

"I rarely see them—rarely see anyone, actually. I'm becoming a bit of a recluse in my old age. And here," he said, stopping in front of a small garden gate behind which a steep path led to a small cottage, "is where I am reclusive."

Robert's cottage was a monument to a single man, small, comfortable and shipshape neat, except in his little study which looked like a paper recycling plant. He told her with beguiling candor that he had a penchant for women much younger than himself, but that he had just broken up with a thirty-year-old woman and it had been so messy that he had no intention of ever getting involved in sex again.

"I hope she wasn't pregnant," Liddy said into her mug of tea.

"Good point. Never thought to ask, actually. Unlike you though, if she were, Harriet would be beating on my door demanding money and support." Robert looked at her seriously. "I think you're being remarkably stoical about the situation, if I may say so."

"No, I'm not, not inside. Inside I'm screaming. I mean, how would you feel if you were Martin confronted with this?"

Robert looked pained and for the first time did not meet her eyes as he got up quickly and busied himself with refilling the teapot. He was clearly anxious to avoid the female territory of emotional conjecture.

Liddy held her arm tightly across her stomach as if to prevent the baby ever coming out.

"I'm a bit concerned about Dad," Laura said to Miranda over the telephone. "Apparently, Mum's staying a few more days with the aunts. Aunt Cyn's got a bad cold, and Dad sounded utterly miserable when I rang him. Couldn't you and Richard go up on Sunday and keep him company, check that he's eating properly and everything?"

"Laura, I can't, I'm busy this weekend," Miranda lied, "and, anyway, you know quite well that Dad is a brilliant cook and is perfectly capable of looking after himself. It's only a few days, he'll be fine—just stop fussing."

Miranda could hear herself being unnecessarily snappy. Laura was, as usual, making her feel guilty. It was all right for Laura, she was one of life's nurturers; that's what she did and it came naturally to her, but it was not what Miranda did. Anyway, she didn't have time to worry about her father. Tomorrow was decision day for Leeds and Richard had not yet come back home.

"You've got to sort this out yourself," he had said coldly when she phoned him in the office the day after he stormed out of the house. "Decide on your priorities. I can't help you do that. You know what I want. If you take this job in Leeds, that's it as far as we are concerned. I'm sorry. I do want to be with you, Miranda. I love you, for God's sake, and I want to support you and care for you, but I can only do that if we bat on the same side. We have to deal with the baby thing if we're going to move on, but you've got to want us to do this together. You tell me. I'll be staying with Jonathan if you need to get hold of me." And he had rung off leaving Miranda feeling cold and shaky. She had a dreadful conviction that Richard would never trust her again—but then, why should he; had she ever trusted herself?

At the office, the pressure was also building up.

"You'd be a fool to jettison this opportunity," David said, fixing her with a steely stare. "You would disappoint me and yourself if you don't take up the Leeds offer."

Miranda felt as though she were being wrenched in half. She began to binge and vomit, something she had managed to control for such a long time, but which now gave her strange comfort. Not to go to Leeds would be the first step toward reconciliation with Richard, but this would, in turn, lead down the path of babies—that which she dreaded above all else. To go would keep her safe from babies, but she wanted Richard, she needed Richard. She could not function without him. Every evening she came home from the office willing him to be back, and every evening the flat was empty, cold and loveless.

Laura knew that something was wrong with Miranda, but as usual Miranda had retreated, snarling, into a large black hole where she could not be reached. Laura felt she should try harder to get to her sister, but she just could not summon up the energy, not this evening. It had been a very bad day.

It had started with a doctor's appointment.

"Now, your miscarriage was when?" The doctor peered, mystified, into the bright green screen of his new computer. "Bloody thing," he mumbled. "Can't get the hang of it at all."

"Three months ago." Laura knew exactly. "And since then, nothing. It's not fair. Why, the one time I manage to conceive, do I lose it?"

The doctor won his battle with the computer. "Right, yes, here you are. Now, you've seen the consultant and he's confident that there is no reason why you should not conceive again, but I see tests were not run on your husband? . . ." His voice rose in a question and he paused as he saw Laura with tears in her eyes shaking her head vehemently. He spoke gently to her. "It is very important that you should *both* want another baby, Mrs. Byford. You must talk to your husband and perhaps it would help for you both to come in and see me and we'll take it from there."

As Laura stood up to leave, the doctor said cheerfully, "Of course, it's probably just a matter of time. You're how old? Thirty. And your husband?"

"Thirty-two."

"Yes. I mean you're both young so that's not a problem. And, of course, you've done it before. The great thing is not to get into a state about it. You have the twins and Rebecca.

You're more fortunate than all the childless couples trying for a baby." He looked at her over the top of his glasses and Laura felt that he, too, was gently chiding her for being greedy. "Take a relaxing holiday together without the children. Actually"—he smiled—"someone was telling me the other day they had read an article about how the afternoon was a good time to conceive. Probably a lot of nonsense, but you could always give it a try."

Despondent and desperate, Laura drove home from the doctor's office, thinking how horrified Fergus would be if she suddenly started suggesting afternoon sex. Even at the beginning of their relationship, Fergus would have considered going to bed in daylight hours both unconventional and self-indulgent; he was, after all, a farmer. In those days they might have laughed together at the doctor's suggestion because they had been such friends then.

Laura had always been a little afraid of men; it was Miranda who had the social life, the erotic affairs and the messy endings. Fergus was safe and solid, he made her feel comfortable and she married him when she was nineteen. He seemed to love her in a quiet uncomplicated way and Laura had been so happy—it was all she had ever wanted. They had started married life in the farm cottage and it was her doll's house come to life and she had loved playing houses and looking after Fergus. Then, he had had the time to teach her how to look after orphan lambs and she became adept at bringing small half-dead animals to life and caring for them till they could go back to the fields. She kept bees, grew vegetables: Fergus bought her chickens and ducks and then, at the very same age her mother had conceived her, Laura fell pregnant with the twins and she thought she might burst with all the contentment in her life. But life changed when Fergus's father died suddenly, Vivien moved out of the farmhouse and they moved in.

Sole responsibility for the farm seemed to weigh heavy on

Fergus and, nowadays, the short time he seemed to be in the house, he lay exhausted in his chair, socked feet up on the ottoman in front of him, his eyes shut as if fending off the nuisance of any kind of conversation.

The house was quiet and empty when she got home from the doctor's and she longed for someone to put their arms round her, to hold her tight and listen to her. She stood by the telephone for some time with the address book open in front of her, nearly dialing the Cornwall number. She stretched out her hand to pick up the receiver just as it rang out, making her jump. For a heady moment she knew it was Mum ringing her because she would know that Laura needed her, but it wasn't; it was an ice cream order. Laura put down the phone, collected her burning pain, buried it back even deeper inside her and went about her chores.

The ice cream business was entirely her own. It had been her idea and she was very proud of it. This summer's orders had surpassed all those ever taken since it was established three years ago. She delivered five tubs of ice cream to a house at the far end of the village and was walking past the small estate on the outskirts, when Mrs. Fairley almost flung herself in front of her. Her face was red and sweaty and Laura thought she had been running. It was only when the young woman began talking, she realized that her face was suffused with anger.

"Mrs. Byford. Could yer come and collect that bundle of rubbish."

"Sorry?" Laura stopped.

"Them toys you shoved on the doorstep as though we were the council tip or something."

"I just thought they might come in useful. The children have grown out of them. You know what children are like . . ." Laura smiled conspiratorially at her. "They get bored so quickly and their old toys just fill up the place."

"Well, we don't want 'em, thank yer. If my kids need toys I

buy 'em meself. If yer don't want them, I'll sling 'em in the bin. And I don't want any more of yer bleedin' rubbish. OK?"

She turned round and stalked off. Laura stood still for a moment in shock; her eyes burnt with the tears that threatened to spill out. She wanted to run after Mrs. Fairley and explain that she hadn't meant it like that; she hadn't meant to upset her. She would have followed her, but she saw Rebecca's school bus coming round the corner. She walked slowly toward the bus stop feeling misconstrued and wounded.

And then, much later, just after Miranda had rang off, Jake's headmaster rang up to say that he had been missing since before afternoon prep. Today, Laura's world, which she tried to keep so safe and secure, seemed to be falling apart.

Jake was standing against the doorjamb, school bag at his feet, sniveling, his face pale, when Alex opened the door.

"Good God," he said involuntarily.

Jake looked up uneasily at him, as if unsure about his welcome. "I couldn't think where else to come." He wavered.

Alex picked up the bag and ushered the boy through the door. "Oh, you poor little sod. Do you really hate school this much?" Jake shrugged. Now he was here, his misery came out in sulkiness.

It was Mungo, turning up from rehearsal just after Jake's arrival, who rustled around with oven-ready fries and baked beans and it was Mungo who made up a bed on the sofa.

Alex rang up Laura.

"Laura, I've got Jake here. He appears to have run away from school."

"Thank heavens he's safe." Alex heard Laura shout to Fergus. "He's found. He's at Alex's." She turned back to the telephone. "Why has he come to *you?*"

"Easier to get to London than Wiltshire, I suppose."

"Yes, yes, that'll be it." Laura sounded relieved. "I'll come and get him now. I'll be with you in a couple of hours."

Alex looked across at Jake, sitting on the sofa with a tray on his lap. He could hear Mungo talking softly to him and his heart turned over for the ashen-faced little boy.

"He's completely exhausted. Why don't you let him stay tonight and collect him first thing tomorrow?"

"I want him home now, Alex," Laura said in a teary voice. "I want to cuddle him."

"Be sensible, Laura. He's nearly asleep. We'll look after him, I promise you, and I'm on a late shift tomorrow."

Laura asked to speak to Jake and the boy spoke monosyllabically into the phone.

He handed the receiver back to Alex. "She wants to talk to you."

Laura spoke ferociously through a veil of tears. "Well, that's it. Fergus will have to listen to me now. I knew Jake was unhappy. I've been telling Fergus for months. I'm going to take him away from that awful school and he can come home. Where he should be." Then, more gently, she said, "I'll come up tomorrow morning as soon as I've put Becs on the bus. Look after him for me, will you?"

Slowly and diffidently, Jake talked to Mungo while Alex was on the phone. He was being bullied. Not *really* badly, he said, but just enough to make him hate being at school. There were so many tests the other boys put the new boys through and he was finding some of them a bit scary.

"It's not, you know, sexual, is it?" Alex asked Mungo later when they were in bed and Jake was asleep on the sofa.

"I don't think so. It seems to be good old-fashioned new-boy bullying. He'll be OK. Bloody brave of him to run, I'd say."

Later that night, Alex woke up and found himself sobbing into Mungo's shoulder. He cried for Jake, for every other child who was scared and hurt by people; he cried for himself as a little boy and for himself as an adult. Mungo held him tightly and he felt safe again.

*   *   *

When Jake's headmaster had rung, Laura was more frightened than she ever remembered. Then, after Alex rang, she was angry—with everyone: angry with the school, with Fergus for making him go there, with herself for letting it happen and, a little bit, with Alex because Jake had run to him. Only when she calmed down did she realize that, unlike getting pregnant and unlike Mrs. Fairley, it was in her power to resolve Jake's situation.

"You must send the boy back immediately," her mother-in-law pronounced. "It's just like getting back on a horse. Do it immediately before the rot sets in."

Vivien had come round from her dower cottage at the other end of the village as soon as Fergus had rung to tell her Jake was missing.

"That's probably quite a good idea," Fergus said, looking warily at Laura.

"No. He is coming back here first for a few days. Anyway, for the weekend," Laura said confrontationally. "It will give us the opportunity to talk to him properly and find out what he really wants."

"Yes, maybe that *is* a better idea," Fergus said miserably, caught between the two warring women.

"Oh, I shouldn't bring him back here, dear," Vivien spoke officiously. "Much better to take him straight back to school. You can't let a child of that age make those sort of decisions. It's ridiculous, he's much too young. It's probably a silly quarrel with a friend. Don't you think so, Fergus?"

Fergus nodded and Laura glared at him, willing him to stand up to his mother. Fergus did stand up, but only to amble out to the porch. "I've got to go and get something from the shed," he mumbled. Then he looked at Laura. "Look, you do what you think best, Laura."

Laura smiled at him gratefully; then he spoilt it by saying, "I'm sure you'll sort it out."

And Laura wanted to shout at him, No, no, no, *we'll* sort it out. Please let us do this *together.* But she didn't shout aloud, not in front of Vivien, and Fergus couldn't hear what she was saying inside.

"I suppose you must do what you think right," Vivien said coolly, gathering her smart brown handbag under her arm, "but I'd send him back forthwith. I think you're just making a rod for your back. You don't want the boy making this sort of fuss every time he has a disagreement with a friend. You should listen to Fergus, Laura, he went to that school, he knows the form." She couldn't resist one last parting shot. "I cannot for the life of me understand why he should choose to go to your brother of all places—not particularly suitable, I would have thought."

Laura had the unusual experience of feeling defensive about her brother's lifestyle.

Miranda hated herself for calling out every time she came into the flat. "Hello."

The silence enveloped and oppressed her.

It was Saturday, the day she had thought, had *willed* Richard to come back and hear the answer she had given her boss. But everything was as she had left it this morning when she went to the gym: her sad single mug on the draining board, the bed unmade. Richard had obviously been into the flat during the day to remove a few more clothes. He had also taken his laptop and his half-written novel. Miranda found that particularly unbearable.

She couldn't bear the dark emptiness. She telephoned her father—he had always been her first choice for succor.

"Hello, Dad." She clutched the telephone receiver so tightly her curled fingers looked skeletal.

"Mirry, darling, what's the matter?"

Martin's voice was full of concern; he always knew when Miranda was beating herself up.

"Richard has moved out. He wants babies. I don't want babies. I hate myself so much. I'm alone, I can't be alone, I'm frightened of being alone. I don't know what to do. It's all rubbish. I'm all rubbish."

"You know you're not rubbish, my darling, you're a wonderful person." Martin spoke softly.

"You're only saying that because I'm your daughter."

"Yes," agreed Martin, "I am. That's what parents are for—to think their children are wonderful. You must talk to Richard, you know you must." If there was a note of desperate urgency in her father's voice, Miranda was not attuned to pick it up.

"I can't. He's absolutely set on babies and I can't have them."

"Now, darling, that's not true; you *could* have them. You just don't want to."

"But why should I? I've never wanted babies. It's Richard that does and I don't think he wants me without babies any longer. He won't understand how I feel."

Martin spoke gently. "But do you really tell him? I mean *really*. Don't disappear from him, darling, don't let a wall build up between you . . ."

Half an hour later Miranda was calm. Martin, as he always did, had softly talked her down from her rising hysteria. She held the phone, listening to the dial tone long after he had rung off, willing him to be back on the line just for her.

She telephoned Alex.

"I was trying to ring you," he said, his voice, like Martin's, concerned and loving. "I've just spoken to Dad. I thought you must be in a bad way if he actually rang me. Anyway, I'm to look after you, so stop slopping round your empty flat and get yourself round here to be looked after."

"Welcome to runaway house," he said cheerfully as he let her in ten minutes later. "Jake ran away from school on Thursday. Laura picked him up yesterday morning."

Miranda fought her way through the waggling hairy bodies of the dogs and sank down onto the sofa.

"Is he OK?" she asked vaguely.

"Oh, he'll be fine. Laura has really got the bit between her teeth now. If Jake doesn't want to go back to that school, she'll make sure he doesn't. The white witch is trying to interfere, but I think Laura is holding her own." Alex gave Miranda a drink and she took it without thanks.

"I hate the flat when it's empty," she said.

"Mungo was brilliant with Jake—" Alex threw an admiring look at Mungo. "—He talked to him for hours. He's a natural parent, I'm happy to say."

"Oh, right," Miranda murmured. "I've just thought, I haven't put out the rubbish. Richard always does that."

Mungo grinned at them both. "I think I'll leave you two great communicators of our time to have your separate conversations together. I'll see you later." He ruffled Alex's hair.

"Where are you going?" Alex asked anxiously.

"Karen's—she wants me to sign something." He picked up his coat and left the room.

"I wonder," Alex said as he sat down beside Miranda.

"Wonder what?" Miranda asked in a tone of voice that suggested she didn't really care about the answer.

"Where he really is going." Alex stood up again and twiddled his glass nervously. "I hate it when he's rehearsing a new play, Mirry. I just never *know*."

"Richard isn't coming back," Miranda said disconsolately.

Alex, still in his own head, gazed at her vaguely.

"I'm sure he is," he said soothingly. "You know Mungo and Karen are married?"

"Married? For real?"

"No, for her British residency. She's Canadian."

"So, you're not jealous of *her* then?"

"No, of course not. But she would cover for him if he was off shagging someone else."

"I wonder if Richard has found someone else to shag." Miranda gulped into her drink.

Alex stood up and pulled a small bundle out of a jar on the mantelpiece.

"Hey, Mirry," he said with a gentle smile, "here's an idea. Let's have some puff and first you talk and I'll listen. Then we'll have some more puff and *I'll* talk and *you* listen. OK?"

"Richard wants a baby," Miranda said.

"So do I," Alex said immediately. Miranda glared at him and he put up his hands. "Sorry, sorry—your turn."

So Miranda talked while Alex rolled a spliff and passed it between them.

"Dad says I should go back to counseling," she finished, "if I really want to make it work with Richard. He said that you should never, never stop working hard in any relationship because relationships and the people in them are always changing and if you're not careful you lose track of them and then perhaps it's too late to go back."

Alex sat very still for a moment. Then he spoke slowly and sadly. "He's right. You know I loved Dad so much when I was little, all those silly games he used to play with us. And he spent hours teaching us to ride bikes and cook flapjacks. He treated us all the same. Do you remember Laura's dolls? You were never interested in them, but I loved playing with them—when Laura let me. Then one day Dad suddenly started wanting to play football with me. He made me do that awful Duke of Edinburgh Award thing. Do you remember that? I think he expected me to be all boyish and I didn't know how to tell him I didn't want to be. We sort of stopped talking and now we never really get around to saying anything to each other. That's why I was so surprised when he rang me this evening about looking after you. I've always thought that he believes Richard would be the perfect son, the one I'm not. They get on so well together, Richard seems so *sorted*—he achieves everything he wants."

"Except bloody babies," Miranda said passionately.

"Yes, well, babies." Alex inhaled deeply and slowly let out the smoke with a ponderous sigh. "You're lucky to have the option. It's more than I've got."

Miranda looked at him in bewilderment. "What do you want a baby for?"

Alex shrugged. "I don't know. Why not? Just because I'm gay doesn't mean that one day I wouldn't like to be a parent. Men can want babies just as much as women."

"Tell me about it." Miranda groaned.

Alex changed the subject. "You don't want to lose Richard—he's a good bloke. I mean, surely you can have one baby. You've been designed to have them; you've got all the right engineering."

"But not the mental bit," Miranda said in despair. "I can't have a . . . a thing growing inside me, and then having to push it out. What would it do to my body? It's a horrible idea. I can't do it, Alex, not even for Richard."

"Dad's right. You could go and talk to someone who would help you," Alex said gently.

"Oh, Christ. I spent most of my adolescence talking to people about my body. No one can tell me any more than I know already. Self-hatred . . . dah, dah, dah. Oh, God, it's so boring. Why can't Richard and I just go on as we are?"

"Because men have a right to babies. Honestly, I mean it. If I could get pregnant, I'd have lots."

Miranda looked at her beautiful brother and said sadly, "The trouble is, you and I have been put into the wrong bodies."

Alex handed Miranda the dog-end of the spliff. "Yes, well, now where do you think Mungo *really* is?"

*　　*　　*

Cyn had demanded a television in her bedroom.

"Ring up a shop and organize someone to come and install one of those portable ones," she had said grandly. "I can't stand you two Edith Cavells trying to amuse me any longer. I'd rather watch my wildlife programs."

"I hope she doesn't take to her bed forever," Cleo said anxiously.

But, by Monday morning, Cyn was getting better and considerably more obstreperous. She had obviously forgotten that she had ever been grateful for Liddy being there.

"That thing seems to be growing very fast." She eyed Liddy's bump. "I hope to God you're not going to have it here. You'd better go home."

"It's not due for weeks yet," Liddy pointed out. "But you needn't worry, I'm going home either tomorrow or the next day."

Cyn rolled her eyes. "Thank heavens for that," she said disagreeably. "Now go away do, and leave me in peace."

"I should stop fretting about Cyn. She's getting better," Liddy said to Cleo when she returned downstairs. "The vitriol is flooding back and she's wearing mascara again."

The volume on Cyn's television in her bedroom was turned up high and sounds of a cooking program filtered down to Cleo and Liddy in the kitchen.

"I'm so relieved. I was becoming quite worried," Cleo said.

She was standing at the sink, mashing bread and milk in a bowl for three seagulls who were stamping up and down on the kitchen steps. A cat was sitting on the table watching the birds warily.

"Don't you ever worry that the cats will attack the gulls or the gulls the cats?" Liddy asked, looking at the gulls' prehistoric-looking claws and their cruel, curvy beaks.

"Good gracious, no. The cats wouldn't dare. They know the

gullies are family—aren't you, sweets?" Cleo cooed at the birds as she took the bowl outside. She came back inside. "They're terrified of them, actually," she admitted, as she stroked one of the cats on the table who now stood up and arched its back languorously.

"Now Cyn is on the mend I should really go home," Liddy said. "I missed my last hospital appointment so I should get to Friday's clinic."

"Yes, you most certainly must, darling. You've been so kind to stay, especially now of all times . . ." Cleo stopped, unsure of continuing, and her face crinkled up with anxiety.

"I'm sorry," Liddy said humbly. "I know I've upset you with all this. Cyn was angry I told you and she was right, I shouldn't have bothered you with it all—"

"Oh, but of course you should have done. I'm your family. I should be able to help you." Cleo spoke sadly, in short sentences as though reciting a previously prepared list. "I keep wondering what your mother would say to you, what advice she would give you, but I'm not your mother. I'm nobody's mother, never have been. I feel so helpless. This is all outside my bounds of experience—babies and everything. I do know Martin has always loved you, whatever he's done recently, and you love him."

Liddy nodded. "I do, so much. I don't know why I keep forgetting to remember that."

Cleo patted Liddy's arm. "See. It will be all right. And I'm glad you came. We've adored having you to stay, honestly. Cyn hasn't had so much fun for ages. I love Cyn dearly, but she always has been a bully. Used to reduce your mother to tears all the time, which of course made her worse than ever. But you take it without flinching and give it back sometimes and she likes that." She stopped and looked straight at Liddy. "You have such a lovely family, darling. Go back and fight for it."

Liddy smiled at her aunt gratefully. "I'm going to, but first we must get Cyn up on her feet. I don't want you wearing your-self out running around after her."

"That's not going to be very easy," Cleo said dolefully. "She's rather taken to being an invalid."

It was Avril who suggested a way of getting Cyn out of bed.

"If you ask me, she'll stay there forever if we don't do some-thing. She's having a high old time, telly in her bedroom, drinks and food brought to her bedside—she's loving every minute. You need a man to come round. She'll come down-stairs for that and she likes to get dolled up for men."

"But she hates men. She always complaining about them," Liddy protested.

"Yup, can't stand 'em apparently, but get her sitting next to a good-looking, intelligent one and she flirts away like billyo." Avril shrugged at Liddy. "Don't ask me. I don't understand those two either."

Liddy suggested Robert as a dinner guest. He would come the next day and Liddy would be free to go home on Wednesday. Cleo thought it a splendid idea and Robert was utterly enchanted. "I can't tell you by how much my standing in the village will go up," he said. "Dinner with the 'queer ladies.' Oh, happy day, I say."

Over the weekend, Robert and Liddy had shared a couple of walks, during which conversation had been kept light between them with only passing references to Liddy's predicament.

"If I was writing the novel, I would have you and your hus-band falling into each other's arms with forgiveness," he said comfortingly. But Liddy had a shrewd idea that he was not speaking the truth.

Liddy rang Martin to tell him she was coming home on Wednesday. She waited for his voice to lighten, for him to sound pleased.

"Actually, Liddy"—the forbidding tone in his voice made her immediately fearful—"I was about to ring you. I've arranged to go away for a bit." He sounded momentarily defensive. "You knew I was going to go before, but then you went to Cornwall. I want to do some walking on the west coast of Scotland and I thought I'd take a couple of weeks. I can't settle here at the moment."

Liddy knew that he still needed to be apart from her.

"What about the shop?" she heard herself ask involuntarily.

Martin sounded irritated at such a trivial question. "The shop? Oh, Hannah can manage. I'm going on my own, Liddy, I promise." He second-guessed her. "I really need to be alone and away from everything—get some air in my lungs, do some evaluation and pull my head together. I need to do this, not just for me. This is best for both of us."

Empty commonplace words, Liddy thought bitterly, and so often repeated in a relationship.

"How do you think this makes me feel," Liddy began to shout, "sitting here while you graciously decide between me and *her*?"

"Liddy, it's not like that, not at all. This has made me look at the whole of my life, not just you and me and Fay. It's the shop, too, and what I want for the future. I feel as though I've come to some sort of crossroads and I need to think it out. If you're honest with yourself, I think you'd find that you feel the same. There has to be a reason why we have both done what we've done."

"You don't understand," Liddy said desperately. "Barney was nothing to me—an aberration, a bit of silly fun. I can't tell you how much I regret the whole thing."

"Barney." Martin rolled the word around thoughtfully as though seeking the man's identity. "This is not about him, Liddy, it really isn't. Whatever he was or wasn't to you doesn't matter very much to me at the moment and I don't want to know about it. This sounds very selfish, but I feel just now that this is about me. Until I've had time to think about me, I can't really deal with what you've got to work out. I'm sorry," he said as an afterthought.

Liddy was shocked into momentary silence by Martin's uncharacteristic selfishness. What had happened to him? How long had all this been seething and bubbling inside him? He went on talking over her thoughts. "No, we need this time apart—we both do, Liddy. Then we'll talk properly. I promise." There was a note of finality in Martin's voice.

"But I love you, Martin."

"Liddy, I know we love each other, but I'm not sure it isn't just a habit now."

"But it's a good habit, isn't it?"

Martin's voice was still stony. "But not enough, maybe." He spoke slowly as if to make her understand. "Liddy, I don't know exactly what I do want at the moment. I need to think about it. I'll see you at home in a couple of weeks." And he put down the phone abruptly.

Liddy knew exactly what *she* wanted but, just now, it didn't seem to be in her gift to achieve it.

As Avril had predicted, Cyn struggled downstairs for Robert on Tuesday. She called for Avril to wash her hair in the morning and emerged from the bathroom with her thinning hair dyed an unlikely color of reddish sand.

Complaining loudly, Cyn arrived in the sitting room at drinks time dressed in black satin trousers, a tailored white blouse and with the full regalia of her makeup.

"I can't think why you wanted to invite the bloody man to supper," she grumbled. "I don't even know him."

Cleo rolled her eyes, delighted to see Cyn upright, and disappeared back into the kitchen to finish the cooking.

"Come and sit over here," Cyn commanded, when Liddy

ushered Robert in. She waved a lordly hand, nails newly painted pearly pink. "Let me look at you properly. For God's sake, don't hover, man. I can't stand hoverers."

"I'm quite anxious not to sit on a cat," Robert said with a glance at the piles of sleeping cats dotted around the room.

"You can move cats, you know," Cyn said, "or are you one of those ghastly people who don't like cats?"

"I adore cats," Robert lied gravely.

"Why haven't you got any then? You haven't, I know because I asked Liddy."

"Darling, do stop bullying the man." Cleo came in with Cyn's pink gin and a glass of wine for Liddy. "What will you have to drink, Robert?"

"Whisky, I should think," Cyn declared forcefully. "Proper men drink whisky. And I do hope you've got some decent wine, Cleo." She turned to Robert. "Cleo hasn't the first idea about good wine, or anything else much, come to that."

"She's getting better by the minute," Cleo whispered happily to Liddy in the kitchen.

Cyn monopolized Robert all evening, using him to vent her spleen on Cleo and Liddy; her heavily made-up eyes glittered, her lipstick slewed off her mouth, and she continually swept her gnarled hand coquettishly across her hair. Liddy watched her performance with amusement, wondering at Cyn's strange flirtation that seemed, in some way, almost masculine in its aggression.

"Of course, Cleo and Liddy are blood, but nothing to do with me, either of them. They're both as soft as each other. Liddy gets herself into trouble—at her age." Cyn rolled her eyes theatrically. "And, of course, we seemed to have taken her in, like we're some sort of hostel for unmarried women."

Robert deflected the conversation by asking Cyn about her past.

"What a truly nice man he is," Cleo said quietly to Liddy as they listened to Cyn's raucous account of her work in the housing department just after the war.

"I mean I wasn't educated, but I was tough. It was my job to house people and by God I did, even if it meant bending the rules. My colleagues were so wet; they never got anything done."

Robert kept asking leading questions and Cyn grew ever more garrulous.

"Father never liked me very much. My sister, Marjorie, was sent off to study physical education at college, but I was just left at home until the war. I wanted to go to drama school. I should have been an actress. I've got it all in here." She thumped her chest dramatically and doubled over with coughing.

"Oh, Christ, it's so ghastly getting old," she said when she regained her breath. "Next time you come," she looked at Robert and frowned, "whatever your name is, I can never remember names, I'll tell you about my father. Wonderful man. He couldn't stand my mother. A very stupid woman." She stood up with exaggerated difficulty.

"I'm still not well, so I shall take myself off to bed. Come along, Cleo," she trumpeted imperiously. She turned back at the door. "Give the man a nightcap, Lydia. One for the road."

Liddy walked across the room to pour a whisky and felt her womb contract slightly. She suddenly felt very frail, utterly occupied by the baby—it lay still and heavy as though it were about to fall through her shaky legs.

"Cyn is quite something," Robert said, taking the glass from her. "They both are. Your aunt is so lavender and pink and Cyn so black and white. Such a contrast and so wonderfully devoted to each other. They are truly marvelous old ladies."

"You know my mother used to get terribly protective of Cleo when Cyn was horrid to her," Liddy said, remembering how her mother used to fret about it. "She thought Cleo should just leave Cyn. But I always knew they loved each other. Cyn was the one who brought in the coal and paid the bills and Cleo cooked and looked after the cats. It was a surprisingly even relationship. My father died when I was a baby and these two were the only real 'couple' that I had in my life."

"They do love each other, you can tell that at once. They are together by choice, both of them." He glanced across at Liddy and drained his glass. "You're exhausted. You should be in bed; you've got a long drive tomorrow."

As Liddy stood up, she felt the water pour down her legs. She gasped and looked down at the puddle at her feet and the splashes around the frill of the chair's loose cover. Stunned, it took her some moments to understand what had happened.

"Oh, God, my waters have broken." She looked at Robert and saw her panic reflected in his eyes as he rose to his feet. "I'm having the baby, help me," she moaned. "It's too soon. I'm not ready."

Chapter

S I X

Robert drove Liddy to the hospital. Hunched over the wheel, he periodically let out small sentences of comfort as Liddy sat beside him, twisting to accommodate her backache and whimpering in a constant lament, "I can't have it, it's too early, it's too small."

The hospital staff took over the moment Robert helped Liddy into Accident and Emergency.

"Um . . . did you . . . er . . . want me to stay?" He shuffled his feet awkwardly as she was helped into a wheelchair.

Liddy, pain and adrenaline now coursing through her, said breathlessly, yet rather formally, "You have done quite enough. Thank you very much." And Robert had left with obvious relief.

"Not the father then?" the midwife said. "Where's he?"

"Don't ask," Liddy said wearily. "You don't want to know."

As her body squeezed and shuddered, Liddy was confounded by how she, like every other mother, could have completely forgotten the sheer force of giving birth. Through the long hours of the night and the next morning, she felt an overwhelming sense of loneliness that never abated even during the worst pain. She wanted Martin to be there.

The baby was born just after midday—a small but whole little girl whom Liddy was allowed to hold for only a moment before she was immediately whisked off to special care. "A few breathing problems," the young obstetrician said, and Liddy felt the first plunging panic of new motherhood.

"Try not to worry," she said kindly. "We would expect this in a premature baby. She's responding well. As soon as we've made you comfortable, you'll be taken down to see her."

Making her comfortable, Liddy knew from experience, was a hospital euphemism for painful stitching. She turned her head on the pillow and allowed herself to cry.

"You've done us older women proud, you have," the middle-aged midwife said when she eventually handed Liddy a cup of tea.

On the ward, surrounded by new mothers fluttering around, proud and excited, Liddy lay on her bed: she was sore, she ached all over and she was disabled with tiredness. And now she had the baby. It was here, *she* was here, a living baby. Liddy wanted her beside her and her whole being was taken up with willing her baby to breathe. Some primordial force was concentrating her mind on the survival of her baby, pushing out all extraneous thought.

"Your aunt has rung," a nurse told her sometime during that long afternoon. "She is coming in to see you this evening."

Not until the pediatrician arrived at her bedside and told her that they were very pleased with her baby's progress and hopeful that she would be breathing on her own and out of special care in a few days, did Liddy's mind begin to race with the implications of her new responsibility. The natural elation of being a new mother was clouded by the fear of what she had done, how she had done it and an overpowering exhaustion at the sheer physical task of looking after a new baby.

"How am I going to manage?" she whimpered at a young nurse who was checking her blood pressure.

"You'll be fine in a few days," the nurse cooed mindlessly, unaware of the turmoil inside Liddy. "What are you going to call Baby, then?"

A name. She hadn't thought about it properly. Thinking of names before the birth would have made the baby too real.

"I always wanted a Dorcas. Yes, maybe Dorcas."

The nurse gave a vacuous smile. "That's unusual. Never heard that name before."

Liddy wasn't at all sure it was the right name, but she couldn't summon up the energy to think of others. She minded having to decide on her own; it had never occurred to her that choosing the baby's name by herself would be so significant.

Cleo appeared halfway through evening visiting hours. She smelled of scent and the outside world as she leaned over to kiss Liddy—her bracelets clattering as she squeezed Liddy's hand in apology.

"I'm sorry I couldn't get here sooner. I had to give Cyn her supper. Robert gave me a lift."

Liddy looked behind Cleo, expecting him to be there.

"He doesn't want to come up. I think he's a bit embarrassed, you know." She looked out of place, sitting by Liddy's bed in the plain white ward, like a butterfly landing on a nettle.

"The sister insisted on taking me down to the unit to see the baby. They seemed very pleased with her, but"—she looked at Liddy carefully—"they said you've been very upset and anxious about her."

"I was . . . well, I still am, but I'm just terribly tired, I think." Liddy could hear herself sound fretful.

"I'm sure you are, darling," Cleo soothed. "You know, I don't think I ever thought she'd be real. I don't know why, it all just seemed—"

"A figment of my imagination?"

Cleo laughed.

"Well, you know what I mean. Anyway, she's lovely, darling. I couldn't believe your note when I got up this morning. Cyn, of course, decided immediately that it was indigestion after the dinner I cooked."

"How is Cyn today?"

"Much restored," Cleo said fondly, "having a fine time complaining about your inconsiderate behavior. Have you got hold of Martin?"

Liddy shook her head. "I don't know where to start and anyway I want to give me and the baby some time . . ." If Cleo picked up that Liddy was still not convinced that her baby would survive, she chose not to comment. Instead, she said cheerfully, "Now, what are you going to call her?"

"Dorcas?"

"No, darling. Not if her surname is to be Claver, too many *C*s and *A*s."

The baby's surname was something else Liddy had not thought about. "I should like to call her Gwendolyn after you."

Cleo shuddered. "Oh, no, darling, why do you think I'm called Cleo? What about your mother's name? Elizabeth? Or your grandmother had a pretty name. Ella?"

"I honestly don't know," Liddy said wearily. "I just can't think."

At three o'clock in the morning, still fighting the sleeping pill, Liddy decided to call the baby Hope; it seemed an optimistic, forward-looking name. Now, with a name of her own, Hope suddenly became a person that belonged to her. And Liddy cried for hours.

The next morning Liddy was bleeding heavily and running a temperature. The gynecologist was called.

"We're not terribly pleased with what is happening down below with you," he said in a bluff voice. "Think we need to keep an eye on you for a few days. Baby's doing well, I gather, and you'll still be able to feed her yourself, but you need to keep your feet up and get some rest. We like to look after you older mums," he said more kindly. "Make sure you're quite strong and prepared before you leave."

Liddy was grateful. She dreaded getting upright, into outdoor clothes and being a proper person in charge of herself and a baby.

"I'd really like to stay here until Hope is eighteen," she said, smiling feebly at the doctor. It wasn't a joke, but the doctor laughed.

Alex knew he was behaving badly—he could put himself outside his body and watch his behavior with astonishment and disgust. Mungo had been out till late for the last four nights and Alex, on his own every evening, had allowed his imagination to run wild. Each time Mungo came in, alight with the work he had been doing, Alex would turn on him. The frustrations of a hateful job and the boredom of a lonely evening by himself built up until it all spilled out like a saucepan boiling over.

"For fuck's sake, Alex," Mungo would say, "you could at least wait until I've had some drink or drugs before you attack me."

Alex would gradually calm down and an uneasy truce would exist between them until they went to bed and had glorious sex. Afterwards, Alex would curl up beside Mungo and promise never to yell again. And he believed himself completely.

"He hasn't got time for a lover," Drusilla pointed out practically when she came round one evening.

"There's someone called Terry. He talks about him a lot," Alex said morosely. "He gets his stuff from Terry."

"So?"

"Well, you know—"

"Sweetheart, I get my stuff from a funny little man with no

teeth and three strands of hair. I don't shag him. *Believe.* I've told you before. Get a decent job." Drusilla sighed impatiently. "You're just suffering from an underactive life and an overactive imagination."

Alex went to Mungo's first night. The play was running at a small fringe theater in south London and Alex had to travel on a densely packed evening train. He felt out of place and worthless in his smart linen suit alongside creased and work-stained commuters.

Karen and Ship were in the foyer when Alex arrived.

"I didn't know you were coming."

"Nor did I until Ship had me actually here," Karen said gloomily. "It's bound to be the same old crap. I loathe the theater. Let's go and have a large drink."

The moment the lights went down, Alex became rigid with nervousness for Mungo. He dug the nails of his left hand into the palm of his right and worried that he might cough or sneeze and that Mungo would recognize it as his.

In the interval, Ship said it was a very important play. Karen said it was rubbish.

"Mungo's brilliant, isn't he?" Alex breathed.

Ship looked at him sympathetically. "Yeah, he's really good. Don't listen to Karen. She's been asleep most of the time."

Alex sat transfixed and when it was over, he clapped wildly at the curtain calls, his face alight with pride and love—and envy.

"I want to be up there," he murmured to Ship.

She turned to him in amazement. "You don't really, do you?"

They waited for Mungo in the bar when the performance was over. He came out, still wet from a shower, his eyes bright and glittering, his body taut and springy. Alex watched him walk across the room accepting congratulations from a couple at a table and he instinctively clasped his groin.

"Oh, look, both my wives," Mungo said, when he arrived at their table. He kissed Alex and Karen. "And the Ship that didn't pass in the night after all. How nice of you all to be here."

Mungo was on a high; he talked and laughed loudly. Some of the cast came and joined them and when Karen and Ship left, Alex felt left out of the party. He covertly watched Terry and Mungo, occasionally leaning against each other, touching each other's arms, reliving the performance, talking about shared moments that had nothing to do with him. And he seethed with anger at his exclusion.

Alex hadn't realized that Mungo always gave Terry a lift in his car and he was ashamed at the disappointment he felt. This would usually have been the time that he and Mungo would discuss Mungo's performance.

"Are you sure I was OK?" he would always ask and Alex would be so proud that Mungo needed his approbation.

This evening, with Terry lying sprawled out on the back-seat, the conversation was about a girl in the cast who was auditioning for a television part and Alex sat in sulky silence as Mungo drove through London. They stopped at a garage for Terry to get some cigarettes.

"Terry's going to crash on our sofa tonight. His flatmates are having a party and he wants to get some kip," Mungo said.

Alex's jaw tightened. "Whatever," he said.

"Lighten up, would you," Mungo said.

"I just feel so out of it." He could hear the whine in his voice.

Mungo stroked his thigh in silence for a moment and then said gently, "You have absolutely nothing to feel jealous about. I promise you that."

But in the early hours of the morning as he lay in the bed listening to Mungo and Terry talking in drink-induced rhetoric, Alex was not so sure. He felt like a small child watching the party through a window.

*   *   *

"What does Jake want to do?" Martin asked. Laura had the impression that he was not completely concentrating. She had tried to get hold of her mother and was a bit nonplussed to find she wasn't there. Aunt Cleo told her that Liddy was spending a few days in St. Ives looking around art galleries. So she had rung her father. He sounded rushed.

"Actually, you've literally only just caught me," he said. "I'm just leaving for a walking holiday in Scotland."

"Whatever for?" Laura forgot the purpose of her call for a moment.

"Just a little holiday—with an old friend from university," Martin lied down the phone. He hadn't wanted to speak to any of his children just now, afraid that their justification for needing him would cloud his thoughts.

Martin was being very calm about Jake's flight from school; Laura sat on her bed and spoke quietly into the phone so that Jake in the next bedroom could not hear their conversation.

"He won't really talk much. He just sits in his room playing on his computer."

"Is Tamsin coming back at the weekend? He might talk to her, they're very close."

"Yes she is, and he might." Laura sounded momentarily happier. "And Alex has rung to see how he is. He seems really concerned about him."

"Don't sound so surprised, darling. Alex is a very kind and caring person." Laura, too intent on her own unhappiness, failed to hear the wistfulness in her father's voice.

"I'm sure you will work something out, darling—you always do."

"Of course, Vivien has to have her say, too," Laura said angrily. "She's the one paying for him to go to this bloody school and Fergus doesn't seem to know what we should do. He hardly talks to me, let alone to Jake."

"I expect he's just as worried as you."

"Well, he should share it with me," Laura protested. "We should be a united front."

"Darling," Martin said, and Laura could hear him beginning to withdraw from their conversation, "some people need longer to be really sure about things. Give Fergus some more time, and Jake, too, perhaps. I know you'll sort it out for the best and I shall ring to find out as soon as I get back."

Laura couldn't help feeling slightly betrayed by her father's distraction.

Laura had won her battle and Jake was still at home. Fergus plodded around the farm miserably and Laura knew that he was heavy with the knowledge that there was what he would call a situation and that his life would not run smoothly until it had been resolved.

"I don't like Jake being unhappy any more than you do," he said, moved to unusual hostility, when Laura had goaded him enough on the subject. "I just feel he will hate himself for giving up so easily."

Vivien added to Laura's distress. "You're just prolonging the poor boy's agony," she said brutally. "He's obviously got to go back to school in the end. He's got to learn to accept discipline, just like everyone else. He can't be permitted to run away just because things get a bit tough for him. The sooner he gets back and knuckles down properly, the better. Believe me. I know."

But Laura was determined. She was going to win this fight—she had to for Jake's sake. Being able to do something did much to mitigate her misery over the feeling of unease she was suffering; she felt her defenses had been broken over the last few days and that she was floundering to regain some feeling of right. Laura had consulted her local friends and visited a private day school. She had even looked at the local com-

prehensive school, secretly quite appalled by the sheer number
of pupils milling around the dreary 1960s buildings.

Fergus did not accompany her but he was gentle with her
when she told him about her visits. "I think you're jumping the
gun a bit, Laura love, I really do. No good doing this sort of
thing in a rush, you know, no matter how miserable he is.
We've got to make sure we get this right for him. Let him go
back and finish the term—it's only a week—and then we'll see.
The masters will keep a very good eye on him. He'd have to go
back and collect his stuff, anyway," he added practically. And he
tramped off across the fields to check his sheep.

Laura had wanted Jake to come with her to see the schools
and was disconcerted by his apparent indifference. She wondered if she should take him to the doctor. Was he depressed?
Had something really dreadful happened to him at school,
something that might scar him for life? She was making her
stand, but she felt alone and unsupported and everything
seemed to be slipping through her fingers. And, on top of
everything else, Miranda was coming down for the weekend.

"Bring out the beautiful butterfly in yourself," Marguerite's
treacle voice flowed over the prone women in the studio and
Miranda tried hard not to let go of a very unbeautiful fart. It
was difficult, she was finding, not to fart when you were lying
on your back with your legs up against a wall. She concentrated on finding this elusive beautiful butterfly in herself, but
could only think about Richard.

"That's a start," he had said grudgingly, when she had told
him that she had refused the Leeds job. "But Miranda," he
went on in a dogged voice, "we have to resolve the baby problem once and for all. I really mean it."

Marguerite's weekly Women's Awareness course was the
first step toward Miranda addressing the problem. "Woman
for Woman" was, according to the leaflet she had picked up

in the library, "a dynamic, interactive and visioning transformational group in which women come together to search for their own wisdom." Resisting the temptation to rewrite the leaflet in less nauseating English, Miranda had decided to try the course in preference to starting the long journey of counseling yet again.

"Your father's right," Richard argued. "You should get some professional help. I'll come with you," he offered.

He had come back home earlier in the week on the understanding that Miranda would talk honestly and openly to him, but he was, in Miranda's view, punishing her by sleeping in the spare room.

"How can I come to terms with what I feel about my body when you won't even sleep beside it any longer," she had screamed at him.

"Darling girl," Richard had said sadly, "I love your body, don't you see. But we have to sort this out first because it's getting bigger and bigger in both our heads and it is coming between us. Speak to me properly about it, tell me everything that you're frightened of," he pleaded. "Let me help you. Nothing can be as bad as you think."

But Miranda knew that it could be. She tried to talk to Richard; little by little she felt that she *was* letting him inside her but, like a nervous pony, at the last minute she shied away from the big fence. She just could not risk sharing her very worst feelings with him. Once he found out about the horrid mess inside her, it would be the end for them, she knew it.

So here she was, lying in a room with eight other women in footless tights and T-shirts, learning how to love herself, which might, she hoped, lead to her clearing up the mess inside her so she could give Richard what he really wanted. She was pretty sure at the moment, though, that she would not be returning to this particular group. There had been a lot of preliminary talk about "soul" purpose, wellBeing (with a capital *B* in the middle), kinship, insight and empowerment. Now they were meditating and Marguerite was wandering emotionally between them, stroking their heads and telling them how beautiful they all were. The whole effect was slightly spoiled, Miranda thought, by the over-whelming smell of sweat that eight, no nine counting Marguerite, beautiful women had managed to generate in the small room.

"Find the child inside yourself." Marguerite wafted past Miranda's head.

But I'm a child everywhere, Miranda screamed silently, not just inside. I need to be looked after. I want to be just me and Richard.

Ship rang Alex.

"You don't fancy a couple of days in a garden, do you?"

"Sunbathing with a drink? Yes."

"No, making one. Well, refurbishing it for my sister. She's just moved into a large house in Clapham. She's about to drop her fourth child, her husband is away and she is completely freaked about the state of the garden. I said I'd go and help her, but I don't know a thing about gardens."

"Well, nor do I really."

"You know about plants, you're always growing things. Please, Alex. Just for Saturday and Sunday. Tessa will pay you."

"I'll do Saturday. Mungo's got a matinée, but I really want to be with him on Sunday. It's his day off."

Mungo and Alex were in the middle of a row when Ship picked up Alex early on Saturday morning. Mungo wanted Alex and him to meet some of the cast in a pub on Sunday and Alex, half-dressed, had looked at Mungo in bed and screamed at him. "I don't believe it. You've been with that lot all week. Don't you want to be just *us* for one day?"

Mungo sighed and pulled a pillow over his head. "Oh, fuck off, Alex, you jealous little queen."

Alex sat tense and silent, biting his lip all the way to Clapham, but the sight of such a large garden and one that needed so much doing to it went a long way to restoring his spirits.

"I can't believe such a big garden exists in the middle of London," he said. "It's fantastic. I would love to live here."

"Yes," Ship said doubtfully. "I suppose. It looks a mess to me. What are we going to do to it?"

Alex took command. They spent the whole day clearing, cutting and mowing and Alex was completely absorbed in the task. The sun burnt his skin and his back ached, but he reveled in the job. Tessa's young children ran around hindering the operation, but only adding to Alex's pleasure. He was delighted when he uncovered straggly little shrubs hidden by heavy curtains of honeysuckle and clematis; enchanted when he found a little stone path buried by long grass and he was completely beside himself when, at the bottom of the garden, Ship came across a small pond.

"You're really into this, aren't you?" Ship said to him wonderingly as he knelt down and enthusiastically plunged his arm into the pool of rank water.

"Oh, what! This is brilliant. Look, it's perfectly sound. We can clean it out, fill it up and your sister can have fish."

"Oh, yes, and have her small children drown in it, too," Ship said sarcastically.

Alex made a face. "Oh, forgot about that." He thought for a moment and his face cleared. "Wire netting, or what about this? Put big stones in the pond and make it a really shallow pond, sort of Chinesey."

On the way home they stopped off at a pub with a small garden overlooking Wandsworth Common. Alex sat at the table while Ship went in for the drinks. He was tired, he was filthy, he was sunburnt and he probably smelled revolting, but he felt happy, satisfied. He had a contented feeling that, for the first time for ages, he really fitted into his body properly, as though all the awkward corners had been filled up. He sighed happily.

Ship came back with the drinks.

"I've been thinking," she said, handing him a glass. "You're really good with the gardening shit. You sort of know instinctively what to do."

"I should have thought about the children and the pond, though, shouldn't I?"

Ship opened a bag of chips and attacked the contents voraciously and inelegantly. "God, I'm hungry. You were good with those kids today. They liked you."

"I liked them. I like all kids, really."

Ship looked at him curiously, her head on one side. "You genuinely would like one of your own, wouldn't you?"

"Yeah. I think I would, one day."

"And Mungo?"

Alex shrugged unhappily. "Difficult to tell at the moment. He is completely zoned into working and the play." Alex's good humor began to slip away.

Ship leaned forward, her sunglasses glinting in the sun.

"Kids aren't all they're cracked up to be, you know," she said seriously. "They're only lent to you for a while. They grow up and piss off and where does that leave you?"

"I think my elder sister is finding that actually," Alex said, thinking of Laura. "She wants to keep her children at home. Her son ran away from boarding school last week. He came to us," he added proudly. "He's very unhappy there apparently. Laura's fighting her husband to let him go to school locally."

"Has she asked her son what *he* really wants?" Ship, the teacher, inquired.

It was Richard who suggested that Miranda spend the weekend with her sister. "Go and talk to Laura," he ordered. "She knows you and she knows about motherhood. If anyone can allay your fears, she can."

Miranda wanted to believe he was right, and she agreed to go for his sake. Trying to please was a novel experience for her and it was the greatest strain, particularly as she knew Laura would never understand her torment.

"Honestly, you forget the pain of birth immediately," Laura said gently. "That's nature's way of making sure you have more."

Miranda endeavored to explain, without letting too much go, that it wasn't just about the pain of birth and Laura tried to understand. She saw Miranda watching Rebecca roughly tying a bonnet on the old kitchen cat and she spoke quietly.

"Oh, Miranda, you mustn't be frightened of something being wrong with the baby. I know we have Rebecca, but there is no reason why your baby should have a disability. And, you know, in those circumstances you manage, you really do. To begin with, I thought my world had caved in. I thought I wasn't going to be able to cope." The muscles in Laura's jaw tightened. "Not by myself. Fergus took it very badly . . ." She stumbled to a halt, but, receiving no response from Miranda, she continued in a determinedly cheerful voice, "Anyway, I got on with it and it stopped being so terrible and, now, not one of us would be without Becs." Laura bent down and kissed Rebecca on the top of her head and the child clambered heavily up onto her mother's lap. Laura looked at Miranda almost defiantly, but Miranda was too bound up with her own thoughts to notice. She had never even got as far as thinking about her baby not being whole and normal—she couldn't see past the horror of the first nine months, the baby growing like some slimy, coiled serpent inside her.

"Come with me to do my church duty, will you?" Laura asked casually on Saturday morning and Miranda, bored and rather regretting coming to stay, accepted the invitation.

Miranda couldn't remember when she had last been in a church. The musty smell of wood, leather and tallow enveloped her as she followed Laura through the heavy oak door. Every sound they made was magnified in the huge hollowness of the building. Laura disappeared into the vestry to collect cleaning things and Miranda, without thinking about it, found herself slipping into a pew and just sitting. The great place seemed full of echoes from generations past; in this minute she could believe that there really was a God who knew, who decided, who loved, who forgave; she could believe that life did go on in one continuous circle. She looked up at the large stained-glass window above the altar: like bright fruit gums, the colors made geometrical reflections on the white altar cloth.

"Magnificent window, isn't it?" Laura appeared by her side. "We're very proud of it. The original was damaged in the war and this was designed by a local artist." She spoke proprietorially to Miranda, as though her sister were a tourist. Personally, Miranda preferred the plain leaded windows running along the sides of the church, the originals probably vandalized during the Reformation. She liked the way these simple windows let the sun through, untainted by color, to warm the old wood of the pews.

Laura handed her a watering can. "Could you fill up the vases. There's a tap in the vestry if you need more."

Miranda was surprised to find that she would have preferred just to sit and enjoy this strange feeling of being nowhere. But Laura liked people to be busy and Miranda took the watering can and instructions from her out of a long-standing habit of doing what Laura told her.

"You want to get on with it, if you're going to," Laura said suddenly as she vigorously polished the brass on the lectern, her whole body wobbling with the effort.

Miranda, filling a large vase of sickly smelling lilies nearby, looked blankly at her sister.

"Babies," Laura said impatiently. "Richard likes children. He's very good with ours."

Miranda, in the heavy peace of the church, tried once more. "I hate the idea of being pregnant . . . ," she began hesitantly. "You know, I'm not good with how I feel about my body. . . ." She petered out, wishing more than anything that she could tell Laura in simple straight words.

Laura looked up from the lectern and spoke kindly. "You mustn't worry about that. I know I'm not a good example," she looked down deprecatingly at her own full body, "but most people do get their figure back after babies. I know you. You'll work at it, unlike me, and you'll be back as slim and beautiful as ever in no time." Miranda wasn't hearing Laura's words, or the wistfulness in her voice. "Nature takes over your body when you're pregnant." Miranda shuddered and opened her mouth to stop Laura, but she rolled on. "You really will *want* to eat all the right things and look after yourself and the baby. You really will surprise yourself at how naturally you nourish and nurture the baby. Honestly, Mirry, you'll feel so fulfilled. Believe me, I know you can't imagine it, probably don't believe it, but you really will—even you—you'll be overtaken by it."

"Overtaken." Laura had said it.

Miranda tried, once again, to explain. "It's not just—"

But Laura interrupted her with a short mirthless laugh. "The trouble with babies, of course, is that they grow up. You can't keep them. They grow up and you don't have to look after them anymore. They leave you all by yourself." Laura spoke almost ferociously. "Do you remember when we were little," she went on, "I wanted a pygmy elephant? I only wanted a *pygmy* one because I thought that being so small, it would never grow up."

"No, Mum and Dad would never have agreed to a full-size elephant," Miranda said gravely and then laughed, characteristically taking flight from her sister's sudden intensity with a glib remark.

Laura paused as if trying to understand what Miranda had said; then she laughed politely. "Oh, yes well . . . anyway," and she had bustled off to some other bit of brass, as if anxious to avoid saying what was on her mind.

Laura needed Miranda to come to the church with her. Ever since she had met Mrs. Fairley, she had tried to avoid being alone in public. She was scared that everyone in the village would know that she had antagonized Mrs. Fairley and think that she had tried to play the lady of the manor. Although she knew her intentions had only been honorable, it did not make her feel better in any way. And then there was the perpetual anxiety about Jake, who seemed so unhappy, even at home. *And* she had her period again. She wanted to tell someone about the large lump of failure that was lodged deep inside her; she wanted it dispersed with comfort. She wanted to say that Fergus was never really *with* her and how terribly lonely you can be with someone who is physically so close, yet who refuses to let you into their heart. She wanted to tell Miranda how Fergus seemed so very far away. But she had been foolish—and perhaps unfair, too, she would admit—to expect Miranda to show any real tenderness and to comfort. She never had been able to; had never found it easy to reach out to someone else.

In the large silence of the church on that Saturday morning, both Miranda and Laura were aware of failing to share something with each other. Once again, family history had beaten their needs and neither of them could begin to understand or even discover what was really happening deep in the other.

*   *   *

It was, as Martin had suggested it would be, Tamsin who rescued Jake from his cocoon of miserable silence. She came
bouncing home on Friday night, happy to be home and happy
in the knowledge that she would return to school on Sunday
night. Jake responded slightly to Tamsin's energy and on
Saturday morning they took themselves off to one of the barns
to make a camp.

That evening, Tamsin found Laura weeding the vegetable
garden. She hung around, hopping from one foot to the other,
picking strawberries and cramming them into her mouth. Bent
over the warm earth, the powerful scent of nearby nicotianas
and geraniums filled Laura's head.

"Mum, Jake wants to go back to school," Tamsin said suddenly.

Laura looked up at her daughter's freckled face. It seemed
to spangle with health and contentment in the bright light of
the evening sun. She wished Jake's face would sparkle like that
again.

"What?"

"He wants to go back to school. It's fun at the end of
term . . ." Tamsin paused uncertainly, as though concerned
that she might be divulging something private.

Laura stopped her weeding and sat back on her haunches.
"But he ran away, darling."

Tamsin shrugged and grabbed some more strawberries, suddenly anxious to remove herself from the conversation and
negate any responsibility for the situation.

"I don't know. You ask him then."

So Laura did. Again. And this time Jake talked.

"I *don't* like school awfully," Jake explained tentatively, "but
I don't think I like any school awfully. Everyone bullies newcaps—it's the done thing. They're not *specially* horrid to me
really. I ran away, but"—and he looked at his mother ner-

vously—"I thought I'd be sent back straightaway, see. It wasn't such a big deal," he added sadly.

"But you don't run away, all the way to London, if it's not a big deal, surely?" Laura said incredulously.

"Paul dared me. Said I'd be top of the newcaps if I did. I thought you'd send me back. I *wanted* to go back, actually, but you made me stay here. Then you and Dad kept quarreling and I didn't know what to do."

Laura felt completely lost. She had always thought she knew the right thing that had to be done and this time she'd failed. Just as she had failed to understand Miranda, as she'd failed to conceive, as she had failed to help Mrs. Fairley—and now she had failed Jake, too. She suddenly felt very small and terribly unconfident.

Jake went back to school. Laura let him go with a sad, heavy heart and Fergus never once said to Laura, "I told you so."

In fact, he didn't say anything much.

"Hope? Hope? How ridiculous," Cyn said. "That's a boat's name." She peered into the Moses basket and eyed the baby with disgust. "Ugly little thing, isn't it?"

Liddy, just back from hospital, felt a tired and feeble irritation at Cyn's rudeness.

She struggled to keep her sense of humor. "She's beautiful," she said protectively. "Not as immediately beautiful as a kitten, I grant you, but, as human babies go, she's really rather beautiful."

Cyn shrugged. "Well, you'd know, I suppose. Parents are always so stupid about their offspring." Cyn wrinkled her face and adopted a whiny drawl. "*If my child had any faults, I'd be the first person to know.* That's what you all say. Absolute nonsense, of course. It always amazes me that perfectly sane people become completely moronic once they've had one of these. Really, Lydia," she added, "this is all most inconsiderate of you."

"It has come as much of a shock to me as it has to you," Liddy said tetchily. "I really hadn't planned on this."

And she also hadn't planned on being in hospital for over a week. For the first few days after the birth, she had felt weak and ill. After a couple of days of pain, she had been wheeled into the operating room. "Give you a bit of scrape and clean down below," the gynecologist had said breezily. Liddy was beginning to hate him. As she recovered, she dragged herself into the dreary, institutionalized dayroom where new mothers, young enough to be her daughters, sat around, discussing their babies to the background of permanent television. She felt a strange combination of relief and foreboding when she and Hope were eventually discharged on Thursday morning.

Liddy felt the tears well up in her eyes—there really was no one to give her and Hope a proper warm welcome home. She felt abandoned and very weary.

"No, I suppose it's fair to say that you didn't plan it," Cyn admitted clumsily. "I'm glad you're both all right, anyway." She picked up a copy of *Hello!* and rustled it briskly. "But don't let it make a noise near me. I cannot bear screaming babies."

Liddy had relearned the skills of caring for a newborn baby in hospital. She had forgotten how the hours ran into each other, how the same tasks were repeated over and over again in a monotonous cycle through day and night. She had forgotten the huge power of a baby crying—the power of noise: the power over the mother, the mother's breasts and the mother's heart. Toward the end of her stay in hospital she had begun to feel a little stronger, but she relished the vacuum hospital offered, grateful that she could relinquish any real responsibilities and that her life had been put temporarily on hold. Now she was out, she and Hope were on their own, and everything ahead of her began to crowd in.

One clear thought, though. She must go home and wait for Martin.

When she was sure that Hope was asleep, Liddy rang Laura. Prepared by Cleo, she briefly mentioned the trip to St. Ives, before saying, "Cyn's completely recovered. I'm going home, probably on Sunday." She spoke briskly, almost as though she believed that Laura might be able to tell she had had a baby just by the tone of her voice. She asked after the children and Miranda and Alex.

But Laura sounded distrait. "They're fine, fine. Look, Mum. I'll ring you when you get back. I'm sorry I can't talk now, I'm knee deep in the village fête. It's the day after tomorrow and the bunting still needs to be mended. Oh, by the way," she added, "I got a postcard from Dad this morning from Kinlochbervie. Sounds beautiful up there."

Liddy wanted to ask if Martin had mentioned when he would be home, but she knew she couldn't.

She rang Mary next. "Liddy, that's amazing. I wondered why I hadn't heard from you. I can't believe it. Hope. That's a nice name. As in Hope it's going to be all right?"

"Something like that," Liddy said with a small smile.

"How are you feeling?" Mary asked.

"Dead from the thighs up, exhausted and a bit tearful," Liddy said.

"That's natural. When are you coming home?"

"Early on Sunday. It's a quiet day to drive and I want to be there before Martin gets back. He's gone walking, you know."

"Yes. I was in the shop the other day and I heard Hannah tell someone."

"Did . . . ," Liddy started nervously. "Did you notice if Fay was in her shop?"

"Oh, yes, she's around. She hasn't gone with him."

Liddy felt she was forcibly dragging Mary into the conversation. "I've got to prove to Martin that I can be what he wants—the perfect wife."

Mary laughed then. "There is no such thing as a perfect wife, Lid, and you've certainly never been one."

"No, I know that, but I've been thinking about why we loved each other in the first place. I loved his gentleness, his calmness and kindness. I think he loved me because I was independent. I think he liked my creative side; he always wanted to look after the children so that I could do my jewelry. I want to show him how we can put *why* this happened behind us and move forward together with Hope . . . If it's not too late," she added with a break in her voice.

"But you have to give him some practical solutions. He needs to know how your life with a new baby is going to be managed. I mean, are you going to stay at home and look after her or are you going to work?"

"I read a magazine article in the hospital about a woman who imports jewelry from the Arctic Circle," Liddy said. "She designs the stuff based on traditional Arctic designs and she has a group of workers up there that make it for her. Apparently she's making a fortune. I thought I could do something like that." Liddy listened to herself, momentarily sounding positive and she tried to hold on to it. But it faded as the picture of Martin telling her that he loved Fay came up in front of her.

"I can't lose Martin," she cried despairingly at Mary. "I love him too much. I want to be at home with *him*. I feel so alone."

Mary, as ever, picked up the plea and knew what to do.

"Would it help if I came down by train and then we drove back together? The thing is, I don't think I could get down until Sunday evening. But we could drive back early on Monday. I could share the driving, help with Hope and I'll be with you when you get home."

Mary's kindness and thoughtfulness overwhelmed Liddy and she burst into noisy sobs that woke up her baby.

*   * `   *

But Mary never did come down to Portlisk—because on
Saturday night, Cleo fell over and broke her hip and on
Sunday, Laura and the three children dropped into the White
House on their way to their rented holiday cottage farther
down the coast.

Chapter

SEVEN

Liddy heard the soft rustling noise as she went into her bathroom in the middle of the night. Since she had been staying here, she had become familiar with the gentle creakings of the old house and the odd sound of a cat skittering along the long corridors. It was only when she had settled Hope down after her feed that Liddy became aware of an unusual sound—a suggestion of a whimper, of a quiet moan. She walked down the corridor to investigate.

Cleo was lying at the top of the stairs, one of her legs at an awkward angle, her gauzy nightdress and satin dressing-gown rucked inelegantly around her waist. Liddy's first thought was to bend down and pull the material gently over the thin, blue-veined legs, wanting, immediately, to restore her aunt's dignity.

Cleo's face puckered up in confusion and her soft blue eyes, strangely pale without makeup, filled with tears.

"I can't seem to move. I'm sorry to be such a nuisance, darling," she whispered painfully, her words thick and fuzzy. "I don't know what happened. I just fell and I can't get up. It hurts."

Liddy fetched a rug and phoned the ambulance. At Cleo's

request, she woke Cyn who emerged from her bedroom, her face thick with hastily applied powder, and sat in a chair beside Cleo, castigating her fluently for falling over.

"Really, Cleo, you should be more careful. You can't go crashing around in the middle of the night at your age," she scolded, her anxiety showing through the crossness in her voice. "It's those wretched old slippers of yours. I told you to get some new ones months ago, but you wouldn't listen and now look what's happened."

She wanted to go in the ambulance with Cleo. The paramedic gently tried to dissuade her, but it wasn't until Cleo murmured about the cats, that Cyn acquiesced and then insisted that Liddy and Hope went with Cleo instead.

"Look after her properly," she commanded gruffly.

The ambulance man told her that Cleo had broken her right hip and Liddy, looking at her aunt's narrow body lying on the stretcher, could only wonder that her thin little frame had ever been strong enough to keep Cleo upright.

At the hospital, the doctor confirmed the injury, but added that Cleo had probably fallen as a result of a small stroke.

An uneasy truce had established itself between Richard and Miranda: they still slept in different rooms and Richard seemed to be working most of his waking hours. The little time they did share was, on the whole, companionable, but unrewarding—neither made any mention of the great round issue they both knew was hovering above their heads.

Miranda was conscious that Richard was waiting for her; the clock was ticking and he was ready to spring. But it was, most definitely, her move and she was quite unable to make it. How long Richard would wait was, she knew, as yet an unknown quantity. At work, Miranda was in gentle disgrace—only now, when it was too late, did she realize that she had been groomed to fly high in the company, and her refusal to accept the Leeds job had baffled her boss and left her outgrown in her present job with no immediate prospect of another on this particular magazine. Her volume of short stories lay abandoned on the table at home. Real life had taken over from fiction.

Would she now spend the rest of her life at this desk, writing the same sort of lifestyle articles and subediting other people's copy? Should she look for another job? The answer to these questions lay tied up deep inside the burning issue of Richard and his baby—and that, Miranda realized, was how she thought of it—Richard's baby.

"Do you think you'll ever get your figure back—honestly?" Miranda asked Megan, one of her passing acquaintances at the local gym.

Megan was a cheerful young Australian girl with big breasts, a small pot belly and a three-month-old baby.

"Gawd no. That's gone, along with uninterrupted sleep and an unworried mind, but hey, I'm goin' have another soon— I'm just going through the motions with this." She cast a disparaging look at the rows of tight muscular legs on the cycling machines outside the door. "Anyway it gives Bill a chance to bond with Spike while I'm here, and he cooks the dinner."

Miranda asked Megan what she never managed to ask Laura.

"What's it *really* like being pregnant and having it?"

"Like having a sitting tenant that exercises to loud music. When you evict it, it's like trying to take a stone out of a litchi—more stone than skin if you know what I mean." Megan laughed uproariously and poured her breasts into a large white bra. "Let me tell you, babies are like choccies: once you've had one, you won't want to stop."

Miranda tried to believe it. She found herself covertly watching pregnant women, in the street, on the tube—looking for signs of serenity in motherhood. She looked into prams, at crying babies, smiling babies, sleeping babies, and tried to conjure up an image of her baby. She couldn't do it. No baby and now no career; exercise was her only security left.

Old university friends invited her to a party on Friday in Bristol.

"Thought we'd have a bit of a reunion," Cassie said on the phone. "Gerry and I have just bought a house in Clifton. The eternal students now work in a bank—can you believe it? Anyway we're having a housewarming bash. Will you come? Look up your old haunts and that?"

"I think I will go down," Miranda said to Richard. "It might be rather fun." She waited for him to offer to go with her.

"Why not," Richard agreed politely. He took a breath as though about to say something and then appeared to change his mind and say something else. "It'll do you good to see old friends—if you can bear to leave your precious gym, that is," he added with a smile that wasn't quite one.

Miranda wondered if she was really that keen to reunite with a group of friends, many of whom she hadn't seen since leaving university six years ago, or whether it was just a good excuse to get away from the cold, waiting atmosphere of the flat. Arriving at the little terraced house in Clifton, Miranda immediately wished she hadn't come. She reflected on how much she would rather be traveling constantly and being nowhere, than ever arriving anywhere. She toyed momentarily with the fantasy of spending the next twelve hours just driving up and down motorways instead—her mind permitted to stay completely blank.

Now young executive material, Gerry and Cassie were overexcited about showing off their first real home. It was a strange microcosm of their development from university to respectability. Decorated mostly in subdued and tasteful pastel colors, there were little pieces of the house that seemed to refuse to conform, as if fighting for Gerry and Cassie's youth. A faded psychedelic painting of Marc Bolan hung, out of sorts, on a wall alongside a strong, single-image black-and-white photograph of a child with a butterfly on its head; the old Turkish hookah Miranda remembered Gerry picking up in a market sat uneasily on a modern, elegant low glass table; an old chair covered in a stripy cotton blanket looked seedy beside a new upholstered sofa; and the stuffed bear's head with which Cassie had been so pleased six years ago overpowered the small, creamy painted landing at the top of the stairs. This was the house of young professionals who were going down the road to sobriety and sophistication and yet fighting it all the way.

A series of old acquaintances drifted around her all evening.

"Hi. How are you?"

"What are you up to now?"

"Did you see Michael on television the other week?"

"How's the writing coming along?"

"Daniella's married, you know. Can you imagine, he's an *honorable.*"

"Are you still working on the magazine?"

"Do you still live in London?"

"And that delicious man—are you still with him?"

By the middle of the evening, Miranda was past thinking coherently: a constant stream of drinks had been poured down her since her arrival, and the pain that had been lodged inside her for so long appeared to have disappeared in a miasma of retrospective sentimentality. Each familiar face seemed to her to be the person with whom she had had the most fun in all her life and she could feel herself swaying and glittering around the small house, being the party girl that she now felt she had always been. It was many years since she had been so out of control.

"Rand!" A large pair of arms circled Miranda's waist and

turned her round. She looked up into Andy's big hairy face, his twinkly eyes shining out from the most ridiculous bushy eyebrows.

"And!" She smiled up at her old lover.

Andy had been a medical student with whom she had had an affair for nearly a year. She had never questioned that it had been anything other than total commitment on both sides, so she had been mystified when it had turned suddenly acrimonious during her finals. Miranda had then cut herself from him with a cold firmness that had brooked no reconciliation and she had not given him a thought for at least five years—a fact which made her even more surprised by her immediate reaction of pleasure on seeing him.

"Come and talk to me—somewhere quiet." She pulled him drunkenly though the French windows into the garden.

They sat on a stone bench under a dead apple tree hung with guttering nightlights in jam jars.

"So?" Andy looked at Miranda inquiringly. "What's with you nowadays? Are you a famous writer yet?"

Miranda shook her head and felt the drink spin in her head.

"Nope, not yet. I work on a magazine and I live with Richard." Alcohol was making her dangerously voluble. "I love Richard. I couldn't live without him—he looks after me."

Andy looked at her with a soft smile. "Still on that jag, are you, Miranda? You're an adult now—a big girl. It's about time you thought about looking after other people for a change."

Miranda pealed with drunken laughter. "Me? Adult? I don't think so." She turned serious. "I've never been able to look after anyone else."

"No," agreed Andy, "you've always been too busy looking after yourself."

Miranda glossed over the last remark and sailed on in a tide of self-pity.

"Trouble is, Andy, it's baby time. Richard wants babies." She made a hammy disgusted face. "And I really don't. But you see, if I don't, he'll leave me." Miranda clung on to Andy's arm. "I don't see why I *should* have babies, do you?" she whined woozily.

She sensed rather than saw Andy shrug.

"Nope, but then perhaps he doesn't see why he *shouldn't.*"

"But I tell you, I couldn't survive without Richard, I really couldn't."

Miranda was dimly aware of Andy looking at her with an expression something akin to anger.

"Oh, balls. You just like the attention. You're just too demanding for the average male."

"I need to be looked after—I always have," she insisted, wagging a wavery finger at him. "That was the trouble. You never realized that."

Andy chuckled. "No, Miranda, the trouble was, you overplayed your hand and I refused to continue the game. If you remember I got fed up being made to treat you taking your finals as something special—more special than anyone else taking their finals."

"But I'm all right as a person. I am, I am." Miranda was beginning to feel the ground rolling beneath her.

"You are," Andy agreed gravely. "I always thought so, despite you being such hard work. You were the most difficult person I'd ever met, but there was something about you that made me want to look after you, but I wasn't the type to stick at it. The sex was good, though, wasn't it?" he added with a grin.

"There you are, you see, I am all right," Miranda said in confused triumph.

"But you're not as special as you've always thought you are," Andy went on relentlessly. "I left because I had my own life to lead; the bad times began to outweigh the good ones. You and I were one-way traffic. I told you things that really mattered, but you never told me anything. I never really knew what was happening inside you. I was just there to feed your neuroses and I got fed up with it."

Miranda blinked at him in surprise. "Amen't I not?" she slurred. "Did you?"

"I did. And it sounds as though this Richard is about to pull the plug on you, too, Miranda."

"It's only because I don't want babies and I'm scared of telling him why I don't because he'll think I'm sick or something."

"Don't have babies then. You don't have to. But don't be a dog in the manger about it." Miranda looked baffled. "Don't be so selfish," Andy went on in his slow soft voice. "Let the poor bugger go and have babies somewhere else. Men who want babies don't have the control that a woman has."

"I need him." Miranda could feel the saliva in her mouth become thin and acid. She fought down the vomit. "You don't understand. I need him most dreadfully."

"Come on, Rand, stop always looking for an adult to let you be a child. You should have grown up by now." Andy spoke disdainfully. "Be honest with the guy, let him choose. You without babies—or zippo—and then get on with your life. It's perfectly normal for some women genuinely not to want babies—or is that too much for you to handle, being normal?"

Miranda's last thought before she crouched down and threw up was that she did want to be normal, but that her ordinariness seemed to be locked up deep inside her and she just couldn't get it out.

Mungo and Alex were having a party. It was Alex's suggestion, by way of an apology for an excessive bout of temper when Mungo went clubbing after a midweek performance. He was also rather proud of a bumper crop of grass he'd grown on the balcony and which he had just harvested.

The cast of the play made up most of the guests because

they had just done the last performance. They all seemed to have brought partners and the flat was heaving and smoky. Drusilla had brought along her second string: a middle-aged man panting for her attention and, more overtly, her body.

"He's *so* wet in real life," she said to Alex, her eyes glittering with cocaine, "but he's *gigantic* in my bed." She swirled off into the group up the other end of the room that was shrieking and dancing to loud eighties disco music.

"God, this party is *so* hetero." Terry sashayed up and Alex forced himself to smile at him. "Good stuff, by the way—quite the little Alan Titchmarsh, aren't you?" He swanned off to the kitchen and Alex watched him put his hand on Mungo's bottom, half-turning to check that he was watching.

"Are you in the biz?" How often Alex was asked that question, and each time he smiled confidently, shook his head and watched the questioner look over his shoulder and then slowly and firmly drift away.

"I can't stand the way actors always talk to you looking over your shoulder, they're so predatory," he complained to Ship when he met her in the passageway.

"At least as a dyke I seem to have some interest value, but I know what you mean," she said sympathetically. She drained her glass. "Karen and Mungo have had a row about something and she's stomped home, so I'm off, too." She kissed Alex on the cheek and held his face in her hand for a moment.

"Hey, cheer up, you. It's a good party."

"For whom?" Alex asked gloomily.

Later he found Drusilla in the bedroom, wrapping white powder in a piece of foil.

"Oh, Druse, not that stuff."

"That Terry is dishing it out—at a price. Luckily Second String is not poor."

"Are they ever, darling?" Alex drawled and holding on to Drusilla's arm, drew her to the doorway.

"Look at him."

"Who?" Drusilla peered blearily.

"Terry, beside Mungo, always there touching him. So attractive and only because he's an *actor*." Alex spat out the words venomously.

Drusilla's coke was beginning to kick in. She sat Alex on the bed and faced him fiercely.

"Alex, you've got to pull yourself together. You are not going to be an actor. You've tried every drama school and they don't want you. Doesn't that tell you something?"

"Oh, please, be brutal, why don't you?" Alex tried to smile as he felt the tears pricking behind his eyelids.

"You don't have to be an actor for Mungo to love you. That little toe-rag Terry isn't going to come between you. I grant you, he's trying his best, but he won't. *Believe*. Mungo loves you, it's obvious he does." Drusilla spoke with the conviction of someone who was experiencing a drug-induced clarity of the head. "But," she went on relentlessly, "he is going to get well pissed off if you keep coming the bitter housewife with him. You're not committed enough to be an actor—you just think you want to be one. Let this one go and find something to do with your life that is all yours." Drusilla picked up her bag.

"Lecture over, darling boy. I'm off to shag. Thanks for the party." She dropped a kiss on the top of Alex's head and pranced out of the room.

Alex was standing by the sitting-room window, looking out at the damp summer drizzle, the smell of hot, wet London pavement wafting up. The noise of the party faded to the back of his head and he stroked the leaves of his precious oleander absentmindedly as he thought about Drusilla. She was right, of course; he knew perfectly well that he was no actor. He thought of his auditions, nightmare hours of shaking knees and sweaty palms as he stumbled through his pieces, watching the panel of faces in front of him looking first interested, then bored and finally sympathetic as his confidence ebbed away like water from a broken tap.

Someone lurched into him with such force, Alex's hand tumbled the heavy earthenware pot to the ground. Terry, his movements now clumsy and uncoordinated, grinned at him apishly and then down at the smashed pot and bent plant.

"Oops, sorry, lovey."

Alex turned and, without thought and in one fluid movement, hit Terry in the face. The shock on Terry's face mirrored the shock that Alex felt at his action. Terry buckled back and fell heavily onto the broken crock.

Alex just stood and watched people converge on the scene as though he had no part in it. Someone shrieked. He was conscious of blood spurting from Terry's arm and someone helping him up; he saw Mungo take command and draw Terry out of the room and the space around the window suddenly cleared as the party began to crank up again.

Alex bent down and through a blur of tears picked up his precious plant. Someone knelt beside him and began collecting the jagged pieces of pot.

"It'll be all right. It's been well rooted. You can repot it."

Alex looked up at the man beside him. "Thanks. It's an oleander. I grew it from a cutting."

"I know. I've got a large one on my patio."

Alex gratefully focused on the subject so dear to his heart. "Does it survive the winter outside?"

"Mine's more mature than this one, but I bubble-wrap the pot; seems all right. I'm Harvey, by the way."

"Alex. I don't know what happened; I didn't mean to hit him." Alex held the plant protectively in his hand.

"I might well have done the same." Harvey had a soft quiet voice. His big hands continued methodically to collect the piles of earthenware. "Have you got a dustpan and brush?"

Alex went into the kitchen, passing the bathroom door.

Terry was sitting on the lavatory seat holding out his arm and Mungo was tying a towel around it. There was evidence of a great deal of blood. Alex stood at the door. Terry stared at him without speaking. Mungo looked up, his face devoid of expression.

"He needs stitches. Someone has just gone to fetch their car. Thank God for a teetotaller in this hellhole."

"I—," Alex began, but Mungo frowned at him. "Not now, Alex."

Peremptorily dismissed, Alex turned away and went to find the dustpan and brush.

He was bending over the cupboard under the sink when he felt someone loom up behind him.

"You should have resisted the temptation, babe." Mungo's voice seemed to come from a great distance above him. He looked up and saw Mungo's face grinning at him. "Still, you only just pipped me at the post, I can tell you. The little pain is going to be OK, so don't stress," he added, as he disappeared through the kitchen door.

"We should pot this up now," Harvey said, when Alex returned to the window.

Carrying the oleander protectively in his hand, Harvey followed Alex through the kitchen into the tiny leaded Victorian sunroom attached to the balcony.

"This is great," he said, looking at Alex's neat shelves of plants and pots. "What a joy to find something like this in an upstairs flat."

As Alex planted, Harvey examined each plant with interest.

"You're a real gardener. That particular hibiscus is very hard to grow, but this specimen looks very sturdy."

He looked at Alex. "Do you do this for a living?"

"No, absolutely not." Alex stopped, but Harvey looked at him questioningly, forcing him to expand.

"I'm trying to get into drama school." It struck Alex forcibly that he had responded automatically and he was interested to hear his voice lacking its usual conviction.

Harvey raised his eyebrows. "Oh, an actor. A nightmare life." He grinned. "I can say that because I know. I'm married to one. Kate's in the play with Mungo."

"Are you not in the profession, then?" Alex asked, patting the soil around his precious oleander and placing it safely on a high shelf.

"Good God, no. Do I look as though I am?"

Alex looked at Harvey's heavy frame, his dark weathered skin, his baggy corduroy trousers and old-fashioned Viyella shirt and then, without thinking, looked down at his hands, now caressing a lush, velvety plant. The hands were hard and ingrained with dirt.

Harvey watched Alex study him with amusement.

"Yes, you're right, I'm a manual worker."

Alex shook his head in denial.

"I'm a gardener," Harvey went on. "My hobby and my work—bit of a perfect life really." He leaned over and examined a bird of paradise plant. "*Strelitzia regina*. Beautiful. You could put this out, really. It would like it on the terrace—till the end of September, anyway. I'd better go and find Kate. If you ever want a job," he added casually, "here's my card. Get in touch." He slid out the door leaving Alex looking at the card.

Harvey Grayshoy, Grayshoy's Green Gardens.

Alex left it propped up against the hibiscus and went back to face what was left of the party.

The village fête was in full swing and the sun shone benignly down on the fluttering bunting hung over the village green. The steam roundabout wheezed round, the silver band struggled through a selection of Andrew Lloyd Webber hits and children screamed on the bouncy castle. Laura dashed around, walking in quick, busy steps, collecting money, buying something from every stall, watching the Scottish dancing exhibition by the schoolchildren and taking time to wander round the flower tent and the WI craft stalls.

Everyone she met had something to say to her.

"Better than ever, Mrs. Byford."

"Well done, Laura, a triumph."

"All your hard work has paid off. Wonderful fête."

"You're an amazing organizer, Mrs. Byford. What would the village do without you?"

Mrs. Fairley passed her, dragging her band of small children. She gave Laura a weak, embarrassed smile and Laura hoped she read the beginning of forgiveness in it.

"Mum." Tamsin came up to her in a rush. "I need some more money. I haven't done the tombola yet—*please.*"

"Another pound and that's it." Laura handed her a coin. "And if you win alcohol, give it to Daddy. Is Becs all right?"

"Granny Viv's got her," Tamsin shouted as she sped off. "Thank you."

In the distance Laura could see Fergus organizing bowling for the pig, or side of bacon as it was nowadays. She wondered why he could give up so much more energy and precious farming time to something like that than he could to his children. She caught sight of Vivien, straw hat, Red-Riding-Hood basket, wandering around with Rebecca clutching on to her skirt and skipping around like a large ungainly rag doll. Vivien, who like her son, had had such trouble coming to terms with Rebecca's disability, feeling that it was a reflection on the family's genes and who never quite remembered not to describe her as a Mongol, appeared today to be showing a degree of pride in her youngest granddaughter.

Jake, now happier at school and even happier to be on holiday, was at the wet-sponge stall with a couple of village boys, shrieking as they slung missiles at one of his old primary school teachers.

Checking on the Portaloos at the far end of the field, Laura stopped to look into a pram standing nearby under a tree. A small baby waved its fat, buttery brown limbs as it lay on its back, gurgling at the tassles on the sun canopy making shadows across the pram. Laura looked around, but she couldn't see anyone nearby. She looked back at the baby and its whole face creased up in a chubby, toothless smile. For one terrible moment Laura was overcome with a feeling, the strength of which appalled her; it almost took her breath away. Her hands involuntarily reached out and held on to the pram handle. She wanted to make the baby hers. Every part of her cried out to pick up this baby, nestle it into her arms and just walk away.

"Hello?" A young girl was suddenly beside her, her hand on the pram, looking questioningly at Laura.

"Oh, right. I wasn't sure who it belonged to," Laura stammered. "You have to be so careful nowadays leaving prams, don't you?"

Too late, she realized the admonitory tone in her voice.

"I couldn't take her into those disgusting toilets, could I?" The girl's voice turned harsh and defensive as she barged between Laura and the pram. "I was only a second."

"Oh, Lord, are they really disgusting? I am so sorry. I'd better see to them." Laura rushed through the door and despite the acrid smell coming from the lavatory, stood there for a time, her knees shaking and her head swimming. How nearly had she walked off with that baby? She was not sure.

Collecting herself eventually, she made her way into the safety of the middle of the fête.

"Laura." The vicar came up to her. "We're drawing the raffle and you're wanted on the stage."

A large bunch of flowers was handed to Laura by a diminutive child in a fairy costume and a short speech of thanks and congratulations was made to her by the vicar. Laura looked down at the sea of sunburnt faces, clapping and smiling and felt a small surge of pride. The fête had, as usual, been hard work, but it had paid off, as it always did. She found her family standing below her: Jake looking round and shiny again; Tamsin and Rebecca, jumping up and down, clapping wildly; Vivien elegantly applauding and Fergus—where was he? She cast her eyes to the back of the phalanx of people. Fergus was there—talking out of the side of his mouth to a fellow farmer, but he was looking at her and he was clapping.

She wished, for the thousandth time, that he was coming on holiday with them tomorrow. They were sharing the house with another family and that would be fun, but she wanted Fergus to be there so that they could have a proper family holiday. She and Fergus could have swum together, gone for walks together, like they used to before the farm became the most important thing in his life. Laura loved holidays: she loved the organization, catching the children's excitement as the familiar buckets and spades, the old kite, the beach ball, the picnic baskets and the sleeping bags were all brought out of the attic and piled high in the gun room, ready to be squashed into the back of the large old Volvo. And she loved arriving at the sparsely furnished holiday house and making it cozy and comfortable—all their own for two weeks. Tomorrow, Rebecca would wake everyone early and all three children would come shrieking into the big bed and after breakfast they would roll off down the drive and on to Cornwall in a competitive bid to get to the cottage before the other family.

In fact, if they made really good time, Laura thought, they might pay a surprise visit on Aunt Cleo and Aunt Cyn. Mum had probably left by now and they might be missing the company.

Cyn was in the sitting room when Liddy returned from the hospital early in the morning. She was still in her masculine, black silk dressing gown, but in full makeup. Liddy got the impression that Cyn had not been back to bed after the ambulance left, but had sat, completely still, on her sitting-room chair, smoking cigarettes and watching the sun edge up over the cliffs across the river.

Liddy had talked to the hospital staff nurse before she left.

"We need to run a few tests and they won't operate on the hip until she is stabilized. We'll observe and monitor her." The nurse had a cool, clean, reliable air about her that made Liddy feel she wanted a nurse all for herself. "The consultant will see her this morning and he'll decide the best time to operate." She looked down at Hope in her basket. "This is no place for such a new baby and Miss Nye needs some rest. Take this little one home. We'll ring you in good time if they do decide to operate."

"Can I bring her partner to see her before the operation?" Liddy asked.

"If you feel that he won't be upset."

Liddy did not bother to correct the nurse's misapprehension.

"Some of the elderly become quite distressed at all the machinery and that often has a bad effect on the patient."

"I think this partner is made of sterner stuff," Liddy said with a ghost of a smile.

"Why don't you go home and get some rest? The duty staff will ring you when we know more."

Liddy had left Cleo, quiet and uncomplaining, in the hard white hospital bed, hooked up to machines that clicked and pulsed in a strangely comforting way. Cleo's eyes looked scared, but her pale lips managed a crooked smile as she gestured to Liddy to go. As Liddy bent down to kiss her, she whispered thickly, "Look after Cyn, she can be so difficult, but she does worry, really. Tell her I'll be back soon."

*   *   *

Cyn struggled out of the chair as Liddy came into the room.

"Well?"

"She seems OK. The surgeon is seeing her this afternoon. They'll have to operate on her hip."

"OK, OK," Cyn bellowed at her. "What sort of medical word is that? You're hopeless, Lydia, I knew I should have gone with her. I want to see her. We must go and see her now."

It was with great difficulty that Liddy persuaded Cyn to go upstairs and lie down.

"We can go and see her later."

"I won't sleep," Cyn said pugnaciously; then with a glimmer of a smile, "I haven't been up at this hour since the war, you know. Simply odious time of day, I've always thought."

Liddy noticed how stiff and lame Cyn was as she hobbled toward the door.

"Don't you dare feed the cats," she said as she went up the stairs. "You won't do it properly. Anyway, they don't expect breakfast till midday. Avril will do it when she comes in."

Left in the sitting room, Liddy telephoned Mary and tried to keep her voice from howling with frustration.

"I don't know what to do. Cleo might be in hospital for weeks. I can't leave now, I simply can't. I just don't know what to do. I want to go home."

But even Mary could not solve this one.

Liddy flopped into a chair. She heard the village church bells begin to ring. Cyn was mistaken, she realized, it was Sunday, not one of Avril's days, and she felt suddenly exhausted as though life had come to a full stop. She watched the river below her coming to life. The ferry, full of holidaymakers in brightly colored clothes, plowed its way to and fro across the water, some of the small sailing craft hoisted their sails and began to edge upstream and a lone Jet Skier made a crude, ugly noise that faded as it disappeared into the open sea. Liddy took comfort in the security of the scene below her. In her tired, muddled thoughts she felt so alone, so responsible and so tired. Liddy's eyes began to close and her brain settled into blissful oblivion.

Hope woke her up in the middle of the morning and she dragged herself out of the chair to feed her, the memories of the night before crowding into her mind in a heap.

She was bathing the baby when she heard Cyn walking heavily and slowly downstairs into the kitchen. She heard her talking to the cats and crashing tin plates around as she clumsily performed the unfamiliar task of feeding them.

Cyn returned to her chair in the sitting room and was sitting there expectantly when Liddy came down, having settled Hope.

"I usually have two slices of brown toast cut into triangles with marmalade and a glass of milk for breakfast. I'll have it down here this morning," she announced loudly, her lip trembling slightly. "Cleo will have laid out my tray in the pantry last night." Then, in a childlike voice, she asked, "Will Cleo be home today?"

The hospital rang in the middle of the afternoon. Liddy listened to what the doctor had to say.

Small strokes are a warning. In many cases the patient will not have another for months or, maybe, years, but sometimes a small stroke is followed almost immediately by a massive, fatal one. Cleo had suffered such a stroke an hour ago and the team had done all they could, but they had been unable to resuscitate her. Cleo was dead. There would have to be a postmortem, but the family could visit Cleo in the Chapel of Rest tomorrow. Liddy sat motionless on the small chair by the hall telephone.

Cyn had been upstairs when the phone rang; now she came downstairs carrying a small leather case.

"That was the hospital, was it? Can we go now? Cleo must be wanting her things."

Liddy told her—straight and simple as Cyn would want to hear it.

Cyn said nothing. Sitting on the stairs, she opened the case and took out a pile of makeup, holding in her old, trembly hands a little round jar of eye shadow, a lipstick, a powder compact and the fluffy powder puff attached to the silk handkerchief. She let it all tumble into her lap.

"She wants her makeup," she said. "She'll need that."

Liddy tried to persuade Cyn to lie down.

"Why should I want to lie down?" Cyn sounded confused.

"I could make some tea," Liddy tried.

Cyn looked at her watch.

"Yes, it is teatime. Cleo always makes the tea." Then she said brokenly, "I don't want tea. Cleo won't be here for tea."

She sat for a moment, her head bowed, her hands fiddling with the makeup in her lap. She put it all back in the bag and slowly and stiffly stood up,

"I think I shall sit in Cleo's garden. Get me a chair—the red one I use. You can sit with me," she added—and it was an order, "but for God's sake don't talk to me and don't bring that baby with you."

Liddy set out two chairs in the little sunken garden that had been Cleo's very favorite place. The hot sun on the roses made their scent overpowering, and ever after Liddy would connect the heady smell of roses with what happened that afternoon.

Hope, as if knowing, remained sleeping longer than usual in her basket on the conservatory windowsill nearby, and Liddy and Cyn sat in silence, neither, seemingly, able to cry. Liddy felt numb. Cleo not being there, or anywhere, was still vague, unreal; what her brain seemed to be concentrating on was the mechanics of death and how it must be she that dealt with it all. Martin would have known what to do first. Should she be at the hospital? Should she suggest that she take Cyn there now? What should she do next? She must get hold of Martin. That was the most important thing.

The late-afternoon sun was hot and tactlessly bright. The shipyard was mercifully quiet, but the sounds of children playing on the little river beach floated up from below and somewhere, downriver, a large boat could be heard chugging toward the sea. As if by some feline telegraph system, the cats slowly gathered round them. Silently insinuating themselves into the little garden, they lay among the hostas at the shady end, their eyes watchful on the two figures just sitting there, staring out across the river.

Cyn began to talk.

"No one told me. Why didn't they tell me she was going to die? I would have said good-bye. I didn't expect it. They should have told me."

"They didn't know."

Cyn looked at Liddy as though she had forgotten she was there.

"Of course they knew, Lydia. They're medical people. They know if someone is going to die. They should have told me," she said stubbornly. "I would have said good-bye *properly*. I'm not stupid." She pronounced the word *shtpid*. "I should have been told," she repeated over and over again.

It was Cyn's angry pain that made the tears eventually come to Liddy's eyes. She wept silently, only too aware that Cyn remained dry-eyed, sitting bolt upright in her chair.

As if sensing her mother's sadness, Hope woke up and screamed.

"Sorry," Liddy mumbled, wiping her eyes as she stood up. "I'll go and feed her."

"Feed her here." Cyn turned to look at Liddy, her eyes bright with unshed tears. It was the first time, Liddy noticed, that Cyn had not called the baby *it*.

"Go and get her," she demanded again. "Go *on*, Lydia. Stop her making that wretched noise."

Liddy did as she was told.

Which was why, when Laura, with her three children behind her, tripped up the little garden path, she found her mother breastfeeding a baby.

Chapter

EIGHT

Sometimes your eyes see something that the brain refuses to accept. In a split second, the brain can produce logical reasons for what the eyes are seeing. Laura's brain accepted that her mother was holding a baby, but it refused to acknowledge that she was feeding the baby from her own breast. Her mother was holding someone's baby and her shirt was undone because it was a hot day. For Laura the journey toward the two figures sitting in the sunken garden happened in slow motion. For Liddy, it happened so quickly that, without any clear thought, she pulled Hope away from her nipple and covered up her breast. Had she planned, somewhere in the deep recesses of her mind, to pretend Hope wasn't hers? Was that the idea that had been slowly germinating inside her all this time? She didn't know. It was just an automatic action of survival and for a moment she and Laura were freeze-framed, looking at each other—neither knowing what to do next. Liddy knew she would never forget those seconds in which she looked into her daughter's eyes and watched her slowly register that Liddy had been breastfeeding the baby.

Laura and the children spoke together.

"Granny," they shouted in surprise as Laura turned to Cyn.

"Hello, Aunt Cyn. We're on our way to a cottage in Forrick and we thought we'd call in on you." She used her polite society voice, clipped and expressionless.

"Where's Aunt Cleo?"

As if suddenly aware of something outside their received wisdom, something not at all right, the children hesitated, a few steps away from Liddy, their faces uncertain as they watched the adults all try to make sense of the situation. Liddy saw Tamsin hold on to Rebecca as if worried that she might cross this new line that divided them from their grandmother.

Liddy stood up and shifted Hope on to one arm.

"Laura, I'm so sorry," she started and then saw by the alarm on Laura's face that she thought her mother was going to make some acknowledgment of the baby. "I'm sorry, but I'm afraid Aunt Cleo died in hospital this afternoon." Her words came out in a hurry.

Cyn continued to stare out across the river.

"Oh, no," Laura said, and her soft blue eyes filled with tears. She turned to Cyn. "I'm so sorry. What happened?"

"Oh, good God, what a stupid question, child. You've just been told—she died," Cyn said furiously, still not looking at Laura.

"She had a small stroke in the night and fell over," Liddy explained, relieved to be talking about Cleo and not Hope. "She broke her hip and was taken to hospital and this afternoon, apparently, she had a massive stroke. She wouldn't have felt anything."

They all stood in silence for a moment.

"Baby, baby?" Rebecca shook herself free of Tamsin and bounced toward Liddy.

Everyone except Jake and Cyn moved.

Liddy took a step back, shielding the baby from Rebecca's

uncontrolled movements. Laura and Tamsin came forward to take Rebecca.

"Darlings," Liddy said, forcing a near normal voice, "it's a lovely surprise to see you, but I must talk to your mother." She looked at Laura who was just staring blankly at Hope in Liddy's arms. Liddy looked down and saw that her shirt had fallen away from her breast. She buttoned it up awkwardly with one hand, the buttons going into the wrong holes.

"May the children go and watch television in the study?" she asked Cyn.

Cyn shrugged and spoke in a dull monotone. "Why ask me? What have I got to do with anything anymore?"

"Are you cold? Do you want to go in?"

"I'm perfectly all right, Lydia. Do stop fussing me."

Liddy felt it was like moving chess pieces. Cyn, Laura, the children all seemed inanimate, wooden pieces waiting to be put somewhere by her. Only Hope was warm and alive as she wriggled and began to complain about her interrupted meal. Liddy led the silent children into the small study that housed the television and took the opportunity to give them each a kiss.

"It's a lovely surprise to see you." She tried to sound gay, but Tamsin and Jake, overcome by the atmosphere of the afternoon, accepted her kiss nervously and remained silent. Only Rebecca flung her arms around Liddy and Hope.

"We're going to the seaside," she said indistinctly. She regarded Hope with interest and took her hand and squeezed it hard. "Baby, baby."

"Careful, Becs, darling." She looked at her two eldest grandchildren who were playing with the television remote control, heads down, concentrating.

"I'll come and talk to you when I've had a bit of a chat with Mum. All right?" She closed the door on the silent children.

Laura was watching Cyn from the sitting-room window.

"Will she be all right out there?" She spoke without turning round.

"She's in shock. She just wants to be quiet, I think. I must ring the hospital and find out whether, if she wants to, she can go and see Cleo." Liddy wanted to prolong the talk about practicalities. "I shall have to organize the funeral. I don't suppose Cyn will want to do that." She would have continued to babble if Hope had not suddenly started crying, looking for her mother's breast.

Laura turned round and spoke fiercely.

"Why is there a baby? Why are you still here? I thought you were going home. Did Aunt Cyn call you back? You should have rung us." It seemed that she, too, needed to concentrate on the comparative normality of the death rather than on the life that was now wriggling in Liddy's arms.

This grown woman, Liddy thought, is my daughter. I am her mother and I have to tell her what she desperately wants to know and yet so desperately doesn't.

Something is going to start any moment, Laura thought. Something bad that I know has to start, but I don't want it to start. I want to go home. I want it to be like it was at breakfast this morning.

"Laura," Liddy said gently. "Come and sit down."

In her wildest, most dreadful dreams, Liddy had not envisaged this: that it would be Laura. In her plan, it was to be Martin and she, as a united front, who would have talked to their children, explained about Hope carefully and made them understand—together, she and Martin. Now it was just her.

For one desperate, unthinking moment, she thought of saying it wasn't her baby, that she hadn't been breastfeeding it and that Laura had been stupidly mistaken if she thought that. But then she looked at the little scrap in her arms, her little open mouth wildly searching for food—her daughter, too—and she couldn't do that to Hope. It was, she was to think afterwards, the first time she confirmed to herself that Hope was as precious to her and had the same rights as the other children.

Laura stayed by the window, making sure there was distance between them. "Is Dad here? He never said." She spoke hopelessly and Liddy knew by the way Laura was looking at the baby that the question was about Hope, not Cleo.

"Dad doesn't know, darling."

"Why doesn't Dad know?"

There was no way to make it easier.

"It's not his baby. He is not the father."

"Not his—?" Laura spoke slowly in bewilderment. "I don't understand. Who . . . who is the father, then?"

Liddy was answering questions just as they were asked, like telling children about the facts of life: simply answer the question, don't expand and then they'll understand. She shrugged.

"A young boy I had a silly, short affair with. It was an awful accident. He doesn't even know."

"But we had a family party for you," Laura suddenly wailed; odd, Liddy thought, the first thoughts that come to mind when you are in shock. "We organized the surprise for you. You can't do this to us."

Liddy spoke quietly. "Do you want me to tell you about it?"

Laura shuddered. "No, no, I don't. I don't want to know anything." She was silent. Tears began to roll down her cheeks and she struggled with the words, "What have you done? You've destroyed our family."

Another thought struck Laura. "Aunt Cleo. She *knew*."

Liddy nodded. Hope became more agitated, wanting the rest of her meal. Liddy, unable to breastfeed in front of her adult daughter, jigged Hope about under her arm.

Laura forced herself to watch.

"That's my half sister," she said slowly, becoming suddenly incredulous, "and my children's aunt." She turned away in what Liddy recognized as utter disgust.

The room seemed so heavy with drama, Liddy felt claustrophobic and panicky. She wanted to extricate herself, but she couldn't leave Laura alone. She couldn't help Laura get through this, but she couldn't abandon her either. In a funny way, she half expected Laura to take charge as she usually did, but she just stood silently and self-contained, looking out the window—her whole body, Liddy thought, physically rejecting her.

Liddy wanted to cuddle her, but she had Hope crying in her arms. Laura and Hope. Two daughters, two different needs and neither reconcilable. She felt torn in two.

"I'm just going to take Hope upstairs," Liddy said almost diffidently.

Laura turned round.

"Hope?" she questioned, as though she couldn't put the baby and the name together. Liddy nodded silently. She hovered for a moment, uncertain whether to go, whether to ask Laura to come with her.

"Do you . . . do you want to come with me?" she asked eventually.

"No, I don't," Laura said flatly. "I want to go and find my children."

Liddy went upstairs and finished feeding Hope. She changed her and put her down and then lay on her bed and cried in harmony with her baby daughter. She cried for Laura, for Hope, for Cleo, for herself and she cried most of all because she wanted Martin to be here.

Left alone in the quiet sitting room Laura struggled with what had been put before her. Disbelief had turned into anger. Anger that her mother had spoiled her wonderful family. Anger that now she, Laura, knew about it all, it had, in some way, become her responsibility. Should she tell Miranda and Alex? She must tell them about Cleo, of course, but she wouldn't tell them about the baby straightaway. Maybe, she thought wildly, if she didn't tell anyone about it, she might wake up from this awful dream and find that it wasn't real and she was not here after all.

Laura took herself in hand.

Of course it is real and I am here, she thought crossly. Think about the practicalities, she scolded herself. There would be the funeral to organize; the family would be together then and the others would find out. But she should tell them. They had to know what she knew, what their mother had done to them all; it wouldn't be fair otherwise. And what about Dad? Poor, poor Dad, on his lovely holiday with no idea what Mum had done to him.

She must drive now to the cottage, take the children to start their holiday. Laura looked at her watch. Melissa would probably have arrived already. She would be unpacking the groceries, making someone else's house their temporary home; her children would be skipping around, arguing over the bedrooms and begging to go down to the beach. She must take her children to join them—a little piece of normality in a world that had suddenly gone topsy-turvy. Tomorrow she could leave the children with Melissa and come back to help her mother with the funeral arrangements. She could drive Aunt Cyn to the hospital. She probably would want to see Aunt Cleo. Laura's mind slowly cleared and began to right itself as she made her plans. Laura took refuge in the practicalities and gradually, very gradually, she began to take charge of herself.

Liddy watched from her bedroom window as Laura shepherded the children down the path. Rebecca turned to wave at the house, but Jake and Tamsin trudged ahead of their mother, heads bowed, not looking back. Laura had called up the stairs to say that she was leaving and that she would telephone tomorrow. Her voice made it clear that she did not want Liddy to come down and see them off. Everything had gone horribly wrong.

Liddy waited until she saw the desolate little band of people reach the bottom of the stone steps outside the house before she ventured downstairs. Cyn was still in her chair. The sun had moved round and her chair was in shade. She looked up as Liddy approached.

"They've gone, then?"

Liddy nodded. "I'm sorry about that. I had no idea that they were coming."

"No, I imagine not. Lau . . . ra"—she drew out the name meditatively—"a soppy name. Even as a little girl she was always the one I liked least."

Liddy felt a surge of protectiveness and would have remonstrated had she not seen the evening sun fall upon Cyn's ravaged face as she got up stiffly from the chair and moved toward the house. She must have been crying alone in the sunken garden while Liddy and Laura were inside.

They walked into the sitting room, a posse of cats following them. Cyn stumbled and Liddy helped her into her chair.

"I'll have Cleo's stick," Cyn said. "Go and get it. It'll be in her bedroom. She should have used it last night." Her chin wobbled.

Liddy went upstairs. The covers on Cleo's bed were pushed back, her pillow was still dented with the outline of her head and a glass half full of water stood on the table beside the bed. Liddy felt the tears well up.

"Why did you go?" she said out loud. "Why did you have to go?"

Downstairs, Liddy handed Cyn the ebony stick with the silver handle. Cyn held on to the handle tightly.

"I must get you some supper," Liddy said gently.

"Cleo would have got something in for this evening." Cyn let the tears trickle, unchecked, down her cheeks. "She was here yesterday evening. She was here," she moaned. She stopped as suddenly as she had started, sat upright, thrusting out her bosom and tossing her head.

"I need a drink." She fitted her cigarette into a holder. "I'll have my usual. You can have one, too," she added graciously.

Liddy mixed a pink gin in the little green-stemmed glass that Cyn always used and then went into the kitchen to see if there was some wine in the fridge. There were three lamb chops on a plate on the middle shelf. Liddy's hand shook as she closed the fridge door.

"Would you trust me to feed the cats?" she called.

"Certainly not. I'll do them in a minute."

Liddy went back to the sitting room. They sat in silence.

Liddy was aware of Cyn leaning over and scrabbling in a drawer. She stood up to help her.

"That box. Pass me that box." Cyn pointed to a small silver snuff box. Liddy handed it to her and Cyn held it tight in her hand.

"She gave that to me. She bought it for me in a shop in Bodmin. I told her it was a reproduction. She never could tell the real thing."

Liddy sat silently.

"She was mine, you know," Cyn spoke aggressively. "I suppose I shall have to give her back to you. Bloody families, always claim their own."

"We'll do everything the way you want it," Liddy said.

"What?" Cyn looked crossly confused. "Oh, you're talking about the funeral. Good God, I don't care about that. Cleo's gone. It's of no importance to me what you do with her now. Of course she'd like her ashes buried in the garden along with all our past cats, but it's up to you lot—nothing to do with me."

"Would you like to see her?"

"See her? Whatever for?" Cyn looked outraged. "It's only a dead body. It's not Cleo. Just get on with it as quickly as possible. Do what you like. No doubt your revolting family will all want to come down." Her lip trembled again. "Cleo would have liked that."

Liddy served supper on trays. Cyn ate silently and with surprising gusto. When she had finished, she stood up stiffly.

"You can feed the cats," she said grudgingly, "and you'd better throw away the other chop." She went up the stairs, leaning heavily on Cleo's stick.

Left alone in the darkening room, Liddy set about tracking down Martin. There was no way of stopping the sequence of events now, and she felt that she was struggling to keep control over the situation.

She rang home in hope—yet dread—that Martin might have returned. Liddy let the phone ring long after she stopped expecting it to be answered. She felt that she was, somehow, in a race with Laura. She must get to Martin first. There was only one avenue to pursue now and that was to ring Fay—just in case she knew where he was.

"He does have my mobile phone," Fay said in a voice devoid of all expression. "I lent it to him. I thought he shouldn't be walking alone up there without some form of outside contact if he got into trouble."

Liddy's immediate relief that Fay was not about to flow into self-justification or apology was now crushed by the hideous proprietorial tone in her voice.

"I'm afraid my aunt died this afternoon. I need to get hold of him." She spoke formally, but Fay's voice softened as she spoke.

"Oh, Liddy, I am sorry. How dreadful for you."

She gave Liddy the number and as Liddy, anxious to terminate the difficult conversation, was saying good-bye, she interrupted her. "Liddy, I just want to say. I haven't spoken to Martin since he's been away. He made it clear he wanted to be completely cut off from everything and—"

Whatever she was going to say next, Liddy did not want to hear and she put the telephone down as Fay was speaking. She went upstairs to look at Hope and, strangely, found herself wondering what Fay would be doing if she were in Liddy's situation.

Martin was actually in the car when she rang—on his way home, he said. He went on talking.

"I've come home early. I've done nothing but walk and think for days, Liddy, and I know I've been selfish and bound up in myself about this. I do want to change my life; I want us to do new things and I want us to make decisions together. If you still want me, that is," he said humbly.

"You're right, of course," he went on, before Liddy could do anything more than mumble a few indistinguishable words, "our marriage *is* worth saving. I've known all along really, I just . . . lost the plot for a while—we both did. We love each other, we always have. I want us to try to put all of this behind us—not just for the sake of the children, but for us and everything we've had for all these years. I shall be home tonight and I can't wait to see you—"

Liddy listened to him saying everything that she wanted to hear—and she felt bleaker than she ever thought she could.

"Martin," she interrupted him, "I'm not at home. I'm still in Portlisk. Cleo died this afternoon."

"Oh, God, no. Liddy, I'm so sorry. I had no idea. I thought you said she was all right."

"She had a small stroke in the night and fell over. Broke her hip," Liddy said dully. "Then she had a final stroke in hospital, this afternoon. Please come down, Martin." Her voice broke. "I don't know really what to do. Cyn is so—"

"Of course I'm coming. I'll get home, grab a couple of hours' sleep and I should be with you tomorrow afternoon, early evening." Martin sounded calm and comforting.

"Will you be all right till then? Isn't Laura at her cottage by now? Weren't they driving down today? Have you told the children? I'll be there tomorrow, anyway, and we'll do everything together. You just try to get some sleep. You must be exhausted."

Martin the protector . . . who was so certain that they loved each other and who wanted to make it work between them.

Liddy did not sleep. With Cleo, the last bit of her own family had gone and now she felt alone and without any anchor. She heard Cyn get up and go downstairs. She heard her come back up again a couple of hours later. She wondered if Laura was lying awake in her little cottage. She thought about Miranda and Alex. Did they know about Hope now? Had Laura told them? The inevitable had arrived as it surely would, but it would be all right when Martin came, wouldn't it? They would be together and together they would help Laura and the others to come to terms with a death and a birth. But she still wanted Cleo, and Cleo was not there for her anymore. Tears of loss rolled into Liddy's damp pillow.

Avril arrived in the morning, pale and tearful. She had only heard of Cleo's death through a friend of hers who was a nurse at the hospital.

"Typical of this place," Cyn said. "Nothing is private."

But Liddy was mortified that, in the turmoil of yesterday, Avril had completely slipped her mind.

Cyn refused to go to the hospital with Liddy. She made it quite clear that she had no desire to visit Cleo.

"I've seen enough dead bodies," she said harshly. "They're all the same and nothing to do with the people who lived in them. I wanted to see her alive, not dead." She turned away from Liddy, her shoulders shaking.

Liddy left Avril to look after her while she went to the hospital. Some sort of auxiliary helper, self-important in a green overall, took her to the chapel and watched Hope while Liddy went in. Somehow she hadn't expected Cleo to look so like herself, yet so vulnerable without her makeup; she looked very small and very alone. Liddy hated the idea of Cleo being all by herself for the next few days. She had been feeling that Cleo had deserted her; now as she leaned forward to kiss her pale forehead, Liddy felt it was she who was deserting Cleo just when she needed her most.

The mechanism of death—the practicalities, the arrangements, came into operation smoothly and quietly. Everyone knew what to do and gently steered Liddy through the procedure. In a short space of time, she had signed forms and taken possession of the small bag of Cleo's things. She couldn't bear to look inside the bag.

The local undertaker took her through the funeral options and they agreed to hold it on Friday. He seemed unperturbed when Liddy pointed out that Cleo was agnostic and would have hated being prayed and sung over.

"Talk to your family," he advised. "It can be as plain and secular as you like. It's entirely up to you. You don't even need a priest there if you don't want one."

The telephone was ringing when Liddy got into the house. Cyn was sitting in her chair, staring out of the window.

"Tell them to go away. I don't want to talk to anyone," she said.

Liddy picked up the phone.

"Liddy, it's Robert."

She was pleased to hear his warm voice.

"Oh, Robert, hello."

"I've just heard about Cleo. Avril told me. I am so sorry. How is Cyn?"

"Oh, well, you know—"

"Should I come up?"

Liddy glanced over at Cyn's hunched back, her head sunk into her neck like a tortoise.

"No, I think not, thank you very much. My daughter came yesterday and Martin is coming this evening."

There was silence at the other end of the telephone. She could almost hear Robert working through the implications.

"Ah," he said eventually.

"Are you in this afternoon?"

He sounded evasive.

"Ye-es. Yes, I think I am."

Liddy chose to ignore the distinct unwelcome in his voice.

"I might drop in if that would be all right."

"Fine. It would be nice to see you," he said politely.

Liddy managed to produce a tuna-fish salad for lunch. Cyn's appetite seemed to have diminished and she fed the fish off her fork to the cats that surrounded her.

"They're missing Cleo," Cyn said, strangely defensive. "Did I hear you say that Martin was coming down this evening?"

Liddy nodded and Cyn rolled her eyes.

"Christ, I suppose they're all going to descend now, are they?"

"It's whatever you want, Cyn."

"Oh, don't be so bloody stupid, Lydia," Cyn snapped. "Cleo's *your* family." Then, for the first time, Liddy's situation must have struck her and her voice turned surprisingly gentle. "Now they'll all know about this, I suppose." She gestured toward the Moses basket.

"Yes. I imagine Laura has already told the others."

"No doubt," Cyn said definitely and drew a line under the conversation. "You can have this week, Lydia, to use this house with your family, but I want you all out and to be left alone as soon as it is all over. Is that understood?" She paused for a moment and suddenly her anger became visible; it shot through her body in a violent shudder.

"I told you, Lydia, when you arrived that Cleo would not be able to cope with your squalid problems." Cyn's lips were tight as the words spilt out, almost involuntarily.

Liddy felt as though she had received a physical blow to her body. Was Cyn implying that it was her fault? Had her being here with Hope dealt Cleo's stroke? She could feel the sweat on her upper lip and her hands shook. She had nothing to say: how piteously inadequate sorry would sound now.

Cyn's flash of anger dispersed as quickly as it arrived and she continued in her normal voice.

"As you know, Cleo and I left this house to each other. You can take any family rubbish you want. I just want to be rid of you all as soon as possible and to be left alone. Why should you care about me now that Cleo is no longer here?"

Liddy tried to protest, but Cyn would not let her in. "Oh, please don't waste your breath on polite little noises. I know perfectly well what you all think of me and the feeling is entirely mutual, let me assure you. I shall sell the house and go back to London. I never liked it down here. I will have more than enough money and I'll go back to Kensington and buy a small flat. Of course, most of our friends are probably dead by now, but at least there are proper people in London—not like in this hateful place."

She struggled to her feet. Liddy watched her limp stiffly across the room and thought how terribly she had aged in the last twenty-four hours. It was hard to see how she would really cope in a London flat—Cyn with no family, no friends and who had had Cleo waiting on her for fifty years.

And then Liddy realized that *they* were Cyn's family. She had been the matching half of Cleo and Cleo had loved her just as much as Cyn had loved Cleo. She might fight it, but Liddy and her family were all that Cyn had. She was now their responsibility, for Cleo's sake.

As if reading her thoughts, Cyn drew herself up straight and rested on the stick and said haughtily, "And don't think I want you lot looking after me. I can manage without your nauseating family caterwauling around me. I am no relation"—she rolled her eyes—"thank God, and I shall be quite happy never to set eyes on you lot again, so just don't get any ideas about visiting me and all that to-do. I can manage quite well without ever seeing any of you ever again. And I always told Cleo so," she finished triumphantly and then looked at Liddy expectantly.

Liddy merely nodded her head meekly.

"I'm going to my room for the rest of the day," Cyn went on, "and I do not want to be disturbed. You can make me a cup of tea at half-past four. Just a cup. Don't you dare try and make a proper tea, not like she made," she added fiercely. "You'll only make a mess of it, like you make a mess of everything."

Laura rang. She spoke briskly, making sure there were no spaces in the conversation for Liddy to do anything other than respond to what she was saying. How was Aunt Cyn? Here was her telephone number. Could she help with the funeral arrangements? She had already made a couple of dishes to put in the freezer for when the family came down. She had told Miranda and Alex about Cleo. She emphasized "Cleo" as if to inform her mother that she had not included the arrival of Hope in her conversation with her siblings; she would tell them when the funeral was, so Liddy needn't bother to ring them. Liddy recognized the warning. Laura was protecting Miranda and Alex. And what about Dad, Laura inquired, does he know? Laura came to a halt then and the silence lay heavy between them.

"He's coming down tonight."

"Right." For a moment, Laura sounded nonplussed; then she retrieved the control. "Well, I was going to pop over with this food, but I can put it in the freezer here. But we should discuss the service, hymns and everything, whatever Aunt Cyn wants. And shouldn't we put it in the *Times*? There might be old friends who want to come. We should think about what we provide after the service—"

"Laura, darling," Liddy gently interrupted the gabbling flow, "Cleo wouldn't want any fuss—she certainly doesn't want hymns. I'm sure Cyn won't even go to the funeral, and as for old friends, if they have any left, Cyn won't want to see them. I think it should just be us and anyone from the village who wants to come. We don't need to do anything elaborate—just keep it very simple."

But Laura desperately needed things to organize—the more physical tasks she undertook, the more she could crowd the other thoughts out of her mind.

"Mirry, it's Alex. Has Laura phoned you?"

"About Aunt Cleo? Yes. Isn't it sad, so sudden. Mum was still down there apparently."

"Did she sound odd to you?"

"Laura was phoning from her cottage. I didn't speak to Mum."

"No, not Mum. I meant did Laura sound off?"

Miranda thought. "I don't know. I don't think so. She says we should all go down to Cornwall for the funeral. Have you spoken to Dad?"

"Dad? No, of course not. He's away."

"I expect Mum will get hold of him and he'll go down. So what shall we do?"

"I told Laura I'd ring Mum tonight." Alex paused and then said, "That's what I mean. Laura was a bit odd about that. She was most insistent that we should not bother Mum and that she would ring us about the funeral. She was really very emphatic. I expect she knows what's best—she's down there. Shall we go down together? I should think Dad and Mum will come back afterwards, but I might stay on with Laura. I quite fancy a few days by the sea."

Liddy called into the village shop to buy something for supper.

"We were so sorry to hear about Miss Nye. So sudden,"

Maureen in the shop said. "She was such a lovely lady, always so pleasant." The implication of the less pleasantness of Cyn floated over the counter.

Maureen came round and bent over the basket. "This is the new baby, then: girl, isn't it?" She stroked Hope's cheek. "She's a very bonny little thing. Is she good?" The two women were probably about the same age and Maureen looked up at Liddy with a shy smile. Liddy recognized and acknowledged the empathy with a small half-smile and raised eyebrows. She heard herself say very normally and quite cheerfully, "As good as any newborn baby. I'm out of the habit of waking in the night, that's my trouble."

She walked Hope down the hill to Robert's cottage. She would have to get a pram, she supposed. This Moses basket wasn't going to last long, and she'd have to get a cot and clothes and that, she knew from experience, was only the start. How *can* I do all this? she thought wearily as she threaded her way through the little narrow streets. She tried rethinking: How can *we* do this? Martin and her. But the imminence of Martin's arrival was making her think a little less surely, a little less confidently.

Liddy looked down at Hope as she waited for Robert to answer the doorbell. She looked so perfect, lying asleep, all wrapped and compact. Martin loved babies. He would, wouldn't he, through Hope, forgive her and stay with her?

"I'm sure it will be all right," Liddy said uncertainly to Robert as he brought a tea tray out onto his terrace. "But, now that Hope is actually born, it will be an even bigger shock to Martin and I can't tell him something like this gently, can I?"

She was taken aback by the distress that appeared on his face. He put up his hands, warding her off. "I'm sorry. I really can't answer that. I can be no help to you. Now, tell me how Cyn is."

"Angry, shocked, baffled and very, very sad."

"I suppose she hasn't really thought about whether she is going to stay on alone in that great house?"

"Well, she says she's going to move to a flat in London." Liddy shrugged. "But she can't, she's too old to up sticks and go back there. She's too shocked to know what she's thinking, really."

"She's got Avril, of course, and you know I will keep an eye on her when you go home. I suppose you'll go back after the funeral"—Robert looked unsettled—"if everything goes all right with your husband."

"As each hour passes, I become less confident," Liddy said morosely. "I'm scared of telling him, I really am. I mean how would you feel about it?" It was really a rhetorical question, spoken with not much thought of an answer. But Robert frowned and, leaning forward, he spoke severely.

"Look, Liddy, I'm sorry. I don't want to second-guess your husband. It's not a game I play. This is not one of my novels, though I admit to being quite interested in the story." He gripped his hands together and made his knuckles crack. "I'm sorry," he said more gently. "I am at fault. As usual I have got involved, but only academically, not emotionally. Now you've had the baby, and your daughter has found out and your husband is about to, I just can't even begin to imagine what you are all going through. But I can't deal with it—it's out of my ken—too much for me. I'm sorry, *so* sorry," he added mournfully.

Liddy could see it really was all too much for him. He looked cornered, almost hunted. He wanted out. Looking at him now, shifting in his chair, his eyes not quite meeting hers, she could see the change in him: he was embarrassed, uncomfortable, and had absolutely no idea how to deal with her or her situation. He wanted it all to go away; he wanted Liddy to go away. He really didn't want to know anything more.

"I should get back to Cyn," she said awkwardly, leaving her half-finished cup of tea.

Robert rose to his feet, relief showing on his face. "Will you let me know when the funeral is? That is, if it's not just family?"

"Friday at two o'clock. It's just family and village at the crematorium." Without thinking, she went on, "My eldest daughter is busy organizing like she always does." She gave a little smile.

Robert did not smile back.

"To be confronted at the same time by a sudden death and a sudden birth must have been very hard to assimilate," he said somberly.

Cyn was feeding the cats. They oozed around her legs as she piled up their plates, spilling food all over the draining board. Liddy offered to help.

"Don't be ridiculous," Cyn snapped. "What do you know about cats?" But she handed her a bowl of bread and milk. "You take this out to the gullies."

She watched Liddy from the kitchen window and tapped on it violently. "Not there. Don't put it there. Cleo always put it over there."

Liddy returned and began to unpack her shopping.

"I've bought some pasta for supper," she began conversationally.

"We never eat pasta."

"I bought some fish as well. Shall I grill some for you instead?"

As if too tired to keep battling, Cyn shrugged. "Do whatever you want. I'm not hungry anyway." She looked up at the kitchen clock, but it had stopped.

"Cleo always wound it," she said in a tight voice. "What time is it?" She waved a hand at the clock. "Doesn't matter. I'm going to my room to watch television. Your husband will be here soon, I suppose. I don't want to see him. You can bring me some supper if you want." And then, most surprisingly, she turned and Liddy thought she could see something akin to sympathy in her eyes.

"Good luck with the stupid man, Lydia." And she rumbled off upstairs.

Would it have been easier, Liddy was to wonder afterwards, if Martin had, like Laura, found Liddy breastfeeding? If he had been presented with the spectacle of Hope, then she would not have had to start from nowhere.

He arrived just as Liddy was preparing supper for Cyn. Hope was fast asleep upstairs, the house echoed with Cyn's television turned up loud and Liddy, standing in the kitchen, didn't hear him until he pushed open the front door and called her name quietly.

She came to the kitchen door and stood for a moment looking at her husband as he stood in the doorway, the evening sun shining dark orange behind him. The gray flagstoned hallway seemed a million miles long and, as if in a dream, Liddy walked toward him.

Martin dropped his bag and half held out his arms, just slightly unsure of Liddy's response to his arrival.

"Darling," he said, "I am so sorry. You poor thing, this must be such a shock for you."

Liddy went into his arms. She hadn't meant to. She wanted that to happen afterwards, when all the dissembling was over. But it seemed such a long time since anyone had cuddled her and held her safe. For a moment she could feel soothed and loved.

"You poor, poor thing," he repeated into her hair. "You will miss her."

It couldn't be allowed to last, Liddy knew that, much as she wanted it to. She pushed him gently away.

"Come into the sitting room. Cyn's upstairs—she doesn't want to be disturbed. Would you like a drink?" The words came out tight and formal as she drew him into the room.

"How is poor Cyn?" Without waiting for the answer, he began to talk. "I know you're sad, darling," he took her hand, "but I am so pleased to see you. When all this is over and Cyn is settled, I want us to go away together, talk about it all, tell each other *everything*"—he gave a little smile—"everything that has happened to us during all these months we've been away from each other. Be completely honest with each other." His voice was low and loving. Liddy let go of his hand. It had to be now.

"Martin, I've had a baby."

Martin did not even register what she said. "We've got another chance to make it good between us."

Liddy repeated the words.

"Martin, I've just had a baby."

He heard her at last. Dumbfounded he looked at her. "What? You've had a baby. Why didn't you tell me? We've had a baby? Us?" He looked wildly around the room as if expecting to see some proof of a new baby. He understood—but not properly—he looked confused, still not working it out. "But we haven't . . . during the bad time . . ."

The words that she had to say stretched out in front of Liddy. "Not our baby. Mine."

She watched his lips move and no sound come out.

"Martin, you have to listen to me, please." She turned away so that she didn't have to look at him.

"I was pregnant. I never realized. I only found out the day before my birthday. I came down here and she was born prematurely twelve days ago."

The *Coronation Street* theme tune, filtering down from upstairs, filled the silence between them, the soulful music lingering around the room.

Liddy turned round to face Martin.

He stood there, his expression unchanged; only his hands moved, clenching into fists so tightly that the fingers looked white and stiff as though he had been in the sea too long.

"You said it was over. I don't understand," he said flatly. "I don't understand what you're saying." He repeated it like a defiant small boy.

Liddy sat down on the nearest chair; her legs were watery, her hands shaking. She leaned forward, putting her elbows on her knees, rocking slightly to comfort herself.

She spoke rapidly, like gunfire, wanting to get it all out in one long retch.

"Martin, it *is* over. Months ago. I didn't realize I was pregnant until it was too late to do anything about it. I thought I was just menopausal. I was going to tell you but then you said about Fay and I was scared you would choose to go to her if you knew. I was going to tell you as soon as I got home, but then she was born early. And I do love you so much, I really do. I *really* do. It's all so awful. I've made such a mess. I didn't mean to—I'm sorry, Martin."

Martin sat there, rock still and silent.

"Martin, Martin, please say something."

But he stayed silent.

Liddy had to fill the space, so she began talking again.

"I was so scared when my waters broke. I felt so alone and then I was ill and she had breathing problems, but she's fine now. She's asleep upstairs. I've called her Hope—"

"SHUT THE FUCK UP!" Martin got to his feet in a swift straight movement. He towered over her—and Liddy fell back into the chair by the window, now cowering as Martin shouted at her.

"You bitch, Liddy, you utter bitch. Do you have any idea how angry and guilty I have been feeling. I even began to think it was my fault that you were unfaithful to me. I thought about you and whatever his name is, how it was a short-lived thing, and I felt guilty that I had let Fay come so far into my life. Guilty, Liddy, me the guilty one." He paused; his face bent over hers, contorted like a gargoyle, his eyes flashing. "How dare you make *me* feel guilty when you've done this to us. You sit here, calmly telling me, just like that, that you've had another man's baby? Have you any idea what you've done? I'll tell you. You have just ruined all our lives: our children's, my life, yours and your little bastard's. Or will the father come running along and carry you both off? What *do* you think, Liddy? Or can't you think because your brain is still in your cunt?"

Liddy had never before heard Martin use such a crude word. His whole body was shaking with fury and she really believed that he might hit her. She stood up to ward him off.

"You absolute bitch, I hate you. I hate you more than anything in the world." Martin spat out the words at her and, with an obvious attempt at controlling himself, he turned and strode out of the room.

Rooted to the spot for a moment, Liddy heard him pick up his bag and open the front door. This was not how it should be. He couldn't go. They had to talk. He couldn't leave her like this. She rushed out after him.

He was already through the garden gate and at the top of the steep stone steps when she stopped him.

"Martin . . . ," she implored. "Please don't go. Please let us talk."

He moved away from her as if afraid of being contaminated by her.

"Talk?" he said incredulously. "Talk to you? I've absolutely nothing to say to you. I've spent the last week castigating myself for my foolishness for destroying the precious thing we had together and fretting that you would never forgive me for being so stupid. Now I find that I really *have* been stupid. You've made a fool out of me, you and this little fling of yours," he sneered at her. "How do you think that makes me feel now? Betrayed? Angry? You'd be right. So angry I don't even want to see you again, Liddy. I couldn't trust myself near you."

Liddy put out her hand to stop him and he pushed her away violently and roared down the steps.

It all happened so quickly, Liddy was never sure whether it was the violence of his push that sent her rolling all the way down the steps or whether she had just missed her footing. She felt a searing pain in her wrist and she banged her head so hard against the wall that the noise echoed in her brain with a hollow, dead sound and it made her teeth rattle and the vomit rise up inside her mouth. When she came to a halt at the bottom, there was no sign of Martin and for a moment she just lay there, every bit of her hurting more than she could ever believe possible—her shattered world buzzing around inside her hurting head.

Slowly, the pains became specific: her head throbbed; so did her right wrist; so did one of her ankles, and she wasn't sure which one because they both seemed trapped under her body. Too shocked to cry, she slowly unfolded herself and got to her feet. She could not put any pressure on her right leg and she had to support her wrist with the other hand in order to make the pain bearable. She could feel blood trickling down from lacerations on her face, and both her arms and her legs were badly grazed.

She hobbled slowly and painfully over to the wall. Down below she could see Martin get into his car without so much as a backward look and join the queue for the chain ferry. Then, suddenly, he turned the car round. He was coming back for her.

She stood there, throbbing with every sort of pain, and watched as he drove past the bottom of the steps and away through the village.

Chapter

NINE

Liddy had to ask Laura for help. She had only one alternative—and Avril was not answering her telephone. There was no one else to whom she could turn, only Laura. Liddy couldn't use her right arm and hand at all and she could only hobble painfully on her right leg. She tried to manage Hope, but every movement she made had her almost screaming in pain. She fed her one breast and then gave up and telephoned.

"Laura, it's me," she said nervously.

"Hello, Mum." Laura's voice was bright.

"I'm really sorry to bother you, but I've had a fall, hurt my wrist and my foot. I think I should go to hospital and have them strapped up. I haven't given Cyn her supper and I can't really manage here." Liddy knew that she was sounding pathetic.

There was a pause at the end of the telephone and then Laura asked, "Isn't Dad there?"

"No. He has been here, but he's gone."

"Oh." Another short silence, heavy with an unasked question, and then Laura said briskly, "Right, I'll come over now."

Liddy left Hope in her basket. She would wake up any moment and realize that she had only had half her feed. Liddy dragged herself slowly, painful tread by painful tread, across the landing and knocked on Cyn's door.

"Yes."

Liddy opened the door and was blasted by the noise of the television. Cyn was sitting in her armchair in her dressing gown. She had not tied it up properly and it flapped open, showing her large white knickers. Her legs, with loose skin hanging off the bones, looked pathetically vulnerable. She made no effort to cover herself up.

"Now what?" she said irritably.

"I'm afraid I've fallen down and I seem to have hurt my arm and leg quite badly."

Cyn rolled her eyes theatrically. "Oh, splendid. Just what we need. Where's that dopey husband of yours?"

"He's gone."

"Ahh. Not so dopey, then." Cyn sat in thought for a moment. "So what do you want me to do about this? I haven't had supper, you know."

"I know. I've just rung Laura and she's coming over. She'll get you something to eat."

"Oh, I don't want anything to eat," Cyn said contrarily.

"I'll get Laura to drive me to hospital. I think my foot and my wrist will need to be strapped up. I'll have to ask her to stay over, because I can't do a thing." Liddy raised her arm ruefully and then winced as the pain shot through it.

"You really are a most dreadful nuisance, Lydia," Cyn said brutally and then added spitefully, "You can't do a thing anyway; I always said you were useless, but Cleo would have it otherwise."

"You'll be on your own while we're at the hospital. I've tried ringing Avril, but she's not there."

"Will you stop treating me like a halfwit, Lydia. I want to be on my own. It's bad enough listening to that dreadful woman's prattling during the day, without it being forced on me in the evenings."

Liddy knew that Cyn was very fond of Avril, but now she merely nodded in agreement.

"Just go and get it all dealt with, for goodness' sake," Cyn said crossly. "And I'm not at all surprised about Martin," she added. "I've always said he was unforgivably pedestrian—that sort of man simply can't cope with anything out of the ordinary. You should never have married him. I said so at your wedding, but of course no one listened to me."

Liddy was touched that just every now and then Cyn seemed to be aware of what was happening to Liddy. She seemed to dip in and out of her grief to acknowledge, just briefly, the world around her.

Liddy pushed Hope's basket on to the landing with her uninjured arm. The pain brought tears into her eyes, but she had it in her mind that Laura should not have to go into her bedroom and see how Hope belonged in there. It was, she knew, a muddled reasoning, because Laura was inevitably going to have to go into her bedroom.

Laura arrived, jangling her car keys nervously in her hand. She came to the top of the stairs where Liddy was sitting beside the baby.

"I'm sorry about this," Liddy said, wincing as she held up her arm.

Laura looked down at her mother's damaged face.

"Those grazes need cleaning up," she said unemotionally. "How did it happen?"

"I just missed my footing on the steps outside," Liddy said, her voice as dispassionate as Laura's. "I think I might have broken a bone in my wrist." She hesitated. "I'm afraid I can't pick anything up. It's very kind of you."

Laura inclined her head toward her mother in acknowledgment. She didn't look into the basket.

A moment of heavy silence fell between them.

"What about Dad?" The question that Liddy didn't want to answer came out at last.

"He . . . er, has gone away to think. I don't know where exactly. He is—" Liddy wanted to offer further explanation, but a shutter had fallen in front of Laura's eyes and she interrupted her mother brusquely.

"What about Aunt Cyn's supper? Shouldn't I see to that before we go?"

"She doesn't want any." Liddy got painfully to her feet, accidentally bumping against the basket. Hope woke up with a start that made her whole body shudder. She started screaming hungrily.

"I need to feed her before we go. I could only manage one half," Liddy said wearily.

She could no longer protect Laura. Hope had to come first.

Laura supported Liddy downstairs and helped her on to the sofa. She hesitated for a moment and then picked up Hope and propped her against the cushions.

Only then did both women realize that Laura would have to do more; she would have to hold Hope to her mother's breast. Liddy was embarrassed; embarrassed to be showing her breast and having Laura moving it to accommodate Hope; embarrassed to be sharing the intensely personal and intimate experience of breastfeeding in front of her adult daughter.

Liddy had broken her wrist and twisted her ankle. Laura had to look after an unsettled Hope while Liddy was X-rayed and plastered.

Liddy was being wheeled into the waiting room, when she saw Laura with Hope in her arms. She watched Laura as, unaware of Liddy, she bent over the baby murmuring softly, her voice gentle and smiley.

She sensed Liddy's arrival and looked up, the smile gone from her face.

"You're not going to be able to manage Hope by yourself with all that." Laura gestured aggressively at the heavy plaster on Liddy's arm. "Are you?"

It was the first time that she had acknowledged Hope by her name. Liddy shook her head miserably and waited obediently as Laura stood silent for a moment, her brain obviously flicking through the next possible sequence of events.

"Right," she said eventually. "I'm going to drop you home, go to the cottage, get some things and come back. Melissa will look after the children and we'll decide what to do tomorrow."

Emotionally exhausted, and in great physical pain, Liddy could only cling on to her daughter's strength with the utmost gratitude.

Alex listened to his mobile phone answering machine as they left the pub.

"Alex, it's Laura. Oh, where are you? It's ten o'clock. Will you ring me at the cottage. Here's the number. I'll be here until eleven o'clock, then you will have to get me at the White House. Here's that number in case you haven't got it. It's really important. Please, Alex, please ring."

Alex frowned at his phone.

"What's up?" Mungo appeared from behind him and flung his arm around Alex's shoulder; their leather jackets squeaked as they made contact.

"Hairy sort of message from Laura; sounds most unlike her. She wants me to ring her tonight, whatever the time."

"It's probably about your aunt's funeral. You know what Laura's like. I'm for home—phone her there."

"I thought we were going clubbing." Alex was in an expansive mood. Mungo had forgiven him for his behavior at the party and of Terry there was no sign. "He's got a job up north. Went this morning, I think," Mungo had said briefly, and Alex had silently begged the Almighty to keep him up there. This was Mungo's first day out of work and he always found it hard waiting for the telephone to ring, but Alex liked the fact that he, alone, financed their lives at this time; he liked being the man of the house and he liked the fact that Mungo needed him more as his self-confidence gradually dwindled through the long jobless days. This was the time when Alex didn't so much mind his job at the ticket agency but, nevertheless, when a note had arrived from Harvey Grayshoy that morning, reminding him that he would be interested in talking to Alex should he ever think of a career in gardening, Alex stared thoughtfully at the letter for some time before tucking it into his desk drawer.

Alex looked at his watch as they got into the flat. He rang the cottage number. "Laura? It's me. What on earth's happened?"

Alone in the hospital waiting room, holding the baby, speaking her name for the first time, Laura had recognized that Hope was a real, live being who could now never leave her memory and who would always be joined to her. She had held the baby up to her face and smelled the milky smell in the crevices around her neck, she had watched Hope's hand curl round her finger and a sudden love and desire for the baby flooded through her. But then her mother had come in and she had had to return the baby. Now back in the cottage, packing a bag, she felt a huge and resentful anger that her mother had got something that she shouldn't have and that she, Laura, should have. The force of her anger drove her to the telephone to ring Alex and Miranda. She wanted to tell them about Hope so that they could share her anger.

She chose to talk to Alex first. With Alex, she only needed to deal with her own pain. He could deal with his own, unlike Miranda, who would likely want her pain to take precedence.

She was curiously disappointed when she only got Alex's

answering service and her sustained anger carried her on to ring Miranda, who was also out. Listening to the telephone ringing in the obviously empty flat, Laura wondered if Miranda would, after all, care as much as she and Alex; Miranda had always been an island.

Alex rang just as she was leaving the cottage to go to the White House.

"Alex, you and Miranda really must come down to Portlisk now."

"For the funeral?"

"No, that's not till the end of the week, apparently. No, you've got to come now, something's happened with Mum—"

"Mum? What? Is she all right?"

"Oh, yes, she's fine . . . well, you know, she's—"

"Laura, what are you trying to say? What's happened?"

At the Cornwall end of the line, Laura tried to find words that would work. In the end they came out in a rush.

"Alex, she's had a baby and it's not Dad's."

"Sorry. Say that again."

"Mum's had a . . . an illegitimate baby."

"Laura, darling," Alex said slowly, half an eye on Mungo at the other side of the room, talking to the dogs, "what are you talking about? Mum is much too old to have a baby. Are you OK?"

Laura almost stamped her foot. How could she make him understand? "Alex, please listen to me. I have been to Aunt Cleo's house, she is there, with a small baby called Hope."

"Are you sure she wasn't looking after it for someone else?"

"Alex, she was *breastfeeding* it. Anyway, she says it's hers. She's had an affair, Alex." Laura gulped and Alex could hear the tears in her voice. "Poor Dad. He's been to see her and left apparently. She's fallen over and broken her wrist and hurt her ankle. I've got to go and help her with . . . everything. Alex"—Laura's voice grew stronger as she regained control—

"I've got to get back to Portlisk, I can't wait for Miranda to ring me, so you'll have to get hold of her tonight and you must come down first thing tomorrow morning. We all need to be there. We've got to sort this out. If Miranda doesn't want to drive, you can come by train and I'll pick you up from the station."

Alex put down the phone and stared unseeingly at an African violet on the table beside him.

"Hey, Alex." Mungo's loud voice broke into the emptiness of Alex's head. "What did she want?" He crept nearer Alex and touched him on the shoulder. "Hey Alex, hello, what's happened?"

Alex spoke slowly—trying to make sense of what Laura had just told him.

"Um, well . . . um, apparently my mother has had a baby and it's not my father's."

"*Your* mother? No!" Mungo whistled. "Holy shit!"

Fergus didn't know about the baby. Laura had rung him yesterday to tell him about Aunt Cleo and he had expressed polite sorrow and insisted that he come down for the funeral; his upbringing decreeing that one put oneself out for family funerals, if not for your children's holiday. Now she rang him again just before she left the cottage and told him about the baby.

"Good Lord." He sounded shocked. "I'd have thought your father would be firing blanks by now."

"It's not Dad's, Fergus, she's had an affair. Mum's had an affair with another man."

"Good God. No. Surely not?" he said, shock affecting reasoned thought. Then he asked hopelessly, "What can I do?"

"Come down here now," Laura ordered. *"Please,"* she cried.

"Yes. Right. Of course, I'll just . . . um . . . By the way, love, do you know where the dairy checkbook is? I can't find it anywhere."

*   *   *

Fergus put down the telephone and sat for a moment in the cool hall. He knew perfectly well that he had been inadequate in his response to Laura's news. He often didn't know the right thing to say straightaway. Now that he began to digest the information, things were all at once becoming clearer. Of course, that was what had been the matter with Laura lately. She must have known her mother was having an affair and kept it to herself, silly girl. No wonder she had been so tense and snappy recently. Now he came to think of it, Laura hadn't been herself for quite a long time. Fergus wondered if Martin had known about the affair. He thought probably not—as far as he remembered, Martin had seemed his perfectly normal, composed self last time he had seen him. Nice man, didn't deserve this, not at all. Poor old Laura, she must have been beside herself, knowing about her mother and probably too ashamed to tell anyone. Even if they knew, Miranda and Alex wouldn't have been particularly supportive; they tended to be a bit inconsiderate, Fergus always thought. His thoughts slowly churning and taking form in his head, he got up from the chair and ambled toward the kitchen to pour himself a large whisky. He was mightily relieved that everything was explained, that there had been a good reason for Laura's recent behavior. He must think of something to take Laura's mind off everything. Yes, he would have to cheer her up. Actually, he had been kicking an idea around in his head—about expanding her ice cream business, she'd like that.

"Mirry sweetheart. It's me. You'd better sit down, I've got something to tell you. . . ."

The shock that Alex had initially felt was beginning to wear off and there was, Mungo noticed, an element of excitement and drama in his voice as he spoke to his sister.

"But Aunt Cleo is dead," Miranda said in a numb voice, as if that was relevant to what Alex had just told her.

* * *

"I don't know why we have to go down," Miranda grumbled as early next morning she weaved the car through deserted London streets. "I really don't want to know about it. It's disgusting, it makes me feel sick." The words tumbled out of her.

"We're going because Laura needs us," Alex said, staring out of the side window as he tried to disguise the unshed tears which were building up behind his eyes. He had woken at three in the morning to find the adrenaline that had coursed around his body had been replaced with a heavy sadness.

"Talk about it, Alex," Mungo had urged, holding him tightly in the darkness.

"I can't," Alex had mumbled into his lover's shoulder. "I can't. Because I don't *know.*"

Miranda now expertly passed three chugging lorries. "Laura's never needed us," she said bitterly. "She just gets on with it all. She always has."

"Well, she needs us now. It's called family solidarity," Alex said sharply. "This affects us all. Why should Laura have to carry this on her own?"

"She likes to be in charge," Miranda said childishly.

Alex shrugged and kept silent. He was disturbed at how vulnerable Laura had sounded last night. He had lost his constant. Laura had always been there in the background, bossy, managing and the holder of the family's traditions. That he might have lost another constant in his life with his mother having some other man's baby, Alex refused to acknowledge at the moment.

Miranda tried to concentrate on driving. She liked to drive. She was good at it and she enjoyed her superiority over the other drivers.

Richard had not come home last night. He had been out at a magazine function in Docklands and had left a message on the answer machine saying he didn't want to risk driving and would stay the night in the company flat. Coming in after an evening at the gym, Miranda listened to the message and couldn't be bothered to mind. It was only after Alex rang that she began to feel abandoned by Richard. This morning she had left him a note telling him where she was going and asking him to inform her office.

"*It seems my mother has had a baby!*" she wrote dramatically at the bottom. She wondered what he would make of that.

Liddy woke up to Hope crying. She moved under the duvet and felt the heavy plaster on her wrist.

Laura appeared in her bedroom.

"I'll bring her over," she said briefly and picked up the baby.

Liddy struggled to an upright position and took the baby from Laura and between them they settled her on to the breast.

Liddy knew that she had to break the cool politeness that was building up between them.

"Laura, darling—," she began, but Laura talked over her—perfectly pleasantly, but firmly.

"What time does Aunt Cyn have her breakfast?"

"About twelvish. She usually has it in bed, although yesterday she came down and had it in the sitting room, but Avril comes in today, so she will do it. Look, Laura—"

Again Laura talked. "Alex and Miranda are coming down today. I shall have to go back to the children. I can't leave Melissa with them all day. Miranda will have to pull her weight."

Liddy tried to fight Laura's denial. "I need to talk to you, darling. Please, you must listen to me."

Laura took a deep breath, as if summoning up a great courage. "Mum, not now. We have to *arrange* things. Let's concentrate on that. I'm here to help you with . . ." She flapped a hand in the direction of the baby. "Do you bathe her in the mornings or evenings?"

Liddy submitted to a greater power and shrugged.

"Whenever," she said hopelessly.

"Right, I'd better do it this morning. I don't suppose Alex or Miranda will be up to the job."

Laura bustled out of the bedroom and Liddy lay back on her pillows, drained of all regard for herself. Laura had spoken to her dismissively, as an adult might speak to a child. Liddy had suddenly lost control and she felt cowed and humiliated. She wondered if this was how hostages felt at the mercy of their captors, never given an opportunity to justify themselves, to take responsibility for themselves, to reassert themselves.

It got worse during the morning. Laura bathed the baby and then had to help Liddy put on her clothes and dress the lacerations on her legs and face. Liddy felt as helpless as Hope. Any moment now, she thought with a glimmer of humor, Laura would lick her handkerchief and wipe Liddy's mouth for her.

Avril arrived and Liddy, sitting in the study, heard her and Laura in the kitchen, discussing arrangements for the funeral. She wanted to go in and wrest command from Laura, but her body seemed too heavy to move. It was all so terribly surreal as Liddy stared into space, uncertain what to do and trying to assemble the thoughts that were crowding into her head and making it ache.

In her basket, Hope grizzled constantly and sucked her hand loudly.

Avril passed the study door, laden down with a vacuum and an old-fashioned wooden box full of cleaning stuff.

"Shit's hit the fan then?" she said cheerily.

Liddy nodded dumbly and Avril propped herself up against the doorjamb. "Don't you worry, my lovely, they'll get used to it. Eventually. Kids aren't very good at forgiving their mums and dads, but in the end they see that whatever you do you're still the best ones they're ever going to have, so they might as well get on with it. You'll see." Avril's bright voice changed to sadness.

"I can't get used to Cleo not being here and Cyn won't let me touch her bedroom. Laura's insisted she does Cyn's breakfast tray. She's done it up ever so nicely. I'm just going to do upstairs. OK to do your room?"

Liddy nodded and Hope's grizzling turned into angry bellows.

Avril came round the chair to look at her.

"They always pick up the atmosphere, don't they? She looks hungry to me."

"I've just fed her," Liddy said despondently.

"Are you sure you've got the milk?"

Liddy grimaced. "Maybe not."

"Stick her on the bottle, lovely," Avril advised. "Much easier. Must get on. Lots to do."

Liddy rang Mary. "You have to give them time to deal with this, Liddy. All of them. Denial, anger then sadness. Only then will it begin to heal, you know that."

"I have never felt so wrong and bad as I do at the moment," Liddy said.

"They will punish you, Liddy. You don't have to punish yourself as well, you know."

But Liddy thought that maybe it was easier to punish yourself.

Avril came into the room as Liddy put down the telephone.

"Just called into Cyn. She's not good today. She won't come out of her bedroom, she says. Place smells as though she's been smoking all night. Laura is up there being torn off a strip for putting one of Cleo's roses on the tray."

"I'm sorry. I gather Cyn is rather rough this morning. She doesn't really mean it." Liddy wanted to apologize for everything and apologizing for Cyn, apologizing for someone other than herself, gave her back a small moment of dominance.

"Well, it's a very upsetting time for her," Laura said, putting Liddy smartly back on the ropes. "Anyway, she wants to stay in her room until the funeral is over. She doesn't want to know anything about it. She's asked Avril to come in and feed the cats every evening because she can't trust any of us." Liddy felt that Laura was a little chagrined that even she, of all people, could not be trusted with the task. "She wants you to go and see her sometime today, but not during the racing at Kempton Park apparently, oh and not during *Neighbours*, *David Attenborough* and *Question Time.*"

Liddy opened her mouth to speak, but Laura was leaving the room.

"I'm going to get on with the washing. There's a pile of it in the laundry room. And then I'll go down to the shop. You had better make a list. We need more nappies." Laura ran over Liddy like a giant steam-roller.

Liddy waited all afternoon for Alex and Miranda to arrive. They were later than Laura expected and Liddy was fearful that they had had an accident.

"Stopped off for a pub lunch probably," Laura sniffed.

Laura helped her to feed Hope, and Liddy began to stop caring about the unnatural intimacy of her eldest daughter helping her to breastfeed. Hope fought the breast angrily.

"I'm afraid I don't have enough milk for her," Liddy said sadly, looking down at her small red-faced daughter.

"Right. I'll go down to the shop and get some bottles and formula." Laura leapt at the idea. Liddy understood that Laura would be much happier and more settled if she didn't have to confront her mother breastfeeding.

Left alone in the sitting room with nothing to do, Liddy felt imprisoned; she longed to be able to go for a walk and be alone.

She must have been dozing when the doorbell rang. She woke with a start, conscious of the dribble down her chin where it had rested against her good hand. She heard Avril go to the door and a male voice that was not Alex's.

Robert came into the room with a bunch of flowers.

"Hel . . . Good Lord," he said, looking at her. "What on earth has happened to you?"

"I fell down the steps outside."

Robert raised his eyebrows. "Are you all right?"

"Fine. It looks worse than it is," Liddy lied.

Robert shifted a bit and waved the flowers in an embarrassed fashion. "I . . . er, just came to visit Cyn, bring her these flowers, see how she is bearing up, you know."

Liddy looked at him hopelessly.

"She won't want to see you," Avril informed him. "She doesn't want anyone going near her, she says, but I'll go and try for you."

Robert sat down on the edge of an armchair and he and Liddy looked at each other in silence.

"You'll have to wait until she's put on her makeup," Liddy said in an attempt to lighten the atmosphere between them.

Robert gave a small smile. "Are you really all right?"

"No, not really, but things can only get worse, I feel."

"I'm sorry, Liddy. I wasn't very"—he searched for the right word—"helpful yesterday. It's a bad fault of mine—opting out when things get difficult, too hot to handle, you know the sort of thing." He gave a guilty laugh. "I just want an easy life, I suppose."

"You and every man since Adam, believe me," Liddy was surprised to hear herself snarl.

"Yes, well," Robert said nervously, "I'm sorry. And if there is anything I can do, I would like to, really." He sounded as though he meant it.

Avril came back. "Yup, you have an audience. She's put on her makeup and is ready to receive you. 'I can't think why the bloody man wants to come and see *me*' is what she actually said, but it seems you're favorite because you're nothing to do with 'Cleo's ruddy family.' " Avril smiled at Liddy, wanting to take the sting out of the remark.

Miranda and Alex appeared in the early evening. They had, in fact, arrived at the chain ferry in the afternoon, but Alex insisted they stopped for a cream tea.

"A what?" Miranda looked at him in disbelief.

"We always used to have a cream tea here before we went to see Aunt Cleo," Alex had said stubbornly. It was his way of postponing the inevitable.

"It isn't quite how it used to be though, is it?" Miranda sat opposite Alex, refusing scones and cakes and sipping distastefully at a cup of tea.

They had driven down mostly in silence, both of them busy with their own thoughts, neither bothering to instigate any conversation.

The small café had not changed in all the time they'd been coming here. Still the same little tables covered in bright red gingham, the same copper pans on the wall, the same gray stone Cornish pixies on the mantelpiece. Miranda seemed too big for the place. Alex felt she was like a coiled spring, desperate to unwind; she kept fidgeting her legs as though at any moment she would jump up and pace the floor.

"Did you tell Richard?" he asked.

"What?" Miranda talked in staccato. "No, he wasn't at home when I left." She paused. "Actually I left him a note. Did you tell Mungo?"

Alex's mouth was full. He was finding enormous comfort in the solid, familiar cream tea.

"Of course I did."

"What did he say?"

"Holy shit." He smiled at the recollection.

Miranda looked at Alex coldly. "Don't you hate her? Aren't you angry? Aren't you disgusted?"

Alex puzzled for a moment. "No," he said slowly. "I was thinking about that on the way down. I don't think I am—not yet, anyway. I don't know how I feel, except a bit bewildered, a bit scared, I think, and mostly just sad. But," he added honestly, "I don't really know who I'm sad for. I was thinking a lot about Dad, too. Whether he knew, what he feels, you know."

"I just don't see how it could have happened." Miranda's eyes were glittering dangerously. Alex could see her tenuous hold on control was slipping. "How could she do it to us, and to Dad? At her age. And who with? Do we know him? I couldn't bear it if we knew him. Is she going to live with him?" The questions, once they started, came tumbling out of Miranda in a voice that became louder and louder.

Alex put out an arm to stop the flow, aware of the other customers looking toward them as they noticed Miranda's distress. He suddenly felt terribly grown up and protective of his big sister.

"Mirry, sweet, we don't know anything yet. Let's just get there and find out. That's what Mungo said. He said we shouldn't judge until we knew about everything."

"It's horrible." Miranda shuddered. "Horrible, horrible, horrible. I don't want to see her—or it."

Alex paid the bill and led Miranda out of the café. He sat her gently on a bench overlooking the river and watched the chain ferry clunk on to its mooring.

"She's too old. She can't. She can't do this to us," Miranda suddenly screeched in animal protest. But the river wind took the strength out of her voice and carried it away.

"Come on, Mirry, let's go." Alex had never felt really in charge of anyone before. It was a curiously good feeling.

Miranda stood up and they walked toward the car. She stopped suddenly. "Alex, I can't stay in that house, not with a baby—not that baby. We've got to find somewhere to stay in the village; there must be somewhere we can stay."

"I doubt it. It's the middle of the season. Anyway, it's not fair on Laura if we don't stay. We need to be together."

"Why?" Miranda sneered. "We're not together sort of children. We never have been."

Alex noticed her use of the word *children* and he said crossly, "We're not children anymore, Mirry. We're adults."

Me, I said that? I really said that? he was to think afterwards.

Miranda looked at him uncomprehendingly. "We're *her* children. And I'm not being selfish." Her anger suddenly left her and her whole being deflated like an old party balloon. "I don't want this to happen. Don't make it have happened," she wailed.

Alex put his arm around his sister's shoulders and held on to her tightly as he watched the ferry start back across the river without them on it.

"Come on, Mirry. None of us wanted this to happen. It's awful for us all, but most awful for Dad. And, if you think about it, it must be awful for Mum as well."

Miranda looked at him in amazement. "But it's *her* fault. She didn't have to have the baby."

He cajoled her into the car and they sat there at the head of the queue waiting for the ferry to get to the other side of the river and come back again.

Alex wanted Mungo. He felt he was beginning to lose control of his sister: his command was slipping away and he wanted Mungo to be here to look after him, to cradle him in his powerful arms and take away this awful responsibility that seemed to have abruptly landed on him. He could not cope with Miranda anymore; he wanted to get to Laura so that she could take over and give him time to think about his own feelings.

"Laura, Laura, darling. We must talk about this." Liddy tentatively touched Laura's arm in an attempt to stop the whirlwind that was her eldest daughter pounding around, polishing the sitting-room furniture. "Avril does that. Please, darling, stop, come and sit down with me. *Please*," she implored. But Laura brushed her off impatiently.

"I don't think Avril does very much," she muttered crossly. "This furniture obviously hasn't been properly polished for ages. I expect the dining-room table is in the same state. I'll have do that, too." She bustled angrily out of the room.

Laura allowed herself to acknowledge that although she couldn't bear Liddy being so submissive and so guilty, she couldn't give her permission to become her mother again. She didn't want the power that this situation had given her, yet she was unable to relinquish it. She wanted Liddy to grab it from her, to become her mother again, but Liddy just sat there. Why was she being so pathetic? Parents shouldn't be *pathetic*. They were the real adults of the family; they were always there—the security—and now, suddenly, that security was lost. She needed her parents to be whole, proper people—together. She had tried to model her life on theirs and now she felt let down by them, as though somehow they had fooled her by pretending all along. She didn't want to feel angry, she didn't want to feel lost and she didn't want to hate her mother. But she did; she hated her for making everything grubby and sullied. It was all so *strange* and so *bad*. She didn't understand: why had Mum had the baby? Why didn't she just get rid of it, if she didn't want it? Where was the father? Why wasn't she with him? Why had she done this to Dad? They loved each other. So much she didn't understand, yet so much she didn't want to know. She longed for it all to go away. Strange surges of anger at her father for letting this happen kept rising unbidden in Laura's head. She hated these thoughts, she had always hated confusion—so she kept busy. Busy putting clean sheets on beds, busy shopping, busy cooking, busy making up bottles of milk for Hope—so many jobs, yet none of them could drive the thoughts away.

*   *   *

Liddy, on the other hand, found herself without any tasks to perform. The midwife, unaware of the hurt and pain this new baby had caused, visited Liddy for a checkup and sympathized with her injuries.

"It's handy that your elder daughter is staying so near, isn't it?" she said cozily. "I always think daughters are there to help their mothers." She bent over Hope in her basket.

"And now your lucky mummy has another little girl to help her, hasn't she, my lovely?" Liddy felt an unreasonable hatred for the woman who was trying hard to combine sympathy for a bereavement with encouragement for a newly delivered mother.

The midwife suggested she visit Cyn while she was there.

"I'll just pop in on her—see how she's bearing up at this sad time," she said cozily.

She helped Liddy into Cyn's room and inquired after Cyn's well-being. Cyn merely snarled at her.

"Well, Miss Trenton, just remember, time is a great healer. I'll say cheerio then. I don't need to see Mrs. Claver again." Undaunted, she left with a smile and Cyn turned to Liddy.

"Don't you ever force that unspeakable woman on me again, Lydia," she said fiercely.

Cyn was sitting in front of the blaring television. The bed was a sea of gently breathing multicolored fur as the cats lay entwined, covering every bit of bedspread.

"I suppose now your family have descended on us, you're not even thinking about Cleo," Cyn said to her. "That Robert at least had the decency to come and see me."

"I do think about Cleo," Liddy said, tears welling up. "I want her to be here. I miss her so much."

"Yes, you probably do," Cyn acknowledged. "Of course, you only came down to see her when it suited *you*," she added unjustly. "I'm not coming downstairs until you've all gone," she went on. "You know I can't stand your family, Lydia, and they certainly don't want to see me. I just want to stay here and think about . . . her." She turned back to the television, her loose jaw set in a hard line. She waved her hand at Liddy dismissively. "Oh, just go and sort yourselves out and then go *away*, for Christ's sake."

Liddy hobbled out, feeling completely alone and utterly rejected. This, she thought, was probably the longest day of her life. And Martin was still not back home. She had tried ringing him several times.

Laura kissed them both. They usually didn't kiss and Miranda shied away slightly.

"How are you, Laura?" Alex heard himself ask foolishly.

"Fine, fine," she answered, just as foolishly.

The three of them stood for a moment in the doorway, frozen in inactivity, a mutual agreement to put off the next bit of their lives.

"You'd better come in," Laura said politely and then added nervously, "Mum's in the sitting room."

"Here they are at last, Mum," Laura said as she ushered them in. She hovered uncertainly, wanting to flee to the kitchen, yet desperate to protect Miranda and Alex from what they had to face.

Alex could see the pain and fear in his mother's face and his heart turned over for her. He was astonished at the force of love for her that welled up inside him.

"Hello, Mum." He tripped forward and kissed his mother's upturned face. He leaned over to look into the basket by her side.

"So what is it called?" He was aware of sounding a little too jovial. He put out a hand to touch the sleeping baby and was shocked to see quite how much his hand was shaking.

"Hope," Liddy said simply, looking at the back of Alex's

213

neck as he bent over the basket. She had loved the back of his neck when he was little; it was always warm and sweet-smelling. She looked past Alex at Miranda, hovering by the door.

"Hello, darling," she said cautiously.

Miranda's face twisted viciously. "How could you do this?" she shouted, two red spots appearing on her usually pale cheeks. "How could you? How could you? It's disgusting. You're too old. You, you cow. I hate you. I hate you."

She rushed out into the hall and fell against the coats hanging in thick folds on the pegs. She buried her face in the warm and woolly material and the tears ran down her cheeks. Liddy felt strangely cleansed by Miranda's public anger. It was a welcome respite from Laura's silent control and it seemed absolutely right. It was also a known, familiar reaction from her daughter; she had been subjected to Miranda's temper for twenty-eight years. She understood it and expected it. Listening to Miranda, the deadly numbness that Liddy had been feeling all day, slowly rolled away down her body, just like taking off a pair of tights.

Tears poured down her cheeks unchecked and her lips shook so, she could hardly get the words out.

"I'm sorry. I'm so very sorry for you, for Dad and for Hope." She glanced down at the basket and then looked up at her three adult children. "And for me, too. Can't you understand how I feel? I didn't know I was pregnant. I have made the most terrible mistake and I feel too old and too tired to put it right. I can just see the years stretching ahead and I feel so lonely. I just can't do it." She bowed her head and repeated, "I can't, I really can't."

Laura and Alex, and Miranda, still in the hall with her head buried in the coats, all three heard Liddy very clearly and in each one of them a small seed of an idea was firmly planted.

Chapter

TEN

Martin had never felt so out of control. When he rushed from the White House, all he could think of was to get as far away as possible from Liddy. In the space of only five minutes, the woman he had always loved had become a monster. His hands were clammy and shaking and his legs gave way as he collapsed into his car. He had driven to the chain ferry before realizing that he didn't want to take the return journey. He had to get out of this village—he felt the whole place was tainted—but not the way he had come. He didn't want to remember how, only about an hour ago, he had been standing on the deck of the ferry, looking down at the oily river slapping against the sides and castigating himself for nearly losing Liddy.

He had believed then that she really loved him and that he had been very stupid and very close to destroying something so precious. He had dared to believe that she would forgive him, make plans with him and that they would move forward into the future even stronger than before. As he had watched the village of Portlisk come nearer and nearer and looked up at the seagulls sweeping above him in the blue evening sky, he had even thought they might move to the sea, somewhere near here perhaps. He had looked at the White House on the hill, knowing that Liddy was there waiting for him and needing him.

Scotland had been good for him—the sheer expanse of raw nature around him had made him feel small and unimportant. He had walked on great grassy cliff tops, their vastness rolling behind and ahead of him, the icy clear colors of the sea below him washing on to the glittering sands of crushed shells and he had felt he was coming back down to earth after a journey hurtling around in a wild fantasy world. He felt he had been caught up in a whirlwind of madness that had been embodied in Fay and he had suddenly found himself definite that this madness was over. As he walked, he remembered Liddy: Liddy as a young woman bent over her work, serious, intent, completely absorbed; as a young mother playing silly games with the children, proud of Laura, worrying about Miranda, laughing with Alex. He thought of Liddy in bed with him, large and sensuous—and he wanted that Liddy back. And he had come to get her.

Tears now began to pour down Martin's face as he thought of how he had been made a fool of by this woman that he loved—for whom he had chosen to put everything else behind him.

He turned the car sharply away from the ferry and took the road out of the other end of the village, unaware of his direction except away from the pain. A few minutes later, he flung open the door and threw up in a ditch. On and on he retched until he felt he had completely emptied himself.

He sat back in the driving seat, waiting for the shaking to stop. He desperately wanted to go home, but he knew he was too tired to drive all that way twice in one day. He would find somewhere to stay tonight and go home tomorrow. And after that? He just could not begin to think.

At half past nine Martin gave up trying to find anywhere to stay. The effort of getting out of his car each time he came to a village, to be told there were no vacancies, was just too much. He bought a bottle of whisky, parked his car in the gateway of a field, turned on Radio 3 and began to drink.

The dawn woke him as the sun poured through the car windscreen on to his tearstained, drink-sodden face. His back ached, his head throbbed and his eyes were dry and gritty. He forced himself to eat a large, greasy breakfast in a transport café and then drove slowly northward, back to the Midlands.

Letting himself into the house and hearing the grandfather clock ticking, he was almost surprised to find everything as he had left it. He expected, almost wanted it to have changed, just as, in one awful moment, his life had changed. He wanted the house violated and ruined in some way—to parallel his own feelings of violation and ruin.

He threw the keys onto the hall table and dragged himself upstairs and threw himself onto the bed. Then he got up and rummaged in a drawer. He found the necklace that Liddy had made when Laura was born. Of all the pieces of jewelry she had made, this delicate topaz-and-silver piece was his favorite. He fell asleep with it clasped in his hand like a child with a favorite toy.

It was dusk when he woke up. He lay still, looking up at the ceiling, assimilating the last twenty-four hours.

How had it happened? He and Liddy used to be good together. When had it started falling to pieces? Martin dredged his memory for the reasons he and Liddy had divided without each other knowing. They had been happy when the children were small: he was content to let Liddy work, selling her jewelry and doing a few lucrative teaching jobs, while he cared for the children and the bookshop in tandem. It had all worked so well—though he never had remembered the right way to put on the girls' tights. Martin wondered why that thought had entered, unbidden, into his head. He rolled over on his side and held his stomach, aching with the desire to be back there with their children very small again and Liddy and he so happy. Life had been full and simple in those days. But what happened? Was it Miranda's dramas? Alex's homosexuality? Laura's Down's syndrome child? Had they not been together over it all? And when the three children grew up and needed them less, why had he and Liddy not talked? They had the time now, but somehow they had drifted apart. Did they really have nothing left to talk about now that their children were adults? Or was it just that they both filled the gap left by the children by being busy with their own lives and forgetting to make time for each other?

And then was Liddy being honest? Did she really perhaps love the father of her child? Was he still in her life? Another question entered Martin's heaving head. Which had happened first, Fay or the father of Liddy's baby?

But what the hell does it matter? he thought wearily as he swung himself off the bed and went in to the shower. Nothing matters now.

He suddenly desired company—he needed someone to remind him that the world was still spinning outside his misery, someone to confirm that he could still speak out loud and someone to set him upright again.

Martin dialed Fay's number.

"Christ." Fay opened the door. "You look terrible."

She smelled of expensive scent, her gray silk dress moved like liquid around her slim figure and her hands were soft as she took Martin's arm and led him to the sofa. He thought of her as a beautiful safe box into which he wanted to climb and then close down the lid.

"Drink first, I think," she said.

"I had half a bottle of whisky in my car last night," Martin said, leaning forward, clenching his fists against his knees.

"Lucky you weren't Breathalyzed on the motorway then."

Fay, with her usual elegant, fluid movements, poured out a glass of whisky and handed it to him. "Here. Another one isn't going to make any difference. By the way," she added, looking down at him with a tender expression on her face, "I would just like to say, I missed you while you were away."

Martin looked into his drink.

"I've got it all wrong," he said miserably.

Fay was noncommittal. "Have you?"

"I thought I was getting it right, but I shouldn't have trusted her." He looked up at Fay. "I trust you."

"I hope so," Fay said lightly as she sat down. "Enough to tell me what's happened?"

"My wife has had a baby by another man," was how he started. He stared at her, waiting for her to speak, to make some comment on this cataclysmic statement. He waited for her to reach out and comfort him. But Fay didn't respond. She sat quietly and Martin found himself talking into her silence, his eyes fixed on the little silver carriage clock on the mantelpiece. When he ground to a halt, she stayed quite still beside him, slowly turning the crystal glass in her hand; Martin could see the rainbow prisms glinting in her lap.

"God, poor Liddy," Fay said eventually and then, almost to herself, "It's not fair, is it?"

Martin looked at Fay incredulously. "What?"

"Well, I mean she wasn't doing anything more than we were, was she?"

"But she's had a *baby*." Martin was baffled by Fay's response.

"That's very bad luck. *I* could have got pregnant. But I didn't."

"Of course you didn't."

Fay shook his arm gently. "That's not the point, Martin. It

could have happened to me. I'm not saying it would, but it could have, just as it did to Liddy. It is bad luck for her and now, after yesterday I imagine, she is probably feeling it is a tragedy."

Martin looked at her curiously. "Why are you defending her? Is this a 'women must stick together' sort of thing?"

Fay frowned at him. "Liddy and I were acquaintances long before you and I were lovers. But she had nothing to do with how I feel about you. I thought about writing to her, you know."

"Did you? Why?"

"Because . . ." Fay hesitated, as though trying to make what she wanted to say completely clear in her head before she uttered the words. "Because Liddy had nothing to do with you and me; she never came into my equation. I forced myself not to think about her. She was your responsibility, not mine. The thing is, Martin, I love you very much, but I knew at that party, when I saw your family all around you and when I saw the misery in both of you, that our relationship would end. You and Liddy have so much more than we could ever have. I'm glad I was there when you were lost and I don't regret the little bit I've had of you, not for one moment, but it was only temporary and I suppose, deep down, I've always known that." Fay paused and gave a sad smile. "It doesn't make it any easier for me, of course. After the party, I wanted to tell her that you and she were safe and worth fighting for."

"But we're not. Not now, and I'm not fighting anything, any more. I was honest with her"—he caught Fay's small frown and put up his hand—"eventually, I know, I know. But I was completely honest about how I wanted to change the future and I told her how I felt about you. Was she honest with me? No, she wasn't. She told me about her affair, but omitted to tell me the most important thing—that she was pregnant with another man's baby. I can never forgive her for that, Fay. I can't."

"Martin, honestly, I probably wouldn't have been able to

think straight in her situation either. It must have been awful for her. She must have panicked when she realized it was too late to have an abortion. The father wasn't around—"

"If that is really true."

Fay shrugged. "Well, I don't know about that, but from what you're saying, he doesn't seem to be around. He's not with her, is he? She must feel so alone. Anyway, what I'm trying to explain is that she was terribly scared, I expect. I would have been. She didn't know how you would respond to a baby suddenly about to come into your lives, did she?"

"My God," Martin said suddenly, "I bet she thought I would adopt it when I saw it." He frowned in disgust. "Of course, that's what she thought. Good old lovable Martin, who would do anything for her. He loves children, he'll look after it. Of course he will. She doesn't love me, she just *needs* me."

Fay held him in her arms and tried to contain his bitterness.

They slept together that night, Martin banging violently into Fay as though trying to evict the devils inside him.

"That was definitely sex, not making love," Fay said as she lay underneath him, feeling his heart pounding between their sweaty skins.

Martin rolled over.

"God, I'm sorry. That was unforgivable," he said, his hands over his eyes.

"It doesn't matter." Fay stroked his head. "I don't mind which bit of you I have."

Martin's shoulders began to shake and he rolled over into her shoulder. She could feel his tears running into her armpits.

"Oh, Fay, I can't, I can't, I can't."

And whether he meant he couldn't with Liddy or he couldn't with her, Fay did not want to ask.

*   *   *

221

Alex and Laura tried to make Miranda go to bed upstairs.

"I'm not staying in this house, I'm not," Miranda protested, now completely beyond herself.

"You'll have to," Laura said practically. "There's nowhere else to go. The village is completely full."

She made Miranda a hot drink, but Miranda left it on the kitchen table and went out in the garden.

"I'll have to stay," Laura said to Alex as they watched their sister pacing up and down the lawn outside. "Miranda can't help Mum—she's in too much of a state."

"I can, though."

Laura looked at Alex in surprise and shook her head. "No, Alex. The baby needs looking after properly. And Mum . . . she needs help, too."

"And?" Alex was becoming cross. "What makes you think I can't do it? Because I'm a man? Just go, Laura. Trust me, I can manage and I can manage Miranda, too, I honestly can. You should go back to your kids. Just go." Alex grinned at his sister. "And you can ring up and check on me every hour, if you want."

Laura didn't return Alex's grin and he listened with patience to her anxious and comprehensive list of instructions. He found that he was rather looking forward to caring for the baby.

Miranda was like a nervous pony, shying away from any comfort Alex tried to give her. She adamantly refused to reenter the house and Alex, knowing her so well, eventually gave in.

"Is there really nowhere she can stay in the village?" he asked Liddy desperately. He was embarrassed for both Miranda and his mother in this situation, but Liddy surprisingly had a possible solution. She rang Robert and stammered out her request, conscious that she was asking a great deal. Her concern for Miranda, though, cut through her embarrassment and pride, and if Robert was horrified and unwilling, he never said so, for which Liddy was unutterably grateful.

Robert came up to fetch Miranda and walk her to his house. She saw a tall crumpled man with a safe, kind face; he saw a tall, thin, nervy girl with blinding hurt in her eyes and he made gentle meaningless conversation as they walked down the hill.

In Robert's front garden, Bonnie greeted them enthusiastically.

"Down, Bonnie. I'm sorry," Robert apologized to the silent girl.

Unexpectedly Miranda smiled. "I don't mind. I like dogs."

Robert looked at her quizzically. "You said that as though you liked dogs specifically more than you liked something else."

Miranda surprised herself by saying, "I do. Most particularly families, at the moment."

"Ah. I know that feeling. Dogs are so undemanding. They never have a crisis, do they?"

Miranda smiled. He *was* a nice man. She turned to look at the sea view which, unlike at the White House, was at the same level as the garden. She gazed upward at the crumbling tower on the cliffs to her left and she watched silently for a moment the ships moving slowly across the horizon in the distance. She wished passionately that she was on one of them, steaming to some uncomplicated far-off place.

Standing behind her, Robert watched her back and thought he had never seen such a tight little buttoned-up body. His heart went out to her and he was surprised at the force of his feeling. He had not wanted this waif foisted on him in the first place, but now he found himself wanting to make her better.

"I'm so sorry about Cleo. And"—he hesitated—"I'm sorry about everything else, too."

Miranda turned and looked at him, surprised; then a thought struck her.

Robert caught the thought and understood it. He held up his hands. "No, no, not me."

"Sorry," Miranda mumbled, looking away.

Miranda wanted to be alone, but Robert moved forward to stand beside her.

"This is very beautiful, isn't it?" he said proudly. "I know this view so well, but I always wonder at it."

"When I was little it always seemed to be raining up there on the cliffs." Miranda remembered the summer holidays of her childhood. "I suppose because if it was sunny, we were on the beach. I used to like holidays here. They were sort of—" Miranda searched for the right word. "—they were *clean*." She looked at Robert. "Do you know what I mean? I felt washed and shiny when I was here." She flapped her hand in frustration. "Oh, I don't know what I'm trying to say."

"I know exactly what you mean," Robert agreed. "The seaside and big places like these cliffs do have a sort of cleansing effect. It's like they sweep out all the rubbish from your head and leave space for other things, don't you think?"

They stood in silence.

"I met your mother up there on the cliffs," Robert said suddenly. "She told me straightaway about everything and what a mess she had made of it all and how unhappy she was about it—"

"She could never be as unhappy as she has made all of us," interrupted Miranda.

"Oh, I think she could," Robert said gently. "Have you never made a terrible mistake and thought that there was absolutely no way out? But, you know, what struck me most about your mother was her determination to make it right again and her belief in herself that she could."

"I don't suppose she's thinking that now, not now that we all know about it and hate her for it." Robert, dismayed at the threatening tone in Miranda's voice, decided not to pursue the subject.

A soft breeze started to make goose pimples on Miranda's bare arms.

"Come on." Robert touched her shoulder. "Let me show you your room." He picked up her bag and they walked down the steep garden path. Miranda suddenly had a desire to skip down the hill holding Robert's hand and swinging on it—just as she used to do with her father.

Liddy was beginning to find a way of operating with Hope, despite not having a working arm and ankle. But when she did need help, she found it more comfortable to be helpless with Alex than with Laura. Alex, for his part, found that he was calm and easy with the small scrap of baby and couldn't wait to tell Mungo how competent he was.

"I could make rather a good mother," he said as he changed Hope's nappy in the morning. "I must tell Mungo I don't mind getting pregnant." It started as a light joke, but then, catching sight of his mother's stricken face, he got bogged down in the sentence and tailed off unhappily.

"Sorry, Mum," he mumbled.

Liddy shrugged and managed a halfhearted smile.

Alex went to see Aunt Cyn in her bedroom.

"Oh, you're here, are you? And the other one's here, too, I suppose."

"Yes, but she stayed with someone in the village last night. I'm so sorry about Aunt Cleo. It's very kind of you to put up with us all, Aunt Cyn."

Cyn shrugged. "I don't have any say in the matter. Not until Cleo is buried, anyway." Cyn stumbled over the words. "I suppose you are her family and should be in this house, but that doesn't mean I want you or that I have to be anywhere near you. And," she said sternly, "I don't want to hear anything about what is happening downstairs, is that clear?"

Alex nodded and Cyn leaned out of her chair and patted the end of her bed.

"Now you're here, you'd better sit down and tell me about

your wasted life. I imagine you're not doing anything sensible with it. You never have."

Alex had forgotten how much he liked Aunt Cyn.

"Nope," he said cheerfully. "I've got a wonderful lover, though."

"Oh, shut up, you revolting child. I don't want to hear any of that disgusting rubbish. I'm talking about a career, you stupid boy. You can't rely on being pretty all your life."

"I still want to be an actor. I'm going to do the rounds of the drama schools again in the autumn."

"Don't be so ridiculous. You can't act. If these schools didn't want you last year, they certainly won't want you this year. You've either got it or you haven't—and you haven't."

Alex hardly winced.

Cyn continued. "You've been spoiled by your abominable parents, that's what's wrong with you. You've all been thoroughly indulged, particularly by that father of yours. Where is the other one, anyway—Miranda?" she asked abruptly. "I see she hasn't had the courtesy to come and visit me."

"She's staying with someone in the village. She's too upset to stay here."

"*She's* upset, huh. And not about Cleo, I imagine—doesn't think about anyone else, does she, that one?"

"No, not really. She never has," Alex said sadly.

"I suppose you're the best of a bad lot. You used to make me laugh and you don't cry when I'm beastly to you like Laura does."

"Well, the thing is," Alex said, turning on his warmest smile, "I don't think you're nearly as nasty as you make out to be."

Cyn looked pleased.

"Go away, you horrible boy," she said with a reluctant smile.

Laura rang up several times during the course of the morning until Alex began to lose his good humor with her.

"Laura, we're managing just fine. Go back to the beach, have a day in the sun with the kids and then you can come and check up on us later."

"I'm sorry," Laura said contritely. "I just can't help worrying. I know you're doing wonderfully. I keep trying to ring Dad," she went on mournfully, "but there's no answer. I've even tried Mary, but she hasn't seen him—no one has. He must know about . . . everything, but I don't know exactly what happened when he came down. He must be so unhappy."

"Laura, leave it. What's between Mum and Dad is for them to deal with, not us. He'll be all right, I'm sure he will—just leave it and go and play on the beach."

Alex surprised himself with his unusually commanding tone. "Have an ice cream for me," he added lightly and then put on a silly voice. "I don't suppose I'll have a moment free today. Babies are *so-o* time consuming."

"Oh, grow up, Alex," Laura said crossly.

Actually, Alex thought he *was* being rather grown up.

Watched by Liddy, he tried his hand at bathing Hope. He hated the way his mother was so grateful for everything and so silently penitent. It was unlike her and he wanted to kick-start her, but he couldn't face the explanations and discussion just yet. He was not, he realized, quite as ready as he thought to take on the situation wholeheartedly.

Liddy tried to get Hope to drink from the bottle, but the baby raged against it. Liddy looked down at the little life propped up on the pillows. This life was starting so inauspiciously. Unknown about and uncared for in pregnancy, Hope had come into a family confused and hurt by her arrival, and now her mother couldn't breastfeed her or even cuddle her properly.

"Oh, come on, *please*," she cried in tearful exasperation.

Alex was clearing up after Hope's bath. He knew that there

227

was a bit of him on the outside, watching with admiration and pleasure as he acted the part—lining up the creams tidily, making up the Moses basket with clean sheets and folding vests so tiny that he marveled at the physical development of a human. He glanced across at Liddy.

"Here, let me try," he said, taking Hope off the pillows. "She can probably smell your milk."

"How on earth do you know that?"

Alex grinned. "I've been reading the baby book in the lavatory. I can do babies, I think." He sat by the window and nestled Hope expertly in his arms. She fought him for a few seconds and then the room was filled with the sound of contented sucking.

"Well, *hell*-o. How clever am I, then?" He smiled at his mother.

Alex took a well-fed, satisfied Hope into the garden. He was surprised at how possessive about her he was beginning to feel. He put her under the tamarisk tree—the tree of life, he thought, a good place for her to be. Before he fastened the cat net over the basket, he stroked the sleeping baby's cheek and wondered at her plump, velvety skin—just like the underside of a rich pink rose petal.

Alex weeded away at the herbaceous border, deadheaded the roses and then moved on to edging the flower beds. He had stripped down to shorts and was completely immersed in the job, enjoying the afternoon sun on his back when Miranda, in leggings and singlet, came into the garden.

"Oh, hello, it's you. I thought you never wanted to come near this place," he added unkindly." He stared at Miranda's red, sweaty face. "What on earth have you been doing?"

"Running, of course. What do you think?" She moved cautiously across the grass toward the Moses basket.

"Is it in there?"

"It's not an it, Mirry, it's a she. Hope. Your half sister."

Miranda looked at him in such bewilderment, Alex wondered for a moment whether she realized Hope was a relation at all. She looked into the basket with an expression usually reserved for people looking into a cage of snakes.

"She's rather pretty," she said with surprise. "Aren't they small? How do they survive?"

"Oh, they're much tougher than they look," Alex said airily, pleased to show off his new skills in baby care.

Miranda straightened up and looked at Alex. "You know what Mum said last night, about her being so tired? Well, I had a thought . . ." She trailed off and then changed the subject. "I rang Richard this morning. He's coming down for the funeral."

"Why didn't you come home, the night before last?" Miranda hadn't really meant to attack Richard like that, not immediately, anyway. Nor had she meant to follow it up quickly with, "I'm not staying at the White House, but I know you didn't ring me last night and I wanted to talk to you."

She heard Richard sigh down the phone. He hadn't rung, it was true. He had put it off until he had the reasonable excuse that it was too late in the evening to bother a house that was mourning a death. But she could have telephoned him.

"Oh, Miranda," he said sadly, "shall we start again? Now, how is Aunt Cyn?"

"Oh, she's OK, I think. But Richard, Mum's had a baby. It's not Dad's." Miranda's voice began to rise. "She's made everything *wrong*."

"Miranda, calm down. Are Laura and Alex with you?"

"Yes. Well, Laura's at her holiday cottage today, but Alex is here and no one knows where Dad is. Laura's been trying to ring him. He knows about it, the baby, but he's gone and Mum's hurt her leg and her arm and can't do *anything*. It's horrible, Richard. Will you come down, please?"

It was as though she had forgotten the lines of battle that had been drawn up between them over the past weeks.

"Well, I'm not sure." Richard hesitated. "I've got a heavy few days. I really couldn't get away till the weekend, if then. When's the funeral?"

For a moment Miranda had no idea what Richard was talking about.

"Oh, that. It's on Friday, but you've got to come down as soon as you can, Richard, because I've had this idea. Mum doesn't want the baby. I know she doesn't, she said so. And I thought, why don't we take it? We could, you know. I'm sure we could manage. Don't you think that's a good idea?"

There was silence at the other end of the telephone.

"Richard?" Miranda said uncertainly. "Richard, you'd love it. It's very pretty."

Richard said quietly down the telephone, "Miranda, I'll come down on Friday for the funeral. I promise."

"But what do you think?" she persisted. "You will think about it, won't you? I think it's fate. I think we're meant to have it. I really do."

"We'll talk when I get down there," he said firmly. "Please give my love and sympathy to everyone."

In their London flat, Richard put down the telephone and slumped in his chair. He had loved Miranda so much. Loved the beautiful, sticklike, mercurial creature with a sharp, angry sense of humor and an unfettered imagination—such a contrast to his previous, more mundane relationships. He had always wanted to be needed and Miranda had really needed him. He had been beguiled by her overwhelming vulnerability, and protecting her and helping her to fight her demons had made him feel good. But he had failed and now she had turned into a monster. He was exhausted. He felt as though he had been on a roller coaster for the last few weeks, but that he had now reached the terminal and could go no further.

*   *   *

Alex rang Mungo.

"I'm missing you," Alex said. "It's difficult here. And I want sex."

"Telephone sex?"

"No, real sex."

"Do you want me to come down?"

"Ummm, yes, please," Alex said dreamily.

"Alex, that's not seemly," Mungo reproved. "I think—"

"Mungo," Alex interrupted him. "I've had *such* a good idea. We could have the baby." The words came out in a rush.

"In what way have?" Mungo asked suspiciously.

"We could adopt her. Mum has said she can't face doing it all again, bringing her up and everything and we could look after her."

"I'm not sure we could, you know."

Alex tried a different tack. "It would be a really kind thing to do."

"Could we not find something else to do that would be really kind?" Mungo asked tolerantly, as usual becoming calmer as Alex became more excitable.

"She's so sweet. She's called Hope."

"As in springs eternal, eh?"

"Oh, Mungo." Alex, the quote lost on him, wriggled against the hall table. "Please just think about it. *Please*." He felt a thrill of pleasure as Mungo gave one of his deep fruity chuckles.

"You're hopeless, Alex, you really are. I'll come down to be with you for the funeral, if you like and if that's all right with your family."

"What family?" Alex's voice turned sharp. "This dysfunctional family, which didn't even know it was dysfunctional until a couple of days ago, has splintered into little bits. Dad's not answering the phone, Miranda is more neurotic than ever and won't stay in the house, Laura is in overdrive and Mum just sits around looking morose and battered. It's so awful, Mungo, please come. It's on Friday. No one will care who is at the funeral and who isn't, believe me."

"You got it. One thing though, darling boy. Just please don't get us a baby until we've talked properly. OK?"

Mungo put down the phone, laughing, completely unaware that his lover was deadly serious about the baby.

He idly stroked the dogs panting at his side. "And by the way," he said softly, "I forgot to say, I love you very much, Alex."

Laura rang Fergus. "Fergus, we need to discuss something very important."

There was a pause. Laura imagined Fergus, probably on the farm office telephone and probably half reading the invoices in front of him.

"Children are all right, aren't they?"

"Yes, yes, they're fine. Listen, I think we may have to take over this baby. Mum obviously can't cope."

"Hey, hey, steady on, Laura." Fergus sounded alarmed. "You're not serious, surely? We've got our own family. We can't just take on another child willy-nilly."

"Somebody has got to look after it and we're the only ones in this family who are capable of it. It's really up to us; we've got all the stuff and we've got the room. . . . It'll be nice to have a baby in the house again," she added casually.

"Hang on, hang on. You're going too fast for me. We need to discuss this properly."

"Oh, of course we do, I know that," Laura said impatiently. "I was just preparing you for what might have to happen."

"But, love, I don't understand. What about Martin in all this? Have you talked to your mother? Are you quite sure she wants to give away her child? I really can't believe she would."

"Fergus, Mum is in a *state*. She doesn't know what she's doing, but she can't manage, that's patently obvious."

"It's a bit of a facer this," Fergus said unhappily. "I don't know what to think. I really don't."

"Well, we'll obviously discuss it properly when you come down for the funeral, but it's got to be sorted out pretty quickly."

Fergus sat at the desk long after he had put down the phone, staring at the cattle-feed calendar on the farm office wall in disbelief. What on earth had happened to this normal, sane family? And what was Laura thinking of? The strain of all this must have really got to her. She obviously wasn't thinking straight. So unlike her. He pulled a pile of papers toward him with a sigh and undid his fountain pen. Laura was usually so steady and level-headed; he had always relied on her good sense and understanding of people. This idea of hers was quite uncharacteristic and also, in Fergus's view, complete madness.

Martin emerged from the safety net of Fay the next morning, now as nauseated with himself as he was with Liddy. When he returned home, his mind was blank, empty, completely squeezed dry. Almost without being aware of what he was doing, he walked round the house touching furniture and favorite pieces of china. It was only as he stood by the piano looking at the gallery of photograph frames that he came to think about the children. The horror and the contempt he felt at himself for being so selfish and self-absorbed was matched by the anger he felt for Liddy whose fault, he believed, this was entirely. Looking down at his hand holding a photograph frame, Martin saw that it was clenched and shaking and he knew he had never felt such misery as he did now. Liddy had brought him right down to her level and made him think only of himself and not of his precious Laura, Miranda and Alex. Did they know? How were they feeling? Would Miranda be able to cope? Particularly Miranda, although

Liddy's theory had been that their middle daughter must, in fact, be the toughest of them all to sustain all that anger for so long.

It occurred to Martin that he was already thinking about Liddy in the past.

He telephoned Miranda, but there was no answer. Laura's friend answered the cottage phone and told him that Laura was at the White House. He had a brief conversation with each of his grandchildren, his heart turning over as he listened to their excited babbling—felt their exuberant innocence. Not prepared to ring the White House, Martin dialed Alex's number. Mungo answered cheerily. "Yo-o."

"Oh, um . . . hi. Is that Mungo? It's Martin, Alex's father."

Martin was grateful that Mungo appeared to be neither embarrassed nor sympathetic. "He's gone down to Cornwall with Miranda."

"How are they both? Are they all right?" Martin had to ask.

Mungo thought for a moment. "I haven't seen Miranda, but I've spoken to Alex. He seems to have got over the initial shock." Mungo was keeping the conversation as general as he could.

"Right, good . . ." Martin hesitated, unwilling to drag Mungo into the web of family intrigue. "Look, if you speak to Alex could you tell him . . . tell him I'm driving down to Cornwall tomorrow. I don't know where I'll stay, but I will be at the funeral on Friday. Tell him . . ." Martin could not find the words.

Mungo found them for him.

"I'll tell him you love him, shall I?" he said cheerfully, with no trace of sentimentality.

Martin had tears in his eyes as he put down the phone.

He was going to Cleo's funeral—for his children's sake. He sat down and wrote a short letter to Liddy.

* * *

Alex was pruning the long box hedge. Liddy lay in the sun on a chaise longue and watched him snapping the shears at the long branches.

"Will you read a poem at the funeral tomorrow?" she asked Alex. "I thought, perhaps, John Donne: 'They are all gone into a world of lingering light!' Do you know it?"

Alex shook his head.

"But will you? Do you mind?" Liddy was insistent.

Alex shrugged. "Yes, OK, if you really want me to."

"It's hard to know what to do," Liddy said. "Cyn couldn't care less, as long as we don't sing hymns over Cleo. She is absolutely refusing to come. I thought we should have Handel's *Water Music*. What do you think?"

Alex stopped shearing and looked at her.

"Shouldn't someone speak about Aunt Cleo and her life or something?"

"It should be me," Liddy said unhappily, "but I don't know if I can."

She idly watched the postman come up the path as she tussled with the idea of speaking in front of her family. She had a vision of them all in their chairs, faces upturned to her and anger, disappointment and even hatred in their eyes.

"Cleo was very special to you and you were her nearest living relation," Alex said primly as he made his way over to the postman. "You've known her all your life—you are really the only person who should do it. But," he said unwillingly, as he came back with a handful of letters, "I will do it if you really feel you can't."

"Letter from Dad," he said dispassionately, holding out an envelope to her. His face was expressionless as though he wanted to disassociate himself from whatever would happen after Liddy had opened the letter. But he stayed nearby. He picked up the bug spray he had been using earlier and started spraying the roses.

"Alex, don't do that. Hope will breathe in the spray." Liddy spoke sharply and Alex was taken aback by her tone, shocked even. He had got used to their reversed roles. He was in charge of his mother and of Hope at the moment; he shouldn't be told what to do.

Liddy read the letter and put it back into the envelope. "Your father's coming down for the funeral," she said, her voice carefully without expression.

"Oh, right." Alex was still sulking at his reprimand.

"He is very concerned about you children, but he doesn't mention Hope," Liddy went on quietly, almost to herself. She bent over the basket and held Hope's little hand; the baby's fingers which Alex thought seemed so long and disproportionate, curled around her mother's finger and Alex felt a jolt of something he could only identify as jealousy. But was he jealous of his mother's caress or was he jealous because he wanted the little hand clasped round *his* finger?

Alex found Miranda and Laura sitting at the kitchen table, drinking coffee. Laura had a notebook in front of her, Miranda was watching the seagulls on the roofs below the kitchen window.

"I hate seagulls. Close up, they look so scary."

"I don't know whether any of the village will expect to come back here after the funeral," Laura said, "but we should have tea and cakes ready, I suppose, in case they do—and some wine perhaps." She sighed. "It's all so difficult. Mum isn't doing anything. Aunt Cyn doesn't want to know. The announcement hasn't even been put in the *Times*, you know. How will distant friends know?"

"Laura," Miranda said in a superior voice, "Aunt Cleo was in her nineties and Aunt Cyn hasn't got any friends, so there aren't many people left to come to the funeral."

"But there must be some. I wish Aunt Cyn would involve herself. She would be able to grieve properly then."

"I think you should leave her alone and let her do what she wants." Miranda got up and put her empty mug on the draining board. "You probably have quite a different outlook on death when you're imminently facing it yourself."

"Miranda, you can't say that." Laura looked pained and automatically got up to put the mug in the dishwasher. "I just want it to be nice for her," she went on, "help her through it, but how can I if she doesn't *say?*"

"I really shouldn't worry," Miranda said. "It's only a funeral; the star of the show won't care what happens."

Laura looked at her in distaste. "Really, Miranda."

"Well, it's true. This family has got much more to worry about than whether the village approves of Aunt Cleo's funeral."

Alex broke into their conversation. "Dad won't want to know about the baby, I know he won't, and Mum just isn't able to cope. So"—he paused for effect, hands on hips—"so, Mungo and I are going to take Hope."

His two sisters looked at him.

Miranda took in what Alex had said and felt a tremor of shock. This wasn't right at all.

"No, no," she said. "You can't. Richard and I are going to have her. He wants a baby, he's always wanted one, but I can't be pregnant. We need the baby. It's important. I've spoken to Richard. He's very happy about it."

"Well, I've spoken to Mungo," Alex said. "We've been thinking of having a baby. I'm going to give up my job to look after her."

"How can you?" Miranda scoffed at him. "Mungo is an actor—you'll both be out of work and have no money."

"You hate babies," Alex began to shout at her. "You can't look after one—you haven't even touched Hope. You still call her *it.*"

"Richard will be brilliant with her." Miranda emphasized

her and looked at Alex triumphantly. "Anyway, Richard and I can afford to have help with her. We'll get a nanny."

"She can't be brought up by a nanny, for God's sake."

"Don't be so ridiculous, both of you." Laura's sensible voice cut in between them. "Neither of you can have her; of course you can't. You wouldn't have a clue how to bring her up properly. No, no, it's all arranged. Hope will come to me. It's much better for her. We've got the space, I've got the experience and it will be good for her to grow up with other children. There's no question about it, I was talking to Fergus about it only last night."

The three of them glared at each other round the kitchen table.

Chapter

ELEVEN

Liddy was aware that she was behaving like the victim, although she knew that it was her family who were the real victims and she the aggressor—the cause of their victimization. But her foot was gradually improving and she was beginning to work out a way of doing things with her plastered wrist in an attempt to retrieve command of her life.

She was in the kitchen trying to make up some bottles for Hope; she moved herself around slowly and heavily, using the table and chairs to take her weight.

This is what it will be like when I'm old and infirm and living by myself in some poky basement flat, she thought sorrowfully.

"Here, let me do that." Laura appeared at the kitchen door and dumped a pile of washing on the table. Without waiting for a reply, she took the bottle out of Liddy's hand and continued the task with smooth ease.

Liddy remonstrated feebly, but in the slipstream of Laura's energy, she gave up and sat down.

"I think this is a very good thing," Laura said, waving the bottle. "Much better idea."

"I've never not breastfed my babies," Liddy said sadly.

"You're too tired; it's not good for either of you," Laura said quickly, as if afraid of the conversation moving into territory that would demand some acknowledgment that Hope had the same rights as Liddy's other children. "Anyway," she went on, shaking the bottles vigorously, her back firmly turned toward Liddy, "I've been meaning to say that of course I will take in Hope for you. It will be good for her to be with the other children and I have the time to care for her properly. Now, I suppose I could take her back to the cottage after the funeral, but if you could hold on to her till the end of our three weeks, it would probably be easier."

Liddy's first reaction was that while she understood each individual word Laura spoke perfectly well, when she tried to put them together, she could not digest the sum total of them.

"I'm sorry, Laura, I don't understand what you mean. Why should you have Hope?"

Laura turned round then and faced her mother.

"Neither Miranda nor Alex would be able to cope with her, Mum. They have no experience. Obviously taking her home with me is the best option."

"No," Liddy persevered, stunned by the conversation. "What I mean is, why should anyone have Hope? I've got her."

"Oh, Mum," Laura said patronizingly. "You can't manage a baby, not properly and not on your own. You said as much yourself. No, we can give her a proper family life. She would be brought up as one of ours. I've discussed it with Fergus, of course, and he agrees with me entirely."

"It was none of your business to discuss it with Fergus," Liddy said sharply. She could feel her heart beating hard and she could sense the sweat breaking out on her upper lip. She welcomed her outrage at the presumption of her eldest daughter; apathy left her as she fought to protect Hope. "Someone else having Hope is not and never has been an option. Is that clear?"

Liddy's voice rang out, cold and strong, but Laura wanted to be reasonable.

"Mum." Laura sat down opposite Liddy and put on her helpful voice. "I don't know how this whole thing came about—and I don't want to. But we have to deal with the situation as it is. You said you didn't think you could cope with bringing up another baby. We all heard you say it. And look at you—I'm watching you trying to care for Hope. It's hard work. I can see."

Liddy could feel her momentary surge of strength ebb away under the onslaught of her eldest daughter's bullying.

"Don't be silly, darling. Every new mother is tired and thinks they can't cope. You know that. And I've hurt my ankle and my wrist, which is why it's so difficult for me at the moment."

"But why did you fall down in the first place?" Laura said kindly. "Because you were exhausted. And you might have been carrying Hope when you fell; did you think of that? No, honestly, Mum, you really must think what is best for Hope. We can give her a normal good life and you'll be able to see her grow up and be part of her upbringing, like a granny, like you are with my children. It's best all round—you must see that."

Laura stood up, confident that she had made her point clear enough.

"I'm going to the supermarket to get some things for tomorrow. I expect some people will want to come back here afterwards. I'll pick up some stuff for Hope, if you make me a list of what we need."

We, Liddy thought. It's already what *we* need, and Laura wants it to become *I*, and then she will have taken over completely.

Laura paused in the doorway. "I'll just go up and ask Aunt Cyn if she wants anything. Mum, when you've had time to think about it properly, you'll realize how sensible it is—for everyone. Of course, when she's old enough, we would have to tell Hope the truth."

"But she's my baby," Liddy said obdurately, still not believing that she was having to say this. "She's mine and you're not having her, Laura."

Laura stood over her mother and spoke gently and earnestly. "I'm just saying it's not fair on Hope; you'll be an elderly single mother. You don't even know where you're going to live. I really want to help. She'd be so happy with us. The farm is a perfect place to bring up children—so much freedom. We would all love her as though she were our own. Think about it, Mum, I'm sure you'll come to see that it's the answer—for everyone."

Liddy wondered when, exactly, in the sequence of events, it had become received wisdom that Martin would definitely not be back and that she would definitely never be able to cope.

Miranda came into the sitting room as Liddy was trying to make Hope accept the bottle. She came in slowly as though unsure of her welcome and stood by the window, her long fingers playing with the curtains.

"Are you all right at Robert's?" Liddy asked politely.

Miranda didn't answer the question.

"I can't help being angry," she said gruffly instead.

Liddy recognized Miranda's defensive apology—she had been on the receiving end of so many. This one had come unexpectedly and it was very welcome.

"No, I know. I am sorry, darling—I am sorry about it all . . ." She would have continued, but Miranda leaned forward to look at Hope, who was wriggling in anger at still being offered a cold rubber teat instead of a warm nipple.

"She doesn't look very happy."

"I can't really feed her myself. I've not got enough milk," Liddy said.

Miranda shuddered. "It's a horrible idea, breastfeeding."

"No, it's not; it's perfectly natural and much better for the baby," Liddy said sadly.

Miranda continued to hover above her. She had something to say.

"Mum," she started slowly, "you know Richard has always wanted a baby? Well, we had this idea that perhaps we could take"—here she gestured toward the baby—"and look after it for you. I just can't be pregnant, you see. I'd be hopeless at it—you know me." Miranda began to speak fast. "And Richard is angry with me about it and I want him to stay with me. It's just this baby thing that comes between us all the time and I thought, well, we could have the baby. I mean, it would be good for both of us, wouldn't it? You don't want to be looking after a baby at your age and Richard and I can afford to give it a good life. We'd get a really good nanny and Richard will be a brilliant father. We could be a real family." Miranda's eyes had started shining as the idea gathered momentum. "What do you think?"

"I think you're . . ." Liddy almost said *mad,* but from old habit stopped herself before Miranda could use the word to wreak havoc. "I think you have misunderstood. I have no intention of giving you Hope."

"No, of course not." In a fraction of the time Liddy took to speak, Miranda had become tight and angry; her chin was up, her head tossed as she scowled at her mother. "Because in this family I have never been given anything I really, really wanted."

Liddy felt almost winded at the apparent injustice of Miranda's statement. Was that really true? Did Miranda really believe that she had been missed out? But then it didn't matter if Liddy felt it was not true: if Miranda felt it, then it was valid. Liddy wanted to put her arms round her, hold her tight and squeeze out all the spike and hurt.

"Mira—"

Miranda would not let her in. "I suppose you'll give it to

Laura; you trust *her*. Or even Alex—you'd give him anything *he* wanted, you always have. Just don't bother about what *I* want. My relationship is going to break up. Richard will leave me, I know he will. If I had the baby it would be all right again, but I don't suppose you care, do you? You never have. Why start now?" Miranda flounced out, her body rigid with fury.

Liddy was left breathless. Hope looked silently up at her with big blue eyes—even she seemed to have been subdued by Miranda's outburst.

She should have expected it. First Laura, then Miranda—of course Alex would follow. He never let his sisters get away with something he wanted.

He sought out Liddy, who was sitting in the garden. She had, for the first time, picked up a book that she'd found in the study bookcase. Only when she put it facedown on her knees, as she saw Alex walk across the lawn, did she notice that the author was Robert Trevland.

"It's a beautiful day, isn't it?" Alex said chattily, as he flung himself onto the grass at her feet. "How are the wounds?"

"Getting better, I think."

"Good, good," he said abstractedly. He plucked at the grass. "Do you think Dad will come back?" he asked casually.

"He's coming back for the funeral."

"No, I meant . . . you know, you and him?"

Liddy shrugged and moved her head in what could have been a shake or a nod.

"He would if you didn't have Hope, wouldn't he?"

"Alex, darling, I really don't know. He and I will have to sort it out. When his anger has died down."

"Mum . . . ," Alex started slowly, "I have an idea."

Et tu, Brute, Liddy thought sadly.

Alex began to talk bouncily.

"You see, it's a bit of a coincidence actually. Mungo and I

244

have been discussing the possibility of having a baby. The idea was to find a female friend who would have it for us, but it occurred to me that we could take little Hope here. I know she wouldn't biologically be either of ours, but she is my half sister and I know we could give her *such* a happy life. I mean, you wouldn't have any hang-ups about her being brought up by two gay men, would you? Not if I was one of them?"

Alex's confidence left Liddy speechless.

"What do you think?" Alex pursued her. "We would look after her between us; I know we could do it. And you could come and see us whenever you want. She would be like your granddaughter. You could have all the fun of her without wearing yourself out when you should be beginning to take life easy. And you and Dad could get yourselves together again. You know you want that and I bet he does, too—you just need some space. And you could go back to work and everything would be normal again. Don't you think that's a *really* good idea?"

Alex was looking at her beguilingly, as he always did, so sure that she would give him exactly what he desired.

"Alex, no. I can't. What are you all thinking? I've never said I planned to give Hope away."

"You said you couldn't cope, you did. You said you were so tired and that you couldn't imagine the next eighteen years. I have the perfect answer for all of us." He appeared mystified that his mother could not see this obvious solution.

"No, Alex, no, no, no," Liddy said, putting her hands over her ears in a childlike gesture. "I didn't mean it in that way. I have just had a baby—of course I'm tired. But I'm not that old, for God's sake. I can manage. I *want* to manage," she said desperately.

Alex stood up. He was, she noticed, typically unthwarted by her refusal.

"Think about it, Mum," he said, echoing Laura's words. "It's a brilliant idea, it'll work for all of us, I promise you."

After he left, Robert's book slipped off Liddy's knees as she tried to make sense of her three adult children. Only Miranda had not dissembled at all. She wanted the baby wholly for her own ends and she had demanded honestly. Laura as always assumed, so sure that she was right. Alex could not believe that he wouldn't get what he wanted eventually—and yet he, the child who since his teens had had a nonrelationship with his father, had been the only one who'd had a thought for Martin.

Had her three children taken over her life and was this to be her punishment for destroying their security?

Miranda wandered into Robert's kitchen, a cozy, cabinlike room full of wood and clean white machinery. Robert was having lunch. A loaf of bread and a bowl sat on the table, Radio 4 played in the background and a large kitchen clock ticked loudly over the Raeburn. Miranda suddenly longed to be properly part of this quiet place.

"Hello, you," he said, looking up at Miranda.

"Am I interrupting anything?"

"Nope, not at all. Soup, bread and cheese, followed by coffee is what I'm looking at. Does that interest you at all?"

"No, I won't, thank you, I'll have some coffee with you later," Miranda said stiffly. She hated being offered food without warning.

Robert gave her a quick glance. "Right. Well, come and sit down at least and talk to me while I eat. Where have you been this morning? I heard you go out."

Miranda remained silent, twisting her hands in her lap while Robert ate his soup.

"Had a bit of a row with Mum, actually," she said eventually. Robert nodded encouragingly. "You see, I thought that my partner and I could take the baby off her hands. When we arrived, she said she was so tired and that she couldn't face the future, so I thought it would solve our problem."

"Problem?"

"Yes. The thing is, Richard—he's my partner; we've lived together for two years—he really wants a baby and I absolutely don't. I might, I suppose, just about be able to handle having a live baby, if you know what I mean. It's not that I *hate* children. I just don't want one taking over my life. And most particularly not from the inside. But I can't tell anyone how bad I feel inside. I don't want anyone to know—they'll hate me. And I *don't* want to be pregnant—ever. So, I had this idea that we could take Mum's baby."

"What does Richard think?"

"He said we should discuss it when he comes down, but I know he just longs to have babies and I think this is the perfect solution."

"What did your mother say?"

Miranda liked the way Robert preferred to get the whole picture before he spoke on the subject. He asked a question, received an answer and then asked another.

"Oh, she won't let me have it. She'll give it to Laura, or Alex even, rather than to me, I know. They both want it as well. She thinks Laura will look after it properly, but she can never resist Alex. Either way I won't get a look in—as usual."

"Perhaps your mother wants to keep her baby."

"She said she didn't. She said she was too tired and too old. And Dad has left her, so she'd be on her own."

"Would you be able to look after the baby?"

Miranda frowned. "Obviously we would have full-time help. Richard will love looking after it at weekends and," she added aggressively, "I might even get to like being a mother eventually, you don't know."

"I don't," Robert agreed, "and it's possible that you might, but do you *really* want to, that was my question."

"Richard would love it. And I love Richard. He might not stay with me if I keep refusing to get pregnant."

Robert looked at Miranda over a spoonful of soup. "But is that fair on the baby? Or the two of you, come to that?"

"Oh, nothing is ever fair," Miranda said with a catch in her voice. "Not for me. Why can't I want to have babies like everyone else?"

"Oh, my dear girl." Robert put down his spoon, stretched across the table and held on to Miranda's arm. For once she didn't move away. "You're not alone—lots of people don't want children. Me for one."

"But you said you had children."

"Two. Two boys conceived under duress. My wife wanted them as strongly as I didn't want them. She would have left me if I hadn't agreed, so I did. It was the most foolish thing to have done. It is my greatest regret. Our relationship never, ever recovered. She died with us both being angry at each other. I love my children, of course I do, but I couldn't help resenting them and their dependence on me. Good Lord, I could only just about look after myself. I am a very selfish man, Miranda. Are you selfish?"

The question was asked in such a calm and measured voice, Miranda answered in kind, without thinking.

"Yes, I suppose I am. We're all selfish in our family. But you know, I have to work so hard to make *me* work, if you see what I mean. You don't know what it's like. I've always been looked after by people. I certainly can't look after somebody else, because I have to spend all my time concentrating on myself so that I can be like other people."

Robert got up and put the kettle on. Bonnie, who had been sleeping at his feet, stood up, too, and looked expectantly at him and he pushed her aside with his knee.

"Do you like animals?" he asked abruptly.

"I don't know," she said simply. "I've never really thought."

"I don't much," Robert said, "but I got Bonnie to stop me becoming a mad old man all by myself. The boys come to see me occasionally but not often, and I wanted to test myself to see if I could be selfless when it came to somebody else—if I could look after somebody without losing anything of myself."

"That's it," Miranda broke in. "That's it. I know what you mean. I'm frightened of losing me in someone else. I haven't got any of me to spare for anyone else really," she added sadly.

"The thing about a dog though, I found," Robert went on, "is that it never makes *emotional* demands on you, so in the end it's not a very good test. It's very easy to see to someone's physical needs, but it's when they require your mind that it becomes complex and fatiguing. So, you see," he said regretfully, "I've left it too late. I've settled into being a selfish, self-contained man locked away inside myself with no hope of getting out."

"I never *want* to be selfish," Miranda said miserably. "This is me *not* being selfish. I'm doing this for Richard. He needs to have a baby . . . I'm sorry, I shouldn't be going on to you about all this—"

"No, I'm pleased you did." Robert put a cup of coffee in front of Miranda and pushed a jug of milk and a sugar bowl toward her. "It rather redeems my behavior toward your mother. I started being a friend to her, but I didn't want to discuss the nitty-gritty of her problem. It wasn't real to me, you see. Once again, I was outside looking in, an uninvolved observer." He talked in a melancholy monotone. "Always uninvolved and shutting people out who want to get near." He paused and looked at Miranda questioningly and she nodded slowly.

"And then," he went on, "when the baby was born and Cleo died, and when your elder sister found out about the baby, it all seemed suddenly very real and very complicated and I backed away. I was terrified of being asked for something that I couldn't give. I couldn't cope with a real life drama. I write detective fiction. I'm not so good with the real world. I'm too selfish to give my mind to anyone. And that," he finished, "is why I'm a lonely old man."

They sat together in silence. Miranda studied the man opposite her and wondered how old he was. Unbidden, a thought came into her head—she wondered what he would be like when making love.

"I'm nearly sixty," he said, uncannily reading her thoughts. She hoped he hadn't read the last bit. "And you're what, twenty-six?"

"Twenty-eight."

"I'm nearly thirty years older than you then." Miranda detected a note of sadness in his voice. "And today I wish I were younger."

Laura met Fergus at the station. He looked out of place as he alighted from the train—diminished and insignificant as though, by using public transport, all status had been taken away from him.

"The children are on the beach with Melissa. I thought we might find a little pub on the way home and have a drink," Laura said.

"Good idea." Fergus automatically moved toward the driver's seat of the car and then, changing his mind, went round to the passenger side. "Mother sends her love and her condolences. She's staying at the house for a couple of nights"—he smiled affectionately—"delighted to be back at the farm, but I've told her to keep away from the office . . ."

Laura let him ramble on until she found a pub.

"We should do this more often," she said, when they were sitting in the garden with drinks in front of them.

"We should," agreed Fergus, so reasonably that Laura couldn't bear it any longer.

She had tried to be gentle, she had bitten back the words that were just aching to spill out of her as soon as she saw him, but Fergus, agreeing to something that he would obviously never sustain, unplugged the cork.

"Fergus, we have to take the baby—Hope," she corrected herself. "Mum is absolutely desperate and we can help her out. Miranda and Alex think they should have her, but that is ridiculous, and I've told them so. They just think it's a romantic idea. Neither of them know how to bring up a baby—not like we do."

Fergus put out a hand to stop Laura's rush. "Laura, Laura, Laura, calm down. It's all right. I know what this is all about. Since you telephoned, I've been thinking a lot and I've come up with a solution."

Laura felt a tremor of heady elation ripple through her. It was going to be all right after all. She had thought Fergus didn't understand, but he did. In her head she was taking out the carefully wrapped bundles of baby clothes and organizing them into neat piles in the small chest of drawers that was still decorated with nursery transfers. She was painting the little bedroom next to theirs, scrubbing out the family pram and she was wondering if they still had the old stair gate.

Fergus was talking. "I know you've been a bit tense lately and I'm not at all surprised now that I know what has been going on with your mother. And I know you feel a bit sad and redundant now that the children have gone away to school and Rebecca's out all day. So"—he looked at her triumphantly—"I've been working on a plan to expand your ice cream business."

Laura stared at him, dumbfounded. He wasn't *really* saying this, was he?

Fergus bent over and scrabbled in his bag. Laura looked at the top of his head, at the little line of dandruff along his parting and the line of pale skin at the back of his neck where the sun never reached. She suddenly felt he was a complete stranger to her. He sat up and flourished a paper folder. His face was smiling and glowing with enthusiasm.

"Here they are. I've been doing some business forecasts and cash-flow charts. I thought you might like to study them while you're down here. It would mean some initial expenditure on the old milking shed to increase the dairy area, and eventually you would need, I hope, to take on some extra help, possibly part-time to begin with—"

Rage, resentment and hurt began to bubble up in Laura and she moved quickly to suppress it.

"You're not even beginning to understand the situation, Fergus," she said in a controlled, curt voice as she got to her feet, "but we can't talk about this now. I promised the children that you'd be back in time for their tea. Come *on*." Laura temporarily packed away the conversation.

"I keep telling you, I really don't want to hear about anything that is happening downstairs." Cyn was adamant and refusing to move.

"Please come down," Liddy begged. "I don't want you to feel you can't come downstairs."

"Can't? Can't?" Cyn was outraged. "Of course I can come down. It is my house, Lydia, in case that has slipped your mind. The thing is, I won't. Not while your dreadful family are all flapping about like hysterical peahens. All Laura can do is come and tell me about paste sandwiches and cups of tea for the village. Why should I give the village a cup of tea? They've never given me anything. They don't care about me; they've never liked me. They'd much rather I had been the one to die, not Cleo. I might as well die. There is no point in me living now. I couldn't care less what Laura gives them all to eat; she can poison them for all I care. All they're coming for is to nose and poke round the house."

"Come downstairs for a little," Liddy begged. "Laura's picking up Fergus, Miranda's staying with Robert Trevland and Alex is outside gardening."

"I suppose they're all making a fuss about this baby thing, are they?" Cyn suddenly shot at her.

Liddy felt a desperate need to talk.

"They all want her. They want to take Hope away from me. Each one thinks that they can give her a better life and I'm beginning to think that maybe they're right." As she spoke, Liddy could already hear Cyn saying contemptuously, "Well, let them then."

But she didn't.

"Oh, Lydia, do stop being so feeble," Cyn said tetchily. "God help you if you had had to live through the war. You've got no backbone, any of you. The trouble with you lot now is that you all seem to have the time and the inclination to think about yourselves and that's all you ever do: worry about this, worry about that, read about it, talk about it, watch it on television. It's boring and self-indulgent. You think you're all *so* special nowadays. Everything is a drama, everything is *oh so* important in your own lives. But *everything*, my dear Lydia, good and bad, passes in the end if you just get on with life, believe me. 'Play the ball as it lies,' my father used to say and he was a proper man, not like these namby-pamby men you get nowadays. That baby is your daughter. I presume you must love her—that's what mothers do, apparently. Stop being so unspeakably moist, Lydia. Stop letting everyone else run your life. Just pull yourself together and get on with it." As rapidly as she had started, Cyn came to a halt and waved her hand dismissively. "Oh, I really can't be bothered with you all. I don't want to know about it. Why don't you all start thinking about Cleo for a change? Don't you care? Any of you? Miranda hasn't even been to see me, you know, but then she always was even more selfish than the rest of you. Get back to your vile family and tell Avril I don't want any tea. I can't be bothered. Why should I eat now?" Cyn's lips were shaking and her eyes were wet.

*   *   *

Much later, Liddy passed Cleo's bedroom. The door was open and she peered in. Cyn was sitting on a chair pulled up to the bed which was covered in old photographs laid out carefully like a collage.

Cyn looked up as Liddy came in.

"She was such a beautiful young girl," she said sadly. "I don't know what she thought she was doing with me—she could have done so much better, you know."

She held up a tattered black-and-white photograph and stared at it. "We had been sharing a flat for three years"—her voice was low, as though she was talking to herself—"when I went off to live in north London with a friend. It was just after the war. Cleo never made a fuss." Cyn glared briefly at Liddy. "We didn't in those days. She stayed in the flat by herself and got on with her life. Then one day I came back. She never reproached me—we just went back to how it was. That's why we ended up in this ghastly place. Cleo always wanted to live here, you know. We used to come down to the village for holidays and Cleo was passionate about it. I could just about stand a fortnight here—then I missed pavements and the theater. She always wanted a garden like her mother's, so when we retired I knew that I owed it to her to come down here and have one—because all those years ago, she had forgiven me when she really didn't have to. She was the most gracious person, Lydia, that either you or I will ever know. I want her back."

Cyn suddenly poked Liddy with Cleo's stick. "You lot don't know anything."

Liddy crept away, leaving Cyn with her photographs and her memories, and wondered if perhaps she really didn't know anything anymore.

The demands of her adult children came back to Liddy in the middle of the night as she tried to fulfill her newborn baby's demands.

It should be easier to satisfy Hope's needs, she thought unhappily as she tried to bring up the baby's wind. Hope had taken the bottle, but now her back was arched, rigid with locked air and her face was mottled with her screaming. Liddy ached in her bones with deep fatigue; tears of frustration ran down her cheeks and she was frightened of how easily she might have shaken Hope in impotent rage, if she hadn't got one arm in plaster. The strength of her hopelessness scared her. Hope suddenly relinquished the battle and gave in to exhaustion. She lay against the pillows and closed her eyes, her chest pumping in and out in breaths that seemed too big for her little body.

Liddy, drained, lay beside her in the welcome silence and thought about the future—the milestones of a child: the first day at school she would be so much older than all the other mothers, they would assume she was the grandmother. She would be sixty-eight when Hope left school. Liddy moved along Hope's life: baby-sitters, measles, tea parties, sleepovers, summer holidays, parents' open evenings, after-school activities, loud music, drugs, boyfriends, exams, staying out late. Would she have the energy or the patience to bring up a child on her own? Looking down at Hope lying like a starfish, open and vulnerable, beside her, Liddy wondered whether her children were not right after all. How could she manage? She would be so alone. She wanted Martin.

Woozy with weariness, Liddy's thoughts grew foggy.

She *could* let one of her other children bring up Hope. She could imagine the immediate relief and the freedom, the mountain that stood in front of her reduced to a simple plateau. But why did they want Hope? And which child had the greater right to her and which the greater need of her?

Laura thinks it would be most sensible for her to have Hope. Perhaps it would. There was an established family structure into which Hope could be slotted with no upheaval. Laura has a great sense of duty, but she wants this baby badly. Is this, in some way, connected to Rebecca? Or to Jake and Tamsin going off to school? Laura wants Hope to be a replacement. Why should Hope be a replacement? Then there was Miranda: the daughter that she had always tried to please, for whom she tried to make things simple. Had she, by doing that, Liddy wondered now, prevented Miranda seeing that it was only she who could make herself happy? Could Hope be the one last thing that she could give Miranda that might just make her happy and stable? But would Miranda cope with a child? She talks of a nanny, but why should Hope be brought up by a nanny? Richard would love and cherish her, but she would have to cope with a mother who might pass on to Hope all her own insecurities, anger and self-hatred.

And Alex, dear, dear Alex. Half asleep, Liddy found herself smiling as she thought of him, so warm, so giving and so loving of Hope—the only one who has shown no anger toward her, either suppressed or overt. He seems suddenly so grown up. But then maybe there was a hidden agenda deep inside her son. There was, she knew, a deep resentment inside Alex that Martin had never openly accepted his homosexuality. It wasn't that Martin disapproved—not at all. He had just never felt the need to talk about it, but Alex, bound up in his sexuality and coming to terms with it himself, never understood that. Martin and Alex had been inseparable until Alex became adolescent, but then they had slowly and inexorably drifted apart, not in anger nor disappointment with each other, just through omission and misunderstanding. So does Alex want Hope to make his own proper family: to prove to his father that he could be as good a parent as he and that he could sustain it through Hope's life? Why should Hope be brought up as part of a competition? Liddy was too tired to sleep. Her muddled thoughts pounded around her head till she wondered if she was on a sort of mental loop. And what about

Barney? Should she try to find him? Liddy looked down at the sleeping baby in her arms. One day Hope would want to know her real father and maybe it was right that he should know that she existed. Would Barney want Hope? Would he want to live with Liddy? She didn't want to live with Barney, or alone. She wanted to live with Martin, but Martin and Hope together was now, perhaps, no longer a possibility. She must, *must* do the right thing for Hope.

Images of Hope revolved wildly in Liddy's mind—a happy Hope smiling, in turn, with Laura, Miranda and Alex; a wretched Hope with herself—round and round went the misty pictures, becoming more confused and irrational until she had completely lost all vision of the right thing for Hope.

In the few hours that Liddy slept, before being woken by Hope, wet and hungry on the pillow beside her, she dreamt that Cleo was a baby, sitting on Barney's lap and trying to read a school report upside down.

Chapter

TWELVE

Jake sat on the hard wooden chair and gazed at the coffin which held his great-great-great-aunt Cleo. He wondered what she looked like inside. Would she be wearing clothes or would she be wearing those white sheet things that wound round you? He remembered Aunt Cleo as being very pale and smelling nice. He didn't suppose she still smelled nice now.

All Mum's family were here, except Aunt Cyn. He was a bit nervous with Aunt Cyn; he didn't like the way she had crackly circles of brown skin round her eyes and the way her makeup went into deep orange lines on her face. She drew her own eyebrows, too. She looked like an ugly doll and her smile often wasn't a proper one.

Aunt Cleo, though, she was always kind and absolutely no one else at school had an aunt that was so many greats.

Jake had never been to a funeral before, and he knew he shouldn't be, but he was excited about the experience. He would tell his friend Paul about it next term. This was a strange place, sort of like a church, but also like the dinner hall at school. They had been sitting here for quite a long time while other people arrived. There was some sad music playing and everyone was looking smart—except for him and his sisters. They had only got seaside clothes with them and Tam and Becs looked all sunshiny in their flowery trousers and T-shirts. Becs had wanted to wear her bright red sun hat this morning and Mum had shouted at her.

It was a funny holiday this one, a bit spooky really. Mum was really stressed out and she kept disappearing. Granny had a baby. Jake thought a bit about that. It was puzzling him; grandmothers don't have babies, so why did his have one? No one seemed pleased to see the baby.

Uncle Richard had winked at Jake when he came in, but now he was just sitting there beside Aunt Miranda, looking sad and staring at the coffin. Jake thought he was probably thinking about Aunt Cleo because he was that sort of person.

Dad was sitting next to Rebecca and trying to make her sit still and there was an empty chair beside her for Mum who was standing at the back. Dad looked like he always did when he had to sit still in a suit, sort of uncomfortable and fidgety and a bit cross that he wasn't in his dirty blue jersey and big gum boots and out on the farm.

Granny and Grandpa both looked quiet and sad and they weren't sitting next to each other, which was odd. Granny had a *bona* big plaster on her arm and a bandage round her leg. Jake wondered where the baby had got to.

Uncle Alex was sitting next to his friend Mungo. When Jake had first met Mungo, he'd said, "Don't you dare call me uncle." So he never did. He liked Mungo, except he thought that Mungo felt perhaps he should be more grown up than he was. He was much more grown up at school, which was all right now, but when he was at home it was easier to be like Mum wanted him to be.

There was some rustling at the back and then Mum came to sit beside Dad. She patted Becs. His mother was a great patter.

Uncle Alex got up and stood in front of them. He didn't

look at the coffin at all, even when he was talking about Aunt Cleo, which Jake thought was rather impolite. He said how much everyone loved Aunt Cleo and what a happy life she had had. Jake wondered how Uncle Alex knew that. He said that everyone should be quiet for a minute to think about her and about Aunt Cyn.

Jake looked at his hands while everyone was silent. If he swiveled his eyes, he could see Tamsin pretending to play the piano on her knees.

He wondered if they should be crying.

Then Uncle Alex said a long poem, the sort of poem Jake supposed he would do in an English lesson when he was in Year 10 or something. He didn't understand a word of it.

There was a bit of a silence; someone coughed and most people fidgeted on their chairs. It was all a bit embarrassing, really. Uncle Alex looked at Granny, who nodded at him and then the music came on again and the curtains at one end of the coffin opened and Aunt Cleo in her box slowly slid away. He wondered if the bunches of flowers on the top would be burnt as well. It made him feel a bit sick. He wanted Tamsin to feel the same.

"She's being burnt now," he whispered.

Tamsin looked at him and he was quite pleased to see that she looked rather alarmed.

"What, *here?*"

Jake wanted to tell her about how there would be a big fire just the other side of the curtains and how they might smell Great-Aunt Cleo burning; he would say it smelt like the roast pork smell of Sunday lunch, but then he saw his mother glaring at him.

It wasn't at all like being in church because no one seemed to know what to do. He liked proper church; he liked the way there was always someone who was in charge and everything happened the same way every Sunday. But here everyone seemed to be waiting for someone else to do something. Then a man from the back came forward and led them out through a different door, by where the coffin had been. Everyone was walking with their heads down and no one said anything.

Tamsin whispered that she didn't want to go past the flames, so Jake made her walk on the other side of him and he felt good about being not scared and protective. Everyone hung around outside looking at the flowers. He noticed that Aunt Cleo didn't have enough flowers to fill the space that said Cleo Nye and he felt sad for her; it was a bit like having a party and no one coming to it. The grown-ups were talking and shaking hands with other people who he didn't know; it was a bit boring. Becs kept trying to pick the flowers. The sun was very hot and he wanted to go to the beach now like a proper summer holiday. Dad was going to take them back after this; Mum had said they didn't have to go to the party afterwards and Dad had promised that he was going to come to the beach with them and Jake was going to show him how good he was at bodysurfing.

Granny came up to talk to them. She was different than she'd been that day when they had seen her on their way to the cottage. She hardly noticed them then, and he remembered thinking she looked scared but he couldn't think why. Today she was more like Granny usually was. He liked Granny better than Granny Viv because Granny Viv was always telling him what was expected of him and Granny let him make jewelry; he liked using the soldering thing. He thought he might do design and technology for GCSE if he was allowed.

Rebecca held on to Granny and wouldn't let her go. It was very hot and very boring standing here; Jake just longed for his dad to drive them off to the beach.

Granny gave Rebecca a flower from one of the bunches and Mum came up and looked cross. She told them to go and get in the car and then she started bossing Granny, too.

It was, Jake thought as he raced his sisters to the car, as though Mum was now in charge of Granny and he found that very odd. It must be something to do with this new baby.

Something gave way inside Liddy as she watched the coffin disappear behind the curtains. When women give birth, their bodies give the baby one last shot of hormones: some female babies have a little spot of blood in their vaginas like a period; sometimes little boys are born with a tiny erection; it's like a kick start and for Liddy, Cleo's final journey, her final goodbye, her disintegration into a small urn of ashes made something unblock inside her—as though she were starting up again like an engine that had lain idle and had now burst into life.

Liddy had felt a jolt of relief when she saw Martin come into the crematorium; it was followed almost immediately by a crumbling sadness and feeling of rejection as she watched him carefully choose a chair within the family circle, but well away from where she was sitting. She saw him look twice at her still grazed face and she saw him take in the plastered wrist. He acknowledged her with a tight movement of his lips. Liddy looked round at her family and wondered if this could be the last time that they were all together.

She watched Laura being the gracious hostess at the door, turning back occasionally to look at her family. Fergus had his serious occasion face on and he was concentrating on stopping Rebecca from fidgeting.

When Robert arrived she noticed Miranda acknowledge him with a smile. Richard looked pale and remote and Liddy had the impression that he had already absented himself from the family. She stared at the panoramic view of Cornish hills framed by the large window that took up the whole wall in front of them. Cleo would have loved to look through the window at her precious Cornish countryside; she would have loved the flowers that Alex had so carefully cut from her garden, fashioned into simple bunches and placed on top of her coffin.

Liddy looked over at Alex. She had seen him and Mungo greet each other when Mungo had arrived. Unembarrassed, they had hugged and kissed each other and Liddy had watched Alex's body language change. He became floppy and acquiescent in his lover's embrace and she marveled, yet again, at how her son—the lotus-eater—had in the last few days so manfully responded to looking after her.

Tears poured down Liddy's cheeks as her last vestige of childhood disappeared through the curtains with Cleo. When it was over she sat for a while, feeling the emptiness inside her change slowly into something powerful. It was Mungo who came over to her and helped her out of the building; the tears continued to pour silently down her cheeks, cleansing her and renewing her. Out in the bright sunlight, she felt reborn and suddenly bold and vigorous; the mist had rolled away and she felt a clear control of her life.

"Back to tea with the Borgias then," she said to Mungo with a grin.

There was a surprising amount of people squashed into the sitting room. On the surface, almost on automatic pilot, Laura was wondering if there would be enough food to go round. Inside, she was desperately wanting to be with Fergus on the beach. They needed to finish their important conversation. She knew she mustn't waste her energy on the rage she had felt about the silly ice cream business. That anger had settled in a place buried inside her and now she was anxious for everyone to leave so that she could return to Fergus and calmly explain to him, yet again, why it would be the natural and best thing for them to take on Hope. She truly believed that she could make him understand. She would appeal to his sense of duty. And the arrangements had to be made immediately, before it became messy for the whole family, particularly for Mum. It was absolutely ludicrous, Laura thought, as she walked through the room with a tray of teacups, that Miranda and Alex should even think of having Hope. Look at them both, not handing round the tea and cakes as they should be; just behaving, as usual, like guests.

Of Richard there was no sign, which surprised Laura. She could usually rely on him to be there for family occasions. And where was Dad? He had looked simply dreadful at the crematorium. Alex and Mungo were talking to somebody from the village over by the sofa and they kept touching each other and smiling private smiles. Laura was disappointed to see Alex reverting to his usual silly self now that Mungo had appeared. She felt Alex had really proved himself with Hope, though that, of course, in no way meant that he should ever think of having her permanently.

Laura took her empty tray back to the kitchen. Avril was pouring out tea and piling sandwiches on plates. Laura automatically rearranged them onto another plate and, intent on the job, didn't see Avril roll her eyes at her.

"You should be in there, Avril," she said, nodding toward the sitting room. "None of us knows the people from the village."

Avril wrinkled her nose. "Nah, I'd rather be in here. Anyway, I'm going to take some tea to Cyn. She's just sitting there, all dressed in black and not even her television on." Avril's little face creased in concern. "I'm ever so worried about her. When you've all gone and that, she'll be so lonely. I know she says she hates you all, but she doesn't mean it really. You're all she's got now." Avril smiled affectionately. "She's ever so fond of Alex."

It's always Alex, Laura thought irritably, as she pushed a cat off the draining board. "Yes, well," she said briskly, "I expect Mum will stay down with her for a while." After all, Laura wondered to herself, where else would she go?

Mungo came into the kitchen and Laura introduced him to Avril. In a beige, collarless linen suit, white open-necked shirt and expensive trainers, Laura thought he had dressed like a rock star, not like someone attending a family funeral.

"I've been sent in for a few bottles of wine and some beer. It seems more popular than tea," he said cheerfully.

Laura pursed her lips and silently removed some bottles of wine and beer from the fridge. She fossicked in a drawer, looking for an opener.

"Here, I'll open them." Mungo took the beer and couldn't resist grinning at Laura. "Give them to me. I'll open them with my teeth."

Laura raised her eyebrows and flounced out of the room with a tray of tea.

"A bit uptight that one sometimes," Avril remarked.

"Just a bit," Mungo agreed. "Want a drink?"

Avril nodded. "I'll have some beer and I think I'll take Cyn up her gin—she might prefer that to tea."

Alex bounded into the kitchen. "Have you met Mungo, Av? He is my true love." Alex laughed happily at them both.

"Laura introduced us," Avril said, responding with an affectionate smile.

"With difficulty, I expect," Alex said cheerfully.

"She did look as though her mouth was full of feathers," agreed Avril. She picked up a small tray. "I'm going upstairs to be with Cyn, since no one else seems to be thinking of her. You can manage down here, can't you?"

Left alone, Alex turned to Mungo. "Well, what do you think then?"

Mungo looked mystified. "About what, specifically?"

"The baby idea, of course." Alex spoke impatiently, as though Mungo were being deliberately obtuse. "What do you think?"

A genuine look of distress crossed Mungo's face.

"Oh, God, Alex, I am sorry. I really hadn't realized that you were serious." He spoke quietly and sadly. "I don't honestly think—"

Alex heard what Mungo was beginning to say, but he refused to listen. "It's just meant to be, I know it is. You wait till you see her. She's absolutely adorable."

"But what about your mother? I really can't believe she is the sort of person who wants to give her own baby away. Does she know you want Hope?"

"Of course," Alex said blithely. "And she is upset and a bit doubtful, too. She would be, wouldn't she, but I know she'll agree in the end. I mean what else can she do? Apart from the fact that she's exhausted at the very idea of bringing up another child, Dad will never come back while she has Hope." Alex's face darkened as he remembered his father. "Have you seen how awful he looks, I feel sorry for him." Mungo frowned at him gently and took a swig of beer. "Just at the moment, I think you should feel sorry for all your family," he said unexpectedly. "The funny thing is that from where I'm standing you actually all love each other very much. You're a very strong and united collection of people: hysterical, selfish, manipulative, completely fucked up but, hey, that's a family for you."

Alex looked at him for a moment, as if to argue the point, then changed tack.

"Which is why it is my duty to take Hope," he said triumphantly. "And I can manage. I've really enjoyed looking after her these few days. I want to do it forever."

Mungo sighed. "Alex, Alex. No. This is just not realistic. It would be an enormous commitment and it would be your commitment, not mine—" Alex made to interrupt him, but Mungo held up his hand and spoke seriously. "No, listen. I thought you were going to try for drama school again this autumn. Not with a baby you aren't, really not."

"I know that," Alex said dismissively, "and I would give up all idea of acting."

"And, in this great plan of yours, how are you proposing to finance you and the baby?"

"I shall find some work I can do from home, and I'm sure Mum would always help." Alex spoke sullenly, turning his back on Mungo to disguise the tears that were welling up.

Mungo put his arms around Alex and nuzzled into the back of his neck, giving him little light kisses.

"Oh, look, my darling boy. I love you. I love you so very much and of course I want to give you everything that you want," he whispered and Alex could feel his heart beating faster and his groin lurch, "and I'm not saying that I wouldn't have bought into this if you'd really thought about it, but I know you haven't. You are falling into the hetero trap of wanting babies because you can't think what else to do. My mum did that and now that we've all left her, she lives in a vacuum—she never had anything else in her life before babies and now she has even less. You think you've been handed a solution on a plate, but you haven't. Because of what you and I are, we have to be *more* than sure that we want children. We have to have thought down every path and alleyway before we do something as big as this." He took hold of Alex's hand. "One day, I promise you, but not now—not till we have both got our acts together. It wouldn't be fair on any baby, let alone your mother's."

"But I wanted Hope," Alex sobbed.

Miranda was talking to Robert and one of the ladies from the village shop when she felt Richard clamp his hand round her wrist.

"Could we have a moment, Miranda?" he said, smiling politely at the other two.

They went out into the garden; it seemed tropically hot and

bright after the cool sitting room. Miranda went to sit down on the terrace wall overlooking the river, but Richard kept walking.

"Away from the house," he said, and they walked in silence to the far end of the garden, to the orchard where the cats' graveyard lay under the old twisted apple trees.

"Have you thought about the baby?" Miranda asked eagerly.

Richard gestured toward an empty teacup on an old bench. "Oh, yes. I've been sitting here thinking for some time."

"It is the best thing to do, I know it is." Miranda sat down and patted the bench beside her.

"Is it? For whom?" Richard remained standing, distancing himself.

"For you and for me and for the baby, too, of course."

"And your mother? What about her?" Richard asked coldly.

"She doesn't care. Look what she's done to us."

He glared down at her. "For someone so convinced of her own physical flaws, you are remarkably unforgiving of other people's imperfections."

"I'm not, but this is my fifty-year-old mother who has had a baby. It's repulsive." Miranda shuddered.

"Is it that she is your mother, or more that she has gone through what you consider to be the disgusting performance of having a baby?" Miranda opened her mouth to speak, but Richard went on in a clipped voice. "No, I'm genuinely interested to know, Miranda, I really am. You see, I thought I understood you. I believed that I was the one who could give you the confidence I thought you lacked, could help you believe in what you have to offer. But you're too strong for me—you don't want to change. I realize now that you have more self-esteem than I've ever had; you are quite remarkably dedicated to *you*. But I've also realized that you haven't actually been *using* me; you just take people's care of you as your proper due. No, I'm afraid I'm the one who has been using you. By looking after you, I was massaging my own ego. This was never an equal partnership, Miranda, and it's taken me too long to find that out."

"Did you ever love me then?" she asked tonelessly.

Richard's voice softened. "Oh, so much. I saw you at that party and I thought you were the most sexy, exotic creature in the world. Then I found that you were vulnerable and full of insecurities and I was convinced that I'd been put on this earth with the sole purpose of looking after you. When you and I moved in together, it was the happiest day of my life. Yes, Miranda, I did love you."

Miranda refused to acknowledge the past tense.

"I love you, too, and I think this is fate," she declared loudly, as though she had not heard what Richard was saying. "I know it is, in fact. We've been given the chance to have a baby and I don't have to be pregnant. I would be so bad at being pregnant, Richard, I really would," Miranda pleaded. "This way," she said brightly, "you can have what you want and we'll be OK."

"No, Miranda, we won't be OK," Richard said in a chill voice that at last Miranda did register.

She spoke in a barely controlled screech. "Listen to me, Richard. You don't understand. It *will* be OK, I promise you. I want it to work. I love you."

"Not enough, Miranda." Richard spoke sadly. "Loving goes with giving, you know. You don't love me enough to give me something that I really want and I'm not just talking about babies, I'm talking about you. You wouldn't give me *you*. I know there is so much going on inside you and I was there to help, but you wouldn't talk to me, tell me everything. You were always separate, never together with me. You shut up like a clam and wouldn't let me in there. You just didn't ever *give*, Miranda."

"But that's what I'm doing, I'm *giving* you a baby."

Richard shot her a look full of contempt. "But, Miranda, I don't want to be given just any baby. I want ours—yours and mine. What you've offered me is a serious indictment of our relationship. It is totally repugnant and it sickens me. Hope is not the solution for you that you think she is. And she most certainly is not the solution for me."

His voice sounded flat and final. He moved his arm, as though he was going to touch her, and then drew back.

"I'm sorry, Miranda. I can't go on battling to get into you. I thought I could keep trying, but I can't anymore, I've had enough. I'm sorry. I really think there is no answer for us any longer. I wish there was, but there isn't."

And he walked away, leaving Miranda on the bench under the trees.

Liddy was in her bedroom waiting for Avril's daughter, who had been baby-sitting, to bring Hope back. As soon as they had returned, Laura had whisked her up here with a cup of tea as though she was some sort of invalid to be kept away from everyone.

"Such a difficult day for you," Laura had murmured in a soothing voice. "I can deal with downstairs. You rest here."

Liddy had no intention of resting; fearful that her energy would evaporate as rapidly as it had arrived, she was changing her clothes. She stripped herself of the loose summer dress she was wearing and rummaged around in the wardrobe for a T-shirt and skirt. The skirt was tight, but wearable, but the T-shirt fitted perfectly. Liddy allowed herself only a moment to mourn her now almost milkless breasts.

She sat in front of the mirror and stared at her face. She looked a heap: there was a line of gray hair sprinkled like frost along the roots at the top of her head. She pulled the sides of her hair away from her cheeks; there, too, were blocks of gray mixed in with streaks of old auburn hair-dye now faded to an unnatural pink. Her tanned face looked clean and scrubbed—and plain, very plain. Liddy reached for her makeup, unused for so long, and, supporting her heavy plastered arm, began, with difficulty, to apply a new face to match her new inside.

There was a knock at the door and Avril came in with Hope's basket.

"Been as good as gold, apparently," she said, dumping it on the bed. She chucked Hope under the chin and the baby's arms batted the air. "Took her bottle, too, no trouble. My Jane says she'll mind for you any time; she is completely taken, wants to steal her away she says, doesn't she, my little lovely?"

"Everyone seems to want to steal Hope away from me," Liddy said. "But they can't," she added robustly.

Avril looked up at her.

"Hey. Getting your spirit back, then?" she said, nodding her head approvingly. "Good for you, my lovely, it's about bloody time, I'd say."

Liddy took a small package from the dressing-table drawer. She unwrapped the soft tissue paper and looked at the delicately worked silver-and-garnet necklace. Hope's necklace—the one Liddy had made in a burst of creative optimism before the baby was born and everything became so dark and disordered. Avril did up the clasp for her and looked into the mirror over Liddy's head.

"You've polished up very nice," she said appreciatively.

"Not too bad. Scarf round the head to hide the gray, a bit of makeup to hide the aging, a tighter skirt and earrings and bangles," Liddy said into the mirror, smiling at Avril. "And a sudden desire to fight for my family. I feel a completely different person." She stood up. "I think I forgot that I am the mother of four children and hostess of this funeral. Avril, would you mind helping me with Hope's basket?"

* * *

Laura watched with surprise as her mother came downstairs, talking to Avril and using the banister for support. She saw her point to a corner of the sitting room and Avril put down Hope's basket. Laura frowned. She shouldn't be put there—that was not a good place—people were smoking in the room. She stepped forward to move the basket and became caught up in the circle of villagers to whom Liddy had gravitated.

"So, to which of your young does that little one belong?" someone asked Liddy,

"None. She's mine," Liddy said clearly. Laura watched the faces surrounding Liddy and recognized with shame the disbelief and disapproval in their expressions.

"Shall I take her, Mum?" Laura stepped forward.

Liddy looked at her in surprise. "Where would you want to take her?"

"Well, I just thought perhaps out of this smoky room."

"No, she's fine where she is, thank you." Liddy spoke firmly.

Laura tried to disguise her mortification at her mother's sharp response. "Right. Well, if you don't need me, I'll see how the sandwiches are going."

Robert had been watching the brief interchange thoughtfully. "Is it my imagination or am I sensing a shift in the family dynamics?"

Liddy smiled at him. "Yes, I think you do. Something changed today. It's time to stop being a doormat."

"I think so," Robert said, nodding his head approvingly. "Miranda told me about her idea, yesterday." Liddy looked at him, puzzled. "About the baby."

"Oh, that." Liddy was pleased to realize that she was, for the first time, feeling completely unthreatened. "She's not the only one with that idea. All three want Hope, apparently."

Robert looked interested. "I say, what a dichotomy—sort of Solomon-like in its complexity."

"No, not at all," Liddy said happily. "There is no dichotomy. It's all very simple. None of them can have Hope—because she's mine."

Liddy was surprised to see so many people: maybe Cyn was right and they had come to poke and pry. She moved painfully around the room making polite conversation. Her foot was aching like hell and she was probably doing untold damage by walking on it so much today, but she needed to be upright. She was looking for Martin—she must try again with him. She was not going to give up. She wondered if he had talked to the children.

Liddy moved out of the chattering sitting room into the study—it was empty and quiet and the armchair looked very comfortable. She sat down and put her foot up on a stool; the release of pressure on the swollen limb was blissful. She closed her eyes for a moment.

"Mum. Oh, there you are!" Miranda almost threw herself into the room. "I've got to talk to you." Liddy recognized her repressed hysteria and sat up in the chair, ready to take on the bombardment.

"You've got to say yes." Miranda paced up and down the room. "You've got to. I know when he sees it, he will want it. He's going to go if you don't."

"Miranda." Liddy put out her hand as Miranda paced past her. She raised her voice. "Miranda, calm down, sit down and tell me what you're talking about."

Miranda looked at her in hurt surprise. "You know what I'm talking about. It's Richard. If I had Hope, there is a chance that he won't leave me like he says."

Liddy struggled from the deep cushions of the chair and drew herself up to a standing position. She faced her daughter. "No, Miranda, I am not giving Hope to you. Apart from any-

273

thing else, if Richard will only stay if you have Hope, then I can assure you that your relationship is not destined to work—"

"I can't live without Richard. I can't manage." Miranda was wringing her hands in pent-up fear and frustration.

"Mum, I think you ought to be more careful who you tell about Hope. I'm sure they're quite shocked." Laura appeared at the door and talked over Miranda and Liddy. "Should you be standing up, Mum?" She moved forward as if to help Liddy into a chair. Liddy pushed her away.

"For God's sake, Laura, will you stop being so bloody officious."

"Raised voices I can hear?" Alex loomed up behind Laura with Hope in his arms.

"What's going on here, then?" he inquired cheerfully.

"And will you please put Hope back in her basket at once, Alex, and then come back here."

Liddy began to speak in a quiet scream. Silenced by his mother's ferocity, Alex left the room and returned without the baby. "Hope is my baby. I love her as much as I love all of you. I am going to care for her, so you can all get your ideas for taking her over out of your head. She is mine. She has not been put onto this earth to sort out a relationship, or as a present for you, or as a replacement for growing children."

She closed her mouth tight and for a moment there was silence in the room.

Laura was the first to speak. "I'm not trying to replace anyone, Mum. I am trying to help *you*. It is the most sensible plan. I think we all feel this is too much for you in the circumstances and I think it would be better for everyone in the family if Hope was brought up as one of mine."

It was her eldest daughter's overbearing and high-handed tone that finally pushed Liddy over the edge. Her voice seemed to explode in her own ears as she burst out. "I am sorry if it embarrasses you that your middle-aged mother has had a baby, but that is the way it is. I'm not saying that I haven't made a mess of it, but it is for *me*, not you, to sort out. And I am not going to allow Hope to be parceled away and passed off as someone else's just because you are ashamed of her. Things can't always happen safely and conventionally, Laura, and you really do not have to be the guardian of this family's morals. Just get on with your own life and stop interfering with everyone else's."

Laura, ashen-faced, stared at her mother in horror, then turned and rushed out of the room.

Liddy knew that she had spoken in pent-up anger and with no thought of sifting the words first, and she knew that she had hurt Laura immeasurably. But none of them was to realize quite how hurt Laura was until some time later.

They were all to agree afterwards that if Laura had been drinking, no one had seen her do so. And none of them actually saw her take Hope out of her basket or go up the wide staircase. It was only when she was standing majestically at the top of the stairs, that the guests, who were beginning to drift toward the front door, registered her being there. She held Hope in her arms, showing the baby to the assembled company below her.

"This," she announced in loud strident tones so that everyone immediately looked up at her, "this is my mother's baby by another man. It is her illegitimate child."

Liddy heard her from the study, where she had stayed after her outburst. Miranda and Alex heard her from the sitting room and the three of them converged in the hall. "She can't really manage a baby," Laura went on, in a softer voice now that she had everyone's attention. "She is too old and it wouldn't be fair to Hope. Yes, she's called it Hope"—she looked around as though inviting a response—"but she refuses to give the child any hope. My father clearly won't have anything to do with it, so she would rather it was brought up by a single elderly parent than in a family where there are already three young children."

Liddy, moving with difficulty, tried to push her way through the bodies in the wide hall.

"Don't come up, Mum." Laura noticed Liddy as she reached the bottom of the stairs and she hugged Hope to her. "I need you to listen to me. The thing is"—her voice became almost conversational as she looked away from Liddy—"all three of us want Hope. Now, Miranda can promise her a nanny—that's good, isn't it? We approve of nannies nowadays, because apparently it's terribly important that women work, so that they can afford a nice house for their child and the very expensive nanny; and they can take the child, and the nanny, of course, on exotic holidays. They can give the child trendy toys, extra French lessons and tennis coaching. In fact Miranda could give Hope everything that money can buy—except, of course, a true mother who would get up in the night when she was teething, a mother who would know how to fill a wet afternoon with entertaining games or run tea parties for other children who whine, wet their pants and want to go home. The nanny would do all that and Miranda would just pop in to kiss her baby good night before she went out for the evening."

"Laura." Miranda pushed past Liddy, who was still hesitating on the bottom stair.

"Shut up! Shut up!" Laura shouted. She looked at Miranda and clasped Hope tightly to her breast.

"You don't like reality, do you, Miranda? And you don't *really* care for this baby, do you? You've never cared for anyone but yourself. Stay there. I haven't finished," she added fiercely. "Now Alex," she continued when she was sure that Miranda was standing still, "would like Hope because Alex is gay." Laura spat out the word *gay*. "He feels that he and his partner have a right to have a baby even though two men can't physically have

one themselves. Never mind that the child would be surrounded by homosexuals of both sexes and that it would have
to cope with all the other children in the school playground
knowing that she didn't have a proper mother like everyone
else. No, their baby would have two mothers, or maybe two
fathers—I don't know how gay parents categorize themselves.
Does it matter? It's not natural, either way. And how would
they cope with her when she became an adolescent? Well, they
wouldn't, let me tell you." Laura spoke with disdain. "They
would have to come to me, wouldn't they? Because I am
already bringing up two girls. I have the experience that they
will never have."

Alex stood behind Miranda.

"Laura," he shouted urgently, taking two steps up the staircase.

"No, Alex. Not this time. This time you won't get what you
want. See how you like that for a change." Laura's lips folded
back across her teeth in a travesty of a smile. The baby, swad-
dled in a blanket, began to wriggle and fret in Laura's arms.

Liddy, realizing with a stab of panic that Hope might be in
danger of being suffocated, made a move forward.

Laura moved back a step. "I haven't finished. You have to
listen," she repeated in a breathless voice.

Liddy caught sight of Martin by the front door and they
exchanged a glance, a united glance of two parents watching
one of their precious children in trouble. She saw him violently push past people in an effort to reach the bottom of the
stairs. "Laura, darling," he called, "come here, we need to—"

She looked down at him contemptuously. "Dad. Do you
know how ashamed I am of you both? You let Mum do this. It
was your fault, too, you know. You must have known she was
having an affair. She's ruined everything and you let her do it.
We were a normal, happy family—everything was fine, but not
anymore. Don't come up. I haven't finished," Laura said to

Martin as he reached the stairs. "I'm asking you. You can't refuse me—not in front of all these people."

Hope began to cry and the sound cut through Liddy—her half-empty breasts contracted in response to her baby's wail.

"Please, Laura." Liddy, sick with fright now, hobbled slowly up to the stairs. "Please let me take Hope and we'll talk about it. Please, darling."

Laura held Hope even tighter.

"You don't deserve her. None of you deserve her." She looked down at the baby and relaxed her grip slightly.

Liddy stopped, unsure quite how unstable Laura had become.

"Not content with destroying our three lives, you've decided to destroy yet another of your children's lives." Suddenly the anger seemed to leave Laura and her voice became sad and lilt-ing. "I should have her, you know, whatever Fergus says, I *should* have her." She looked down at Hope, momentarily quiet in her arms. "I will love her. I'll care for her, bring her up as part of a happy, loving family. I know about babies and children, that's what I *do*. I should be the one that has her. I want her so much." Laura looked up from Hope and tears began to run down her cheeks.

"Please let me have her," she mewed piteously. "Please, *Mummy*, please." And the unexpected use of the redundant, childish sobriquet seemed, at that moment, very poignant.

It was Miranda who came out of the trance in which everyone seemed to be caught. She recognized Laura's derangement—it was only too familiar to her. She could sense her distraction, feel the panic making a big noise in Laura's head. She knew from experience how the temporary unbal-ance of Laura's mind would make everything cloudy and swirly, how her heart would be beating too fast, how she would feel trapped, unable to retreat, and how she wouldn't be sure of anything anymore. All at once Miranda knew that she could help Laura, because she *understood*. Her mind was quite clear as she moved slowly, stair by stair, her hand stretched out as though facing a cornered animal.

"Laura, I know how you're feeling," she said softly. "Listen to me carefully. Take some big breaths. Come on, Laura, a big breath in and then out. Why don't you give me Hope? Let me take her just for a moment and then we can talk."

Laura's movements were becoming more agitated as she pulled the baby tighter to her. Now everyone could see Hope fighting in her blanket, struggling to fill her lungs.

"No. If you have her you'll never give her back."

"I will," Miranda spoke slowly and clearly. "I will give her back. I promise."

Laura jiggled the baby violently and Hope began to howl again, great gusts of baby screaming. Laura looked at her sister with a mixed expression of contempt and sadness.

"No, you won't. You never give me anything back. You only take—just like him." She looked past Miranda to Alex and whimpered. "I'm not going to let Mum give her to either of you. Hope should be my baby. I love her. I'll care for her. She should be mine and yet my mother won't give her to me. She won't let me have her and I want her—"

"Give Hope to me at once, Laura." Cyn appeared behind Laura, a stumpy, dark figure, awkwardly holding out her arms for the baby. She spoke again, her strong, icy voice rising above the howls of the baby. "We have had quite enough of this absurd behavior. Stop being so selfish. This is Cleo's day, not yours, or the baby's. Now give her to me, immediately, before you suffocate the poor thing."

Chapter

THIRTEEN

Laura slowly turned to look at Cyn.

"You don't want this baby. You hate babies," she said in a puzzled voice. "You hate everyone."

A half-smile flickered across Cyn's face—gone almost as soon as it was there.

"I want you to give me the baby, Laura." She spoke slowly and clearly.

"I'm not going to hurt her. I love her."

"I know you do," Cyn said briskly. "Now give her to me."

"What will you do with her?"

"I shall give her to her mother, of course. That's where she should be—with her mother. Now give her to me at once."

Caught in the current of Cyn's forcefulness, Laura gently and carefully handed the baby to Cyn, who held it stiffly in her arms. The gathering in the hall took a collective breath.

Cyn looked down at the sea of faces below her.

"Lydia," she called sharply, "you appear to have two wretched daughters up here who need you very badly. It is about time that you dealt with them properly."

Ignoring the pain in her foot, Liddy almost ran up the

stairs and took Hope from Cyn. Laura swayed beside her and Liddy put her plastered arm out to steady her. Supporting each other they moved slowly across the landing into Liddy's bedroom.

"Now," Cyn said, in her natural cantankerous tone and fixing the upturned faces below her with a glare, "*you* can all go home. I never wanted you here in the first place. You've got what you came for; you have seen inside the house, you have enjoyed my hospitality and I don't suppose any of you have thought about Cleo for one moment. You don't care, so please go at once and you don't ever have to bother coming back." She stood at the top of the stairs eyeing the guests balefully as, in a group, they made their way out, unsure, in the light of what had just happened, who to thank for the hospitality.

"I'm sorry, I want her. I just want her," Laura moaned as Liddy put Hope down on the bed and guided Laura on to the pillows at the other end. She was looking after her daughter now—as it should be. Laura's distress had enabled her, finally, to take repossession of her role as carer. She covered her with the bedspread and sat down silently beside her. Her two daughters lay either end of the bed, both on their backs, eyes unfocused, still and silent. Liddy willed her youngest daughter not to cry and her eldest daughter to talk.

Laura began to talk—slowly, hesitantly the words were forced out through her tight lips. And once she started, the momentum gathered until all the untapped fury, unhappiness and loneliness that had built up inside her for so long poured out in a stream of words that followed each other so fast, they became one huge wave of misery.

The empty sitting room seemed to Alex to be echoing with the voices that had only recently filled it. Miranda and his father were nowhere to be seen; they appeared to have slipped away with the tide of departing guests. He could hear Avril in the kitchen, and picking up some empty cups and plates he took them in to her.

She and Mungo were washing up, talking in muted voices. As he put the china on the draining board, Alex saw Martin standing at the garden wall looking out over the river. Even from the back he looked defeated: his suited shoulders were hunched, his neck sunk deep between them.

"Go on, then," Mungo said, pushing him gently. "Go and tell him how much you love him."

Alex went out through the back door and walked toward his father. He noticed an unnatural patch of scalp showing through Martin's normally thick hair.

"Dad," he said quietly.

Martin turned round.

"Oh, Alex, it's you." The sadness in his eyes made Alex want to reach out to him and hold him.

"Are you all right?" They both spoke at once and then smiled at each other.

"She is bitterly unhappy." Even as he spoke, Alex was not sure to which "she" he was referring.

"I know," Martin said simply. They stood together, shoulder to shoulder, in silence.

"It was my fault just as much as your mother's," Martin said suddenly. "Nothing is ever just one person's fault." He looked at Alex. "Like with us. It's both our faults, you know—that you and I don't know each other as well as we used to. I love you very much, but it went wrong somewhere between us playing football together and you going out clubbing." He gave a rueful little smile.

His father was right, Alex knew that. He could have involved his father in his life, but he had chosen to sulk instead and the gulf between them had expanded till neither could make the leap.

"I was bullish. I thought you disapproved of me," he admitted.

"And I wanted you to have your space. I thought you might feel I was putting heterosexual pressure on you," Martin said apologetically. "I wanted you to feel comfortable with me, but all I succeeded in doing was to make us both uncomfortable. No parent ever sets out to get it wrong with their children," he went on quietly. "You try to do the right thing, but you can't always succeed and the trouble with the young is that they don't have the time to help you work it out—they're too busy growing up and leaving you behind."

Alex turned to his father and touched him gently on his arm.

"It happens, I suppose. But it's never too late—is it?" he asked anxiously.

"Never," Martin said, covering Alex's hand with his.

"Oh, Dad. I do love you. But I never did much like playing football, you know."

"Me neither," Martin said with a grin.

Alex gave his father a kiss.

Martin walked back into the house and Alex stayed sitting on the wall, his eyes nearly blinded by the bright evening sun on the water, thinking how much he loved his father and what a waste of years they had behind them. He was wondering idly if he would like to live by the sea when Mungo came up and put his arm around him. "Hiya, pigeon. Just occasionally your family has a magnificent moment. And that, back there, was a couple of them."

"Poor old Laura. She really does want Hope," Alex said.

"And what about you?"

Alex shrugged. "Yes. And no, as well." He laid his head on Mungo's shoulder. "Not yet, anyway."

Mungo gently stroked his head.

"Oh, really, you two. Must you canoodle out here in public?

It's quite revolting." Cyn, leaning heavily on Cleo's stick, was making slow progress across the garden.

Alex turned and grinned at her. "I said he was beautiful, didn't I?"

"Don't be so ridiculous, Alex. I don't care what he is. Just do stop mauling each other all the time." She pointed with her stick to a wicker chair. "And get me that chair and bring it over here."

"You were brilliant with Laura, Aunt Cyn—," Alex started, but Cyn interrupted him, waving her hand dismissively.

"Nonsense. It was just a matter of being the only sane person there at the time. You really are an odious collection."

Mungo returned with the chair and tried to help Cyn. She shook him off.

"Leave me alone, for goodness' sake. I'm perfectly able to manage." Then she smiled at him.

"At least you've got some manners, which is more than can be said for this lot," she remarked grudgingly. "I thought their mother was the epitome of selfishness until these three came down and started their demanding like spoiled little children."

Alex began to protest, but Cyn glared at him. "Be quiet, you."

Alex subsided silently.

Cyn looked round the garden. "You've worked hard here, Alex. Cleo loved her garden. All her life she dreamt of having one of her very own. I'm glad she wasn't disappointed. You've made it look nice and she would like that. She had green fingers, like you, but you wouldn't know that. None of you really knew her. Not like I did," she added sorrowfully.

The three of them shared the silence.

"I'll pay for you to go to college, Alex, if that's what gardeners do nowadays," Cyn said abruptly. "You should stop fannying around trying to be an actor. I've always said you'd be a lousy actor—you do it off stage too much." She smiled unexpectedly.

"I should know. If the truth be told, I was exactly the same. Oh, I was going to be a great actress, furious with my father for not helping me, but now I'm probably glad I was never found out." She changed the subject back to Alex as if to prevent further personal disclosures. "Of all Lydia's children you are the most redeemable and I've got more money now than I know what to do with. You can be a gardener. It'll keep you out of trouble and, in return, you can come down here occasionally and make sure my gardener is keeping Cleo's garden as she would have liked it."

"That's a heavenly idea, Alex. Are you listening to this?" Mungo said.

Cyn shrugged. "Probably not—he's an arrogant little bugger, always was. Anyway, it's up to you. If you decide to take up my offer, it's there. You might as well do something useful with my money and God knows you've frittered your life away up until now. You're a silly boy, but at least you're not stupid like your sisters." She glared at Alex as he began to stutter out his thanks. "Oh, do go away both of you. I'm tired and I want to be on my own."

Miranda waited long enough to see Hope safely in Cyn's arms before she turned away from the stairs to look for Richard. When Laura had started speaking, she had thought she had seen him by the front door, but now that it was all over she couldn't see him through the bodies that pressed together in the hall, anxiously trying to remove themselves. He wasn't in the sitting room, or the kitchen, or the study. She went out into the garden and found him at the front gate. He appeared to be hesitating at the top of the stone steps, car keys in his hand.

He watched Miranda come toward him.

"Richard, Richard, what are you doing?"

Miranda already knew the answer; she could see it in his eyes.

"I was debating in my mind whether I would hate myself if I just left you this." He took an envelope out of his pocket and looked at her sadly. "You really tried with Laura back there," he added gently.

"I was worried about Hope. I thought she might be going to be suffocated and then none of us could have had her." As she spoke she watched Richard's eyes, and Miranda realized the wrong words had spilled out.

"I didn't mean it like that, Richard, I didn't, honestly. I just knew how Laura was feeling inside."

But it was too late.

A shutter went down over his face, but his voice was strangely tender. "I know how you felt, Miranda, but I have to go. I told you before that I must. I am sorry. I'm sorry about so much: that it has to be today, of all days; that it has to be now, this moment, with no more discussion or argument; I'm sorry that I can't help you any more and that I'm giving up on us."

Miranda put out her hand toward him in panic.

"No, Richard, you don't understand, I'll do what you want. I'll have our own baby. I will, I will. You'll help me and it'll be OK. Please don't go."

Richard took her hand and said in a sad voice, "It's too late, Miranda. It won't work, not now. It wouldn't work for you or for me and certainly not for the baby that you would give birth to so unwillingly. I must break out of this awful circle that you and I have created. We both must."

"I can't be without you. I can't," Miranda keened, her stomach so tight that she thought she might be sick at any moment.

"And I can't be with you anymore," Richard went on ruthlessly. "I know this is the right thing for both of us. You need to be free of me, just as much as I need to be free of you. You'll come to realize that, Miranda, in time. I promise you, you will." Richard broke away from her and then leaned forward and kissed her forehead. It was as though a great fog was slowly beginning to clear from Miranda's head. As she felt Richard's lips on her skin, somewhere, through the heavy mass of pain that was churning inside her, she thought she caught brief glimpses of clear space. She felt herself quiet and become composed, her shoulders dropped and her hands stopped shaking.

"I know," she said calmly. "I'm trying to understand." And now, she realized, she really did understand. She leaned forward and lightly touched his arm. "I am so sorry," she whispered.

Richard's look of despair and anguish reflected Miranda's.

"So am I," he said miserably as he turned and ran down the steps. "Very sorry."

Always so many sorrys in her life. Miranda turned away and threw up violently in the bushes.

Martin went into the house and found Liddy sitting by the telephone.

"Laura's asleep. I've just phoned Fergus," she said wearily, "and he's coming over now to collect her."

"I was going to offer to drive her back," Martin said. "Poor Laura. What can we do?" he added pleadingly.

Liddy rubbed her eyes. "I don't know. It's between her and Fergus. Only they can help each other. That's why I wanted him to come here. They need time together; they seem to have grown apart—forgotten to talk to each other." She looked up at Martin and said ruefully, "Familiar at all?" Martin winced in acknowledgment. "She's been unhappy for so long," Liddy went on. "She's been trying to get pregnant without Fergus knowing and she's had a miscarriage. So this"—Liddy couldn't say the words—"this was just the last straw."

"Oh, God, poor Laura. Why didn't she say, at least to us?"

Liddy answered sadly, "I think she's been trying to. We were just too busy with our own last straws to hear her."

"Oh, my God," Martin muttered, stricken. "How could we?"

They looked at each other for a moment, aware that they had both failed the child they shared.

"Liddy . . . ," Martin started. A distant and blurry memory of that night had been sliding in and out of his mind ever since he saw Liddy, damaged and bandaged, at the crematorium. It was a sensation similar to one of being drunk—nauseous waves that made his head roll and a recollection that seemed just around the corner of his mind, just out of sight. Had it been him? Could he remember shoving her out of the way as he desperately tried to escape?

Liddy remained silent. He gestured toward her wrist.

"I didn't—?" The horror of what he might have done prevented him from speaking it out loud.

"I fell down the stone steps," she said briefly.

"I didn't . . . did I . . . was it?"

"Yes. It was when you left the house last time and I don't know whether you pushed me away or whether I tripped." Liddy spoke matter-of-factly. "It doesn't matter—whichever."

Martin slumped against the hall chiffonier and put his hand over his eyes.

"Oh, Christ, what have we done to each other?"

Liddy noticed the hairless patch on the side of his head. She put out a hand and touched it gently. Martin lifted his head and smiled weakly at her.

"Loss of hair caused by stress, apparently. I suppose I'm lucky not to have woken up one morning with all my hair on the pillow beside me."

"Oh, Martin," was all Liddy could say bleakly.

Miranda came through the front door and confronted Martin and Liddy in the hall.

"Richard has gone," she said blankly. "We're finished. Over."

She looked at Liddy and spoke almost courteously—without

anger. "We just *might* have sorted it out, if you hadn't ruined everything. You made everything impossible."

"That's enough, Miranda," Martin cut in. "You don't understand."

Alex and Mungo arrived in the hall with Fergus behind them.

"Mirry." Alex moved toward his sister.

"Richard's gone. He's gone forever," Miranda repeated.

"Listen to me, Miranda, and you, too, Alex." Martin moved nearer to Liddy and he seemed to fill the space in the hall.

"Liddy and I are sorry. We have both done wrong to each other. Yes, me, too, only rather less publicly and dramatically than your mother. I am to blame just as much: you must be as angry with me as you are with her. I'm sorry you all got caught in the fallout, but this is something the two of us have to sort out. Parents have their own roads to travel. They don't just come to a grinding halt when they have children. We have a life after you've all left us, you know. You cannot expect us to stay the same; we change, move on, just as you do. You can't keep us any more than we can keep you. You are not on the same journey as us. Leave us alone. You expect your parents to be able to give you everything you want, but we can't. We couldn't, even when you were little. Now you demand bigger things, much bigger things than Smarties and cuddles, and we can't always give them, but you still expect them and stamp your feet when you're thwarted. You have been bullying your mother, all of you. Miranda, you threaten; Alex, you charm; and Laura tries to take over. But it has to stop. Whatever happens now between your mother and me does not negate in any way the happiness that we have all had as a family. Just give us a chance to sort out our life without any interference from you."

"I don't think I've got much of a life anymore," Miranda said with a broken sob.

"Of course you have, darling." Liddy spoke sharply, buoyed up by Martin's sudden burst of vigor. "You don't need Richard to depend on. You must get on, grow up and take responsibility for yourself. You, too, Alex. Don't spend your life hanging around waiting for something or someone to happen—and Fergus, Laura needs you, she *really* needs you; she has something to tell you and you must listen to her and be her friend again. Don't let yourselves grow apart. Don't lose the habit of talking," Liddy said vehemently. "It happens slowly and you don't really notice until it's too late." Looking at Martin, she said softly, "And then it's a lot of hard work to put it all back together again."

Martin gave her an almost imperceptible nod of his head.

She turned to Miranda and Alex. "Hope is your half-sister, and she will need you all as she grows up. Be there for her. She is part of you all. And I love her so much." Liddy's voice shook with tears. "Just like I love all of you so much."

She turned away and Martin put his hand out to her protectively.

"Are you going to stay with Mum?" Miranda looked at her father in astonishment. "After this?"

"That has nothing to do with you, Miranda. It's for me and Liddy to work out," Martin said firmly. "We're adults and you're adults, so leave us to sort out our lives and go away and live yours."

"Oh, hoo-bloody-rah. Thank the Lord for that." Cyn's voice bellowed out from behind Martin. She had come through the back door and now stood in the passageway, leaning on her stick, a large black cat, tail upright, twining around her legs. "Someone has said something sensible at last. Now bugger off, the lot of you and leave me alone, for God's sake. You're an unspeakable family, quite loathsome and nothing but trouble, I've always said so."

HOPE

I hated it when Mum told me that my great-great-aunt Cyn had died. She was trying not to cry and her mouth went in funny shapes and I would rather she had cried properly. I liked Aunt Cyn, but she could be a bit scary when she sounded cross. Last holidays her words didn't always make sense like they used to. She was really, really old and kept forgetting what she was saying; sometimes she would say the same things over and over again, usually about the war and stuff. She had lots and lots of cats. I wonder what will happen to them now.

Mum has made the whole family come down to Cornwall for the funeral and everyone is staying at the White House. I know we're meant to be sad, but I like everyone being here together. Tamsin has had her belly-button pierced and every-one hates it—except for Alex who says he is going to have his done as well. Mungo's here. He's been let off filming for the day and the men who brought Aunt Cyn's coffin recognized him. I saw them nudge each other. I bet they want his auto-graph. I go and stay with Alex and Mungo in London a lot and Alex takes me shopping and we walk the dogs. He lets me play on his brilliant new computer. I want to make gardens like him. You can talk to Alex about anything and he always listens. He's funny, too, though at the moment I can tell he's awfully sad about Aunt Cyn.

Jake told me that Aunt Cyn's coffin would slide through the curtains and would be taken on a conveyor-belt thing to a big fire. I wondered if you could smell burning, but he said you couldn't. When our aunt Cleo died, he said, he thought it would be like the smell of meat cooking, but it isn't at all.

I am sitting between Rebecca and Marcus and she is telling him not to make a noise, but she's making much more noise telling him not to than he is making it. I go and stay at the farm quite often because Marcus is only fourteen months, five days and seven hours younger than me, even though he's my nephew. My friend Sophy thinks it's really cool that I'm only ten and I'm Tamsin and Jake's aunt and they're nearly twenty.

Laura, my eldest sister, has just sat down. She has been making sausage rolls all morning for the party afterwards. She is Marcus's mum and the twins' and Rebecca's. Fergus gave her a surprise birthday party when she was forty last year and we all helped him get it ready. She was so happy when she found out, she cried heaps.

My other sister, Miranda, is sitting in front of me. When we stay at the White House we see her a lot. She lives in the village, all alone in a tiny cottage with her dog, Paper, and she writes these brilliant children's stories; they're really, really good, which is odd because she hasn't got any children of her own. Her friend Robert lives in the village, too, and he is teaching me how to draw cartoons. He is sitting between Miranda and Avril and he's got his arm round Avril because she is crying. I don't like Avril crying because she is usually always smiling.

Aunt Cyn is the first person I know who's dead, but my dad explained how it was all right because she was so old. He's not my real dad. He adopted me when I was a year old. My mum is my real mum, though. Dad looks after me a lot because Mum makes all this jewelry and sometimes she goes away to sell it. Some of it is all right, but a bit *old*, though she did make me a really cool silver bracelet for my birthday.

Mum is standing up in front of us. She reads a poem, which I don't understand, and then she talks a lot about Aunt Cyn and Aunt Cleo. Aunt Cleo died just after I was born, so I don't remember her at all. Aunt Cyn used to talk about her a lot. They were really good friends.

I thought we wouldn't ever come back to the White House now that Aunt Cyn is dead, but Marcus said he'd heard his mum say that she's given the house to me. It's funny to think I'm going to have a house of my own—at my age. Aunt Cyn said she was going to give the house to a cats' home when she died, because she didn't think our family deserved to have anything from her. She was always saying that we were all a nuisance and utterly feeble and that she didn't like our family one bit, but I think she was just pretending. . . .

Lucy Clare is the mother of four grown children. She lives with her husband in London. *Hoping for Hope* is her first novel.